LILLY BARRETT

Forever Noah's

Lilly Barrett

ISBN 10: 0-6481388-0-1
ISBN 13: 978-0-6481388-0-8

Editing by Melissa Van Natta
Book design and formatting by Swish Design & Editing
Cover design by Soxsational Cover Art

Cover image Copyright 2015

Dedication

For My Mum
Who taught me the joy of reading
I'm sure she's still devouring a
Mills and Boon up in heaven

Chapter ONE

Noah

How the hell did this happen?

We've gone from having an incredible Christmas day together in the snow to the worst day of our lives. She doesn't need this kind of stress so soon after her rape. Shit. Maybe it's my fault. Maybe I was too rough with her. She's twelve weeks pregnant. I should've been more careful. Oh God, she can't lose our babies now. Surely he wouldn't do that to us. She's been through so much shit these last few months, she needs a break. First the broken engagement, then the car accident, kidnapping, rape and now pregnant with our triplets. Enough is enough.

I've ordered her to bed to rest up. The bleeding is still ongoing, but now we're stuck out in the middle of nowhere in a blizzard with no hope of getting to a hospital. No cell phone or internet reception either.

I've spent the better part of a day laying with her on the large king size bed as she watches daytime talk shows on the large flat screen opposite the bed. I've been putting the final touches on the presentation that I'm doing for the Canadian mining company executives in Vancouver on Saturday. Working on my laptop has allowed me to keep an eye on her and make sure she's okay.

So much for our week in the snow. This was supposed to be a carefree break for her to rest up and recover. Well she's definitely resting now. I've told her that her feet aren't allowed to touch the floor for the duration of our stay. I know that she's putting on a brave face for me, but I held her last night when she cried herself to sleep. My heart was breaking for her, and there's not a fucking thing I can do to help her besides just be here for her. So that's what I'm doing. I'll just continue to silently pray to every deity that I know to let her carry these babies to term. If she needs to stay in bed for the rest of the pregnancy, I'll make sure that she does. Anything to keep Mia and my sons safe.

I glance outside at the bleak scene, watching the howling wind throw snow around and move the branches of the trees, dumping snow on the ground as they sway with the force. I'm dying to get out of here and get her to a hospital to get checked. We need to see an OBGYN to reassure us that our babies are ok. Our OBGYN in Perth is out of the question, since our cabin is so remote.

If this doesn't get better soon, we will fly back to Western Australia and see our OBGYN, Dr. Christine Brittain. The presentation that we've come halfway round the world for will have to wait, or I could do it by Skype as I planned to originally. I can use the private jet that has a bed and she can sleep the whole way home if necessary.

I glance over just as she pushes the blankets off her and lifts her legs over the side of the bed. In an instant my laptop is dumped on the bed cover and my arm shoots across the bed to grab her around her upper arm. "Where do you think you're going?" I growl at her softly.

"Noah, I need to pee. It's six steps away, I can manage on my own."

"Not gonna happen Babe. Don't move. I'll carry you."

I can hear her resigned sigh as she sits where she is while I come around to pick her up and carry her to the bathroom. When I set her down she shoos me out of the door, closing it behind me. I stand outside the door and wait for her to finish and as soon as I hear her washing her hands I open it and stand behind her waiting for her to be done. "Do you want to go back to bed or would you like to come downstairs and lay on the sofa while I cook us some dinner?"

"Yeah that sounds good. I could actually sit on a stool in the kitchen and help if you want me to."

"Nope. You rest on the sofa in front of the fire and keep warm. I must say Hun, those cute duck PJ's are growing on me. You look adorable in them."

"Wanna grab my robe from the bed then and I'll supervise while you cook, though I'd much rather help. What are we having?"

"I thought I'd do Mum's chicken casserole though it won't be as good as mums, that's a given, but I promise it'll be edible. I don't know what she does, but hers is always better than mine." I tell her as I hold out her robe for her to slip her arms in, then pick her up and slowly carry her downstairs, laying her on the huge leather sofa in front of the fireplace. I cover her with a blanket from the back of the sofa and throw another log on to each fire to keep the house warm. Striding out to the kitchen I get out what I need and spend the next 20 minutes chatting to her through the doorway as I get dinner prepared.

As predicted it's definitely edible and Mia eats hers on the sofa, balancing her plate on her lap as I settle in to the armchair nearby. I'm happy that she hasn't been sick for two days now and her appetite's still very healthy. I don't know where she puts all this food. There's not an ounce of fat on her. Those boys of mine must be eating it all, and I smile at the picture in my head of my babies with their knives and forks digging in as they float around the womb. Mia glances over at me as I'm still lost in my head.

"What's that smirk for? What are you thinking over there?" she asks, shoveling food into her mouth, enjoying every bite. I can hear her soft moans as she eats and I'm doing my best to ignore them. It's hard enough being so close to her and not touching, without hearing those noises. The same sounds she makes when we make love. The ones that drive me crazy.

"Just thinking about our boys and how much they're making you eat. I think they'll all end up huge and you'll be a skeleton in a few months." I tell her, a grin breaking over my face. "How is the bleeding? I meant to ask before, but got side-tracked by your ducky pajamas. Has it settled at all?"

"Yeah it seems to be okay now. No bleeding at all. God Noah, that was freaking scary. I never want that to happen again. Hopefully it was just a glitch and everything will be fine from now on."

I let out a huge sigh of relief as I realize that this means our babies are safe for the time being. She hasn't complained of any cramps today like she did last night, so I am hoping that means things are getting better. I still want her to go and get checked as soon as we can get out of here though. I'll be worrying till I can see them on the ultrasound and know that they're alright. Our three little hungry peanuts.

"Regardless, you'll rest up and do nothing for the rest of the week, or the rest of the pregnancy if that's what you need to do. We'll do what we need to do to keep you all healthy."

She gives me a smirk between mouthfuls, her crystal green eyes shining with humor. "Yes Boss. Whatever you say."

Putting down my plate on the side table beside my chair, I get up and step over to her, pulling her forward slightly so that I can lay a kiss on her forehead.

"Glad you're playing nice. We'll get you sorted at the hospital and take it from there okay? If we need to go home, then that's what we'll do. Hopefully this storm won't last too much longer and we can get back to Vancouver soon."

"I hate having to do nothing. This is gonna drive me crazy. You'll have to give me something to do while I can't get up and about. By the time we get back to Perth this should just be a distant memory. I'll go and see my own Doc as soon as we get home. Then if everything's alright I'll be fine to go back to work."

I raise my eyebrow as I look over at her from my chair. "Yeah maybe not. I don't want you to overdo it after this scare. Once we make sure they're okay then we'll talk about it more. I'd prefer you didn't go back to work, at least for a while. I'd be happier if you stayed home and laid around for a while just to make sure everything's fine."

I can see her shaking her head even before I've finished speaking. "Not gonna happen. If the bleeding doesn't start again and the babies are okay, then there's no reason for me not to be at work. I'm not on the end of a shovel digging ditches all day. I have a lovely comfy chair that I sit in and I know my boss will keep a close eye on me."

"You got that right. I told you before. First sign of trouble and you're out of there. That still stands." I inform her around a mouthful of food. "If Christine gives you the all clear then you can come back to work for a while if you really want to."

"Gee thanks!" she says, sarcasm dripping from her words. "*WHEN* she says that I'm fine, I'll be back for a long time yet. I'm only 3 months. I can work right up to the last month hopefully."

"Okay, but if she says that you need to rest up, promise me that you won't fight her about it. Promise that you'll take her advice and stay home and lay around doing nothing, if that's what she tells you to do."

Her face softens as she smiles widely and assures me with a nod of her head. "Yeah of course. I'll do whatever she says. No question. Hopefully she won't tell me that though. I'd hate to be stuck in bed for the rest of this pregnancy."

"I know, and so long as everything's fine there's no need for you to be, but we both know carrying three babies is a lot different to carrying one. A lot more can go wrong so we'll need to go to the hospital here before we leave just to make sure that you're all okay and fine to travel home. Hopefully they can tell us why you started bleeding so suddenly as well, but FYI, no sex till we're sure it wasn't caused by that. If I have to go without for the next 6 months, then I'll cope.

"I won't!" She sputters at me. "It wasn't because of that Noah. Don't go blaming yourself for this too. It just happened. From what I've read, spotting is quite common in early pregnancy and especially with multiples. We may never know what caused it, and I'm okay with that if it just never happens again and our babies are safe and healthy."

"Yeah me too. Must admit. One of the scariest moments of my life. Not a night I want to go through again. Please make sure my boys are on board with that too."

"I honestly hope that they're three girls and they'll be the bane of your life when they grow up."

"Huh. Had enough practice with Scarlett, believe me. She started slamming doors at 12 and didn't stop till she was 18 and went to Uni. Don't want to do that again, especially with three of them. Nope make sure they're boys. That I can do, boys are much more user friendly."

"User friendly?! What are they power drills??!!" she laughs at the thought.

We spend the rest of the evening cuddled up on the sofa and listening to the driving sleet outside and the raging storm. It hasn't abated at all and while we were in Vancouver they were predicting this blizzard with talk of it lasting a few days. It's been going since yesterday afternoon so hopefully it'll start to die down soon. Getting out of here might be a bit harder than we thought though with the amount of snow that's been dumped. As long as the bleeding doesn't start again I'm happy to laze around enjoying the warmth of the fires in the living room. The house is amazing. It's been built to keep the whole house warm, with the huge stone walls conducting heat to the upper story of the home.

I'm laying along the sofa with my legs stretched out in front of me and my back resting against Noah's chest, a pillow behind me. He has his right arm wrapped across the front of my chest with his other hand holding his kindle up so he can read.

I'll be grateful to Noah forever for bringing me here for our first white Christmas. Even with the scare last night I've enjoyed every moment of our stay and just being together like this.

"Noah?" I ask quietly as I can see he's engrossed in his new Kindle that I bought him for Christmas.

"Mmm?" he replies, distractedly.

"Thanks for arranging this for us. I don't think I said it before. I just love that we're here and I've had the best Christmas ever. If last night hadn't happened, it would've been perfect."

Leaning over to kiss me gently he smiles down at me before touching my lips with his own. "You're welcome Baby. I've loved it too...well except for last night obviously."

"Do you think we could come back again one day and maybe bring the kids with us? Can you imagine how much fun this snow would be for a child? It'd be awesome." I smile to myself, turning back to my kindle again.

"Of course we can. We'll have to wait till they're older obviously, but it's a great idea. Maybe we could come back for our 5th wedding anniversary in a few years."

"We aren't married yet! Already you're planning ahead to our wedding anniversary?!" I scoff at him over my shoulder.

"Soon as I can arrange it, we will be. Semantics, Babe. I don't want to wait a second longer than I have to."

"Well you may have to wait a bit, if we can't make it to Vegas like we planned. We might have to change our venue and maybe just get married at home on the farm with our immediate family. How does that sound?"

Leaning down to kiss the top of my head gently he says, "Perfect."

I love this man with all my heart and it's about to burst right now it's so full. I snuggle back into him, content in the knowledge that my babies are fine and I have the best fiancé in the whole world. Everything is as it should be in my universe.

Noah carries me up to our room, places me gently down on the bed and goes to brush his teeth and change out of his clothes. Even with the stone wall behind us, the night's get cool and he's taken to wearing his sleep pants and a cotton t-shirt to keep him warm. Normally he sleeps naked, but it gets chilly up here by morning.

Once he's finished I get carried in and placed in front of the vanity in the large bathroom. I brush my teeth and pee, grateful that there's still no sign of blood. It won't stop me worrying about them, but I'm reassured somewhat now that the bleeding's stopped, along with the cramps that worried me last night. I spent the whole night panicking that I would miscarry here in the middle of nowhere and nothing Noah said eased my mind. I appreciated his support, but at that stage nothing was gonna me feel any better.

The next morning brings sunshine, but there's still a ferocious, roaring, gale force wind outside when we wake up. The winter wonderland is so beautiful it hurts my eyes to look at it, even with tinting on the window. The wind has blown a lot of the snow from the tree branches exposing their green leaves which shine brightly against the stark white background.

Noah rolls over to kiss me good morning and pushes himself upright in the bed as he takes in the sight through the huge floor to ceiling window beside our bed.

"Wow. That looks awesome. At least it's not snowing anymore. We might be able to get out of here today if that wind dies down some more. I don't want to take any chances with you if it's not necessary. We can wait another day if you feel alright."

"So far, so good." I reassure him, leaning back against his shoulder and gazing out the window as he wraps an arm over me pulling me close. "Though I really, really need to pee...again! I seem to spend half my life peeing at the moment. I hope this improves soon. I need to buy a book when we get home. Something that tells me everything that's gonna happen in advance so that I'm prepared."

"I spent a bit of time doing some research on the internet before we left home. It was an eye opener, that's for sure. Did you realize that the babies can poop while they're still inside your belly? That one blew me away!"

I jab at his chest with an elbow. "Ewwww... that's disgusting! Why would you tell me that? See, I could happily go the rest of my life without knowing that piece of information. Now I'll I can think about is them pooping!"

He chuckles loudly behind me pulling my long braid out from under him and placing it over my shoulder into my lap.

"I suppose this means a haircut for sure. No way am I gonna have time to look after all this with three newborns. I'll be lucky if I get a shower every day!" I declare as I pick up the end of my knee length dark hard.

I hear a long sigh as he takes in my words and knows I'm right. "I think that's true, though I hate the thought of you cutting it all off. Can we wait till the last possible moment before you do it? I love your hair and I'll miss it when it's gone. What about just getting it cut up to your bum? That way it's still manageable, but long as well."

"Yeah that sounds like a good idea. I'll wait till it really annoys me then I'll go. Maybe I could donate it to make wigs for cancer sufferers. There'd be more than enough for at least one."

"Still thinking of others, my little Florence Nightingale. See this is why I adore you."

"Really? I thought it was for my sharp wit and good looks?! Well now I'm disappointed." I laugh loudly, turning to take in his astonished look as he tries to think of a suitable retort.

"It is, and because you're mine. You're gorgeous, smart and witty and I adore everything about you. Even your little piggy toes that you hate."

"Oh don't love them. They're horrid. I hate my toes!" I declare forcefully. My toes are the one thing that I hate about my body. Everybody has something that they hate right?

"They're the prettiest toes ever because they're yours." He replies as he bends down to place another kiss on the back of my head. "Well I suppose I ought to get up and cook us some breakfast. What do you feel like today? My culinary skills are at your service."

"Ha. Right! How about some pancakes if you can make some without a plastic jug of mix. I'll come help you if you want."

"Nope. I can handle it. You shower and dress and I'll bring it up for you. Remember you're resting up still, so back into bed after your shower. I'll even let you walk to the bathroom if you're sure you're okay today."

"Yeah I'm good. I need to get up and around. I think I have a pressure sore on my butt from being in bed all day yesterday."

"Okay, I'll go make us some food. Be back in a while, but if you need me just yell out."

I lean around to kiss him softly on his lips as I push myself up from the bed and walking over to the bathroom quickly. Now I really need to pee. My bladder's about to burst, I think.

Reassured that the bleeding hasn't started up again I shower quickly and run my hand continuously over my small bump. I can't get over the realization that soon that bump will be three squirming, screaming babies. I take a deep breath and tell myself that we can do this...together. I'm sure that Noah's mum, Maxine, will come and help if we need her to for a while. I wonder about feeding three infants at once. How do women breast feed three babies? I really need to do some reading up on this. I don't think I've ever seen a stroller for three either. I need to do some searching of my own on the internet. Being a first time Mum is hard enough, but being a first time Mum with triplets is gonna be so much harder. Now that I've got used to the idea I'm excited about it. I must admit it was a huge shock when we first found out. We only found out because I was savagely raped and had a pregnancy test then an ultrasound which showed two babies. It wasn't till we saw my OBGYN in Perth that we found another one. Noah didn't want me to have any more ultrasounds after that. Each one found another baby.

He's been amazing this week. Not only did he give me the most incredible emerald and diamond engagement ring ever, but he's done everything he could for me since we found out I was pregnant and especially this week, since we've been in Canada. I've actually been managing full nights of deep dreamless sleep since we've been away from home and I hope that continues. I hate having the nightmares where everything is so real I can smell him, feel him violating me and I'm helpless to stop him. It's like reliving it over and over again. All I want to do is put it behind me and move forward into the next chapter of our lives. Jackson's attack changed my life and I need to deal with it so that I'm healthy for these babies and I'm not a mental case for Noah. Going to see the psychologist for the first time was helpful but we didn't really get into the details of the rape. It was all too raw and too soon to talk about. It was hard enough telling the Police the details.

Noah got up and walked out of the room. It was too much for him to take in. He's decided to go and talk to her as soon as we get back too, so that he can be supportive and understanding about what I'm going through. The trauma of the rape has been eclipsed slightly by the news of the pregnancy, but I'm trying my best to just take it day by day or hour by hour if necessary as my doc suggested. So far I've been relatively lucky. She told me of other women who have constant panic attacks and agoraphobia so bad they can't leave the house without being medicated and still others who've tried to commit suicide even because of the shame and the trauma. They don't have a Noah or his family as a support system like I do.

I blow dry my hair and braid it again as I make my way back to the bed and wait for Noah to bring up our breakfast. It's taking him a long time and I really want to go down and check on him, but I know that he wouldn't be happy about it plus the sensible thing to do is stay put. I wouldn't forgive myself if something happened to the babies because I was too impatient to wait for food.

Just as my stomach growls loudly he appears with a large wooden tray, which has two glasses of juice plus a stack of pancakes with a bottle of maple syrup. He places it carefully in the middle of the bed and my mouth waters from the smell of the sweet treat. I pick up a fork, cut into the top pancake and smother it in syrup, cupping my hand under it as I bring it to my mouth. "Mmmm delicious." I tell him around a mouthful of pancake, some of the syrup stuck to my lip.

"My boys hungry today are they?" he grins as he watches me dive in to spear another large mouthful.

"Uh huh. Very!" I tell him between bites. It's true too. I've never eaten so much food before in my life. It seems like I'm constantly hungry since I've been pregnant, and now that the morning sickness has temporarily stopped I can eat anything and everything. I think I agree with Noah and decide these babies must be male. Noah and his brother Logan eat more food than I've ever seen anyone eat on a daily basis, but then they both work it off by exercising – Noah at the gym and Logan by marathon training in the Pilbara.

We chat between bites and I tell Noah a bit about my childhood. I grew up in a country town on a beach and had the best childhood ever. We swam as soon as we could walk and spent most weekends and school holidays at our beach house outside of town. We grew up with our friends, a lot of whom we've known all our lives. Noah's was much the same, but without the beach. He asks about my family and I tell him that we're related to half the town or probably most of them. My mum was from a large family and so was her mother, so I have relatives scattered all over the country.

My sister moved to Adelaide to be near the private schools for my nieces. My Dad followed her when he retired, getting a house only a few streets away from hers. Julie's husband is a mine worker who flies in out to work in the largest uranium mine in Australia, so he's away a lot of the time, leaving Dad to help with the girls who are only in Primary school. My sister works part time at a local nursing home as the Admin Manager, which keeps her pretty busy. I love my nieces Jacie and Courtney whom I try to Skype as often as I can and each time I see them, I swear they've grown another inch or more.

Noah tells me of his childhood on the farm and some of the mischief that they used to get up to when their parents had no idea where they were. Apparently there's a creek that flows all year round not far from the homestead and they spent a lot of time there playing in the water and catching tadpoles and frogs and frightening Scarlett by chasing her with a frog and telling her that it was gonna eat her up. Poor Scarlett now hates frogs because of them! I once again feel sorry for her, having three older brothers to harass her constantly must have been a pain.

Our day flies by as we lay around – first on the bed, then after lunch I move to the sofa downstairs, by move I mean that Noah carries me once again, despite my protest. I lay and watch the flames for a long while just enjoying the warmth and the crackling of the fire.

The wind has died down more and the clouds haven't come back so it looks promising for us to leave tomorrow if we want. I really don't want to leave our haven just yet. I'm loving the solitude and the snow and the house, but I know that we need to get back to get the babies checked, to make sure that they're okay, so we can fly home as planned.

Darkness falls eventually as my stomach once again makes a loud protest at its perceived lack of food. I had a snack of a few cookies an hour or so ago, but now it's hungry again.

Noah pushes me off him carefully and strides out to the kitchen to start dinner for us again. He hates cooking, but he does it willingly at the moment. Tonight's meal is a vegetable and pasta dish, but I think he just found every vegetable in the fridge and chopped them up, mixed in a jar of cheese sauce and added them to the pasta. Simple dishes he excels at, and this one is delicious, but seriously if it was crap I'd still eat it because I'm starving.

Once again he carries me upstairs as I start yawning loudly, despite it still being reasonably early. I glance out at the moonlit area in front of the house and the snow glistens and sparkles despite the lack of bright light. It truly is magical and I wish I'd been able to get out and enjoy it more, but I know that we'll come back and we have some awesome photos of us both in the snow to remember it by.

I settle in to sleep wrapped up in his arms, and I can hear him softly snoring behind me. I lay awake for a long time just taking in the feeling of protection and warmth that I get every time he puts his arms around my body. I sigh deeply at the thought of being able to do this every night for the rest of our lives, and smile to myself, relishing the feeling of happiness that fills me.

I wake up to darkness, in a cold sweat, and it takes me a minute or so to realize where I am. My heart's pounding so hard it feels like it's about to come out of my chest, and I wonder what woke me. I don't remember having a bad dream and even if I did I normally wake up screaming because of the reality of it, not like this. My arms are tingling with pins and needles, I'm trembling all over and unable to stop, I feel nauseous, and I'm nearly hyperventilating. Noah stirs at my movement and forces one eye open to look at me, as I sit upright suddenly. When he sees the terrified look on my face he bolts upright and grabs me, running his hands up and down my arm and hugging me into his wide chest. I wish it helped, but right now I can't breathe with him hugging me like this, my lungs just won't fill with lifesaving oxygen, so I push him away and concentrate on sucking in deep breaths, trying to fill my lungs, as he watches me, but doesn't touch. I raise my hand up to my chest to try to slow my rapid heartbeat, at the same time I focus on his eyes as they look at me with alarm

"C'mon Baby. Just breathe. Slow deep breaths…that's it. Slow it down more…take a slow deep breath in and hold it for the count of three and then let it out slowly…good girl….and again…good. That's it. Slow deep breaths…you're fine…slowly…good." My breathing finally deepens to nearly normal, but my heart is still thumping rapidly in my chest. I shake my arms to try to rid myself of the pins and needles as I concentrate on keeping my breathing under control. It takes a while, but I'm finally able to feel like my lungs are working normally, my heart rate begins to slow considerably and the tingling in my arms disappears. What the hell was that????!!

"I think you just had your first panic attack, Sweetheart. You're okay now. Did you have a nightmare again?" Noah asks as he rubs my back slowly.

"Not that I remember. Fuck Noah, I thought I was having a heart attack! Oh My God. I've never had a panic attack before in my life. That was scary as Hell. I've no idea why it happened either." I reply between sucking in air deeply and blowing it out slowly. Finally, I'm starting to feel like my normal self again and my heart rate's nearly back to normal. "I'm almost positive that I didn't have a nightmare. I'd remember it if I had. I always have before. Now I think about it, Denise said panic attacks come out of nowhere and hit you when you least expect it, but I never expected to have one in my sleep!

"Can I get you something? A glass of water maybe? What do you need Babe?" He says quietly, still rubbing my back slowly, his large hand trailing up and down my spine.

"No I'm good...but thanks. I think I'll just go and splash my face with some water, then try to sleep again if I can."

Chapter THREE

Noah

Shit what the hell do I do? I think I'm shaking more than she is. That was fucking terrifying! Poor Mia. It's not bad enough that bastard damaged her physically, but now she's mentally scarred as well. As soon as we get home we'll both go and see that head doc and see what we do about it. I don't know how to help her and I hate that powerless feeling. I'm a fixer by nature. This sucks...badly. I scrub my hand up over my face and run my fingers through my hair as I wait for her to finish in the bathroom and come back to bed.

As she approaches the bed I reach up to take her hand in mine and pull her gently over to me so that she can spoon against me. I throw the soft doona over her to keep her warm and I hear her contented sigh as she relaxes again.

"You okay now?" I ask her softly as I kiss the back of her exposed neck.

"Yeah I think so. Just a little freaked out still, but I'll be fine. Just don't let go of me okay?" She says snuggling back and wiggling her arse against my dick.

"Never. I've got you Sweetheart. Always." I kiss her again on the spot below her ear that I know she loves and I lay back down and wait for her to fall asleep. Eventually I hear her breathing even out, but I don't sleep. I just lay there holding her close and taking in the sensation of her soft body against mine, the smell of her hair and the warmth from her body. I'd lay down my life for this woman in a heartbeat, but I can't take away what she went through because of me and my fucking computer program. I wish I'd never developed it now. If I knew that it would cause someone to kidnap and rape her repeatedly like Jackson did, then I'd never have touched the bloody thing. I'd have been content with just the Gold Mines that Logan and I own. I'd give up every cent if I could turn back time and change what happened.

I watch the sky brighten through the window as the sun rises and the crisp white snow glistens in the light. It really is spectacular scenery. Maybe next time we come back we can bring the rest of the family as well for a white Christmas. I know Mum and Dad would love it and maybe Mia's Dad and Sister and her family could come as well. I keep it in mind as I gaze out the window at the rising bright sun. I feel Mia stir in my arms and I lean down to kiss the top of her head softly.

"Hey you. How come you're awake so early?" She asks sleepily, snuggling back into me, yawning loudly.

"Watching the sun rise and you sleep and trying to decide which one is more amazing. I decided you win, hands down." I kiss her forehead as she turns to look up at me.

"God I love it when you say things like that. I don't know what I did to deserve you, but I'm thankful every day." She kisses my neck and my chest through my t-shirt and takes a deep sniff of it as she lays her head back on my shoulder.

"Not half as grateful as me gorgeous girl. I don't know what I'd do without you and I never intend to find out." I kiss her hair again lightly as I push her over to lay on her own pillow. "I need to feed my family. What do you feel like today? I cook great toast!"

She giggles at me and my dick instantly hardens. "Toast sounds great thanks Hun, though I don't think we've got any Vegemite so just some Peanut Butter, if there is any."

"Really? Peanut Butter? That's just crap. How can you eat it? It's like eating sludge!" I shiver in distaste. Peanut Butter is fucking disgusting. I've never liked that crap.

"Hey! Don't be picking on my PB, its delicious!" She tells me as she throws the quilt off her and walks over to the bathroom. "I'll have a quick shower then meet you downstairs okay?"

"Righto." I tell her as I take in how cute she looks in her pale blue flannel pajamas with little yellow ducks on them. They are way too big for her. She has the sleeves rolled up and the bottom of the pants as well, but they're her favorites so I just smile at her and leave her to it, heading downstairs to start our breakfast.

Seeing as the wind has died down and the weather is still clear we decide to head back to Vancouver though we aren't due to be back for another two days, but I want to get her to an OBGYN to make sure everything's okay with the babies. The cabin's only just over half hour's drive from the city as the crow flies, but it takes us well over an hour to get out through the thick snow to the freeway back into the main area of town. Mia programs the GPS for the nearest hospital and we head there before going to the hotel.

After an hour or so wait we're taken in for a consult with an OB doctor. He listens as Mia tells him what happened. I stand back in the corner of the small room, close enough for support, but far enough back as to not get in the way. The doc nods at the appropriate times and frowns as she tells him about the sudden bleeding and how scary it was. He wants to do another ultrasound and Mia lays back on the small examination bed and pushes down her sweat pants slightly. The doc notices the yellowing bruises and bite marks on her lower stomach and his eyes fly up to mine in challenge. "Wanna tell me what happened here young lady?" He asks her in his French Canadian accent.

Mia's eyes dart up to meet mine. "Uh......I was raped. It happened a few weeks ago now. We found out about the pregnancy at the same time." She reaches up for my hand and I grab hers tightly moving closer to her side.

"I'm sorry to hear that. I hope you're getting some support from some kind of rape crisis center back home?" He asks her gently once he realizes that I'm not responsible for her injuries.

"Err yeah I am. I have a psychologist that I've just started seeing. The bruises are finally fading now thank goodness."

"In my experience the outside marks fade quickly. It's the inside injuries that you need to take your time with. I'm glad you have a supportive partner. You'll get through this alright if you continue seeing your doctor back in Perth. Now let's have a look at these babies shall we?" He says as he squirts her exposed belly with a cold gel and she jumps as it hits her skin. He chuckles softly and apologies "You'd think we'd heat it up for you wouldn't you?"

Mia smiles at him and agrees as he starts pushing on her pelvis with the camera thing. Soon I can hear rapid thumping and I let out a breath that I didn't realize I was holding as I recognize the sound of their heartbeats. Mia glances up to me as a tear falls to her temple and I reach down to swipe it away.

"Are they all okay doc?" I ask, dreading the answer but knowing that at least one of them has a healthy heartbeat because we can hear it echoing around the room. The probe moves to another angle as he stops to take measurements and clicks some buttons on the machine. Suddenly he moves it slightly again and I can see them on the screen. Three little peanuts floating in a black space. I bend down to kiss Mia who's holding her breath, waiting for the doc to tell us if they're alright.

"Well the good news is that they all appear fine and healthy. They're the right size for your dates and there doesn't appear to be any problems with the placenta so I'm not overly concerned. I would advise just taking it easy for a week or two though just to make sure. Go see your own OB when you get home, but for now everything looks good." He informs us smiling broadly.

Mia immediately bursts into loud sobs as I gather her up in my arms and lay kisses over her face, wiping away her tears with my lips. "It's okay Baby. They're alright. Our babies are fine. Let it out......it's okay."

She looks up at me with watery eyes, trying to control her sobs as she says on a hiccup, "Noah I was so scared. I was sure that something had happened to them."

"I know baby. I was too, but they're all alright." I pepper kisses over her face as she slows her sobbing to the occasional hiccup. "So Doc what happened? What caused the bleeding and can it happen again?"

He looks over at us and smiles. "Sometimes these things just happen. Nobody knows why, and it's a bit hard to diagnose after the event, but the main thing is that they're okay and the bleeding stopped by itself so that's a good thing. I can't say if it'll happen again, but there's no reason to think so. Just take it easy young lady and you should be fine. Good luck for the future." He nods to me as I help Mia to sit up. "I'll just go and do your discharge paperwork, but you can leave as soon as you get dressed. Goodbye son. Take care of her."

"Forever Doc, that's a given." I assure him as he opens the door to leave.

Once Mia's calm enough, we leave the hospital thanking the Doc on the way out, my arm around her protectively as I lead her to the car.

"So Babe. Thank God they're alright. You ready to go to the hotel now or you want to stop and get some lunch first?" I ask as I help her up into the large SUV that we rented. She waits till I'm doing up my seat belt before answering.

"Definitely food first. I'm starving again. I feel like I haven't eaten for days!"

"Okay then. Food it is. What do you feel like? Any preference?"

"Something really unhealthy I think. Lots of grease and carbs to celebrate the good news." She giggles as she tells me.

"You're the boss! Burger King or Maccas?"

"Maccas. I have a craving for a Big Mac, fries, chocolate thick shake and maybe an apple pie as well." She says smiling my way as I back out of the car park. I program the GPS to find us the nearest McDonald's. It's only a few streets away so we get there quickly and Mia devours her Big Mac plus some of mine as I smile at the amount of food she can put away now. She's constantly hungry and eats almost more than I do.

"At this rate we'll need to go get me some maternity pants soon because I won't be able to wear my clothes much longer." She says around a mouthful of my burger.

"Sweetheart you eat whatever you want and we'll go shopping for whatever you need. I don't care. You're gonna need some maternity clothes sooner or later anyway. No way my boys are gonna fit in those track pants for much longer. We still have tomorrow free. If you promise to take it easy for the rest of today, we could go and do a bit of shopping then if you'd like."

"Mmmm. Sounds like a plan. Let's see how it goes. I can always go on Saturday while you're doing the presentation. I don't mind wandering around by myself for a bit."

"Nope. Not gonna happen Sweetheart. Where you go I go, for a while. What if something happened and I'm not there? I'd never forgive myself. I want you resting up in the room on Saturday otherwise I'd just be worrying about you the whole time."

"Noah I'm fine. I promise to take things easy, but I'm quite capable of doing a bit of shopping on my own. You don't need to hold my hand every second of the day. It's fine." She tells me with that determination in her voice that I've come to know when she's getting her back up.

"Humor me Mia. Just till we get home......please?"

"Okay Okay. You win. We'll go tomorrow and do some shopping if the weather's alright...otherwise we can wait till we get home. It doesn't need to be done right now." She throws up her hands in defeat as I smile at my small victory. I know how hard she can dig her heels in when she wants to, so I'm glad that she's giving in on this.

We settle back into our room at the hotel overlooking the shopping district. I arranged to have the same one because I knew it had good views of the Christmas lights for her. I work on my computer while she browses the internet and the chapels available in Vegas. I glance over to see a page full of wedding dresses but she quickly turns it away so that I can't see while I laugh at her.

"Don't laugh at me. You can't see my dress. It's tradition. What do you think? Vegas or the farm? Now that we know that I'm fine, we can go to Vegas on Sunday if you still want to."

"I'm happy to do whatever you want Baby, but I'm fine with the original plan of getting married in Vegas and a party at the farm when we get home. We can fly down first thing on Sunday if you'd like and get married then...wait...when's New Year's Eve?"

"Umm...Sunday? Yeah Sunday...why?"

"Sunday it is then. Show me what you found for us so far. Anything take your fancy? An Elvis impersonator or just a marriage celebrant?"

She turns the laptop my way to show me her choices and explains what they do. No Elvis impersonator though, much to my disappointment. I was really hoping that she'd want to do that. I was looking forward to telling everyone that Elvis married us, but so long as someone marries us legally, then I'm all good. I just want her to be mine...now and forever.

I make a few calls and arrange the jet to take us first thing Sunday morning to Vegas as well as speak to the guy in charge of the chapel that she wants and arrange the ceremony for 4pm to give us time to get there and get ready in plenty of time. I don't want her rushing around on her wedding day. I want her to have time to enjoy it. This also means that we'll have time to shop for her dress tomorrow and a suit for me even though I brought one with me for the presentation. We spend the rest of the afternoon making plans and decide to wander out for a little while and look at some jewelers for rings. Mia assures me that she feels good, but we can make this quick then come back to have some dinner in the room and relax.

Chapter FOUR

Mia

Noah really is so sweet. I wonder if he realizes that every time we walk outside he walks on the outer edge of the sidewalk near the road or that he walks touching me somehow. Either his arm is around me or he's holding my hand or kissing me. I see his eyes dart around for any signs of danger as soon as we leave the hotel, and smile to myself at his protectiveness. I'm not a helpless frail female, but I know that he won't change so I had best get used to this. It's just him being Noah, and I don't think I could love him any more than I do right now. I can't believe that we're heading out to buy our wedding rings.

Wedding rings!

I'm kinda freaking out inside with excitement. I can't stop smiling as we slowly stroll along the crowded path. It's 4pm on a Friday afternoon so the sidewalk is pretty crowded with people rushing to do some last minute shopping before going home or heading out for drinks to celebrate the end of the week. Noah uses his large frame to clear a path for us as we make our way to a Tiffany jewelers only a block or so from our hotel.

My wedding ring is all diamonds and I adore it even though Noah wouldn't let me know how much its worth. He chose a plain wide platinum band for himself. I also caught him looking at Eternity rings to fit around my engagement ring while I was browsing at the sparkling diamond jewelry on display. I see him subtly nod to the assistant who immediately whips out a tray and removes a ring for him to examine. He passes it back to her and she disappears through a nearby door as we wait for them to bring us our rings. I'm not much of a jewelry lover, but it's so much fun just looking around at what they have to offer. It doesn't take long for the assistant to return and I see Noah pocket a small blue box as he quickly passes over his credit card for payment, she passes him the small gift bag that holds our rings in exchange.

As we're walking slowly back Noah notices a Bridal shop nearby and pulls me over to have to a look inside. I have a dress in mind, but I'm not about to show him so I shoo him outside while I look around with the help of a lovely older lady. After a bit of searching I find my ideal dress. It's a tea length strapless dress with a corseted beaded bodice and full tulle skirt. Very Doris Day looking, but absolutely perfect for our ceremony. It has that 1950's look about it. I don't want a long dress that I'll never wear again and this is just ideal. It fits me like a glove as well. I choose some shoes to go with it and pay for it with my credit card as the assistant puts it into a black hanger cover for me so that Noah can't see it. I'm absolutely astounded that I managed to find the perfect dress in the first shop that I went into and I can't help grinning widely as I open the door to an astonished Noah leaning against the shop window.

"I was expecting to pay for it Baby. It's the least I can do. Let me carry it for you. Are you sure you're happy with it? We can always go looking in Vegas when we get there if you want to. I'm sure there's a lot of Bridal shops."

I bring his head down to kiss him lightly. "Nope. I want this one. I love it and I won't change my mind. It's just perfect. Now let's go get you a suit. Can you buy off the rack or will it need to be tailored for you?"

"Normally I have it tailored by a shop in Perth, but I can make do with an off the rack one I think. There's a shop over there we can look in if you're not too tired?" He nods to a shop across the road bearing a famous menswear logo.

We enter and get greeted by a very flamboyant assistant who immediately starts measuring Noah with his eyes, much to his dismay. I smirk to myself as Noah endures the stare while telling him what he needs. The assistant flounces over to a rack and pulls out a few suits in different shades for Noah to try on. He settles on a pale gray silk with white shirt but no tie despite the assistant's desperate efforts to choose one for him. Noah quickly shows me his suit for my approval, but immediately backs away to the dressing room as the assistant comes over in a flurry of hand gestures and swishing hips, accompanied by murmurs of approval. I laugh at Noah's look of discomfort when he comes out changed back into his normal clothes, looking around for any sign of the over-the-top assistant. I nearly pee myself laughing as Noah has to endure a lot of touching when he hands over his suit and shirt for the guy to pack up for him. I can see that he can't wait to get out of here and away from the overly friendly guy helping him.

Once he has his suit hanger and he's paid for it he grabs my hand tightly and almost drags me out of the shop while I'm almost running to keep up with him because he's walking so fast.

"Noah, Hun, slow down a bit!" I laugh at him as we reach the sidewalk.

"Uh Uh. He might still be following us. Oh Fuck, that was creepy! I don't have anything against gay guys, except when they continually paw me unnecessarily. Ewww...he didn't even care that you were there!" He says, glancing back behind him to make sure we aren't being followed.

"Settle Gretel! He's not coming to accost you. We can slow down now. I can't keep up with your long legs."

He slows his pace and leans down to kiss my temple lightly. "Sorry Baby. He freaked me out. You poor thing...I didn't mean to make you run. Shit...are you okay?"

I smile up at him, reassuring him that I'm fine. "Yeah Luv, I'm good, but I think a long hot bath's in order now. It's still freezing out here."

"You can't be cold. You're rugged like an Eskimo. You look like a very pink fluffy marshmallow still...but yeah, a bath sounds good. I need to wash away the feeling of him touching me."

At the innocent words my mind immediately flies back to the time Noah found me in the shower trying to scrub my skin clean after the rape. It must show on my face as he glances over at me and pulls me into his arms for a tight hug.

"Aw Fuck. Sorry Babe. I didn't mean to bring back any bad memories. Shit, I need a filter. Oh God. I'm so sorry." He says between feathering kisses over my pink woolen cap covering my head, and rubbing my back.

I'm trying to maintain control of my emotions as I look up into his deep blue eyes. "It's alright. It's not your fault. I need to toughen up a bit. You shouldn't have to censor your words. I'm okay."

"I can be such a dickhead sometimes. I'm sorry. From now on I'll be more careful, I promise." He says, looking deep into my eyes, his expression serious.

"Noah it's okay. Let's just get out of this weather and get warm and order some food. These boys are hungry again."

While Noah is at the office of the Canadian Mining Company, I stay in the room and watch a DVD and think about our future. The DVD is on in the background, but I'm on the internet doing some research on multiple pregnancy, and checking out cribs and strollers and try not to think about how much this is going to cost us...well cost Noah. Although technically after tomorrow I suppose his money becomes mine as well, though I've never really thought about it before. I have no idea what he's worth, but I presume that if he can afford private jets to fly across the other side of the world then he's worth a lot. One day we'll have that conversation I suppose, but I don't really care. I'm thinking more about the immediate future. When I get back I'll have to put my apartment on the market. It's mortgaged so I won't make that much money on the sale, but what I get will clear my credit card debt and maybe some left over. I'll need to sell my furniture as well. I Google second hand dealers in Perth and decide to call a few when I get home. No point in doing it just yet.

I'm excited about tomorrow. I can't believe that I'm getting married! Everything seems to have happened so quickly. These last few months have just flown by, and they've been the happiest of my life, except for that one day, that was the worst day of my life, when I woke up in a seedy motel room chained to a bed. I push it to the back of my mind as I decide that no negative thoughts are going to get in the way of our happiness tomorrow. I'm determined to make this a great day for us both. I go through my suitcase and pull out all my lingerie to find something suitable for my wedding day. I find a tiny white lacy thong that's perfect. I ring down to the beauty parlor in the lobby and book in for a full wax, massage and facial, giving myself a few minutes to get down there, as they have an open appointment right now. Grabbing up my purse and room key I hurry over to the elevator and wait impatiently for the car to ascend.

My phone starts ringing halfway through my massage and doesn't stop ringing till after my facial. I pull it out of my handbag and unlock it as I pay for my treatments. There's 16 missed calls and 5 text messages telling me to ring him ASAP. I realize I forgot to leave him a note so he'd have no way of knowing where I am. I quickly dial his number and he picks up after the first ring.

"Where the Fuck are you? Are you alright? I got back and you were gone. I've been going out of my mind here!" He barks into the phone before I have a chance to say hello.

"Well, hello to you too. Remember that conversation we had about a filter Noah? You need to engage it right now before I hang up. I'm sorry I've worried you. I'm just downstairs about to come up now....so you'd best calm down a bit and let me explain okay?" I say annoyed at his attitude. "I clean forgot about leaving a note and I should have, but I rushed out so quickly I didn't even think of it. I didn't realize that you'd make it back before I would. I thought you be gone for ages yet." By this time the elevator has arrived and I'm halfway up to our floor. "I'm almost at the room. I'll see you in a sec." I tell him as I disconnect the phone call.

I stride over to the door and before I have a chance to insert my Key card, its yanked open from the inside. Noah pulls me fiercely into his arms and hugs me tight. "Thank Fuck you're alright. I was worried sick. I didn't know where you were. Don't ever do that to me again." He kisses each cheek and the corners of my mouth before slamming his mouth down on mine. I return his kiss, reassuring him that I'm fine. My fingers slide up to his hair and I grab hold of his head pulling him back slightly so that I can speak.

"Hun I'm fine. I just went downstairs to get all pretty for tomorrow. I honestly didn't expect you back so soon, and I thought I had plenty of time. I'm sorry I worried you...I really am, but the next time you talk to me like that you'll be sorry okay?"

"Aw Fuck Baby. I'm sorry. I'm an idiot. I was just scared out of my mind. I pictured you laying in an alley where I couldn't get to you and my imagination was going crazy. Please don't ever do that to me again. If I'd known you were just down in the Day Spa, I wouldn't have reacted like that." He kisses me softly again sliding his lips across mine. "Forgive me?"

"I suppose, ya big moron! Next time I'll leave a note I promise." I lean up to kiss him again. "Soooo tell me. How did it go? Do they want it?"

"Yeah they do and they want me to come back and train them as well, though I think Logan would be more qualified or maybe one of the Tech nerds. They're probably the better choice, but I'll arrange someone to come over in a few weeks once we've signed the contract and handled the details. I wouldn't mind coming back again, but I thought I'd check with you first. It's probably going to be at least a month, maybe two before it's all sorted, but I thought if you felt up to it we could go back to the cabin again. The weather will be nicer by then hopefully, though I know how much you love the snow."

"I'd love to Hun. That sounds great. We could use it as our honeymoon as well. By the way...did you ring Bill and let him know that you won't be back for a few more days?"

"Actually I did and I told him that we won't be back for the rest of the week because I thought we'd stopover in Hawaii for a few days as a proper honeymoon. What do ya think?"

"I think I adore you with all my heart. You're the best future husband that there is. Wow. I hadn't even thought about a honeymoon. I just assumed we'd go straight back to Perth after Vegas." I say, my face showing my gratitude at his gesture.

"My wife deserves a honeymoon and we have to refuel at Hawaii anyway, so I just arranged for us to stay for the rest of the week. I'm glad you approve. I can't wait." He tells me, smiling and wiggling his eyebrows up and down suggestively.

I giggle at him, shaking my head. "You know, technically we shouldn't be sleeping together tonight. It's the night before our wedding. According to tradition, we're supposed to spend it apart."

"Fuck tradition. There is no way I'm letting you out of my sight after today I don't think my heart can take it." He declares, frowning down at me, gently swiping away a lock of hair away from my face.

"Okay. It's a stupid tradition anyway. Let's order some food and relax for the rest of the night."

Chapter FIVE

Noah

We land in Vegas at lunchtime, it's a balmy 80 degrees and the sun is shining brightly. I ordered a car to take us to the hotel. Mia looks out the window in amazement as we cruise up the main strip. I can't wait for her to see it at night with the neon lights shining brightly. Vegas is amazing during the day, but absolutely spectacular at night. She turns her head rapidly trying to take in everything at once as we near the hotel. I chose a hotel that I've stayed at before, so I know it's nice. I ordered a suite for us so we have some privacy.

In a few hour's she's gonna be mine forever and I can't wait.

I take her hand again and raise it to my lips, she glances down at me quickly, with a look of amazement on her beautiful face. I smile over at her, she runs her hand down the side of my face and her thumb over my bottom lip.

"I love you and I can't wait till this afternoon. I promise I'll try my best to make you happy and be a good wife." She looks at me earnestly, I can see the love and adoration shining in her eyes. I lean over and kiss her lips softly, then pull back and look into her crystal green eyes.

"I promise to be the best husband and father I can be, for you and our babies."

She swipes at her cheek as a tear escapes and tells me on a laugh. "Maybe we should save this for the ceremony. I feel like we need a priest to say, "I now pronounce you man and wife" and it'll be over." She gives me a watery smile.

I bark out a laugh as I brush away another tear from her porcelain skin. "Babe we can certainly include it in the spiel if you want to. Not a bad idea. I thought I did well"

"Do we have time to write our own vowels do you think? I'd like that."

"Of course we do. It's your wedding Baby. Whatever you want to do is fine with me and I reckon I could whip up something in an hour or two."

"Well luckily it won't take me long to get ready so I think I can do something half decent as well. I should have thought about this last night. I could have had it done by now." She smiles up at me.

"Won't take long? Babe if you're planning to arrive naked you'd better tell me now so that I'm prepared!" I tell her on a laugh as we walk through the huge entrance to the hotel and over to the reception desk.

"Whhhaaattt?! NOOO! I didn't mean that at all, you sex fiend!" She tells me with a shocked look, elbowing me in the stomach as we make it to the desk and stand in front of the Clerk, who must have heard the last sentence, because she's giving me a strange look as if trying to decide if I'm a threat or not.

Politely we both turn to her and start laughing at her narrowed eyes focused in my direction. "Ummm. We have a suite reservation for Byrne." I tell her trying not to laugh.

After the check in is completed, we make our way up to the suite which is everything I'd hope it would be. We have a living room, dining room and small kitchen with a huge bedroom and bathroom attached as well. A king size bed dominates the bedroom and the bathroom is all marble and glass with a shower for two people and a deep ceramic bathtub.

I follow Mia from room to room as we check it out. She's impressed with the opulence of the suite as I watch her face taking in each room. I told the clerk when I made the booking that we were getting married and someone has thoughtfully left deep red rose petals scattered over the pure white bed cover in a romantic gesture. I make a mental note to leave a big tip as Mia turns to me and hugs me tight, thinking it was my idea.

If I'd actually thought about it I'd be proud, but I'll keep a secret. No need to let on that I didn't plan it. I raise her left hand up to my lips and kiss her engagement ring, then twirl it gently from side to side with my thumb, as I smile at her, happy to take credit. I notice a bouquet of 6 roses with a white ribbon wrapped around them in a tall vase on the dresser. Mia sees them at the same time and I hear her gasp as she realizes that they're her wedding roses.

"Oh My God Noah. You thought of everything!" She squeals as she walks over to touch them, rubbing a petal between her finger and thumb.

I smile at her and decide to double the original tip that I was leaving, silently thanking whoever did this for me.

I've just been elevated to the best fiancé in the universe I think, even though I had nothing to do with the flowers. I won't tell her

that though. I don't mind being the best fiancé in the universe at all.

"So how are we going to do this?" She asks as she turns towards me.

Confused about what she means; I look at her with a blank stare. "Do what Babe?"

"How are we going to manage to get dressed and to the chapel without you seeing my dress till the right time?"

"Oh that. Ummm how about I get dressed out in the living room and you can have the bedroom and bathroom, although they did say that there's a bride's room if you want to use it at the chapel. You can get dressed there if you want."

"Noah that's brilliant." She beams at me then kisses me on the jaw lightly. "That's perfect. I'll get 90% dressed here and then finish getting ready at the chapel."

"There you go talking about being naked again." I tell her on a laugh as she hits me with the back of her hand landing a slap on my chest, and scoffing at me. "Seriously though Baby. Nothing has to happen tonight if you aren't up to it. In fact, I think I'm a bit scared to try again after what happened the last time. We can wait a few weeks to make sure everything's okay if you want."

Her shocked look tells me all I need to know, especially when she sputters, saying, "I don't think so Mr Byrne! My hormones are running rampant at the moment, right now it's taking all my self-control to resist tearing off all your clothes and pushing you down on that gorgeous bed. There will be sex tonight, you can guarantee it."

Gathering her up in my arms I cup the side of her face in my large hand and she leans down into it. "You sure about this Sweetheart?"

"Absolutely. The Doc said the babies are fine so there's no reason to think it'll happen again and I don't intend to abstain for the next 6 months, so you'd better get used to the idea of being ravaged anytime and anywhere."

"Anytime and anywhere? Really? Wow. Now there's an offer I can't refuse. My Mamma raised a gentleman and a gentleman always gives his lady what she asks for." I tell her with a smirk.

"Good. Now shall we go out and grab some lunch and have a quick look around? We don't have to go too far." She tells me, pulling me over to the door.

We get some lunch at an American Diner, complete with jukebox and booths and black and white tiled floor. I devour my hamburger as she struggles to finish hers. Luckily there's no time difference between Vancouver and Las Vegas so there's no jet lag.

I need a few minutes alone to organize our wedding dinner tonight. I slip out to the men's bathroom and make a call to the concierge, who assures me that everything I need will be done by the time we get back to the hotel.

We make our way back to the hotel slowly, taking in the sights along the way. We stand and gaze at the incredible structures that are a feature of the Strip. People crowd the sidewalk as I hold her close to me, arm around her shoulders.

When we get back to the hotel she decides to go shower and start getting ready, as I take my clothes out to the living room. Before she has a chance to get to the bathroom I run over and burst through the door ahead of her, slamming it in her face as she stands there dumbfounded. "HEY!" She shouts through the door.

"Sorry Babe. I'll only be 5 minutes and then it's all yours for the next hour or two." I yell back at her as I start the shower and strip out of my clothes quickly. True to my word it only takes me a few minutes to do what I need to do. I quickly run the electric razor over my stubble and splash on a bit of aftershave and I'm done. I open the door, wrapping the large bath sheet around my hips tightly, heading out to the living room to finish getting dressed.

Mia's sitting on the long sofa playing with her phone when I enter. She jumps up quickly and walks through the bedroom door, stopping to give me a firm kiss on the way past. "It's all yours Sweetheart. Take your time." I tell her as she closes the bedroom door.

"Don't worry I will!" I hear through the closed door and laugh at her.

An hour later she emerges from the bedroom in a simple sundress, clothes bag folded over her arm. She's left her hair down and her face is made up immaculately. She looks stunning even without makeup, but when she applies some she looks amazing, her huge green eyes are highlighted with a smoky dark eye shadow, but the rest of her face looks completely natural though I know it isn't. Smiling up at me she declares that she's ready to go if I am.

What a question. I've been ready for the last 55 minutes, but I told her to take her time, so I won't complain. I don't want to go from being the best fiancé in the universe to the worst in a couple of hours. I take her overnight bag and zippered dress bag and we make our way downstairs. We faxed all of our relevant documentation to the chapel yesterday, so all that remains is stopping at the Clerk's office, to pick up our license. Once that's done we head to the chapel in the large sedan that I rented for the duration of our stay.

Mia gets shown to the Bride's dressing room as I follow our celebrant into the chapel. We don't have any witnesses so the couple who were just married here hang around when he asks them if they wouldn't mind doing the job for us. They're a couple from New York, who eloped to Vegas to get married because their families thought they needed to finish college first.

They decided not to wait and headed off on their own, telling their parents they were going to Vegas for the weekend, but omitting to tell them that they planned to get married while they're here. We chat for a while as they ask questions about Australia. Like most Americans they think we all have pet kangaroos and koalas, but I tell them that most of the kangaroos I see are dead on the side of the road, which makes the groom laugh, but the bride isn't so impressed. I try to explain that kangaroos are considered cute but pests by most people, but nobody ever goes out of their way to harm one, sometimes they just get on the road at the wrong time, especially in the country.

A lady comes out and quietly tells us that the bride is ready if we are. I take my place at the front of the small chapel with the celebrant as the wedding march starts and the door opens at the back of the room revealing my gorgeous bride to be.

She's dressed in an amazing calf length full skirt chiffon dress that fits her snugly from the waist up. It's strapless and fits snugly in the bodice showing just a hint of cleavage. She looks stunning as she walks slowly down the aisle towards me, clutching her red rose bouquet tightly in both hands. She gives me a shy smile and I impatiently walk towards her, needing to touch her. I grab the hand that she holds out for me and raise it to my lips. "You are breathtaking, my gorgeous girl." I tell her quietly, leading her to the front of the chapel.

I see a tear overflow down her cheek and reach up to wipe it away quickly. "No tears today Sweetheart." I tell her as she takes a deep breath, getting her emotions under control quickly.

The celebrant knows that we want to say a few words to each other, so he invites us to do so, smiling at us broadly. He's an older man and reminds me a bit of my Dad. I'm sure he does this 10 times a day, but he makes each couple feel special, like they know him.

I start after dragging in a steadying breath. I look down at her beautiful face and everything I was going to say leaves my mind. "Mia. I can't remember a time I've ever been happier, than the day you came into my life and completely overwhelmed me. I promise to adore and worship you till the day I die and probably beyond. I'll make sure we have a good life. I promise we will raise our children together, as a partnership. You'll never want for a thing materially or emotionally. I'll give you everything I have. I'll work by your side, respecting and needing you every second of every day."

I stop to take a deep breath as emotion fills me and my chest feels like a rock's sitting on it as I think of what's she's been through these last few months. "I love you Baby." I tell her quietly, nearly breaking down as I say it. I can't help myself. I lean down and kiss her softly as I wipe another tear away from her cheek.

She looks up at me and takes a deep shuddering breath before saying, "Noah, I'll love you for an eternity and it still won't be long enough. You rescued me when I didn't even know that I needed to be. I'll be forever grateful that I met you and fell in love with you and that you actually love me back!" She smiles up at me, a hitch in her voice, tears streaming down her face now. It's all I can do to hold back my own tears as I realize that this moment is forever. I lean down to kiss her gently again, giving her time to take a breath.

After a minute she continues, still crying silently, "I love you and these babies more than my own life. I promise to be a good wife to you and the best mother that I can be to our children. I promise to share my life with you till my last breath. I'm thankful that I found my perfect soul mate. I'll love you with all that I am forever, and I'll never let you go."

The celebrant asks for the rings and my best man/witness comes forward with the box containing them. I take them both and pass mine to Mia, keeping hers safe in my palm.

He tells me that I can now place the ring on her finger as I repeat the wedding vows back to him and focus my attention on my bride, slipping the ring all the way up her slim finger, promising to love her till death do us part. She repeats the vows back to me, sliding the ring up over my knuckle and onto my finger as she promises the same. The marriage celebrant pronounces us man and wife and tells me that I can **now** kiss my bride, smirking at me because I've already kissed her a few times before I should have.

I place both my hands on either side of her face and lean into her, touching her soft pink lips with mine over and over again. I deepen the kiss as she meets me, the rest of the room fading away so that it's just us, lips grinding against the others, tongues meeting in the middle. I pull away and take in a gasping breath, as I look down at her.

"Hi Mrs Byrne." I say softly, kissing her quickly again.

As I pull away, she says on a smile, "Hi husband," and I almost strip her out of her amazing dress right there in front of everyone. The celebrant takes the opportunity to step forward a bit and hugs us both as he announces to our two witnesses that he'd like to introduce Mr and Mrs Byrne, to which they give us a great round of applause. We laughingly sign the paperwork and thank our witnesses, Maggie and Zac Pullford from New Jersey. Maggie and Mia give each other a girl hug and Maggie reaches up to place a quick kiss on my cheek as she wishes us all the happiness in the world and I shake hands with Zac telling him the same. I pass him a business card that I found in my wallet and promise to keep in touch, but know that we probably won't.

Mia and I leave after we get a few dozen photos of us all. I want some good ones of her in her wedding dress to put on my desk at the office and at home. We thank the celebrant and his assistant and head back to the car to take us back to the hotel for our wedding night. I hope my plans work out, as I kiss my new bride repeatedly on the way back. I open my door as the car comes to a halt and wait for her to move to the edge of the seat and I reach down to scoop her up in my arms, and she wraps her arms around my neck tightly.

Carrying her through the large glass doors we accept congratulations from total strangers as we pass them, plus a few comments along the lines of "worst mistake ever Dude!" Obviously going through a bad divorce I decide, brushing off the remarks. I even get a few back slaps on the way to the elevator and Mia hides her head against my chest in embarrassment.

Once we're in the elevator and alone again, she immediately changes, kissing me passionately as I hold her firmly against me, my dick hardening to a painful level. As soon as the doors open I almost run to our door. I slide the key in carefully while holding Mia against me with my arm. I push at the door and walk through to the bedroom, sitting her down on the side of the bed. As I requested the curtains have been pulled back, but the lights are off and glowing candles fill the room, the only available light besides the glow of neon from outside the window. Even though it's just dusk, the lights shine brightly up and down the Strip, but I only have eyes for the beautiful woman in front of me.

"You look amazingly gorgeous in that dress Baby, but I can't wait to get you out of it." I tell her as I take off my jacket and throw it over a chair in the corner.

She leans back on her hands as she watches me undo the buttons on my shirt and pull it out of my trousers, with a huge smile on her face. She stands up, walking over to me as I undo my cuff links and throw them on the dresser behind me. Her hands reach up to push the shirt off my shoulders. I stand still, drawing in deep breaths as I wait for her next move. My shirt falls to the ground and I reach down to undo my belt, kicking my shoes off at the same time.

She steps out of hers, much to my disappointment. I had visions of those white shiny stilettos wrapped around my ears later tonight at some point. Maybe I can talk her into putting them back on in a while. I reach around to undo the zip at her back as I bend forward to meet her lips in a desperate kiss. Her arms reach around my neck pulling me down to her so that she can spear her tongue into my mouth, moaning as my dick nearly forces its way out of my tight dress pants. I slowly slide the zip down and the dress falls away, hitting the carpet making a huge white puddle of material.

She stands there in just a tiny white G-string, which barely covers her. She must have read my mind as she steps back into her shoes and I almost cum in my pants at the sight of her. Those long legs go on for miles now, and her luscious tits are on display, nipples hard and crinkled with anticipation. I walk back a few feet to take in the vision before me, running my hands up through my hair as I groan loudly from deep in my chest.

"Holy shit Baby. Just stand there a minute, so that I can look at you." I tell her when I finally find my voice. "Wow! You are exquisite Mrs. Byrne. I'll never forget how you look right now, standing like this before me as my wife. I can hardly believe my good luck. Your body's amazing Sweetheart and I'm dying to touch you."

"Then stop talking Husband, and get over here and do it." She orders me with a breathtaking smile, holding out her hand for me to take.

I walk forward a few paces as I grab it and scoop her up into me, monkey style. She squeals because she wasn't expecting it and wraps her legs and arms around me quickly as I stride through to the huge bathroom where our bath full of bubbles and more rose petals and candles greet us. She looks around the room, taking in the sight of all of the glowing candles and the deep bath that waits for us. "Noah...how...I mean...when? How did you do this?"

"I arranged it at lunchtime with the concierge. I would have ordered us champagne as well, but you can't have any so I thought it'd be mean to watch me drink it all, so we have non-alcoholic white wine. I hope that's okay."

"It's perfect. This is perfect. You're perfect. You've thought of everything! I can't believe it."

"I wanted to make our day one that we won't forget in a hurry. Now take off those Fuck me heels and that indecent scrap of material and I'll help you into the bath." I hold her hand to steady her as she steps out of the heels and then watch as she pushes her underwear down her legs, dropping it to the floor. The sight of her naked in front of me is almost my undoing.

I fall to my knees, grabbing her hips in my large hands, then lean forward to kiss her belly softly over and over again. "Hello my boys. Mum and I just got hitched, and your Daddy is the happiest man in the world right now. I love you guys to the moon and back." I glance up and catch Mia swiping at a stray tear as she looks down at me, love shining from her amazing bright green eyes.

"I love you Noah. Forever and eternity." She tells me quietly, her eyes not leaving mine.

I straighten up, pulling her into me, capturing her lips with mine in a breathless kiss, my hand behind her head. Pulling away to drag in a breath I look into her eyes and tell her, "I love you too Baby. Forever and eternity, and that still won't be long enough. Thank you Mia. For loving me, for having my babies, for being you – my soul mate. Every breath that I take I do it for you, you and our children. I can't wait to get home and start our new life together." I lean forward and kiss the tip of her nose as I wipe away the tears streaming down her cheeks. She reaches back to gather up her hair and winds it all up catching it with her huge alligator clip at the back of her head in a messy bun.

Pulling away from her I undo my trousers and push them down, along with my boxers. Ripping off my socks quickly I reach over to help her into the high oval shaped tub. "Be careful, it's deep." I watch as she settles down into the fragrant water, the smell of roses surrounding us both in the semi darkness. Candles surround the tub and fill every surface, creating a soft light. I step into the tub behind her and gather her up into my arms, settling her back against me as I stretch out my legs alongside hers.

I kiss the back of her head, then move down to her bare neck, peppering kisses along her neck and collarbone to her shoulder and back again. "Have I told you how beautiful you looked in that dress today? I nearly thought I'd have a heart attack when I saw you standing at the door. My heart was pounding so hard I thought it was gonna come through my chest. I don't think I've ever seen anyone so gorgeous before in my life."

"Thanks Hun. You looked pretty spectacular yourself. I was nervous when the door opened and I saw the celebrant, but then I looked at you and my nerves just disappeared. You tend to do that to me…you make me feel safe…like I'm the only person in the world that you see."

"You *are* the only person in the world that I see, and that won't change Sweetheart. Forever and eternity."

She turns around, dragging her legs up to sit on them, and wraps her arms around my neck, playing with my hair gently. I gaze into her vivid eyes, wondering what on earth I ever did to deserve this amazing goddess.

"I adore you, you know that?" She smiles up at me, her gorgeous tits brushing my chest lightly. I bring my hands up to cup them gently, running my thumbs over her large pink nipples, hardening them immediately.

"I know Baby, the feeling's mutual." I tell her as I raise one large breast up to my mouth, sucking in the nipple and twirling my tongue over it again and again. I see her head drop back and a long moan escapes her, making my dick so hard I could pound nails with it. I let her nipple fall out of my mouth with a pop and do the same to the other one. I know that the pregnancy has made then sensitive so I'm careful not to bite them, I just play with the nipple with my lips and tongue. My hand reaches down between her spread legs and I rub her clit lightly. My dick's getting impatient to be inside her, but I need to know that she's okay with this. I don't want to scare her if she's not ready. As much as it'll hurt I won't go any further if she doesn't want me to.

"Babe, I want inside you. I'll be gentle I promise, but if you don't want me to, then that's fine. One word and it all stops okay?"

"Noah..." She drags out my name on a long moan. "Noah I need you inside me...now!"

With that I move my hand out of the way and use it to raise her slightly allowing my dick to line up with her entrance. I slowly push my hips upward and feel her tight pussy wrap around my shaft, and once again I groan at the sensation. I lower my mouth to her nipple again, sucking and licking it as she raises and lowers herself onto me slowly, finding her own pace.

I can feel myself hit the end of her every time she lowers herself and the thought flashes through my mind that this might be hurting the babies, but I push it away quickly as I concentrate on the sensation of her gliding up and down on my hard dick. I hold her hips as movements become faster and more uncoordinated. The sound of our ragged breathing and the splash of the water is the only noise breaking the silence in the room.

I attempt to slow her movements slightly trying to prolong the inevitable. I want to finish, but I don't want to lose this sensation, it's the best feeling in the world. Being inside her tight pussy is like coming home and I thank every God out there that she's okay with us doing this, but more importantly that she wants it as much as I do.

I throw my head back and groan loudly as I feel her tighten around me, her body starts trembling all over. I reach down with one hand and flick her clit with a finger and she shatters in my arms, a scream piercing the silence as her orgasm overcomes her. Her head falls to meet mine, as I lift her slightly, I hold her still as I thrust in and out of her. I keep this up for a few more strokes as I chase my own release, feeling the familiar tingle start in the base of my spine then I feel myself explode into her on a loud grunt and thrust of my hips.

I rub her back gently with one hand as we both come down from our high, dragging in deep breaths together, looking into each other's eyes, our foreheads touching. She runs one hand down the side of my face and traces my lips with her slim finger. I capture her finger with my lips and suck on it lightly as she smiles.

I raise her left hand to my mouth and kiss her wedding band gently, toying with it with my lips.

"Fucking hell Babe, that was incredible. I thought my head was gonna explode, I came so hard." She giggles like a schoolgirl and it does things to my dick. "Mine too." She agrees, still giggling.

"I think we need to get out now. The water's getting cool and I don't want you catching a cold." I tell her pushing her away from me gently. "Stay right there and I'll help you out." I stand up, brushing bubbles and petals off me as I do. She's now at eye level with my semi hard dick and I see her smiling as her tongue comes out to lick over her bottom lip slowly.

In an instant, I've gone from semi hard to cement hard as I step out of the bathtub and onto the carpet, grabbing a towel and wiping myself down quickly as she watches every movement. I wrap it around my hips, my now hard dick tenting the front and I reach out a hand to help her over the side of the wide tub. I reach out and get a towel for her too, wiping her down gently.

I don't bother wrapping it around her, I just pick her up in my arms and carry her over to the bed, placing her down among the deep red petals on the cover, her hair splaying out behind her, now out of its confining hair clip. I take in the sight of her with all that hair. Normally she has it up in a long braid for bed, so I don't get to see it down like this very often. It's like a dark blanket beneath her, and her pale skin looks almost luminous against it.

I crawl up between her legs as she spreads them wider for me and bends her knees out allowing my broad shoulders to fit. I take a moment to kiss her belly, running my hand over her growing baby bump, I still find it amazing that her slight body is gonna give birth to our triplets in a few months. I kiss my way down to her pink center and glide my tongue up and down as she squirms beneath me.

I spear my tongue into her moist pussy with a long groan rumbling from my throat. Raising my eyes, I see her gripping the bed cover with outstretched hands, her eyes are closed, taking in every sensation. I continue licking, sucking and gently biting her clit until she explodes on a scream, her body arching upward as she cums hard. Before she has a chance to come down I thrust into her, and she screams as her back hits the bed.

She runs her hands all over my back, leaving long deep score marks in the flesh there. I try to control my hips so that I don't hurt her as she raises her hips to meet mine, our bodies slamming together. I pull out and quickly flip her over, raising her arse into the air and push back into her again as I grab her hips for leverage. Her back arches and she throws her head back, her hair spilling all over her back and the bed. God I love that hair!

I can feel her thighs start to tremble as I continue on thrusting into her over and over, trying not to slam myself into her like I really want to. I pull out of her and lean down to lick her from her tight pussy to her clit, using my tongue and nose to slide up and down her bare pink center I can feel her getting close as she starts trembling all over and I raise myself back up and over her, covering her back with my front as I slide back into her again with a harsh grunt. Her arms are shaking and she's barely staying up on all fours as she explodes beneath me again and falls back onto the bed. I continue thrusting into her as I feel her pussy clench around me in spasms, bringing on my own release, as my back arches and I throw back my head and a half grunt/cry is forced out of me, my whole body tightening and relaxing slowly. We stay joined like this for a while till I feel her squirming uncomfortably and I throw myself off her to the side.

"Fuck Sweetheart. I have no words...nope...nothing." I smile at her as she opens her eyes slightly, taking in her glazed, well-fucked look. "Are you okay? I didn't hurt you did I?" I frown as she reaches over to run her hand up and down my chest and stomach gently.

"No Baby, you didn't hurt me, but I'm not sure about you covering me like that. It brings back bad memories and makes me uncomfortable, so maybe we won't do that again for a while."

"Ah Shit. I'm sorry Mia. I never even thought about that. You should have said something. I would have moved. I'm so sorry Sweetheart." I tell her as I scrub my hand up over my face and through my hair.

She lifts herself up on to her elbows and looks over at me, her curtain of hair falling down her back and off to the side, pooling on the bed cover. "Hun, its fine. I'm okay. I just made me a bit uncomfortable, that's all. I didn't want you to stop. I would have told you if I did." Leaning over she places an open mouth kiss on my left pec then licks my nipple like a cat lapping up cream. Oh my fucking God. Immediately my dick's hard again. I roll her to her back carefully and support myself with my elbows.

"Again?" She asks incredulously.

"Uh Huh." I say looking down at her, a smile breaking over my face. "Are you up to it? You aren't sore are you? I can wait until tomorrow if you are."

She opens her thighs wider allowing me to settle between them comfortably. "Nope not sore at all. I want my husband to make love to me...again."

"Your husband certainly wants to make love to his beautiful wife." I tell her as I lean down to capture her lips with mine, forcing my tongue into her mouth and tangling with hers.

I move my hips up and down so that my dick rubs against her clit, gathering her moisture as I slowly push into her, relishing the feel of her walls surrounding me. I pull back until only the head of my dick is inside her and I thrust forward just a fraction over and over, teasing her.

"Noah. Just fuck me already...please!" She cries as I spear into her filling her completely. I wait for a moment, enjoying the feeling of her tight pussy around me, then I slowly move back and forward, making love to her with my body, my heart and my soul. I can feel her drag her nails down my back and I'm sure I'll have deep scratches there tomorrow, but I don't care.

The slight pain only adds to the enjoyment as I languidly push back into her and drag my hips back again. I lean down to cover her nipple with my mouth, flicking her tight tip with my tongue as she arches her back, moaning at the sensation. I let it go and do the same to the other one, elongating the nipple even further and allowing it to pop out of my mouth. I lay open mouthed kisses up the middle of her chest to the hollow of her neck, as I continue thrusting slowly in and out of her.

Her thighs are trembling and her body is rigid, as I rock into her, my mouth taking hold of her earlobe and pulling on it gently with my teeth. I kiss her in the spot under her ear that I know she loves and feel her shatter around me, the feeling triggers my own orgasm, my hips jerk forward and cum shoots out of me. I lay there gasping for a minute, supporting myself on my elbows as I gaze down at her flushed face, her breathing as ragged as mine.

"You want to shower or sleep?" I ask her quietly as her eyes study mine.

"Yes" she smiles back at me, grinning.

"Yes?" I ask her, confused, a frown wrinkling my forehead.

She reaches up and pushes my hair off my face running her hand down my cheek as I turn to kiss her palm. "Shower then sleep." She says on a long sigh.

"Right. No worries" I tell her scooting off of her and standing beside the bed. I lean down to scoop her into my arms and carry her back into the bathroom, leaving the lights off, the glow of the candles sufficient to see by.

I place her on her feet and reach in to turn on the shower, pulling her in when it heats up enough. I wash and dry every inch of her, throwing one of my t-shirts over her head to cover her, when I hear a knock at the outer door. I quickly pull on a pair of sweats and open the door to the bellboy who has a rolling trolley with our dinner on it. I ordered it at lunchtime as well and he's right on time. I tip him and he leaves quickly. I push it over to the dining table for us. I ordered us an entrée of roast vegetables with a cheese sauce, a grilled fish and salad for Mia and a huge Texas T-bone steak for me which is so large it hangs over the edge of the long plate.

"I thought we'd eat in here because it's a bit hard to cut a steak on the bed." I say, sitting down beside her at the table. We start on the roast veggies and I realize that despite the huge burger at lunchtime, I'm starving again. Must have worked up an appetite the last few hours.

Chapter SIX

Mia

Our dinner is delicious and we take our covered dessert plate to the bedroom with us. I quickly brush the petals from the cover and slide into the huge bed as Noah does the same on his side, leaning in to kiss my temple as he does.

I watch him lift the cover from the large plate and take in an assortment of mini desserts, my mouth salivating at the sight, despite my stomach being full to capacity. There are tiny pieces of chocolate cake with thick dark icing, little fruit tarts, pavlova, tiny cheesecakes and strawberries dipped in chocolate. Everything is bite sized and there is a huge plate full of them, more than enough for the both of us.

"Oh my God. I could die a happy woman right now!" I exclaim as I reach over to take a cheesecake and lift it to my mouth with two fingers. His grin's as wide as mine as he does the same with a piece of chocolate cake, telling me, "I didn't think I'd be able to fit in another bite, but now I've decided that I definitely can!"

Noah feeds me a small pavlova and I do the same for him because I know it's his favorite. His murmur of appreciation matches my own as I taste the sweet crunchy sugar crust. I lift a chocolate coated strawberry to his mouth and he bites into it, taking it from my fingers. He feeds me one the same way as we lay back against the pillows in contentment. "I think this should be our anniversary tradition. Every year I get to feed you like this, on this day." He informs me, raising a tiny piece of chocolate cake to my mouth. "I'm good with that plan for sure." I smile up at him, opening my mouth to take the rich cake from his fingers.

"Noah this has been the best wedding day I could have ever hoped for. Thank you for doing all this." I tell him lovingly, sweeping my arm around the room, indicating the candles, rose petals, the dessert plate.

"Best day of my life too, Baby." He says planting a kiss on my chocolate covered lips and licking some of the frosting from them. "And you're very welcome. I wanted to make it special for you."

"It was.....the most wonderful day of my life." I glance down to the sparkling rings on my left hand and still can't believe that I'm married to this amazing man beside me, that he wants me even though I'm damaged after the attack.

I thought for sure he'd leave and find someone who deserves him, someone whole, someone without fading bruises and bite marks covering their body. Every time he makes love to me, the memory of Jackson forcing himself inside me fades a bit further, except for the odd moment when it all comes hurtling back and I need to force myself to remember that it's Noah and he'd never hurt me.

I think I'm doing a great job of covering up the lapses, as Noah hasn't said anything, so he can't have noticed. I want him to make love to me, I do, but it's not as easy as it was before the rape. I hope that we can get back there again, where we both aren't thinking of it each time he thrusts into me.

There was a moment or two when I felt him covering my back with his large body that I actually panicked and nearly cried out. It took all of my strength not to. I don't want to scream in terror every time he does something that makes me uncomfortable. He didn't know, it's not his fault. This is my fault. I need to deal with it and I will. No matter what it takes.

We lay in bed feeding each other and drinking our non-alcoholic wine. It tastes like crap, but I drink it anyway. I get up to pee and blow out all the remaining candles in the bathroom and bedroom other than the ones on our bedside drawers. The flickering flames make dancing shadows on the walls as we lean back against the headboard and gaze out at the neon lights through the window. "Are you tired?" Noah asks running his hand down my hair and pulling me in for a quick kiss. "No not really. Not sleepy tired. Why? Don't tell me you're up for round four already?!"

"Baby, I'm always hard and ready to go another round, but no I was actually about to ask if you wanted to go out for a wander, take in the night life a bit. We don't have to go far if you don't want to, I'm happy to stay right here as well. Just thought you'd like to see some of the city while we're here."

I think on the suggestion for a minute, then turn to him and nod rapidly. "Yeah I think I'd like to get out and stretch my legs. I feel like we've been cooped up a lot this holiday. It'll be nice to get out and get some fresh air, but I warn you...you may have to piggyback me home." I throw off the covers and pull out a pair of knickers and a dress, quickly pulling them on as Noah watches me. He only pulls on his sweats again and a t-shirt.

"Going commando are we?!" I laugh at him, watching him pull on joggers with no socks.

"Yeah! After the workout my dick's had tonight it needs to breathe a little. You can't notice anything can you?"

"No you're good." I tell him after checking out his crotch for a lot longer than necessary. "Now that's definitely noticeable!" I grab the hardening thickness of his shaft through the cotton of his sweats.

He removes my hand and takes a deep steadying breath. "You keep doing that and we won't make it out that door for the rest of the week!"

I lean up and give him a quick kiss. "Yes we will. We've a plane to catch in the morning to Hawaii, then you can keep me behind closed doors...or not," frowning I think about what I'm saying. "No on second thought...I'd like to see Hawaii while we're there so you'll have to control yourself."

Striding over to the main doors he swings one wide open as he grabs his wallet and key and stuffs them into his front pocket, ushering me through the door.

The Strip is alive with people and traffic and so many things to see that I don't know where to start. Noah nods in the direction of the famous fountains, we walk arm in arm toward them to have a closer look. Noah tells me the Bellagio's fountains do a show every 15 minutes at night. There are hundreds of people gathered around watching the dancing water and the lights. It's a magical sight, I lean back against Noah's hard chest, his arms are wrapped around me tightly.

Every now and then he bends down to plant a kiss on my head or my temple. We stay and watch the musical event for the entire show then wander slowly down the strip, Noah leading the way. I'm battling to take it all in-the lights, the noise, the people; it's overwhelming. We walk for a while ending up at Fremont Street. We make our way through the famous arcade, stepping off to the side to watch the millions of lights that make up the ceiling display. It's breathtaking, I pull out my phone to video some of the changing colors, Noah stands next to me protectively as people crowd around, filling the area.

"I had no idea this existed Noah! It's just unbelievable. How did you know?" I turn and ask him.

He leans in for a kiss. "I've been to Vegas before Babe. I thought you'd like it. C'mon there's more to see."

We spend an hour or more wandering around, trying not to stumble into people on the sidewalk, I look up at the tall signs more than look where I'm walking. Noah saves me from a few nasty falls as I miss my footing while I'm busy looking around.

We pass a pretzel stand on the way back to the hotel and I pull him to a halt, my stomach growling at the smell of the warm bread.

"Seriously Babe?! You're hungry again??!" He says, eyebrows raised in amazement.

"Yep. I'll have a plain one and a chocolate one please. These boys of yours need fuel. Growing three babies takes a lot of calories." I tell him, my mouth watering at the sight of the large variety before us.

I devour both as we walk slowly back to the hotel, when we make it up to the room it's past midnight and I'm definitely sleepy now. Dragging my dress over my head, I hear Noah order room service for 7am so that we make our flight at 9am. I groan at the thought of another early morning after being up early this morning to fly from Vancouver.

As he strides into the bedroom with a small glass of scotch in his hand, I snuggle down into the soft mattress. "Don't bother waking me in the morning, just haul my arse into the plane and leave me sleeping." I inform him in all seriousness.

I hear him chuckle loudly as he strips out of his clothes and walks over to the bathroom. I raise my head to watch him disappear through the door, admiring that rock hard butt of his. He glances back, catching me looking and laughs loudly, blowing me a kiss.

God I love his body.

I think I fall asleep before he's finished brushing his teeth, because I don't remember him coming to bed, but I wake up to a knock at the door and it takes my brain a while to realize what the sound is.

"Noah." I say, shaking his shoulder. "Noah, someone's at the door." He wakes up and sleepily looks around the room, taking in what I'm saying.

"Oh shit. That's probably breakfast. What time is it? He asks, looking around at the digital clock on his bedside table. "How can it be 7am already? We just went to sleep!" He declares, pushing back the covers and pulling on his sweats. Striding out to open the door I hear a soft murmur of voices, then he comes in with a huge tray full of food, placing it beside me on the bed.

"How many are we expecting for breakfast Luv?" I ask him taking in the mountain of food that's loaded on to the tray.

"After the amount of food you put away yesterday, I thought I'd better order some extra this morning. Dig in." He nods to the food that he's spreading out on the bed cover. I take my plate and load it with some eggs, bacon and pancakes, along with a couple of slices of toast. I devour it and decide that I need a muffin as well, washing it down with a glass of juice. Noah watches me smiling and laughing at the amount that I eat. Almost as much as he does.

We get up, cleaning up the breakfast dishes as we do and leave them on the dining room table for collection later. Noah showers first because I want to wash my hair and we both know that if get in with him neither of us will come out clean...or quickly, and we don't have much time this morning.

I shampoo my hair and condition it before I soap up my body, realizing that my baby bump is more noticeable today. I'm 14 weeks so it's understandable that I'm starting to show. I'm sure that I read that I might feel them kicking from now on. I stand very still and keep my hand over my stomach, trying to feel anything, but I don't. No butterflies or fluttering yet. Soon hopefully.

The flight to Hawaii takes us around five hours and we land to a warm bright tropical heat. The perfume from the hundreds of flowers fills the air. I take in a deep breath as we drive along with the window down. Noah's rented us a house for the remainder of the week and hired a car and driver to take us where we want to go. There's so much I want to see, but I'm happy just to be here for a few days and I know I need to rest after the big day we had yesterday.

I had a quick nap on the plane, but most of the time I spent curled up on Noah's lap like a kitten, snuggling into him. We just talked and held each other. Our flight attendant was Lynda, whom we flown with before. She and Noah fly frequently together, so we chatted about where she's been while we'd been holidaying. Apparently she has family in the south around Louisiana so she spent some time with them, then went on to New Orleans with a friend, before making her way back to Vegas for the flight home via Hawaii. She's been to Hawaii a few times before so she's made arrangements to stay with a friend while she's on the island. The plane won't be the same one that we came over on as it has to fly back again, ours will be a similar one, but bigger and with a bedroom. Lynda will accompany us on the way back to Perth, where she lives too.

Chapter SEVEN

Noah

I know she's tired.

I can tell by the way she moves slowly and practically drags herself up to the rental house. It's a large house on a hillside and I can see the infinity pool from here. There's a staff of four who'll look after us during the day, but they finish after dinner, so we'll have time to ourselves at night. I pick her up and carry her as I push the front door open and kick it closed behind me. I kiss her quickly and let her legs drop to the floor, but I keep the other arm around her shoulders.

"Wanna go up for a nap? You look exhausted. We can look around later if you want." I say as I stand ready to carry her up the wide staircase to the master bedroom.

"No, I think I want to swim and lay around in the sun for a bit. I'm a bit sweaty and that pool looks great." She replies, looking out through the back wall of glass and timber doors. It's one of those doors that fold back to the walls on either side, opening up the whole back of the house to capture the breezes.

"You sure? You can have a sleep first and then a swim. We aren't going anywhere today. You can just laze around all day." I tell her, frowning. She looks a bit paler today than normal. I hope it's just tiredness causing it.

"Yeah I'm tired, but I need to get in that pool. I can hear it calling my name. Then I'll sleep I promise." She reaches up to pull my head down for a kiss, and just as she does a portly lady with graying, long hair tied back in a braid comes hurrying around the corner, wiping her hands on a dishtowel.

"I'm so sorry." She says rapidly, stepping forward with her hand out. I let go of Mia to shake it firmly and then she does the same to Mia. "I'm Rosie, the housekeeper. I didn't hear the car pull up or I would've been straight out to meet you."

We introduce ourselves, Mia forgets her married name and tells her that she's Mia Drummond, before I correct her.

"Oh Shit! Sorry! Rosie, we just got married yesterday. It's going to take me while to get used to having a new surname. Maybe I could be Mia Drummond- Byrne, does that work?" She glances up at me with a raised eyebrow.

 I don't care what the fuck her name is, she can call herself Winnie the Pooh for all I care, so long as she wears my ring and remains my wife. "It works if you have an hour to introduce yourself each time!" I tell her laughing as she screws up her face at me.

Rosie leads us out to the large kitchen where she's preparing our dinner for tonight. She has some fresh fish and a garden salad with a tropical fruit salad for dessert. She sits us down with a cold glass of water and makes us a sandwich with the fresh bread she baked this morning.

I'm watching Mia carefully, but she seems okay, happily chatting with Rosie as she tells us the history of the house and her life story. She has 5 kids scattered across the islands and 2 on the mainland – one in Boston and the other in Washington. That's 7 kids altogether!

After lunch is done Rosie leads us up to the master bedroom. Once again it's a huge room with en-suite, but no bath in this one. She tells us that there is a bath in the guest bathroom down the hall if we want to use it, but I think the pool will be enough. It's huge and hangs out over the edge of the hill so that if you're in it all you can see is mountain and sky, plus the odd scattered house down below.

After offering to hang our clothes for us while we swim, she leaves us to find our swim suits and get changed. Mia goes to the bathroom and comes out in a barely-there bikini in peacock blue and pink. Once again my dick hardens almost instantly, as I take in the sight of my wife. "Noah I've really popped!" She says as I look at her with confusion written all over my face. "My belly. Look at it. It's not flat anymore. It's huge!" She tells me as she runs her hand across the small bump above her bikini bottom.

"Baby I hate to tell you this, but it's gonna get a whole lot bigger than that! It's hardly noticeable. I can't wait till it's big and round and I can feel them kicking." I walk over to her, subtly rearranging my dick in my board shorts. "You look amazing in that. I don't know how I'm gonna keep my hands to myself." I say as I bend to kiss her.

"Well Mister you had better. No hanky panky in front of the housekeeper. I don't know that Rosie would be impressed if she comes across you ravaging me in the pool." Smiling at me she checks her braid to make sure it's secure and walks out of the room in front of me. My eyes follow her arse as we walk down the hallway to the stairs.

"I know what you're doing back there." She tells me glancing over her right shoulder.

"Really? What am I doing Baby?" I say, not moving my eyes up to meet hers, too intent on the cute butt in front of me.

"I can feel your eyes on my arse. Don't think I don't." She laughs as she slowly descends the stairs and I'm sure she's swinging her hips in an exaggerated way, but my eyes follow each movement. I nearly trip on the last stair because I don't expect to hit the floor, as I've been too preoccupied with my wife's gorgeous arse.

I hear her giggle at me as I take a step to make sure I don't fall flat on my face. "Yeah all good!" I tell her with a smirk as she looks back at me.

We walk outside through the door. I stand next to her as I remind her we just had lunch so we need to wait a while before we swim. We head over to the lounges beside the pool and I pull hers under the shade of the large umbrella so that she doesn't get sunburned.

"Want me to put some sunscreen on you Babe?" I ask as I pick up the bottle on the table beside me. She turns over as she lays down and I coat her back with the thick cream, enjoying running my hands all over her. I slide them down her legs and her arms, making sure that she's completely covered and then wait for her to turn over to her back so that I can do the same to her front. Oh, I'm liking this job for sure!

I smear cream on her exposed cleavage and manage to slide my hand into her bikini top running my palm over her nipple before she yanks it out and slaps at it, telling me to behave. I cover her completely with sunscreen then do myself as well. I tan easily, but I don't want to get burned so I make sure I'm covered where I can reach and she helps me with my back.

We lay back and enjoy the warmth of the island, taking in the smell of the fragrant flowers surrounding us. I can see hibiscus, frangipani, daphne and bougainvillea as well as ginger plants and gardenias. I recognize all of those because I had to help mum plant them at the farm years ago. She also came and helped me choose some plants for my garden when I built my house.

Soon I hear Mia breathing softly and evenly beside me. I check that she's covered by the umbrella as I lay back, soaking up the sun's rays. When it gets too warm in the sun I dive into the pool, enjoying the feel of the cool water against my skin. I wipe my hair from my face when I emerge from the clear water and gulp in a cleansing breath. I swim over to the edge of the pool and gaze out at the scenery. It green and lush and I know we're probably on the side of a volcano, but it's a spectacular view. I just hope the volcano doesn't decide to come to life while we're here.

I swim some laps burning off my lunch and wait for Mia to wake up. I get out of the pool a few times to adjust the umbrella so that she's in the shade as she lays sleeping quietly. I'm gonna take her for a check-up as soon as we get back to Perth. I hope it's just because of our last few busy days, but I want to make sure she and the babies are fine. I've been making sure she takes her vitamins every day and she's eating well so I tell myself I'm worrying over nothing, but I need to make certain.

As I'm swimming another long lap I see her stretch like a cat, arms up above her head and back arching. I swim over to the side in front of her and pull myself up out of the pool. Walking over to grab my towel, I shake myself spraying water all over her.

"Fuck Noah!" She squeals, sitting up quickly. "That was cold!"

"Na Babe. It's actually very warm in there. You wanna join me?" I say as I swipe the towel over my face and hair.

"Only if you promise to behave." She says to me, narrowing her beautiful eyes, as I laugh loudly.

"C'mon then. Up you get. Do you feel better after your nap?" I ask holding her hand as she walks down the shallow stairs to immerse herself up to her waist. Sliding forward into the water she says, "Yeah I feel much better now. I needed that, I think."

Catching up to her as she breaststrokes across to the edge of the pool overlooking the steep mountain, I agree with her. She has more color in her cheeks now and she isn't as pale and washed out as she was before. I release a breath that I didn't know I was holding as she joins me hanging over the edge of the glass pool, and gazing out over the hills. You can see for miles up here.

Dinner is wonderful and Rosie comes in as we're finishing dessert and takes our plates, telling us that there is coffee ready if we want one and she'll turn on the dishwasher and leave us to it for the night. We both thank her as she tells us that she'll be back at 7am to get us breakfast. Mia objects first and tells her that we won't be up that early so there's no need. I ask her to wait till at least 9am so that Mia can sleep in, explaining that she's pregnant and needs her rest. After a big hug, in which Mia's engulfed in her large floppy arms, she tells us that she'll be here at 7 as usual, but breakfast can wait till we get up.

We make our way to the living room once she leaves and settle in on the huge soft sofa to watch a movie together. I lay back and Mia snuggles into my side with her arm across my stomach. I watch her as her eyes grow heavy and she struggles to keep them open despite choosing the movie which she declared one of her all-time favorites. I pick her up and carry her up to bed, undressing her without her even noticing. I go back downstairs and lock up the house, turning the movie off and the lights out as I make my way back up to the master bedroom.

I pull her back towards me as I climb in behind her and fall asleep holding her to me tightly.

I wake up to a scream.

Chapter EIGHT

Mia

Fuck, get off me! Don't do this!

Panicking, I kick and scream as loud as I can, trying to dislodge him from on top of me. I punch at him as he grabs my arms and yells my name loudly. How does he know me? Who is he? Why me?

All these things run through my mind in an instant, as I scramble upwards and feel his arms fall away from mine. My eyes fly open to take in Noah's worried face staring at me with alarm. I look around in the darkness trying to figure out where I am and it takes a minute or two for the nightmare to fade away. I burst into sobs as he pulls me into him, trying to calm me, by rubbing his hand up and down my back and kissing the top of my head as I cry loudly into his massive chest.

"It's okay Babe, I'm here. You're alright. It's just a bad dream. It's not real. He's gone. I won't let anyone hurt you ever again, I promise." He tells me over and over that I'm safe.

"Noah it's always so real. It's like he's attacking me all over again. I can see him and smell him and feel him. I hate this! I scream at his chest, pounding on it with my closed fist.

"If you need to hit something to feel better then go for it Sweetheart. Hit me. I promise I can take it. Hit me as much as you want. Make out it's him you're hitting. Let him have it. Really go to town and hit me hard. You'll feel better I reckon."

I lash out before he's finished saying his sentence. I punch him hard then pull back and punch him again with both fists putting everything I have behind the hits. I continue till I'm exhausted and my sobbing has stopped. Noah gathers me into his arms again and kisses my forehead. "I bet that feels better now."

"I just want to stop dreaming. Noah it's exhausting. I can't stop. Why can't I stop? I don't want to see him in my dreams anymore…please…make it stop." My sobs start up again as he leans down and kisses my hair over and over trying to take away my pain. I know he can't, but I want it gone so badly it hurts.

"Hush Baby. Shush…it's okay. I know…I know. I wish I could take them away Babe. *Fuck,* I wish I could. I'd do anything to stop this so you get a good night's sleep."

I sob into his chest until I fall asleep from exhaustion, knowing that there's nothing anyone can do to help me. I just need to work through it. Noah doesn't need to know that I'm hardly sleeping at all, too scared to close my eyes in case the nightmares return. I manage a few hours here and there, but I'm beyond shattered with trying to stay awake night after night to avoid dreaming. I don't think I've had more than one night of deep sleep since the attack. That's why I'm so tired right now.

I wake up to bright sunlight. The tinted windows take the edge off, but I can feel the heat coming in already. I raise my head and look around, wondering what time it is. I get the feeling that it's late. I look over and locate a digital clock on the dresser opposite the bed. It says 1:23pm. That can't be right, maybe it's stopped. I throw on a dress quickly and make my way downstairs as I pass another clock that says the same. Fuck, I can't remember ever sleeping this late. Not even as a teenager. My sister used to sleep till 2 or 3 pm on a Sunday afternoon, after a late Saturday night, but I never did.

I find Rosie before I spot Noah out on a lounger beside the pool, reading his kindle. He looks up and sees me at the same time and puts down his book, coming inside. Rosie asks me what I'd like to eat and I distractedly tell her whatever she has is fine. She pulls out some leftover fruit salad that she obviously made for our breakfast and dishes up a large bowl, placing it in front of me as I sit at the kitchen island bench.

"Hey sleepyhead. How are you feeling? You okay?" He questions, as he bends to kiss me gently.

"God Noah, why didn't you wake me? I've never slept this late before in my life!" I snap at him, startling him with my tone.

"We've both been going up to check on you to make sure you were alright, but I wanted you to sleep as long as you needed to. No point in waking you. We don't have any plans and you need your rest." He shrugs a shoulder and for some reason it annoys the hell out of me.

He thanks Rosie for the mug of hot coffee she places in front of him and I watch him sip it slowly. I'd kill for a strong coffee right now.

"You know that if I have to have decaf then I think it's only fair that you should have to as well." I tell him as he raises one eyebrow. "Really. It's the least you could do." I feel like I'm in full on bitch mode, but I can't help it.

"Ooookkkkaayy." He says with raised eyebrows. He puts down the coffee mug and pushes it across to Rosie on the other side of the island bench. "Rosie could you please make us both a decaf? It won't hurt me to go without caffeine, but if I start snapping at people just remember it's probably from the withdrawals." I wonder if that's a veiled reference to my attitude this morning.

Rosie returns with two mugs full of coffee and pushes them over to us as she smiles widely. I pick mine up and sip it slowly between mouthfuls of fruit. I don't know why I said that. I don't really care if he has coffee or not. Why the hell am I picking on him like this? All he did was leave me to sleep and I must admit I did have a wonderfully restful night when I got back to sleep finally. I should be grateful to him, not berating him in front of the housekeeper. I just can't seem to shake this bad mood.

"You feeling alright? Did you have another bad dream before you woke up?" He asks quietly.

My eyes fly over to Rosie to make sure she didn't hear his words. She's busy washing dishes and totally ignoring us luckily.

"No I didn't have another nightmare. I think one a night's enough don't you? Or did you want to play savior again?" I can't help the hurtful words as they fall out of my mouth.

He raises both eyebrows in amazement and jerks his head back to look at me. My body language tells him everything he needs to know. I'm stiff and almost shoveling in the wonderful fruit salad forcefully.

"Wow. Okay then. Remind me never to let you sleep late again. It's obviously not good for you." He says as he goes to stand up, grabbing his mug of coffee.

I feel a tear slip down my cheek as I realize I'm being a right cow to him and he doesn't deserve it. I hang my head and cry loudly into my hands. God I'm all over the shop today. I can't seem to stick to one emotion at all. It must be the hormones. Poor Noah.

Between sobs I manage to hiccup at him, "Noah I'm sorry. I don't know what's wrong with me." I reach out to stop him leaving. He sits back on his stool and leans forward to kiss my hair, running his hand down my long braid.

"It's alright Baby. I've got a thick hide. I can take it." He smiles at me as I glance up to meet his eyes.

"I'm such a bitch. I don't know what's going on. I don't mean to be, but I can't help it." I tell him as I swipe at my eyes, brushing away the last few tears and shaking my head.

"C'mere." He says, pulling me up to stand between his open thighs and wrapping his arms around my back. He leans over to kiss my lightly, before bringing his hand up to run his fingers down my damp cheek. "I love you. If you want to abuse me over some coffee, I'll take it gladly with no complaints. I think it's just the baby hormones talking Sweetheart. My Mia doesn't snap at people like that. Why don't you go shower and we'll go for a drive and do some sightseeing?"

"Yeah that sounds good. I'll be quick, seeing as I've wasted half a day already by sleeping in. I'd love to go out and have a look around. From what I've seen so far it looks amazing. Can't wait to see the rest of it."

He pulls out his phone and unlocks it. "Okay, I'll tell the driver to bring the car around while you go shower and change."

We head out on a clear blue sunny day. Apparently a storm's forecast for this evening, our driver Lewis tells us, as he takes us into town to have a look around and do a bit of shopping. The shopping district's crowded with tourists who take up every available space on the large beach as well as the sidewalk. The area's surrounded by high rise hotels and apartments casting long shadows over us as the day progresses.

The clouds gather and the wind begins to pick up as we leave a shopping center after doing a bit of browsing and souvenir shopping. I bought my nieces a small Hawaiian doll in a traditional outfit. I'm sure they'll love them. For my sister I get an umbrella, very cheesy, but she'll appreciate it. My dad gets luggage tags.

Noah buys a pearl necklace for his Mum and a tiki mug for his Dad. He gets something for them every time he travels. They love getting little gifts from other countries, and Noah enjoys buying them something.

The driver meets us outside the entrance to the shopping center and we deposit our purchases into the large boot of the car and slide into the back seat. I'm sweating profusely even in my thin sundress. The humidity is dreadful as we turn on the air-conditioner in the car and enjoy the cool breeze coming out of the vents.

I aim one in my direction so that it hits my face. The clouds are low and dark as we pull up to the house and get out. Rosie pulls the front door open for us as we greet her and step inside, enjoying the cool of the air-conditioner in the house after the energy sapping humidity outside. I think I need a shower again or a swim. That'll cool me down.

I head upstairs to change and I'm pulling my sticky damp dress over my head as I hear Noah behind me. Suddenly his large hands cover my bare breasts and run gently over my nipples. I giggle and try to pull away, determined to have my swim with or without him.

"Unhand me, you sex maniac!' I slap at his hands as he lowers his head and begins kissing my neck softly. "Noah I'm all sweaty. I need a swim. Behave!"

Lifting his head slightly he mutters, "So am I, but it's not my fault. You're the one standing there in just your little thong."

"I'm trying to get dressed in my bikini so I can go cool off in the pool and watch the storm come over, if you'd let me! I can't believe this heat. At least at home we get dry heat. I don't think I like this humidity." I tell him still trying to dislodge his hands from my breasts and get his mind off making love. Every time he touches me I just melt, but this time I really, really want a swim.

"Okay. We'll do things your way, but only because I don't want a repeat appearance of that witch that showed up this morning at breakfast...or lunch...or whatever." He says, laughing and waving his hand around.

"Witch?!" I ask on a gasp, pretending to be angry. "I'll have you know that she wasn't a witch. I was just a bit touchy that's all."

"A bit?!" He barks out loudly, stripping out of his cargo shorts and t-shirt and pulling on his swim trunks as I finally get into my bikini and put my braid up securely with an alligator clip. "I hope this is just a passing phase. I can handle crying Mia, but bitchy Mia's a bit more of a problem."

"Really? I hate crying Mia. I feel like I've been crying for weeks nonstop. I don't want to anymore. I want to be happy Mia."

"I'll cope with whichever Mia shows her gorgeous face. I just want a healthy Mia, everything else is negotiable. I'll take bitchy Mia every day if it means that you and our babies are healthy" He says, dropping a kiss on my forehead as he walks to the door.

"I'll remind you of that next time!" I laughingly tell him as I follow him downstairs. "I'm sorry about earlier. I had no right to pick on you like that. It wasn't fair. You can drink whatever coffee you want Hun, I promise I don't really mind."

The water's warm, but refreshing. We float around for a while, watching the dark clouds get closer and listening to the distant thunder as it rumbles over the mountains. Noah swims some laps as I lean against the edge of the pool looking out over the lush valley.

I push off and join him for a while, till I get tired. He can go for hours, but I get tired easily now. These babies are sapping all of my strength, I think. Maybe I need some more vitamins. I'll drink lots of fresh juice and eat a lot of the local tropical fruit, that should help.

I climb out of the pool slowly, wiping water from my face as I carefully navigate the stairs. I suddenly stop dead in my tracks as I feel a fluttering in my stomach. I wait for it to happen again, standing still and holding my breath, my hand flying to cover my stomach. A few seconds later I feel it again...like butterflies in my lower belly. I scream for Noah, who appears at my side in an instant, a look of concern instantly covering his beautiful face.

"Baby what's wrong? What happened?" He asks worriedly, as he follows my gaze to my hand covering my stomach.

"I think they kicked me! Put your hand here where mine is. Maybe they'll do it again. I'm sure that's what it was. It felt like hundred butterflies flying around in there." I tell him in amazement, not prepared for the surge of love that I feel for my unborn children. It overwhelms me and once again, tears fill my eyes as I try to blink them away. He moves my hand to replace it with his, as we stand thigh deep on the steps waiting to see if it'll happen again. Suddenly I feel it and I jerk my eyes to his as his gorgeous blue eyes melt. He felt it too!

"Fuck, that's incredible. When did this start?" He asks breathlessly, staring at my stomach as if he can see inside to his babies. His hand doesn't move. He keeps it there as if wanting it that much can make it happen again.

"Just now. I haven't felt it before. Oh Wow! I felt them moving Noah! That's the most amazing thing ever!" I say excitedly, a wide grin breaking over my face as I look at him.

"It is Sweetheart. I felt them too. You know that now they've started they're just going to play soccer in there from now on?!" He jokes, leaning in for a quick kiss. We stand there for a long while waiting to see if they'll do it again, but I don't feel anything. My bump does seem to have grown slightly though, but it may just be because they changed position. I eventually step up out of the pool and lay down on the cushioned lounge under the umbrella even though the sky is dark and ominous.

I relax for a while, watching Noah swim laps in the pool till the wind picks up and I begin to get cool. Wrapping a towel around me I wander inside and start pulling at the fold back doors to close the open space and protect the house from the rain that's started beating down on the patio. Noah runs inside still wrapping his towel around his hips and finishes closing the doors for me. We stand there looking out at the pounding rain, the valley obliterated by the sheets of water falling from the roof.

"Nothing like a tropical storm to clean things." Noah laughs.

"My God, that started quickly. Looks like we're inside for the rest of the day eh?"

"Well we can't go swimming again. We'll get wet!" He jokes, unwrapping his towel and rubbing it over himself roughly.

I roll my eyes at his feeble joke, "Oh ha ha."

"What? That was funny! It was!" He protests, heading upstairs to change out of his wet trunks.

I follow him up and stand in the doorway as he strips them off walking through to the bathroom. I watch that firm arse of his till it disappears into the shower, deciding to join him and save water.

The rain lasts all night and most of the next day, but we don't mind. It's lovely to just relax and read, listening to the rain pounding on the tin roof. There's no better sound than rain on a tin roof especially when you don't have anywhere to be and can stay inside and just enjoy it.

I'm so relaxed I fall asleep against Noah as we recline on the huge sofa. I left my hair down this morning and he picked up strands, twirling it around his fingers as he concentrated on his book. I didn't realize how relaxing that simple action could be till I woke up an hour later, disorientated and starving.

We have an early dinner of steak and salad, Noah's favorite, Rosie fusses around us, making sure that he has enough to eat and that everything's to our liking. No matter how many times we tell her that we're fine, she loves hovering I think. Eventually Noah convinces her to leave and go home to her family and assures her that we'll be fine. He walks her out to the car with an umbrella because of the driving rain.

"Thank God, I never thought she'd leave." He says, coming back inside and slams the door after shaking off the umbrella. "I hope she's okay driving home in this storm. It's getting pretty bad out there. I'd hate to hear she's wrapped herself around a tree. Maybe we should have offered her a bed for the night so she didn't have to drive?"

I smile at his thoughtfulness. "Noah, I'm sure she'll be fine. She's lived here all her life. She knows how to drive in these conditions. Stop worrying."

"You're right, I know. It's like a hurricane out there. Wait. Do they have hurricanes or cyclones over here?" He says, frowning slightly as he takes his seat to finish his dinner.

"Ummm, hurricanes I think. We're still on American soil."

After our delicious meal, we wander up to bed to watch a movie while we listen to the rain and wind outside. The wind howls and driving rain beats against the bedroom window. It's strange because it isn't cold really, in fact it's still quite warm despite the raging storm.

Noah chooses an action movie and I battle to keep my eyes open after our big day out. You'd think that I'd be wide awake after all the sleep I had today but no…I drift off, snuggled into his shoulder, his arm around me securely. I jolt awake when I suddenly feel the butterflies return in my belly. Rolling to my back I take Noah's hand and place it on my stomach lightly as he looks at me in confusion. Then he grins at me as the babies start moving and he can feel the fluttering against his hand.

"Fuck, that's never gonna get old. I hope they don't keep you awake, but I just love that kicking and it's barely started yet." Leaning down he places a soft kiss on my forehead. My smile's as wide as his. I enjoy the strange feeling of the babies kicking me. I know that in a few months I won't be so happy about it, but right now it's a novelty and I can't wait for it to happen again. I just hope that they don't make a habit of doing this every night, while I'm trying to sleep. I remember my sister complaining about her girls keeping her awake all night towards the end of her pregnancies, so I pray that ours will be more considerate.

Chapter NINE

Noah

My heart's still racing from the feeling of the babies moving around. It's a tangible sign that they're okay and I'm grateful beyond words after the hell that Mia's been through. After the rape and threat of miscarriage my heart's about to explode with the love that I feel for her and our three peanuts. I'm reassured that they're real, when I feel the slight flutters that accompany their movements. To be able to feel them kick, and know that they're fine, is the best feeling in the world. It's indescribable.

I lay there with her sleeping in my arms for a long time, before I fall asleep to the sound of the rain pounding the roof. Mia doesn't move all night and I slip out of bed the next morning trying not to wake her as I shower and dress. I hope she wakes up in a better mood than she did yesterday. I know it was just the hormones making her act like that, but I'm not anxious for a repeat performance.

We spend the day out sightseeing. Lewis takes us to a nearby waterfall and we walk slowly along the path till we reach it. I slow my stride to match Mia's as we near the clear stream the water falls into. They must be 50-foot high and they divide into 3 streams at the top before joining again as it cascades down the edge of the cliff and into the crystal clear small pool at the bottom.

Mia is the first to strip down to her bathing suit. I follow, removing my t-shirt and leaving my board shorts on as we carefully walk into the cool water. It's pretty deep and we enjoy the amazingly clear water. Even in the middle at the deepest part of the pool you can see right to the bottom. The falls are deserted so we make the most of our time, fooling around and laughing at each other like teenagers. Climbing out we lay our towels on the grassy bank and allow the warm sun to dry us as we relax with our eyes closed.

After our hike back to the car Lewis drives us to his favorite restaurant for lunch, where we spend an hour enjoying our fresh food and each other's company. Mia makes that so easy. I love being around her. She's intelligent, well read, witty and nonjudgmental unlike most of the women that I've dated in the past.

Our time in Hawaii soon comes to an end, and as we both step up into the jet following Lynda to our seats for take-off. It's hard to leave this island paradise. It was great to see Mia totally relax for a few days. Maybe I can talk her into taking some time off when we get home, we could go down to the farm for a while. I know Mum, Dad and Scarlett will look after her, though Scarlett is going back to Miami in a week or so to pack up her stuff to start her new job in London. Last time I talked to her she was really excited about it, but I'm sure if I asked her she would come up and drive back down with Mia.

Somehow, I don't think Mia's gonna go for that idea though. She's determined to keep working and I agreed to let her as long as she's medically able and willing. The research that I've been doing into multiple pregnancies says that most are born early and with low birth weight and the mother may have lots more complications during pregnancy.

I need to make sure that Mia's healthy, eating right and that she rests enough. I know she's gonna hate that last part, even though she's been getting really tired rather easily lately.

Perth is having a heat wave when we arrive. Its 9pm and still 38C. Thank god for air-conditioning. The car drops us off at home and I drag in our suitcases, leaving them in the hallway for the moment.

"You want something to eat baby? Hopefully Mrs Grantham's restocked the fridge for us. I rang her and told her when we'd be back and she said she would." I walk over to Mia, who's standing at the back door looking out at the pool that's lit by underwater lights.

She drags her tank top over her head, exposing a pretty blue lace bra. "Not hungry, but that pool looks *really* good. Wanna come for a swim with me?" She continues stripping off her clothes, dumping her shorts and underwear at the door as she walks naked through it, to sit on the edge of the pool. I quickly decide it's a good idea and start tearing my clothes off to join her. I walk out and sit on the edge of the pool with her as she swings her legs back and forward in the warm water. Jumping down into the shallow end, I hold up my hand to help her in as she pushes off the edge and into my arms.

"Well I like this idea of yours. You, me, naked in the pool. I can think of all sorts of ways to entertain ourselves for a while." I kiss her lightly on the lips.

"Yeah I was thinking more along the lines of a swim to cool us off and wear us out so that we'll sleep tonight. I don't know about you, but my body still thinks it's breakfast time. So let me go, so I can swim a few laps." She lightly pushes against my chest, but my arms are wrapped around her firmly and she doesn't move me at all. I smirk at her as I feel my dick hardening against her. "Sure I can't change your mind? I *really* think that we could wear ourselves out in other ways. No swimming involved."

"Sex maniac. I can feel that, don't think I don't! I know what you have in mind, but not just yet. I'm all sweaty and sticky."

"Oh I love it when you talk dirty like that." I tell her with a wry smile. "Okay, I'm willing to compromise. You just lay back and float and enjoy the water while I carry you around, how's that sound?"

"What do you get out of this deal if I say yes?" She eyes me suspiciously, laying back in the water. My arms move to hold her under her shoulders and bum as I start walking backwards with her. "This." I say quietly, taking in her nakedness. Her nipples are tight and her arms outstretched as she allows me to walk around letting the water wash over her. I study her body as I walk slowly, watching her breasts move as the water flows over them. It's all I can do to stop myself from reaching down and taking one in my mouth.

I'm almost drooling as I watch her nipples pebble with the coolness of the night as they leave the water. I can feel her relax against me as my eyes travel down across her stomach and the slight bump above her bare mound. I move my hand from under her bum and push it gently between her thighs from underneath. I feel her legs part slightly as she opens one eye and looks at me curiously. I slowly push my long finger into her as my thumb rubs over her clit and I hear her gasp.

"No fair." She says quietly, looking up at me.

Her arms slide up around my neck as she lowers herself into the water and my hands slip from her, making sure she's steady on her feet in the deeper water. She quickly wraps her legs around my hips as my dick pushes against her entrance, my hips moving forward unconsciously.

I slowly thrust into her as a low moan escapes and I'm not sure if it's from her mouth or mine. I lower my lips to press them against hers, spearing my tongue into her mouth as she parts hers slightly. Her nipples rub against my chest hardening instantly with the friction as I move her slowly up and down, her soft moist walls tight around me. Her head falls back as a long sigh falls from her, my lips now finding her neck and feathering kisses all over every bit of it that I can reach.

"God I love you." I say quietly against her skin, sucking on it gently.

She lifts her head as I pull back and study her flushed face, "I love you too, always have and always will."

I can't help myself. I spear my thick shaft into her, quickening my pace, as she makes those incredible sex noises that she does, telling me that she's getting close. I can feel the tingle starting at the base of my spine, indicating that I'm close too. We continue for a few more strokes, her body slapping against mine in the water as I raise and lower her, holding on to her perfect arse. I feel her thighs tremble as she tightens around me and lets out a soft cry of pleasure. My harsh grunt a few seconds later joins her as I struggle to keep my legs upright as my orgasm rushes over me. I pull her close as my release fills her, needing the contact. We're both dragging in air on deep breaths, coming down from our high. God I fucking love this woman. She was made for me. We just fit. She's everything I never knew I needed. My body was made for hers and hers for mine.

I carry her over to the steps and walk out of the pool carefully, with her still in my arms, her long braid hanging behind us, trailing in the water. Despite the warm night goose bumps cover her, I grab a towel from the outside cupboard and place her down on one of the nearby cushioned lounges, wrapping the towel around her quickly. I kiss her forehead and go get myself another thick towel, rubbing it over my body quickly, then wrapping it around my hips tightly as I bend down to dry her. I run the towel over her lightly, kissing her as I go. It's like I can't get enough. I have to be kissing or tasting her skin. I need the contact of her as much as I need my next breath.

When we're both nearly dry, I pick her up and carry her up to our bedroom, neither of us saying a thing as I lay her back slowly and spend the rest of the night worshiping her gorgeous body over and over again.

The sun wakes me in the morning as it rises and fills the deep blue sky. I can hear the pounding of the waves as we left the door open last night to let in the breeze from the ocean, leaving the security door latched. I move my head slightly and find Mia curled up into my side with her arm over my stomach, leg thrown over mine. I kiss the top of her head lightly, laying back to just enjoy this moment. The feel of her against me, her soft breathing, her hair tickling my arm which is protectively wrapped over her waist. I take a moment to cement this image in my mind, the feel of her, the smell of her shampoo, her soft breathing and the sight of her naked body connected to mine like this. I hear a soft whimper and her breathing starts increasing.

I see her hand move slightly against me as she shakes her head in her sleep. Oh fuck, another nightmare. I kiss her forehead and shake her gently, trying to wake her from her bad dream. I know how much she hates having to relive the memory of that day over and over again in her mind. "Mia, baby wake up." I tell her softly, pushing her shoulder a bit more vigorously. Her eyes fly open and I see the torment in them as she takes a moment to take in her surroundings. "Oh shit." She sighs quietly, tears filling her eyes as she blinks rapidly trying to contain them.

"It's okay now babe. You're safe. You're okay. I've got you. I've always got you." I say as I pull her in to kiss each eye lightly. Fuck I wish she didn't have to go through this. I'd do anything for her to never have to deal with this again, awake or asleep. "First thing tomorrow we'll make an appointment with that head doc and with the baby doc as well. I'll skip out of work and go with you."

"No you don't have to do that. I can get a cab. You'll be busy. You can't keep missing work because of me. You need to be there. I'll be fine. I promise that I'll tell you everything that happens with the OBGYN."

"Nope that one's not negotiable. No matter what, I intend to be at all the baby appointments. I need to see for myself that you and the boys are alright, but if you want to go to the head doc alone that's okay, though I'd rather drive you."

"Noah, I'm a big girl. I've been getting around Perth for a while now. I can do it myself. I'll get a cab if you don't want me to drive, but I'm perfectly capable of going alone."

"I know you are baby. You can drive there if you want. We'll try and make that one late afternoon, then you can come straight home and rest up. I can get a ride with Bill, he lives close by and he won't mind."

"Okay, if you're sure he won't mind, otherwise I can get a cab."

"No, you take the car. Maybe we should look at getting you your own car as well. You're gonna need something to get around in when I go to work and you're home."

She pulls back and studies my face seriously. "You want to buy me a car?"

Kissing her on the tip of her cute nose I say, "Well it's the logical solution. You need your own transport. Is there something that you'd like?"

Thinking long and hard about my question she leans up and kisses my mouth quickly, saying, "Nope, surprise me. My birthday's next month. I'll let you buy me one if you promise you won't go overboard. I don't want a huge Hummer or F350. It has to be a sensible car."

A grin breaks over my face as I hear her agreeing with me. That was easier than I thought it would be. I thought she'd argue with me about it, I already know what I'm gonna buy her, but Jesus, I was hoping she'd say yes to a F350 because I'd really love one of those. Maybe I'll trade in the Sahara for one. No way can you get hurt in one of those, they're as big as a Mack truck.

"Deal." I agree on a nod of my head. "Now as it's officially the last day of our honeymoon, I vote that we spend it in bed together. What do ya think?" I say kissing her softly all over her face as I roll her onto her back, and move to lay between her thighs. Her arms reach around me and she scrapes her nails down my back lightly, sending my dick into overdrive, pre cum dripping down it already.

"I say that's a great plan, but we'll need to get up at some point and do some washing and unpack."

I kiss her nose softly, moving down to her lips as I say, "Spoilsport. It can all wait till I've made love to my gorgeous wife. Now shut up and kiss me."

Chapter TEN

Mia

Noah's idea was great except for the fact that I had to get up and pee a dozen times. We eventually got out of bed and showered around 2pm. He'd made us some pancakes for breakfast and we fed each other as we sat in bed, watching the ocean shimmer in the sunlight and listening to the growing crowd of people filling the beach.

I started a load of washing as Noah unpacked quickly upstairs. I wanted to cook something special for dinner because I knew the rest of the week would be rushed meals. Finding a lamb leg roast in the freezer I defrosted it in the microwave and set about peeling vegetables as I waited for the washing to finish. It was still warm today so the air-conditioner was turned up, blowing a cooling breeze through the house. I'd just slipped on a loose cotton sundress and a pair of knickers as we had no intention of leaving the house.

"Babe where are you?" I hear Noah yell down the stairs.

Continuing to peel the potatoes I reply loudly, "In the kitchen", and he strides towards me, dressed only in board shorts. My head turns at his approach and I gaze at my new husband's body, tanned and taut. His biceps and shoulders are huge, waist narrow and once again I'm reminded of his resemblance to the actor that plays "Thor". He has the same crystal blue eyes that are now raking over me as I stand at the bench, potato still in my hand. "What's up?" I say as a frown crosses my face.

"Nothing much. I just rang Logan to tell him that we're back and he's in town so I invited him for dinner. Is that okay?"

Grabbing another potato and peeling that quickly, I assure him that it's fine. "He's always welcome Hun, they all are. I love your family. I'll just do a few more veggies for him and it's all done."

"Can I help? Anything you need me to do?" He asks as he reaches over to pinch a small carrot from the pile of peeled ones and munches on it loudly.

"No it's all sorted, but you could go and check on the washing for me if you want."

Kissing my neck from behind he heads towards the laundry and I hear him shuffling about in there and the sound of the dryer starting. "Don't forget to open that door in there!" I yell over to him as I hear the sliding door open, allowing the heat from the dryer to vent. I hate using the dryer, but it's too hot to go out and hang the washing so it's a necessary evil today. We both need clean clothes and underwear for the rest of the week.

"I just quickly need to go into the study and catch up on my emails and ring Bill, if you don't need me for anything else right now." He tells me as he walks past me on his way to the large study.

"Nope don't need you right now, but check back again after Logan leaves tonight." I tell him as he stops dead in his tracks, turning towards me as I smile widely at him. His face is a picture of lust and desire. "Woman, don't tease me like that. I may just have to come and take you over the bench. We haven't christened the kitchen yet."

Laughing loudly, I hold up the pumpkin that I'm cutting, "I'm busy at the moment. Later I promise." I say as I wink at him. He shakes his head and laughs, but continues walking to the study, adjusting himself in his board shorts as he walks, muttering something about prick teasers as he closes the door.

I hear the murmur of his voice later as I sit and watch a movie, not really watching it. He must be talking to Bill, I think to myself as the front doorbell rings loudly, startling me from my daydream.

"Logan, hey. Good to see you." I kiss him lightly on the cheek. "C'mon in. Noah's just in the study, but you can go and interrupt him if you want. He's been in there a few hours."

"Hey pretty lady. Have I told you lately how good you look? You know you chose the wrong brother right? My older brother's not as great a catch as I am. I'll help you divorce him so that you can rectify your mistake if you want." He strides into the foyer and starts walking out to the kitchen at the back of the house.

As I go to answer him, I hear Noah boom from the study door. "You disrespecting me and trying to steal my wife in my own home Bro? Seriously?!"

"Yep, I am. I can't believe that you actually convinced her to marry you Dude. She's way too good for you. She needs a proper man to take care of her. I'd willingly do the job; I'm a gentleman like that." He smirks up at Noah, knowing he's pissing him off with his words.

I go and stand next to Noah and wrap my arms around his waist as his arm comes around my shoulder, hugging me into him.

"I've definitely chosen the right brother Logan, but I'll keep your offer in mind should anything crop up and he doesn't measure up or do as he's told."

"Hey! I'm right here, ya know! And Baby, you aren't going anywhere with this smooth talking leech. He's just jealous because the best man won." He smiles down at Logan with a wide grin, hugging me tight.

"Oh the best man hasn't won yet, but I'll keep trying. Sooner or later she'll see the light and leave your sorry arse." Logan tells him ducking quickly out of Noah's way as his arm lashes towards him, trying to slap him upside the head. We all laugh loudly as we head to the living room. I sit beside Noah on the sofa, snuggling into his as his arm drapes my shoulders. Logan sits on the couch across the way.

"So Noah told you about our wedding huh? I wondered how long that'd take." I say, smiling up at my husband, who's grinning widely.

"Ya know I tell him everything Babe. I did wait a few days though, and I haven't said anything to Mum, Dad or Scarlett. Have you told your Dad and Sister yet?"

"No I haven't but I will. It's getting too late now with the time difference. I'll leave it till tomorrow."

"The big dumb ox rang me from Hawaii and told me the good news. Seriously, I'm really happy for you Mia. I don't know why, but I know you love him madly, if he stuffs up though, my offer still stands."

I hear a low growl in Noah's chest as he grates out, "You need to stop this shit right now if you want dinner, otherwise you go hungry, while watching us eat a lamb roast."

"Lamb roast? My favorite I'll be on my best behavior I promise." He replies, grinning at his older brother. I laugh at the bond that they share, being able to joke around like this. Logan's a great guy and I think I need to introduce him to my best friend

Heth, next time she's back from Kalgoorlie. I think they'd get on well. They both have a lot in common.

I get up and check on dinner, deciding to set the table while Noah gets Logan and himself a beer from the fridge. They sit and chat while I get dinner ready. I scoff at their offers of help, preferring to do it myself. We chat as we devour our delicious meal, telling Logan about our wedding, honeymoon and the scary few days we spent at the cabin not knowing if our babies were okay. He wants reassurance that we're going to get checked with our own OBGYN and Noah tells him that he's making an appointment for me first thing in the morning. I roll my eyes at his over-protectiveness, but secretly I love him all the more for it.

The boys clean up while I rest up on the sofa, drinking my water. Noah comes to sit beside me sliding his arm around my shoulder as he sits down. Logan and Noah catch up with the gossip from the mine and Noah tells him about the presentation and how he was asked to come back and train the Canadians on how to use the program once it's installed. They discuss the merits of Noah going instead of one of the tech guys. Noah tells him that he wouldn't mind going back for a few weeks if I can fly and the babies are fine.

"I still can't believe that you're going to be a father, let alone have three of them." Logan tells Noah shaking his head.

"I know." Noah nods, sipping his beer. "I'm still getting used to the idea as well. Did I tell you that they've started kicking? It's just the coolest thing ever Bro. you can actually feel them kicking Mia from the inside." He grins across at his brother, his chest puffing out slightly.

"Oh wow. That's got to be awesome. Does it hurt Mia?" Logan asks, looking over at me.

"No not yet, but I have a feeling that it will as they get much bigger. At the moment it's just like a fluttering sensation. It's amazing." I tell him picking up my water bottle and sipping it.

"I bet it is. I can't wait till they start kicking properly. I'd like to feel that if it's okay with you."

"As soon as they do, I'll let you feel it for sure Logan, if you want to." I tell him, looking to Noah for his consent as well. He nods slightly and smiles down at me. Leaning in for a kiss he tells me, "I can't wait to see them tomorrow on the ultrasound. I love looking at them and making sure they're alright."

"Me too." I tell him softly. "I love that you want to come with me. Thank you."

"I want to be involved at every step, Baby. There's nothing more important than you and these babies." He tells me with a loving look on his face.

"Oh yeah Dude. Definitely fucked, for sure. Pussy whipped now." Logan smirks at him as he lifts his bottle of beer to his lips, taking a long gulp of the cold liquid.

"I don't care. I'll be pussy whipped forever if it means Mia's by my side. One day you'll have a woman that you feel the same way about and I'll sit back and laugh at you. You just wait and see." He tells his brother earnestly, tipping his beer in his direction as he speaks.

Logan doesn't stay late as he knows we need an early night for our first day back in the office tomorrow. I get out the gifts that we bought for Grace and Bill and I put them next to my handbag so that I won't forget them in the morning.

We meet Grace in the elevator at the office. She hugs us both, quickly filling us in on the gossip in the office that we've missed while we were away. I pull out the gift that I bought for her in Canada. It's a snow globe with a moose in the middle and she laughs as she opens the box, promising to treasure it always.

True to his word, Noah arranges an appointment for after lunch with Christine, my OBGYN. She specializes in multiple births so we're really lucky to have her as my Doctor. We leave after a quick lunch together in Noah's office. Sitting in the reception area I glance up to notice the receptionist frowning at me. I'm sure she's wondering about the bruises that I sported when I came in for the first visit. It was just after the rape and I had two black eyes plus a split lip and a dark bruise on my cheek and I'm sure she's still wondering if Noah was responsible. I reach over to grab Noah's hand, trying to show her that he isn't capable of that sort of violence, but I doubt it convinces her.

Christine is happy with the examination, but assures us that we need to have an ultrasound every visit from now on just to keep a close check on their progress. She drags over the machine as Noah and I wait, hands gripped tightly together as we impatiently wait for the probe to stop and show us our three little peanuts. At last we see them as Christine smiles and tells us that everything looks fine and they are actually above the weight and length of most triplets at this stage. I tell her of the movements that I'm feeling and she smiles broadly telling me to enjoy it. Most triplet pregnancies don't go to term.

If we can make it to 30 weeks then we're doing well, any sooner and they would need to spend a long time in the NICU getting stronger before they were allowed home. Discussing my plan to continue working as long as possible, she tells me that we need to take this week by week. A multiple pregnancy is much riskier than a single baby, so if everything is fine then I can continue working, but pre-eclampsia is a common complication as well as gestational diabetes. If either of these things happen then my plans will have to change and I'll need to finish early.

Leaving the doctors surgery, I'm lost in my thoughts as Noah helps me up into the high SUV. He tells me that I can drop him back at the office before going on to my next appointment alone. I get the feeling that he's not happy about me doing this alone, but I tell him that I'm fine and I can find my way easily enough.

It will give me a chance to get home and get some dinner started though I feel bad as I've not only missed half of my work day, but he has been out of the office for nearly two hours as well.

My appointment with Denise Lee, my psychologist, goes well. I tell her about my ongoing nightmares and she suggests some techniques to try to avoid them, but if I can't then I need to be able to talk about them, especially to Noah. He needs to know what I'm dreaming about – good and bad. She wants me to be open, honest and candid with him. Allowing him to share my nightmares will apparently make them less scary to me as time goes on.

I hope she's right. She asks me about panic attacks and I tell her about my experience in Canada when I woke up panicking, and Noah made me focus on my breathing and on him and the panic attack subsided. She nods in understanding and tells me that this is a good technique, quiet, calm, and focused thoughts.

I drive home smiling at my good afternoon. I feel so much better than I did this morning. My babies are fine and growing well and my psychologist is determined to rid me of my bad dreams and I'm hopeful that she can.

I sing along to a song on the radio, a favorite of mine, 'Say Something' by Christina Aguilera and A Great Big World. I rush into the house when I get home and text Noah to tell him that

I'm home and okay. He's in the middle of a conference call with the Canadians if I recall his calendar for today correctly so I'm surprised when he immediately texts me back.

> **Noah:** Glad you're home and okay. I miss you. Xo
> **Me:** I'm good. About to start dinner. Want anything special? X
> **Noah:** Can I have you spread across the bed when I get home? Xxxx
> **Me:** Not on the menu. Try again. ☺
> **Noah:** Can't blame a man for trying. How about a lasagna? Luv you xxx
> **Me:** Lasagna I can do. Luv you too. Xxxxxxxx

I walk up the stairs to get changed out of my work clothes, then walk carefully back down the stairs to the kitchen, pulling out ingredients from the pantry and fridge to start the lasagna.

Noah walks in about 6.30 and I'm immediately pulled into his arms and kissed firmly on the mouth. I smile at him as he releases my lips. I missed him as much as he missed me this afternoon. I can't believe that we can't go a few hours without one another. It was like a physical ache, not having him near me today. "I missed you." I tell him, pulling his head down to kiss him again.

"Not half as much as I missed you, Baby." He says kissing my face and neck softly.

"Dinner is ready when you are, and it won't wait long, so you'd best let me go." I tell him, pulling out of his arms and walking to the stove, quickly opening the oven door and pulling out the lasagna dish after donning oven gloves.

Walking over to me as he pulls his tie loose and throws it on the bench, he wraps me up in his arms from behind and tells me, "That smells delicious Babe. I'm starving."

One thing I've learned about Noah over these last few months is that he's always starving. He was up early this morning and had been to the gym by the time I woke up.

We enjoy our dinner together and chat about what Christine told us today. I'm happy to take things week by week, but we both understand that this is a high risk pregnancy and anything could go wrong at any time. If the babies go full term it'll be a miracle. Most babies come early and by C-Section and have to spend a long time in the NICU as they're low birth weight and their lungs haven't developed enough, so they need constant oxygen and monitoring. We both know the scenarios, but we don't discuss the bad things that may happen, trying to focus on the good things. They're a good size at the moment and all we can do is pray that they remain healthy like this.

Chapter ELEVEN

Noah

Three Months Later

I wait for Mia to arrive and pull into her parking space beside my Sahara. Her Mercedes SUV is smaller than my car, but it's one of the safest on the road and she needs that. I presented it to her for her birthday two months ago and she's been driving it every Monday since. She needs to get to her psychologist appointment which is normally at 4pm on a Monday. I've been a few times as well for my own consult. She's been helping me to understand what Mia went through and how to help her now with her panic attacks and nightmares. Both are becoming more infrequent luckily, but I'm glad that I went to see her. I stride around to the driver's side as she pulls into the parking space and I open her door helping her down from the high vehicle.

"You made good time Baby." I comment as she lowers herself to the ground carefully.

Her belly's getting huge already and she can't see her feet, so she has to do this slowly despite my supporting arm. I run my hand over her pregnant stomach and kiss her quickly, still amazed that there are three little babies in there. She waddles slowly beside me as I push the button for the elevator.

"I would have been here sooner, but I had to stop to pee again before I left. Seems like all I do is eat, pee and sleep. Remind me of this if I start talking about doing it again at some point." She tells me as I help her into the elevator.

"Right. Will do. No more babies because you pee too much." I smile at her, laughing inside. She's so cute.

"I'm serious. Remind me of the sleepless nights, because this lot play footy all night with my bladder. That should be enough to put me off." She says with a determined look on her face. I know what she says is true because I hear her getting up a few times a night.

"God I love you Mia. I don't care if you never want any more. I'll just be happy when these three arrive. We have your appointment at 12 today, don't forget. We get to see if they're boys like I predict, if you still want to know."

"Yeah I think it's a great idea. I'd like to be as prepared as we can before they arrive and knowing the sex of each of them will help." She says, walking slowly to her desk and lowering herself carefully into her chair.

"Now stay there and I'll get you a coffee before I start." I tell her ducking down to kiss her lightly on the top of her head. She looks amazing all round with my babies and I can hardly keep my hands off her. I know she's getting big and uncomfortable, but I love seeing her like this. Hell, we can have a tribe of kids if she wants.

The morning flies by as I'm busy with conference calls and meetings. Mia knocks on my door and reminds me that it's time to leave, as I finish up on a call to China. I quickly say goodbye, thank them, then hang up, grabbing my suit jacket as I leave the office. As usual Mia heads to the ladies as we're walking towards the door and I wait anxiously for her.

We arrive just as Christine calls Mia's name and we follow her down the wide hallway, my hand resting lightly on Mia's back. I help her to sit down then quickly lower myself into my seat, grabbing her hand as I do.

"So Mia, how are you feeling? Any headaches or blurred vision? Swelling of your feet or hands?" Christine asks rounding the desk to stand beside Mia. The last visit two weeks ago, Mia's blood pressure was raised and Christine is concerned about pre-eclampsia. I quickly glance down to Mia's feet, noticeably swollen in her shoes. I try to twirl her rings around her fingers, but I can't do it like I normally can. I frown at the knowledge that this could be serious. The doctor wraps a blood pressure cuff around her arm and checks it as we wait with bated breath for the result.

"Sorry Mia, it's even higher than it was before. I think you need to have complete bed rest for a month and see if that helps. I know this isn't what you wanted, but we don't want you to develop pre-eclampsia and that's where we're heading right now. The safest thing to do would be complete bed rest. Noah you need to make sure that she does it." She tells me, frowning in my direction. I nod my head, indicating I understand how bad this is.

"Right then. Let's have a look at these babies and make sure they're still growing well, and we're finally going to see what sex they are, is that right? You definitely want to know now?" She asks referring to our delay in finding out. At first we didn't want to know; we wanted it to be a surprise, but then Mia thought about it more and decided that she does want to know, so I'm happy either way, so long as they're healthy and she's fine.

Helping Mia step up on to the examination bed, I watch as Christine measures her stomach and feels around to see how the babies are laying. One reason that C-sections are often necessary is that the babies are so cramped in the womb that they can't get into position to be born. She's 27 weeks now and considered safe, but the babies would be premature and need a lot of care, but their chance of survival increases with every week they spend in her belly. The ultrasound probe just shows us a bit of them at a time now because of their size. Christine stops to take more measurements as she runs the probe over Mia's large stomach, telling us that they're all fine and a good size, which is good news. I slowly release a breath that I didn't know I was holding as I grip onto Mia's hand tightly.

She slowly moves the probe and stops now and then as we wait for the sexes to be revealed. "Well looks like baby number one is a boy. You have your son Noah." She tells us with a wide smile. A boy! There's no way to wipe the smirk off my face as I grin down at Mia as she shakes her head at me. "Baby number two doesn't want to co-operate so we'll just move over a bit and check out number three...ah yes...there it is...or isn't as the case may be...this one's a girl. Now let's see if baby number two wants to show us...yeah...another boy...that makes two boys and a girl. Congratulations!"

I bend down and pepper kisses over Mia's gorgeous face as I wipe away her tears. She cries for no reason at all now, but today she actually does have a good reason. Two sons and a daughter...I'm over the moon with happiness. Completely blown away, though I was sure they were all boys. I'm going to have a daughter...well, at least she'll have brothers to look out for her as they grow up.

When we arrive home Mia goes up and showers quickly before pulling on one of my t-shirts and climbing into bed.

"I'm gonna ring Mum and see if she will come up for a few weeks while you're bedridden. I'm sure she won't mind and I'll feel better knowing that she's here with you. Then I'll start dinner okay?" I tell her, pulling out my phone and dialing Mum's mobile.

"Hey Mum, it's me. Yeah I'm good. No, that's why I'm ringing. She's been ordered to bed for the next month and I was wondering if you'd mind coming up to stay for a bit to keep an eye on her for me? Yeah that's fine. Okay. Thanks Mum. Yeah I will. See ya then."

"Mum's coming up tomorrow so she'll be here after lunch, she reckons, if she can get away early. I can work from home tomorrow so that's good. I can look after you till she gets here." I say, leaning in for a quick kiss.

"Noah this is all unnecessary. I can spend the day on the sofa downstairs and rest up. There's a pile of DVDs down there for me to watch till you get home. I feel bad dragging your Mum away from the farm like this." She says, a frown showing on her forehead.

"She loves fussing and this is the ideal opportunity. You know she'd be offended if we didn't ask her, and there's no way I'm leaving you alone at home alone, so get used to the idea. Now what do you feel like for dinner?" I ask as I make a move to get up off the bed.

"Anything you want to cook. I think there's a couple of chicken breasts in the freezer if you want to do them and we can have the leftover roast veggies with them. Can you manage that or do you want me to come down and supervise?"

I glare at her as I walk away, turning back to tell her, "Smart arse. I can manage that. Reheating veggies is a special talent of mine!" I hear her giggle as I walk down the stairs.

Mum arrives about 3pm, bearing gifts for Mia and the babies. She's been busy knitting and has finished 3 sets of white jackets and booties for the munchkins.

As I predicted, Mia is fussed and fawned over and allows Mum to do everything for her so that I can go back to work. They get on famously, which I'm happy about. It would be awful to have a wife and mother that didn't get along.

After two weeks of complete bed rest we return for another consult with Christine, who checks Mia's blood pressure again and it's better, but still raised slightly so she orders Mia back to bed again with clear instructions for me to ring her if I need her, day or night. The babies are now 29 weeks and labor could happen at any time, though there's no sign of it just yet. Another ultrasound tells us that they're still fine, but not head down as of yet. This means that if Mia does go into labor early then she'll need a C-section. We both know that the odds are against a natural birth so we're prepared for it.

After another week of complete bed-rest she's sick of herself and bored and getting moody. She's uncomfortable and the babies keep kicking her all night and she needs to get up and pee 6 times each night. I think she looks amazing, but I can't believe how big she is. No wonder she's uncomfortable.

Mum helped her pack her hospital bag yesterday and it sits by the front door ready to be grabbed as we leave, when labor starts. Luckily Mum was happy to hang around and Dad has been up for a few days here and there visiting, now that they have extra help on the farm. Grace and Heth have popped over and kept her company as well and Scarlett rings nearly every afternoon, which is her morning in London.

We're lying in bed watching a movie as I work on my laptop when Mia suddenly squeals and grabs her stomach. I launch up, tossing the laptop to one side and lean over her slightly wondering what the hell's happening. "You okay Baby? Is it time?"

"No I don't think so. It was just a hard kick. Shit that hurt. One of these boys is going to be a star footballer, I can tell already. Someone has a mean left foot." She says, rubbing over the spot on her belly after she pulls her t-shirt up to check for bruises. I lean down and kiss her belly as another kick lands swiftly against my mouth.

"Hey! Quit that....no kicking Dad in the face!" I say rubbing at my lips, leaning in to place another kiss on her exposed stomach. I can't believe that she hasn't got any stretch marks so far. It's incredible how far the skin can stretch when it needs to, though I've been helping by applying cream every night, which is just another excuse to touch her and run my hands over my babies.

She giggles at me, loving that I'm finally feeling how much they're kicking now. They're quite strong as well. I should know, I sleep with my hand on her stomach every night and they're all having a soccer game in there I swear. It's a wonder Mia gets any sleep at all. I'm exhausted from sleeping with one eye open each night as she gets up to go to the bathroom, trying not to disturb me.

Shit I'm so sick of this bed. I mean, I love it and all, but I can't wait to get up and around again. The only time I'm allowed up is to pee, shower or go for my consult with Christine. We've taken to eating up here with tray tables and I'm grateful for the company. I've read till my eyes have crossed and watched way too much daytime television as well as every DVD that Noah has, plus a heap more that Grace, Heth and Logan have brought over for me. Maxine has been a saint.

I don't know what I would have done without her each day. She intends to stay around for a while after the babies are born to help out and I'm beyond grateful. I know how hard it's going to be to manage three little newborns, so I know that I'll need her assistance. Noah's taking a month off to help, but he'll need to go back to work after that, hopefully by then I'll be fine.

I lay back, trying to sleep, but I know that before I do I'll have to get up and use the bathroom again. Noah's snoring softly behind me as I carefully make my way to the edge of the big bed and push myself upright, supporting my huge stomach as I walk.

Okay I get it. At this point in time I don't care how much it's going to hurt I just want these babies out. I only take two steps towards the bathroom door before I'm bent over, holding my back and my pelvis, not sure which one hurts the most.

The pain nearly tears me in half. I stand up straight and wait for it to pass, before continuing slowly walking to the bathroom. Just as I get into bed again another contraction hits and I smother a cry, not wanting to wake Noah. I know he hasn't been sleeping well and I need to make sure that this is the real thing and not just some Braxton Hicks contractions. I rub my pelvis, trying to suck in some deep breaths and it feels like this one hasn't even finished and another one starts. I decide not to wait any longer. The hospital is about 15 minutes away, so it's better to be safe than sorry. I lean over and shake Noah lightly and instantly his eyes fly open as he sits upright in the bed, looking around, trying to wake himself up quickly.

"Noah it's time...I think." I tell him as a confused looks spreads over his face.

"Time for what?" He asks looking at the digital clock on his bedside table. It shows 2:25am. He scrubs his hands over his face trying to wipe away the last remnants of sleep as he looks at me curiously.

"Hun, I think it's time for the babies to say hi to their family. I've had a few bad contractions. It might be nothing, but I think we'd better go and get checked." I no sooner say the words and he's flying out of bed, pulling on some sweats and a hoodie. He grabs my extra-large robe, helping me to put it on. Maxine must hear us moving around, because instantly she's in our bedroom, still dragging her robe up her arms and looking at us as she waits for an explanation.

"Is it time?" She asks quickly taking in the fact that Noah's dressed and helping me to stand up.

"I think so. I've had a few contractions, but it might be nothing." I say, just as another one punches me low in the stomach and I bend forward trying to ease the pain.

"Give me 5 seconds to get dressed and I'll help you get her downstairs Son." She tells us, quickly striding back to her room to pull on some clothes.

Noah helps me down the stairs because I can't see my feet, so he guides me from the front while Maxine holds me tightly with an arm around my shoulders.

Getting up into the high SUV is extremely difficult and Noah practically lifts and throws me into the front passenger side, slamming my door as soon as my butt hits the seat. I wait for him to get in the driver's seat and for Maxine to climb into the back seat before I tell him to relax. "I'm fine, we might be jumping the gun. Don't panic just yet." I say as I reach over the console to take his hand. He immediately lifts it to his lips, kissing it lightly.

"Are you sure you're okay?" he asks, his voice full of concern and worry showing all over his face as his eyes search mine for reassurance.

"Yeah Baby. I'm good. Don't go running any red lights just yet, alright?" I smile over at him before another contraction starts and I lean forward slightly in my seat, puffing out breaths, trying to breathe through the pain. Noah starts the car and backs out of the driveway quickly, heading for the hospital.

He's driven the route a few times just to make sure it's not full of road works or detours, and we get there quickly. Noah hardly stops the car before turning it off and jumping down to run around to my side, he helps me down carefully. The pains are getting closer together and I'm glad for the wheelchair that arrives before I take a step away from the car. The young orderly helps me to sit and takes me through the glass doors into the waiting room, yelling over to the receptionist to grab my chart and send it up as we make our way to the elevators. Noah holds my hand tightly, reassuring me all the time that we're fine. I try to smile up at him, but it's becoming increasingly difficult to smile at the moment. I'm focused intently on my breathing, trying to get through continuous contractions. Maxine follows with my hospital bag, staying back but close by.

Just as we hit the ward another fierce contraction hits me and I grunt with the pain, a sheen of sweat covering me. The midwife who comes to greet me smiles and assures us that they've been waiting for us to arrive. It's not often they get to deliver triplets apparently. I settle into my bed in a private room while she goes out to notify Christine that I've arrived.

When she comes back she does my BP again and raises her eyebrows at the reading. I explain about it being a concern for the last two months and she nods in understanding. She ushers Maxine out for a minute while she dons gloves and examines me to see how far dilated I am, then checks the position of each baby. Apparently none of them are engaged in the pelvis meaning that I won't be able to deliver them naturally, so they ready me for a C-section as she assures me that this isn't a drill.....that my contractions are real.

Even though I've been mentally preparing myself for this I'm still disappointed when she tells me about the C-section. I was hoping to be able to have a natural birth, but I know it isn't possible now, so I wait for Christine to arrive while Noah paces and Maxine holds my hand, patting it occasionally and smiling at me. I can see the worry in her eyes even though she's trying hard to cover it as she talks excitedly about meeting her grand-babies soon.

Christine arrives in a flurry of activity as the OR orderly comes to collect me, gently lifting me over onto the small trolley as Noah grabs my hand firmly, leaning in to kiss me and say that he's gonna be in there with me, no matter what. The last time I was in an OR I was 5 and had my tonsils removed, so the surroundings are a bit scary, especially when the nurse drags Noah away and guides him to a changing room to get out of his street clothes and into scrubs so that he can be with me in the operating room.

People rush about and the room is full of masked faces as I'm wheeled in. Tears burn my eyes as I realize that all of these people are here for my babies. I see three portable humidicribs lined up along one wall next to three small examination trolleys with large bright lights shining down on them, portable oxygen cylinders attached to the sides. Nurses are busy gloving and pulling out drawers as a masked older man with kind eyes heads in my direction.

"Hello Mia. I'm Mike Evans and I'll be your anesthesiologist tonight. I understand that you want to try an epidural so that you're awake for their arrival, so I'll just get you to roll over a bit more and we can get started." He says, giving off an aura of calm and control, making me relax for the first time since I arrived.

Noah strides over a paper mask covering his face and a disposable cap over his thick hair. The sky blue of the scrubs suits him, making his eyes appear twice as bright as they normally are. He bends down to kiss me through his mask as Dr Evans tells him that he's about to place the needle into my spine and he needs to keep me very still for a little while. Noah leans in and whispers that he loves me and he's looking forward to meeting his children at long last, trying to distract me from the pain of the spinal needle. It's over in a minute luckily, and I lay on my back while the anesthetic is injected and I feel my legs go numb quickly.

As soon as I'm on the operating table I'm completely covered in green drapes which hide me from what's happening down at my stomach. Noah sits on a small stool next to my head as he reaches out and holds my hand under the drape that engulfs it and he kisses me gently over and over.

Now that the pain is gone I have nothing to focus on except his face and the occasional glimpse of Dr Evans as he stands silently to one side, checking on me frequently. I hear Christine's voice asking if I'm okay and ready to meet my babies and both Noah and I reply at the same time. "ABSOLUTELY!".

A babble of laughter fills the packed OR as people scurry about. I hear the nurses counting things on the nearby instrument tray and then Christine tells me that she's about to make her incision. I feel some dragging sensations and then a pulling feeling, but no pain. There's a pressure sensation then I hear a squeal from an infant as the first baby is delivered.

Noah tells me that it's one of the boys as he glances up over the drape separating me from the babies. He has tears in his eyes as he gazes at his son, then back to me. He runs a few fingers over my forehead as his eyes crinkle up in a smile, and I know under that paper mask there are deep dimples showing.

"Is he okay?" I ask, holding my breath because I can't hear him crying anymore and I know that can't be good. Just as Noah's about to answer me we hear another squawk from a newborn and Noah's head shoots up to look at his new baby. I can hear Christine telling us that this is our baby girl. Noah lowers his head back to mine and kisses me through his mask. I know that it's driving him nuts, not being able to touch me, but I'm willing to do whatever it takes to get these children delivered safely. I wait as I feel more pressure below my waist and then a sensation of lightness as the last baby is delivered. This one has a healthy loud cry which drowns out the other two. Already I can separate them by their sounds. Our little girl sounds like a kitten mewling and one boy has a loud wail while the other squawks intermittently. "Baby what's happening? Are they all okay?" I ask, starting to panic because nobody is telling me anything.

Suddenly a bundle of blankets appears at the side of my head containing my loudest crying son. The nurse hands him to Noah carefully and steps back allowing Noah some time with our baby. He looks at me with tears streaming down his face and I realize that I'm sobbing quietly. I don't know when that started, but I'm aching to hold my baby and I know that I can't just yet. Noah brings him close to me so that I can see his little wrinkled up pink face as he continues to complain loudly.

"Hey little man. You're making a lot of noise for someone who's just a few minutes old." Noah tells him, peppering his face with soft kisses. "Baby he's perfect. Look at him. He looks as gorgeous as his Mum." He turns him slightly so that I can study his face, then brings him in close so that I can kiss him. "Hey you. I'm your Mamma. Was it you that was kicking me all these months? You got comfy in there didn't you?!" I tell him as I continue sobbing between words. "The others Noah, are they alright?"

Noah looks up at the exam trolleys and tells me that he can't see them, there's too many people around. He looks up to Christine who doesn't say anything, just continues suturing. I can feel the tug of the needle, but there's no pain. "Noah what's happening? Are they okay? Somebody tell me something!" I say loudly, determined to find out what's going on.

"Baby calm down. They're fine. I'm sure they're okay. They would have said if they weren't. Just be patient for a bit longer. I'm sure they're alright." He leans in and kisses me again, but now panic is starting to set in as nobody agrees with him or replies. All I can hear are the doctors and nurses murmuring things about Apgar scores and I hear the word intubation and I know what that means.

"Dr Evans, can you tell me what's going on please? I need to know. Are they alright? Is something wrong? Please can you find out?" I ask him, desperation sounding in my voice between sobs. He assures me that they look okay and someone will come and see me in a sec. a middle aged man with glasses on strides over to us and nods to Noah, but addresses me.

"Your first baby, the boy, is having a bit of trouble breathing on his own so we're going to put a tube down into his lungs to help him, now this is just a temporary thing. He's strong and healthy otherwise, so I don't foresee any ongoing problems. I'll bring him over quickly before we take him down to the NICU okay?"

"What about our baby girl? Is she alright? Do you know what's happening with her?" I ask struggling to comprehend what he's telling me.

"She looks fine. She took a bit longer to get her Apgar up, but she looks fine now, but we'd like to monitor her overnight down in the NICU, if she's still improving in the morning we'll bring her straight up to you. She looks to be the smallest of the three, but they're all a good weight for multiples. I would guess that they're all over 5 pounds which is a good size. Anyway I'll go get your other son for you before we take him downstairs."

My sobs fill the room as Noah cradles our baby boy in his arm and unconsciously rocks him as he leans in to kiss me gently.

"Don't cry Baby. They're in the best place with the best care. They're Byrnes and Drummonds so they'll be fine. We breed em tough, don't you worry." Lifting his head to look at Christine he asks quickly, "Shit, um sorry! Can I remove this bloody mask now and kiss my wife?" I hear everyone laugh at him as Christine tells him that so long as he doesn't breathe over the draped barrier he can take it off, as she's nearly done.

"Thank Christ for that." He says, tearing it from his face, and immediately leaning in to land his lips on mine, rubbing them across gently. "I love you so much Mia. I can't believe that they're finally here, and they're perfect."

He's interrupted by the pediatrician who came to speak to us before. He is pushing a covered humidicrib towards us as our boy lays quietly, a tube taped to his mouth attached to a machine breathing for him. I sob at the sight of my poor baby, needles poking into his skin for an IV line and a naso-gastric tube taped to his cheek. Noah lays a hand on the side of the crib and softly tells his son that we love him and we'll be down to see him soon. I long to hold him, to touch him, but I know that he's safe and sound and going to get well cared for.

They leave quickly and I can hear our baby girl still mewling quietly. She isn't very loud and I don't know if that's a good or bad thing. I look over to watch Dr. Evans inject something into my IV line and raise an eyebrow in question.

"It's just a mild sedative. Once you've seen your other baby I want you to rest up and recover." He says gently.

A nurse brings over a pink blanket wrapped bundle and places it in Noah's other arm and steps away telling him that she can only stay for a minute or two.

"Look Mia. She looks just like you. Look at all that hair." He says softly, taking in the long black hair covering our baby. She looks to be the smallest, her tiny hand reaching out and latching on to Noah's as he supports both babies. A nurse comes over to take our son away for assessment promising to bring him back soon as we get to the ward. Noah's left with our baby girl who opens her eyes suddenly and gazes into his watery blue ones.

"Hello sweetheart, I'm your Daddy, and this is your Mummy." He tells her, turning her slightly towards me. She makes eye contact immediately and opens her mouth widely in a yawn. "Apparently it's hard work being born." Noah says on a smirk, cradling our baby and patting her back instinctively.

"Noah she's perfect. Look at her. I think she's going to have your eyes, though I know it's too soon to tell. She's just gorgeous. They all are, though I might be biased." I say sleepily, gazing at my daughter lying quietly in her father's arms. A nurse comes to take her from him and promises that we can see her soon, she tells us that she took photos for us of their birth.

She's going to get them developed and bring them to us in a day or so. I can hear Noah thank her softly, but he sounds like he's far away as I drift off to sleep.

When I wake up I'm back in my room and Noah's asleep on a chair, resting his head on the bed beside me, his hand holding mine. The door opens and I turn my groggy head to see Maxine enter quickly. She notices that I'm awake and walks over to the bed, running her hand down my braid and smiling widely. "I've just been down to check on my grandchildren. Mia they're just perfect. The nurses down there say that they're behaving and your boy may have to spend a few days on the oxygen, but he's doing well."

A tear runs down my cheek as I think of my baby, tubes and needles overwhelming his tiny body. "Are you sure they're okay Maxine? The other two are fine? They're only 31 weeks, it's early. They shouldn't be born yet."

"Honey they're just wonderful, I promise you. They're the superstars of the NICU at the moment. Apparently not many triplets or even preemies are born over 5 pounds, and though they're small, they're much bigger than most. You should see some of the tiny little wee things down in that nursery." She shakes her head. "I swear some of them are no bigger than baby rabbits. The poor little mites."

Noah lifts his head sleepily and smiles up at me. "Hey you. How long have you been awake?" He scrubs his hand over his face as he speaks.

"Not long. Have you been down to see them Noah?" I ask anxiously.

"Earlier, while you were sleeping, but I've been sending Mum down to check on them. I wanted to stay here and make sure you were alright." He tells me on a yawn. It's been a long night for all of us. I'm sure Maxine hasn't had any sleep since we left the house.

"I want to go down to check on them if I can. I need to see them for myself." I tell him firmly.

"I'll go and see if you're allowed to go in a wheelchair or I'll push your bed down there if I have to. I'll be back soon okay?" He says, standing up and bending over to kiss my forehead.

As he walks out the door Maxine collapses into a chair.

"You must be exhausted. Why don't you go home and get some rest? I'm sure Noah wouldn't mind you taking the car. I don't think he's intending to go home just yet."

She yawns loudly and walks over to open the blinds, allowing the early morning light to fill the room. "I think you're right, sweetie. I'll go home as soon as Noah gets back. I want to see those babies one more time before I leave, but I'll be back later on today. I need to go and ring everyone and tell them about my beautiful grand-babies. Logan and Scarlett are going to be so happy. They've been hanging by their fingernails waiting for this."

Noah walks back in and tells me that if I can wait for 15 minutes then someone will come and take me downstairs in a wheelchair, so that I can see them. The nurses are having handover at the moment, but as soon as that's done I can go. I try to shuffle my butt back so that I'm sitting up more and I realize that getting out of bed is going to be hard work, and.... I need to pee.

"Noah can you take me to the bathroom? I need to pee...again!" I say quietly.

"No you don't Baby. You have a catheter in. The nurses have been checking it every hour or so since you came back from recovery. It probably just feels like you need to go, but I promise you that you don't." He says as he lifts the bag from the side of my bed to show me.

I shuffle to the side of the bed and Noah swings my legs over the side, holding on to me as I get my balance. I'm as weak as a kitten and every move I make hurts my stomach. I support my wound as I move, but it's still painful. A nurse soon appears with a smile and a wheelchair. She introduces herself as Kate and chats happily while Noah picks me up slowly and transfers me to the wheelchair while she gets the catheter bag and my IV.

I take some deep breaths and hold my stomach, realizing that maybe I should have asked for some pain relief now that the epidurals worn off. We move slowly down the corridor to the elevator and Noah lifts the chair carefully over the bump and I'm grateful.

We quickly get to the 1st floor where my babies are staying and I'm anxious to get to them as soon as the elevator doors open. I can hear the mewling of my baby girl and the bellow of our larger son above the noise of the other babies cries. I glance up at Noah and Maxine, my grin splitting my face as I get closer.

We have to wash our hands with antibacterial lotion and put on a gown over our clothes, but I'll do anything to get close to my children so I comply happily. Noah pushes the wheelchair over to a plastic crib, where our son is crying loudly. I reach out to take his hand as the NICU nurse comes over and lifts him out of the crib for me to hold.

As soon as he's in my arms he quiets and opens his eyes to look into mine. I gaze down at him and I see his resemblance to Noah. He has his nose and mouth and huge hands. I look lovingly down at him as he yawns widely then puts his thumb in his mouth and sucks on it hungrily.

The NICU nurse tells me that this one is always hungry and asks me if I want to try breastfeeding if I'm up to it. I nod tentatively, not really sure of how to attach him, but she helps me to undress and attach him securely. I look up to Noah in amazement as he instantly starts suckling at my breast. "Look at him Hun, he's feeding. This is the most incredible thing ever!" I run my hand up over my son's head. He has a mop of dark hair like his sister, but he's clearly the biggest of the three.

He eventually falls asleep and my nipple falls out of his mouth. Noah picks him up and places him against his shoulder and pats his back gently till he burps loudly. We all laugh at the noise. He could put Noah to shame with burps like that. Maxine has a cuddle before handing him back to me and I lay him across my lap, just looking at him for a long time. I allow Noah to place him back in his crib as I look around trying to see my other babies.

Our daughters mewling cry attracts my attention as Noah pushes me over to her crib. She's awake and clearly not happy. Noah scoops her up after sanitizing his hands again and puts her in my arms gently. I look at my squealing daughter and run my hands over her soft face as she screws it up into a grimace and lets out a cry. I undo the other side of my gown and place her to my breast like the nurse showed me and she attaches and feeds vigorously, her tiny little hand gripping on to my finger while she suckles.

We all watch her as she drinks her fill noisily. Her eyes slowly close as she stops feeding and Noah takes her from me to burp her like he did our son. She takes a bit longer to release her wind, but he persists, patting her back and kissing her tiny head softly. Maxine looks at him as she pulls out her camera and starts snapping pics of them both. He hands her back to me and she takes a few more. Finally, we place her back into her crib and tuck her in securely on her side. Her little face is totally relaxed in sleep and we watch her intently for a while as she twitches and breaths softly.

Our other son is in his covered humidicrib and we can't hold him just yet, but we're allowed to touch him gently after sanitizing our hands again. The NICU pediatrician tells us that he's doing well and is already much stronger than he was at birth a few hours ago. He goes into detail about his oxygen saturation levels and how the machine is pushing air into his lungs with positive pressure, but he doesn't think he's going to need it for much longer. They intend to try to wean him soon and assess him as they do. They're confident that he'll do well and won't be in the NICU for long.

As we leave, I look back tearfully at having to leave them once again. I need to be near them as much as I need to be near Noah. He knows how I'm feeling and gives my shoulder a squeeze as we get into the elevator. Kate tells me that I can come down later today again and see them, but I can also start expressing some milk for them to have while I'm not there and I feel better about not being with them. At least I can do something for them while we aren't together.

Noah lifts me carefully out of the wheelchair and places me back on the bed, arranging the pillows behind me as I lay back. My breakfast soon arrives and Maxine leaves, taking Noah's keys. She says that she went down just after we arrived and moved the car from the entrance and parked it in the car park not far away.

She kisses me gently on the forehead, then hugs Noah tight, patting his arm as her eyes fill with tears of happiness. He wipes at her eyes gently then leans forward, kissing her on the top of her graying hair.

"Go home and get some sleep Mum. I'll call you if anything happens I promise, but they're fine and Mia needs some rest.

Can you please bring me some clean clothes when you come back and I'll shower and change?"

After Maxine leaves, promising to be back later this afternoon, I dig into my scrambled eggs as Noah pinches my toast and spreads it with a thick layer of butter and Vegemite. We share a cup of juice, but he goes to get himself a coffee in the patient's kitchen and sits quietly sipping it beside my bed in the armchair.

"So are we going to give these little munchkins names Baby? Are we going to go with the names that we talked about?" He asks, blowing across his cup to cool his coffee.

"I think so don't you?" I reply, pushing my breakfast tray away from me. "She definitely looks like an Alice to me so that's a given. The boys, I don't know. I was thinking Jake for the noisy one and Callan for the little one. Shall we stick with those or have you come up with another one that you like?"

"No that's the ones we chose so we should stick with them. So, Jake Edward after my middle name, Callan Alexander after your father, and Alice Violet after your gran, right?"

"Yeah I like the sound of those, and they suit them don't they?" I ask, double checking that he's happy with their names.

"They do Baby, they certainly do." He grins at me, showing his approval.

Shuffling my butt back slowly so that I'm sitting up more I can't wait till all of them can spend some time in here with us. I spend the morning sleeping and expressing breast milk for them. The nurses take it down to the NICU for me and tell me that even little Callan will get some of the milk for the antibodies that it contains. Even doing this small thing helps me feel close to them all.

After lunch I can barely keep my eyes open and Noah's face is the last thing I see as I drift off, dreaming of our future with our 3 gorgeous babes.

Chapter THIRTEEN

Noah

I watch Mia as she finally succumbs to sleep, her face relaxing and all of her stress falling away. I can't help myself. I run my hand down the side of her face lightly, needing to touch her porcelain skin. Thank god she's okay.

I was seriously worried in the OR.

That shit was scary.

I could have lost her and the babies. I'll be thankful every day of my life for the skilled professionals in that room. I know how close we were to losing little Callan, but Mia doesn't need to know that.

I interrogated the NICU pediatrician when I was down there by myself early this morning and he told me how close it was and how it was still touch and go till they can prove that he's strong enough to breath on his own. I know that he's in the best hands and that if something happens it won't be from the lack of care. If anyone can help him survive it's these guys. They know their stuff and I trust them. I have to, my son's life is in their hands.

Mia sleeps for a few hours and I just sit and watch her, knowing that as of today our lives will never be the same again. I have a million things running through my mind, but my main thoughts are of her. This sweet adorable woman who came into my life and completely turned it on its head. I don't know what I did to deserve her and those three munchkins downstairs, but I'm overwhelmed with love for them all.

Just as Mia stirs, Christine knocks lightly and pokes her head around the door, asking quietly if she can come in. I nod as Mia stretches and yawns, trying to wake up.

"Hey Mia, congratulations to you both. I've been down to see the babies and they're all doing remarkably well. In fact, I talked to the head pediatrician and we agree that the two of them can come up here with you, but unfortunately the little guy needs to stay for a while down there till they assess him over the next few days." She tells us, smiling brightly. Mia grabs my hand and squeezes it, happy at the news that our babies can come up here and be with us.

"How soon can they be brought up?" She asks quickly.

"Slow down a bit. I'll arrange it as soon as I can, so hopefully very soon. I understand that you've been down to visit already? I don't want you overdoing it too soon. You need to rest and recover so allow Noah and the nurses to spoil you for a while. I don't want you out of bed unless it's absolutely necessary.

Your BP is still quite high and that's a concern. I need you to take it easy. I'll allow one visit a day to the NICU and Noah can take lots of pictures for you, and if you find you aren't resting enough then the babies can go out to the ward Nursery with the other newborns and you can sleep while the nurses look after them." She tells us seriously. "Noah I need you to make sure that she gets enough sleep and if you have any problems at any time you get the nurses to call me immediately okay?"

I frown at the seriousness of her tone, not understanding why she's being so strict about the bed rest. I can see it written all over her face.

"Christine what aren't you telling me?" she asks quietly, worried now. Her tone suggests that there's more to be concerned about than what's she's saying.

She smiles down at her in a reassuring manner and pats her hand gently. "I don't want you to worry. I just want you to rest and get strong enough to look after your adorable children."

I nod in her direction. "Alright. I'll keep a close eye on her for sure, but can I see you outside for a minute?"

We both walk quietly to the door and leave the room.

"Noah what's going on? What did she say? Is something wrong...what aren't you telling me? Whatever it is I want to know." She tells me firmly, her voice raising as her worry increases.

"Babe, calm down. She was just telling me that she's still worried about your high blood pressure. She thinks it should be coming down now after the babies were born. That's why she wants you on complete bed rest still. If it doesn't come down there's a chance that you might have a seizure and that can cause damage to the brain, or you may need to start on medication. So for now just do as your told and get as much sleep as you can. She's going to see about getting the babies up here to put your mind at ease, but I don't want you getting out of this bed okay?"

Huffing out a long breath she nods in agreement, totally destroying the idea of having a shower before dinner arrives tonight. "Can you get me a bowl of water so that I can have a quick wash before Alice and Jake get here?"

"Sure, I'll even help you wash your back." I grin suggestively, wiggling my eyebrows up and down.

"Yeah right. Like that's going to do you any good. I don't think you want to even look at this body right now, let alone lust after it!" I tell him on a laugh.

"Sweetheart you know I always lust after it and I always will, so long as I'm breathing. That won't ever change. You're even more beautiful now because of your strength over the last year. I adore you. Thank you for our babies." I say, kissing her firmly on the mouth, showing her all of my love in that gesture. She reaches her arm up and slides it around my neck, pulling me further into her, returning my kiss.

We break apart at the same time, still looking deeply into each other's eyes. "I love you so much Noah." She tells me earnestly, running her hand over my thick blonde hair. I wonder if any of our children will end up with my hair color?

At the moment they're all dark, but I know that can change. They all look identical except for small things that define each of them. Alice has Mia's features, fine and feminine and Jake is big and boisterous and reminds me of Logan, and Callan looks like a mix of both of us, though we haven't been able to have more than a quick look at him through the clear plexiglass covering of the crib.

. I glance down and see it that Mia has damp spots on her gown, and lean over to get her the breast pump so that she can express her milk for them, especially Callan. As she attaches the electric pump to both of her breasts I study the action as the milk is sucked out into the sterilized bottles attached to the machine. I liken it to milking a cow, but I don't care. If it means my babies get her milk even if she's not around, then she's happy to be a cow for a while. Glancing up at her face, then back down to her breasts, I say, "I've told them they have twelve months max., then they have to give them back."

"Wait...what?? You've put a time limit on breastfeeding?!" She asks me, amused that I've actually thought about this.

"Absolutely, I want those boobs to myself, but I know I have to share them for a while, so they get 12 months, no more." I nod, as though this is important information that she needs to listen to.

"Okay then. Good to know! Did they agree to this caveat or was this a dictatorial decision?" She asks, humoring me.

"Oh no, they agreed. I told them months ago about it and they all kicked me, which told me that they agreed. So 12 months and then they're mine again."

Somehow I don't think I'm going to wait 12 months, not by the way her nipples are pulled into the suction apparatus. I run my tongue out over my lower lip

"Noah did you speak to the pediatrician downstairs? Is Callan going to be okay? Is he going to have any ongoing problems?"

"No Babe, he said that he's hoping to try him off the oxygen in a few days, which is great because normally preemies stay on it for a lot longer than that. He says he's well developed for a 31 weeker, whatever that means. He even said that once you're strong enough you can hold him, even if he still has everything attached. So that's good news, I reckon." She nods in agreement, smiling up at me.

"Noah I think I'm done. Can you please put the lids on the bottles and take them out to Kate if she's still here? She'll take them down and put them in the NICU fridge." She tells me as I tear my eyes away from her engorged breasts and focuses on the small glass bottles. She quickly covers herself while I'm distracted, and lays back, taking a big drink of water as she does. I know she needs to keep up her fluids to help with the breastfeeding so she's been drinking a lot today. I haven't left her side all day and I'm.getting weary, though I'd never say it.

I watch her quickly touch her wedding rings and attempt to twirl them around her finger, but they remain firmly in place. Her fingers are still swollen I notice, and I hope they go down soon. It's got to be uncomfortable having sausages instead of long elegant fingers.

When she wakes up I'm cradling a baby and bouncing him slightly on my shoulder. I see that she's awake and quickly support him under his head and back like the nurses showed me and lay him in her arms. I gaze down at my sleeping son, his little mouth open and breathing softly, his arms jerking around in his sleep. I watch as he screws up his tiny face and his hands ball into fists. I take one of his hands and he wraps it around my finger tightly.

"He's just had a feed not long ago." I say quietly, leaning in close and just staring at him like I am. "You make gorgeous babies Sweetheart. Look at that face. He's perfect." She turns her head slightly and pulls me in for a quick kiss. "I didn't do this alone you know. You helped."

"Okay then, we make gorgeous babies." I smirk.

"That we do." I glance over to Alice's crib and notice her beginning to stir. She's making those gorgeous little baby noises that newborns make and I can see her arm waving about. "I think someone else is awake as well." I say, nodding in her direction.

I walk over and scoops her up in my huge hands, holding her against me firmly. "Hey little girl. You hungry?" I ask, rocking her slowly as she continues to fuss. "Okay, Mum's here. You want some milk don't you?" I hand her down to Mia and we swap babies.

Holding Jake close and supporting his head with my hand, I bring him up to my shoulder. Mia drops one side of her gown and attaches Alice quickly. She continues to fuss for a little while, but soon gets the hang of it and suckles firmly. I watch my daughter, and a wave of emotion rushes through me. Who could believe that you could love three little beings as much as I do? She looks up at me still holding our boy and I can't believe how lucky I am right now. I have everything in the world that anyone could possibly ask for.

She watches me for a little while. She's a pro at this baby stuff already and it's only been one day, though I never doubted that she would be. Anyone can see that she clearly adores all of the babies, and even though she's never been this close to one before she's taken to them, like a duck to water. I turn my head to kiss my son gently as he sleeps on my shoulder and Mia almost melts into a puddle on the bed. A tear escapes and falls down her cheek, landing on Alice's hand. She swipes at her eyes with her other hand as I frown down at her.

"You alright Baby?" I ask walking over to the bed.

"Yeah Hun. I'm good. Just having a little moment." She says, looking up at me with watery eyes and smiling slightly. "I can't believe how good you are with them already. It's like you've done this all before."

I laugh out loud at her comment. "Sweetheart I've never been this close to a newborn in my life except for Logan, Caleb and Scarlett, but they don't count. I'm crapping myself that I'm gonna drop him on his head or something. I have no idea what I'm doing, but he's sleeping and happy so I must be doing something right I figure." I lean around to place another soft kiss on Jake's dark down covered head. Jake's nuzzling at my neck, breathing quickly, tiny mouth open. She grabs my phone and take a few quick photos of us together.

Just as she pulls Alice away and does up her gown again there's a knock on the door and Mum pokes her head around, her face grinning widely when she sees her grand-babies here with us. She's followed in by Dad, who gives us both a beaming smile as he walks over to me, slapping me lightly on the back in greeting. Mum quickly walks over to me and gives me a hug and a kiss on the forehead, and gazes lovingly down at her grandson.

"You can hold him if you want. I've just finished feeding him so he needs burping." I tell her, handing her my baby who's now sound asleep.

"Come here to your Nan, Sweet pea." She coos to him, scooping him up into her arms, then rocking him softly. I watch as Dad gets acquainted with his granddaughter and he and I stand chatting amicably. I hear Mum comment about how good I am with such a tiny baby and I laugh at my father, telling him that I'm actually shit scared right now! I smile at the scene before me. Jake is cradled against Mum and Alice is sleeping in her Poppa's arms contentedly, the only thing missing is little Callan. I look to Mum and ask if she stopped by the NICU on her way in.

"Yes Love, we did. We could only see him in the crib again, but he looks good. They're putting him under the UV lights for a while because he's a bit jaundiced, but the doc told us he's getting stronger every hour so that's good news eh?" she glances up at me.

"He's jaundiced? Why hasn't anyone told us? Noah? I need to go and see him." she says, panic rising in her voice.

"Babe you know what Christine said. One visit a day, the rest of the time you need to stay in bed. I'll go down and see what's happening and I'll take a couple of pics for you, but you're staying right here." I say firmly, striding to the door.

"Oh I'm sorry Love. I didn't mean to scare you. Jaundice is common in babies and easily treated with light therapy. I think it was Caleb or Logan who spent nearly a week under the lights when they were born. It's nothing serious really." Maxine tells Mia, trying to reassure her, but it isn't working. What's normal for a full term baby might be a major thing for a preemie.

"Why's Noah taking so long? I'm nearly to the point of asking Rory to find me a wheelchair so that I can go down there and check on him myself" Mia says, just as I finally step back through the door. I smile at her as I walk over and bends to kiss her lightly on the mouth.

"He's fine Sweetheart. Really. I spoke with the doc and he said this is a normal thing for preemies, something about his liver still maturing and he's confident a few days of the light therapy plus some extra fluids and he'll be fine. He said that if he's still doing well in the morning when you go down then he'll let us hold him. Oh and they weighed him and I forgot to tell you...he's 4lb 12 oz...so nearly 5 pound which is like the benchmark figure. They're already cutting back his oxygen and he's doing well so far with that. Here I got you some photos of him."

I pull out my phone and unlock it. And she nearly snatches it out of my hand in her rush to check on our little boy. She quickly opens the folder and enlarges the first photo. His eyes are covered by a loose net bandage and he still has a tube in his mouth and a feeding tube in, but she can see him. He's bare except for a disposable nappy and a tiny plastic board that's been taped to his arm to keep it straight for the IV line.

"Oh look at him, he's just beautiful. I can't wait to get there in the morning and hold him. He looks so little with all those tubes in him. I can see the yellow tinge to his skin too. You sure he's okay though?" She frowns up at me as I nod at her.

"Yeah Babe, he's good. He's getting the best care and hopefully he'll be strong enough soon to join us up here as well."

Mum rocks Jake as he starts fussing and lays him over her shoulder, patting his back gently. "How are you feeling today Sweetie? How's the belly?" She asks as she glances at Mia.

"I'm good. Got a bit of a headache, but I think that's just because I haven't drunk enough water, but I did have the IV till they removed it this morning. I wish they'd taken the needle out as well, apparently they want to keep it there for a while longer in case I need another IV for any reason. The headache's not bad, though I think I might need to get my eyes checked. I feel like my vision's a bit blurry...like I'm looking at everything through the wrong glasses.

I immediately frown and quickly get up, telling them that I'll be back in a second, as I stride out the door. When I come back with a nurse behind me, she looks over at both of us with a curiosity all over her face.

"Noah what's going on?" she asks as the nurse starts wrapping the Blood pressure cuff around her arm securely. She smiles at her and explains that it could be her high blood pressure causing the symptoms and she just needs to check it again. She frowns as she looks at the digital numbers, but because it's turned away from her, Mia can't see it. I can though and a deep frown creases my forehead as I walk to the bed and sit on the edge of it, taking her hand. "Exactly how long have you had a headache Sweetheart?"

"Ummm I'm not sure...a few hours maybe? Why?" She asks, getting worried as the nurse and I share a look of concern.

"I'll be back in a little while, but maybe we should cancel visitors for now and close the blinds and let Mia rest for a bit." She says kindly, walking towards the door.

Mum and Dad immediately get up to leave, giving me a frown as they hug me and then Mia and tell us that they'll be back tomorrow and remind us that our clean clothes are in the overnight bag near the bathroom door.

I place the babies back in their cribs to sleep, now that they've settled, giving each a soft kiss on the forehead before laying them in their beds and covering them.

"Noah you're scaring me. Why did they have to leave? How high is my BP? I feel okay, I'm just tired I think." She tells me as she lays back against her pillows and closes her eyes.

Bending down to kiss her, I say, "You're fine Baby. You just rest and I'll go and have a shower before dinner arrives." I open the leather overnight bag and pull out some clothes, then open the bathroom door before sleep overcomes her.

Chapter FOURTEEN

Noah

I quickly soap up and rinse, toweling myself off with a scratchy hospital towel and pull on some clean sweats and a t-shirt. I'm combing my hair when I hear a strange gurgling sound from the main room. I open the door and in the dim light I see Mia on the bed having a seizure. She's actually having a fit in front of me and I have no idea what to do about it. My mind is trying to grasp the fact that her limbs are jerking, her fists clenched and legs outstretched.

Oh Holy Fuck! What do I do?

My mind goes completely blank in my panic as I hesitate in the bathroom doorway. I run my hands up through my damp hair and tug on it slightly trying to get my head around the sight of my gorgeous wife fitting. Her whole body's shaking and her head is hyper extended backwards, every muscle rigid. My legs finally move and I run over to the call bell and push it again and again as I pull out the pillows from behind her, moving her down the bed and onto her side. I don't know what to do as I stand there and wait for help to come.

In an instant the room's full of doctors and nurses and I step back out of the way as I see IV lines being hung on the pole of her bed and someone yelling about giving her some Diazepam and Magnesium, but I stand back so that they can do what they need to. Jake starts fussing beside me and I gently scoop him up and lay him on my shoulder, patting his back distractedly. My brain has shut down. This is exactly what Christine was warning me about this morning. She told me to look out for blurred vision, confusion and headaches. Why didn't Mia tell me about her headache before? It's just like her to be not worrying about herself.

Oh My God. I can't lose her now. I just can't. Not after all that we've been through. Not now. I need her to be okay. I can't live without her and raise these babies. They need their mother as much as I need my wife. I can't even contemplate a life without her in it.

I walk around the bodies surrounding the bed as I try to escape the horror in the room. I need Mum and Dad to come back. I need to get my phone. Where the Fuck's my phone? I dig around in my pockets with my free hand, but these are clean sweats. My phone's still on the bathroom vanity. I quickly stride back, dragging my eyes from the sight of Mia jerking around on the bed as they all try to help her. Once my phone's in my hand I rush out to the hallway, trying to drag in a breath. I feel like a huge weight is sitting on my chest and I'm having trouble getting any air into my lungs. I concentrate on my breathing for a minute as I unlock my phone and dial Mum's mobile. She answers on the second ring. "Hey Son. Did I forget something?"

"Mum. Mia's having a fit. I don't know what to do. Where are you?" I tell her, panic evident in my tone.

"Okay. Rory turn around now. We need to go back. Don't panic Noah. She'll be fine. You just hang in till we get there okay? We're only about ten minutes away. Just stay with me alright?"

She says, trying to stay calm herself, but I know her. She'll be as worried as I am.

"Mum this is what Christine warned me about this morning. Mia should have told me about her headache and blurry vision sooner. We might have been able to prevent this happening. Oh Fuck. I can't lose her. I just can't. She has to be alright. Oh God Mum.....she's my world. I can't breathe without her!" I sob into the phone, more scared than I've ever been in my life, and I don't mind admitting it.

Mum makes reassuring noises, but I can hear her snuffling in the background as she does. Jake starts squirming on my shoulder, bringing me back to the here and now. I jiggle him softly and pat his back, leaving my phone cradled between my neck and shoulder firmly as I hear Mum tell me that they're just parking the car and they'll be right with me. I end the call and shove my phone into my pocket and concentrate on Jake. No doubt he's hungry. This boy can eat.

I pat him gently trying to settle him. I walk back in and stand just inside the door as someone pushes against me as they move Mia's bed. I step out of the way and they move it quickly through the door as they tell me that they're taking her up to ICU. I'm torn between needing to feed Jake and being with Mia. I know they won't allow the babies up there with me, so I wait for Mum and Dad to arrive and take over from me.

I stride to the kitchen and pull out a small bottle with Mia's name on it and shove it in the bottle warmer on the bench. I'm doing everything on autopilot at the moment, my brain too overloaded with everything it's had to cope with the last 24 hours. I need to be with Mia. That's my driving thought. That's all I can think about as I grab the bottle and walk quickly back to her room and fall down into the chair, tears streaming down my face. I gently place the bottle into Jake's mouth and he sucks hungrily at it. I watch him and wonder how we'll manage if Mia doesn't pull through this.

Christine left me in no doubt about how serious this could be. Mia could have a stroke or brain damage or her organs can fail. I just hope that she's strong enough to fight this as well. After the shit storm that she's been through she needs to finally catch a break. I need her to. I don't think I'd survive without her.

I look up as the door opens and Mum and Dad rush in, panic all over their faces.

"Where's our girl? How is she?" Mum says in a rush of breath, looking around at the empty room. Alice is still sleeping in her plastic crib in the corner, unaware of the drama that unfolded. It feels like I'm watching a TV soap, that this isn't real, but I shake my head to clear my thoughts as I look down at Jake, who's finished all of his milk.

"They've taken her up to ICU." I glance up as Mum gasps loudly, a sob escaping. "I need to get up there and find out what's happening, but Jake woke up and needed feeding. Can you take over here and I'll go and check on her and be back soon to fill you in?" I hand Jake over carefully as she sits in the chair I just got out of, lifting him onto her shoulder to burp him. "When Alice wakes up she'll need feeding and changing too I think."

"Son they'll be fine. You go and be with your girl. We'll keep an eye on the young'uns here." Dad tells me, patting me on the shoulder in a show of support, his eyes teary as he takes in my tear stained face.

I swipe at my eyes and rush out, not waiting for the elevator. I need to expend some energy so I take the stairs up the two flights to the ICU floor. I pull open the stairway door and stride in, looking around as move down the long corridor, hoping to see Mia in one of the private rooms.

I finally catch a glimpse of her in a bed in front of the nurse's station, which tells me how serious this is immediately. I pull back the curtain a bit more and notice a smiling nurse changing Mia's IV fluid. I walk over to the bed and take Mia's hand in mine, needing the contact.

"Are you her husband?" She asks kindly and I nod in reply.

"She's doing alright so far. No more seizures, which is good. She's sleeping now because of the drugs she was given to stop her fitting. You can sit with her if you want. Her Doctor's expected any minute and she'll be able to fill you in more. At the moment we're concentrating on getting her blood pressure down with some medication. She'll need to stay up here for a while so that we can monitor her and make sure she doesn't seize again."

"Okay. Thanks for that. I'll just sit here with her for a while, till Christine arrives." I tell her as she nods and leaves me alone with my sleeping wife.

"Hey Baby. You scared the hell out of me for a minute there. I don't want you to do it again okay?! I need you to wake up and show me those gorgeous green eyes that I love so much. I need you to be alright Babe. I can't be in this world without you. I don't care what it takes, but I'll make sure that you're healthy again, no matter what." I run my fingers down her cheek gently as I lean in for a soft kiss. "I love you so much Sweetheart. You just have to be okay. I need you and your babies need you too. Jake's gonna be a handful, I can just see it, and Alice will need her Mum for all of that girly shit that you do together, and Callan's gonna need his Mum to take special care of him. Don't you dare leave me Mia. I won't survive. I know it."

Tears stream down my face as I watch her sleep. I swipe at them, but others rapidly take their place. I put my head down on the bed, still holding her hand tightly in mine and I sob hard, not caring who hears or sees me. I need her to wake up and be okay. I'm broken without her. I need her to feel whole again.

"Noah?" I hear from the end of the bed. "Noah? Listen to me. She's going to be alright. Her blood pressure has come down and she's stopped seizing, so that's a good sign." Christine tells me as she places a hand on my shoulder in support. I look up at her, trying to reign in my sobbing, but a few hiccups escape.

"I need to know that she's gonna be alright. She just has to be. I can't do without her. This shit's just too scary. I need her Christine, like I need my next breath. You have to make sure that she's okay. I'll do anything...anything at all."

"I know. You need to realize that she's in the best hands at the moment and receiving the best care possible. We've given her some medication to stop the seizures and to sedate her as well as lower her BP. They all seem to have done the job and she's just sleeping peacefully now. I want her to stay up here for a few days just to make sure that she's alright, but I have no doubt that she's going to be fine. She's a tough girl, this lady. She'll fight for her babies."

"I need her to. I can't imagine my life without her, and those babies need her so much. I wish she'd have said something about her headache sooner and we could have prevented all this." I say as I draw in some deep breaths, trying to control myself.

"Me too. Typical Mia. Always thinking of others and not herself." She says as she watches the monitors showing Mia's heart rate, breathing and blood pressure. I notice that it's considerably lower than it was before and I'm reassured slightly. I just need her to wake up so that I can see for myself that she's okay.

I feel her hand jerk against mine and my eyes fly to her face as her eyelids flutter slightly then open sleepily. She looks around, not understanding where she is and I almost burst into tears again, with joy this time. "Hey Baby." I say softly as she tries to focus on me, and notices Christine sitting in the chair beside me.

"Noah? What's going on? Where am I?" She glances around at the unfamiliar ward with a deep frown. "Where are Alice and Jake?" She asks quickly, worry covering her face.

"Take it easy Baby. They're fine. Mum and Dad are with them downstairs. You're in the ICU. You had a seizure and scared the crap out of us all, but you're gonna be just fine now. They've given you some stuff to lower your blood pressure and Christine thinks it's doing the job." I glance at Christine as she nods and smiles at Mia.

"How do you feel Mia?" She asks her quietly.

"Like I've been hit by a bus." She says as she runs her hand up over her face. "I really had a fit? I'm not epileptic. I don't understand."

"It was the eclampsia Mia. Your high blood pressure caused the fitting, but we've given you some drugs to help it now. You should have told us about the headache and blurred vision sooner and maybe we could have stopped this happening." She admonishes gently.

"I just thought it was a slight headache. It wasn't even a bad one. Just kinda there you know? It never occurred to me to say anything till Maxine asked me, and by then it was probably too late right?"

"I think so. It's fine though. You just need to keep to strict bed rest for the next few days and we'll see how it goes after that. This means that you won't be able to visit the NICU like we planned. I'm sorry about that, but it's necessary for you to have complete bed rest. I'm sure Noah can make sure that you do." She quickly stands up and pats my shoulder again.

"Anyway I'll leave you to it and I'll be back again tomorrow night after I've finished consults, okay? I'll see you then." I watch as she walks to the nurse's station in front of Mia's bed and talks to the two male nurses for a minute then gives me a smile and wave as she heads to the door.

I turn back to Mia and search her face with my eyes. "Never ever scare me like that again. I thought I was gonna lose you. I couldn't think straight. I didn't know what to do and I couldn't breathe without you. I never want to go through that again. I need you so much Baby." I get up and sit on the edge of the bed and lean forward to kiss her firmly, needing to feel her sweet lips against mine again.

She returns the kiss as I rub my lips along hers gently and kiss her over and over, not wanting to let her go. We eventually hear a loud cough from the other end of the bed and I pull away slightly. "We're always getting sprung kissing in hospital rooms. You really need to stop enticing me like that." I tell her, a grin breaking over my face, as she blushes suddenly and swats at my arm. I pull back as I laugh at her face, and I sit back in the chair beside her bed, not letting go of her hand.

The nurse smiles at us and apologizes for interrupting, but she wants to give Mia a quick wash and settle her down for the night. I leave them to it after grabbing more kisses, and head down to check on the babies, and tell Mum and Dad the good news.

As expected Mum bursts into tears of relief and Dad grins widely as I tell that she's gonna be okay. I walk over to the cribs against the wall and scoop up Alice who fidgets for a minute then goes back to sleep. I need to hold her, just to reassure myself that they're fine as well. Mum watches me as she wipes the tears from her eyes. She comes over and places a soft kiss on the back of Alice's head and runs her hand over it gently. "She's such a good girl. Been no trouble at all. Bullfrog here screamed for a while before he belched and fell asleep, but not our Alice. She's a perfect little lady, aren't you sweetheart?" She says, as though Alice is gonna answer her.

I keep touching and stroking her gently while I sit on another chair and lay her along my lap, her head at my knees. I watch her peaceful sleeping face, so like her mother's. She twitches and jerks as she dreams and I can't take my eyes off her perfect little features. Her tiny hand jerks out to wrap around my finger and I marvel at how small it is compared to my own. I hear Mum taking photos with her phone and I'm distracted by the clicking as she does.

She looks at me, smiling widely as I glance up her with a raised eyebrow. "What? I need a lot of photos of my grand-babies, and that one is priceless. Her teeny little hand wrapped around one of your huge fingers. That's a keeper for sure." She informs me.

"I'm gonna go upstairs in a while and see if they'll let me stay with Mia tonight, but if they don't I'll be back soon. Can you stay with these two? I want to quickly run down to the NICU so that I can give her an update on Callan."

"Of course I'll stay. Your Dad can go home and sleep and bring us all some clean clothes in the morning and the nurses have already told me that they'll bring in a foldaway bed so I'm sure they have another if you can't stay upstairs. You must be exhausted my boy. You've had a pretty full-on day."

I laugh loudly at her analogy. "Yeah you could say that! Okay Dad do you want Alice or shall I put her back in her bed?"

"No I'll hold her for a bit though she doesn't have handles yet so I'd better sit down with her, Son." He says, holding his arms out to take her from me as I stand up.

"Okay, if I'm not back in 20 minutes you know I'm staying up there with her." I tell them both, as I walk out the door and close it softly behind me and head for the stairs again. I run down the stairs to the NICU on the next floor and check in on our little man, who's sleeping, but the nurses assure me that he's doing well, and demand an update on Mia's progress after they heard about her seizure earlier tonight.

I make my way down the hallway to where Mia's bed is as a Nurse looks up from her desk and gives me a smile. I pull back the curtain slightly and walk over to the bed which is lit by a small overhead light. She's sleeping again and I stand and watch her for a long time, memorizing every detail of her beautiful face. Her long dark lashes are spread over her cheeks, her pretty eyebrows arched elegantly over her eyes, pale skin and her rosy pink lips almost giving her a Mediterranean look.

I finally sit down in the big armchair beside the bed and take her hand in mine waiting for someone to kick me out, but the head nurse comes over and tells me that so long as I don't get in the way, I can stay with her, and offers to get me a foldaway bed to put beside hers, but that would mean letting go of her hand so I thank her politely but tell her that I'm fine in the chair. I eventually lay my head down on the bed and fall asleep, her hand held firmly in mine.

I wake up to the feeling of fingers running through my hair and I lift my head slowly, getting my bearings. Mia's awake and it's still the middle of the night so I frown at her, wondering why.

"It must be feed time. My boobs need emptying." She tells me, slightly embarrassed.

"Ah right. Of course." I say, realization hitting me that my munchkins downstairs might be kicking up a fuss about now. "I'll take it down to them if you want to pump and dump."

"Yeah the night nurse has just gone to get me a machine. They're rock hard. I think my milk's come in." she tells me, running her hand over her swollen breasts.

I remind myself that they aren't mine just yet as I watch her. "Wait I'm confused...what do you mean your milk's come in? What have we been feeding these kids?" I ask her on a note of surprise.

She laughs softly at my expression of confusion and tells me quietly, "They've been getting colostrum, which is like milk, but it has the antibodies and good stuff in it. Now it's changed to milk and my boobs are as hard as rocks."

I'm dying to check if what she says is true, but I control myself and keep my hands on the bed cover. The nurse soon comes back and helps Mia attach the machine to her beautiful breasts and I see her notice my look of lust as she exposes herself. "Calm down Cowboy." She tells me once the nurse has gone. "12 months remember?!"

"Babe you're gonna have to stop flashing me then if you want me to wait that long. Once again it's all your fault that I'm hard as a fucking cement pillar."

"Noah behave!" She tells me on a laugh.

"I'm behaving, believe me Baby. If I wasn't, these hands would be full of those incredible tits by now." I say, nodding towards her chest.

"These are the babies', not yours." She reminds me, shaking her head at me.

"I know, I know, but you keep whipping them out like that and I can't help myself. One look and I'm fucking hard." I give her my best puppy dog eyes as she laughs at me.

I watch as the bottles fill and Mia becomes sleepy again, struggling to stay awake. I help her cover herself and she lays back exhausted against the pillow and falls asleep instantly. I grab the nearly full bottles of milk and softly tell the nurse that I'm just going downstairs for a minute to deliver them and she nods and smiles at me.

I run down the stairs again and walk quickly to Mia's room just as a wailing noise starts up inside. I push open the door and hand a bottle to Mum as she scoops up Jake after changing his nappy and quickly finds a teat for the bottle and shoves it into his mouth, silencing him immediately.

His soft suckling is the only noise in the room as we look at one another and then down at him, his hand hitting the bottle as he moves it around. "Hey little man, you're a hungry one aren't you?! Your sister's still sleeping and you're bellowing like a lost calf." I bend to kiss his fuzz covered head gently as he opens his eyes and stares at mine, recognizing my voice. "Hey you." I tell him softly. "You be good for Nan, ya hear?"

"He's fine Noah. I can handle him. He's just like you were as a newborn. Demanding food often and a lot of it. Nothing's really changed has it?!" She says on a laugh as she looks up at me with smiling eyes. "How's Mia?"

"Yeah she's okay. Her blood pressure's come down and she hasn't had any more fits so hopefully she's on the mend. She's exhausted though. Could hardly finish expressing her milk, before falling asleep. I'm going to do everything that I can to help her Mum. I promise you that." I say softly looking from her to my son in her arms.

"I know you will love. She's lucky to have you. You're a good man." She tells me seriously.

I look at her studying her face for a minute before replying. "No Mum, I'm lucky to have her. I never knew how to love a woman till she came along. She's the best thing to happen to me. She makes me a better person."

"I know she does, my son. She's a wonderful girl and I love her as much as my own. You know your Dad and I will do whatever we can to help. We're happy to move in and help you both when she comes home. She's going to need a lot of care for a while and I don't mind if I just do the washing, ironing and cooking, so long as I can help somehow."

"I love you Ma......I don't think I tell you enough, but I do, and I know Mia loves you like her own Mum. She's happy that you're staying to help. She knows that she's not gonna be able to do anything much for a while, and we're both grateful for your offer." I say, watching as tears fill her eyes. "Hey now. No crying okay?"

She takes a deep breath in and blows it out as she nods, then lowers her gaze to the sleepy baby, who's fallen asleep with the bottle in his mouth. Carefully removing it she hands him to me and I lay him against my shoulder and rub his back as I stand up. I kiss his little head gently as a huge burp is forced out of him, and we both laugh as he startles himself awake.

"Hey little man. You really do take after your Daddy don't you?!" I say on a laugh as I lay him in his crib and cover him. I can't believe that I could feel so much for these babies in one day...well 9 months and 1 day. My heart feels like it's about to explode out of my chest as I look down on them both as they sleep.

"Go sleep Mum, I'll keep an eye on them for a little while before I go back up to Mia." I promise her as she lays down on the small fold up bed and pulls the blanket up over her. "Okay. No doubt I'll just get to sleep and Alice will wake for her feed, you just wait and see." She says as I turn out the light and the room plunges into semi darkness.

I sit down in the large armchair and just watch them breathing softly, making little squeaks and grunts in their sleep. Alice begins to stir and I get her bottle as Mum sits up supported by her elbow and watches me in the semi dark room. "Do you want me to show you how to change her nappy?" She asks quietly. I walk over and switch on the small light, sorry that I have to disturb her.

"Ummm I think I can figure it. How hard can it be?" I say grabbing a tiny disposable nappy from the pile and unwrapping it. Okay this doesn't look too difficult. I unwrap Alice quickly and remove her wet nappy slipping a clean one under her bum. "Don't forget her cream." Mum says and I search around for the tube I saw her use on her earlier.

Fuck me.

I need to use one of those baby wipe things right? Sooo… wipe first then cream or cream first then wipe? No, that doesn't make any sense, I decide, shaking my head in confusion, as I stand there with a wipe in one hand and the tube of cream in the other and look down at my naked squirming little girl. "MUM!" I say loudly and in an instant she's by my side and pushing me back from the crib.

"Give them to me and I'll show you what to do." She says as she grabs the cream and wipe from my hands. She wipes over Alice's butt while she lifts her legs in one hand and then smothers her groin with the cream. The nappy gets placed under her bum properly and she shows me how to tape it down. Fucking Hell, I wouldn't have done it like that at all.

She reminds me to get the iodine and do her belly button each time I change her as well. She still has a little peg thing on it and it's kinda freaking me out a bit. Is that shit normal? I had no idea that they did that with their belly button. Not sure if I want to touch it, even with a cotton bud.

"One clean little girl." Mum says, kissing her quickly before she passes her over to me.

"Hey there my little duchess. How's Daddy's girl doing huh?" I ask as I kiss her sweet face gently, before sitting down with her and getting her bottle. She sucks it down and I'm amazed at the strength that she's using to keep it in her mouth. I gaze down at her as she stares back at me intently, her hand wrapping over the bottle as if to keep it attached to her mouth. She can give her big brother a run for his money in the drinking stakes. She's a strong little one, just like her mama.

Before she's finished drinking the whole bottle of milk she falls asleep and I remove it and place her gently up on my shoulder to burp her. It doesn't take long and a huge burp erupts out of her mouth, sending her flying backwards slightly. I laugh at her disgusted expression, as if she can't believe that noise came from her. I turn my head to kiss her again and I can feel a huge explosion in the nappy against my hand as I hold her. How the fuck did that come out of her tiny little body, I wonder, as I look over to Mum for help.

She's sound asleep though, so it looks like I'm on my own this time. Okay I can do this. It's easy. Nothing to it. I walk over and lay her gently down in her crib and pick up another nappy as she wriggles and kicks her arms and legs. I can see a black tarry paste oozing out of the leg of her nappy. What the fuck is that??? Is that even normal? I look over to Mum praying for her to wake up and take over, but she stays softly snoring and I don't have the heart to wake her.

"Okay baby girl, looks like it's you and me. We can do this…so long as I don't upchuck we should be fine!" I say quietly, as I carefully unwrap the nappy. I dry retch at the sight of that black tar stuck to her butt, knowing that I'll need to clean it off. I look over to Mum again, but she's still sleeping so I need to get this over and done with.

Wipes. I need lots and lots of wipes. I start pulling them out quickly trying to decide if I have enough yet. Maybe I should have put on some gloves first so this crap doesn't get all over me. Too late now, I say to myself as I carefully run a few bunched up wipes over her little bum. This shit sticks like glue! If that came out of me I'd be seriously worried I reckon!

I continue wiping her butt with the moist towelette thingies and it takes a heap to finally remove the black sticky tar from her butt and her leg. "How could something like that come out of such a sweet baby girl huh?" I ask her as she continues to wave her arms and legs around in annoyance because I'm taking so long.

I hurry and cover her with the cream and hope there's no trace of that black shit left on her because now it'd be on me as well. I quickly cover her with the nappy and do up the tapes firmly, pleased with my efforts. One clean nappy done and dusted. I've so got this! I wrap her in her small blanket and place her on her side in the crib and cover her with another loose rug like Jake's.

Very proud of myself, I wash my hands and run up the stairs again to Mia. I check my watch as I walk to her bed quietly, trying not to disturb the other patients in the area. It's nearly 2 am and I've been awake for 24 hours except for a quick nap earlier with Mia. I'm beginning to flag as my body reminds me that I haven't really eaten today. I can smell toast from the ward kitchen and I walk quietly over and poke my head in the door at the nurse buttering a few slices.

"I don't suppose that you have any more of that? I've just realized that I've been awake since 2am yesterday with no food, and now my stomach's complaining." I watch her smile at me as she says, "Sure. What would you like on it? Vegemite, peanut butter or apricot jam?"

"Vegemite please." I say quietly. "Could I make a coffee as well?"

"Absolutely. Help yourself. There's mugs in that cupboard and coffee and tea on the bench there." She says nodding to the bench on the far wall. I walk over and make myself a hot drink and wait for my toast to cook. She hands it to me and I bite into it gratefully. Once it's gone I finish my coffee and wash my dishes as I thank her and leave her to her meal break. I walk quietly over to Mia's bed noticing that she's sound asleep still. I slowly lower myself into the chair and rest my head on the bed, holding her hand again tightly. She doesn't stir at all and I turn my head to watch her sleeping peacefully. She's the last thing I see before I close my eyes and fall asleep myself.

I stare at Noah as he sleeps peacefully, I raise my hand running it lightly over his gorgeous face. He must be shattered if he's sleeping so soundly on my bed like this. I vaguely remember him coming in last night and sitting down, but I have no idea what time that was. I hope the babies were behaving for them. I feel like I've let them down somehow by not being there to take care of them.

A nurse brings me a wheelchair so that I can go and shower quickly with her assistance before Noah wakes up. I slip out of bed carefully, holding my belly firmly as I slide into the wheelchair. A shower never felt so good I decide once I'm done.

I've even managed to wash my hair, but now I'm seriously exhausted again. I sit in bed and brush my hair firmly, waiting for Noah to wake up. Once it's brushed I braid it again and flip it behind me. It's still damp, but there's not much I can do about that. It'll probably still be damp tomorrow morning, but that's okay.

Noah stirs as a nurse delivers my breakfast tray then comes back again with one for him as well.

"Morning husband." I say softly, waiting for him to wake up completely. "Are you hungry? They brought you a tray if you want some food." I nod at the tray by my feet.

"Thank fuck for that. I'm starving. Wait! How are you feeling this morning Sweetheart?" He says as his eyes lift to the monitor above my bed and he studies the numbers on it. "Hey your blood pressure's down even more today. That's good right?" He drags the tray towards him and uncovers a plate of scrambled eggs on toast and smiles broadly. I nod at him and tell him that I feel good, except for my sore belly.

We eat in silence. I'm starving as well so it doesn't take us long to finish our meals. I ask the nurse, who comes to take away our trays, to bring me the pump so that I can express the morning milk for the babies. Noah watches intently, but behaves himself this time and helps me when I'm finished.

Promising to be back as soon as he's showered and checked on them, he takes the bottles downstairs to feed them, after kissing me firmly. Poor thing must be exhausted, all this running up and down stairs, from me to the babies and then down to the NICU to check on Callan.

An hour or so later he strides in, showered and changed and tells me that they've taken Callan off oxygen to see how he manages on his own and he's gained a little weight so they're really pleased with him. I ache to hold him and I can't wait to go and see him. Noah took some photos of him for me, but it's not the same as holding him in my arms.

The rest of the day is spent with me resting in bed, bored silly and poor Noah running back and forth between wards. Eventually Christine arrives and tells me that she's pleased with my blood pressure and I can be transferred back down to the maternity ward and if I'm still okay in the morning, I can go down to the NICU and see my little man. You couldn't wipe the grin from my face if you tried. I am still grinning as Noah pushes my wheelchair down to the room to my waiting family.

As the door opens widely to let us through I catch sight of my Dad and sister standing back in a corner smiling broadly. Tears fall as I reach out my arms for a hug and my Dad steps forward and leans in grabbing hold of me tightly and squeezing. "What are you doing here?" I manage between sobs. "How...I mean...when??"

"Your husband arranged it. We can only stay a few days, but I needed to come and make sure you were okay for myself when Noah rang and told us. He got us first class tickets from Adelaide on the next plane so that we could be here."

I look up to my husband with love shining in my eyes. "You did this? Did I tell you today that I love you?"

He bends down and kisses my tear streaked cheek. "You have, but I'll never get tired of hearing it. It's the least I could do after what you've been through."

"Thank you...really...this is amazing." I tell him trying to stem my tears. "Come here sis. I need a hug from you too." She steps forward to hug me tight and bends down to look at me seriously.

"Don't ever scare us like that again okay? I nearly had heart failure when Noah told me what happened yesterday. It's bad enough you had to have a C-section, but to have seizures as well...holy crap...that's scary. Are you sure you're okay now? What did the doc say? Should you be out of ICU just yet?" She frowns up at Noah, needing reassurance.

"I'm fine, I promise. My blood pressure is down now with the meds they gave me and so long as I take it easy I should be fine. Still have to have strict bed rest, but the good news is, I can go down and hold my little boy in the morning. How are my angels?" I look over to the sleeping babies in their cribs.

"Mia they're just amazing. We stopped by to see little Callan with Noah earlier and he's so tiny! The doc said he's doing well though and hopefully he won't have to say too long down there. Freakin hell girl...three of them...I had enough trouble coping with one at a time, let alone three of them...good luck with that!" She laughs and we all join in.

Noah lifts me carefully out of the wheelchair and places me on the bed as Maxine transfers the IV to the pole on the bed. I need to keep it in for a few more days apparently just in case they need to add some more medication to it. It's annoying, but necessary and if it means I can stay down here with my babies, then I'll do it without complaining.

Maxine lifts Alice out of her crib while Julie lifts the other and they both bring them over and place one in each of my arms as I settle back into the bed. I missed these two so much, I can't believe it. I smile at my sleeping infants and look over to Noah whose expression is pure contentment, as he smiles back at me. He walks over and sits on the edge of my bed, he pulls back the wrap that surrounds Jake and kisses his head lightly.

"Look at them Noah, aren't they gorgeous? I can't believe that they're finally here at last." I tell him as my eyes glance up to meet his.

"Yeah Baby. They're amazing...just like their Mum." He says leaning forward for a kiss.

Julie smiles at us both, shaking her head lightly. "Geez girl. Where I can I get me one of those? My husband doesn't say things like that! I'm gonna have to send him over for some lessons I think."

I smile up at her and then to Noah who slides his arm around my shoulder and pulls me close as we look down on our sleeping babies. "He's one in a million that's for sure, and he's all mine." I tell her, glancing up at him with a smile.

Maxine steps forward to tell us that they'll go back to the house for a few hours and be back later to check on us. She leans in for a quick kiss on my cheek as I thank her for taking such good care of my children while I couldn't. I can never thank her enough for what she's done. She assures me that she's happy to do it, pats my arm gently and they leave quickly, closing the door quietly behind them. Julie pulls up a chair beside the bed and looks over to Alice, her tiny face screwed up in a grimace. "She's just perfect Mia. They all are." I smile up at her and nod my agreement.

"So how did you get away so quickly? What about the kids?" I ask her.

"They're staying with my in-laws till their Dad gets home tomorrow. Then he can have them for a few days. They'll all love it. I can just see it now...they'll be having Fruit Loops for breakfast, lunch and dinner if that's what they want. You know he spoils them rotten, but it'll be good for them all to spend some time together."

Looking over at my Dad and then down to my big sister I tell them both, "I'm glad you're both here. I couldn't believe it when the door opened and there you were. So much for no excitement today. I bet my blood pressure is sky high again after that."

"Let's hope not Sweetheart. Why don't I take your Dad down to the cafeteria for a coffee and you girls can have some alone time together huh? You want anything while I'm there?"

I look at my Dad as he rises from his chair and walks towards the door with Noah. "No thanks Hun, I'm good. What about you Julie...you want a coffee?"

She smiles over to Noah and nods quickly. "Hell yeah. That sounds great. Dad knows how I have it. I'll stay here and keep an eye on her for you...so take your time...we'll be okay."

Once they're gone we giggle together, knowing that Noah and Dad are in for some "male bonding" time, which means that

Dad's going to give Noah the third degree and make sure that he's good enough for his baby girl, but I think he's already been impressed with Noah arranging for them to be here with me so quickly.

Everything happened so fast I never got a chance to ring Dad or Julie and tell them the news, so I'm grateful that Noah did it and then got them here for me. I can't believe that he did that, but I know he would be thinking of how happy I would be to have them both with me right now and he's right. I'm over the moon about it. It's been so long since we've been together and we have so much to catch up on.

I tell her about the trip to Canada, my almost miscarriage, our wedding in Las Vegas and the wonderful honeymoon in Hawaii and she listens and smiles as I recount our time together.

"Wow sis. I can't believe that you're a world traveler now and on a private jet no less. How awesome is that?! He seems really lovely Mia and I'm happy for you. I can see how much you love each other and you deserve it after the way that arsehole treated you before." She tells me, scooping up a sleeping Jake from my arms and kissing him gently, before laying him on her lap to study his little cherubic face. "I think he's going to make an amazing father to these little angels as well. He seems like he wants to be a hands-on Dad."

"He's incredible with them honestly. For someone who's never been near a baby before he's doing a wonderful job, and Maxine's been so great as well. I'm really lucky to have them."

"Oh she's awesome. Thank god you got a great Ma-in-law, not like mine...though I must admit that she's mellowing in her old age. She doesn't nag me as much as she used to. Maxine is the kind of mother-in-law that we all dream about."

"She's amazing. Nothing's too much trouble for her. She's been incredible to me since the first day we met, she just took me under her wing and decided I was part of the family, whether I liked it or not. Even after the rape she stayed with me at the hospital for as long as I needed her." I can see her spine stiffen as she studies me intently. "What rape? Mia, you never told me that you'd been raped. When was this and why am I only now hearing about it?! Oh my god...what the fuck happened?"

"Oh shit. I shouldn't have said anything. It just kinda slipped out. It was just after I met Noah and we went down to his family farm near Albany. A car ran us off the road and I woke up in a motel chained to a bed. Turns out one of Noah's business competitors had committed suicide and his father blamed Noah and decided to kidnap me for ransom, but he hired the wrong guy to do it. He was awful...he...um...raped me in the motel room, before the cops came with Noah and Logan and rescued me."

Her expression goes from disbelief to anger in an instant. "Oh my fucking God! How did I not know this? Why didn't you tell me? Is the guy still alive or did Noah kill him on the spot?"

"He was arrested. They both were. Noah nearly killed him I think, but they all pulled him off the guy. They're both in jail and waiting for the trial. I'm not looking forward to that, I can tell you, but I know I have to testify against them so that they spend the rest of their lives in jail for what they did. I think if he'd hurt the babies, Noah would have found a way to kill him"

"You were pregnant when it happened?!" She asks incredulously.

"Ummm...yeah I was, but we didn't know it then. I found out the next day while I was in hospital. They did a rape kit and part of it is a pregnancy test. I'm sorry I didn't tell you, but I just couldn't."

She flops back in the seat careful not to disturb Jake. "Holy Shit! I can't believe you never told us. We could have come over then to help. It must have been devastating for you. I can't imagine how bad it must have been."

"It was really shitty, and it was just before we left for Canada, so it was perfect timing actually. I needed to get away and just recover and Noah was just brilliant, but I don't want you saying anything to Dad okay? He doesn't need to know. I'm seeing a psychologist every week and she's been helping me. I was having shocking nightmares and then some panic attacks, but thank god they've improved. I rarely have them now. I'm in a good place."

Her eyes fill with tears as she leans forward to grab my hand. "I had no idea. You know that if I'd known I wouldn't have been here for you....no matter what."

My tears overflow at her crushed look and I second guess the decision I made at the time of the attack, maybe I should have told her. At the time I thought I was doing the right thing. There was nothing she could have done from South Australia.

"I'm sorry I didn't tell you, but I thought I was doing the right thing. Honestly once the trial's over and done with I just want to try to put it all behind me and get on with my life."

"I just wish I'd known when it happened. I feel like I've let you down somehow." She says as her tears fall freely and she swipes her hand across her eyes.

"Please don't. I promise that I'm okay now. Noah and his family have been incredible. I don't think I would have gotten this far without their help and understanding. You've had enough on your plate with the girls and Dad and work. I didn't want to add to your worry."

She gulps in a few deep breaths and nods in understanding. "Okay what's done is done...I won't tell Dad, I promise."

"Thanks Jules." I tell her sincerely. "So...I take it that you and Dad are staying at the house?"

"Yeah we are. Rory came and picked us up from the airport and took us back there to drop off our bags before we came here. He's a lovely man. It was so nice of him to come and get us. We could've caught a cab to the house or even straight here."

"He's gorgeous. He and Maxine have been great the last few months. They've come up and taken care of me when I was on bed rest at home...well Maxine came to stay and Rory came up each weekend. It was amazing how much they've done for us."

"What about the rest of his family? He has a brother and a sister right?"

"Two brothers and Scarlett. Caleb lives in Melbourne so I haven't met him yet, but Logan and Scar are adorable. I actually dated Logan before I fell for Noah....no that's not right. I fell for Noah straight away, but I agreed to a date with Logan to try to stop the feelings that I had for Noah. Obviously that didn't work!" I smile at the memory of my first date with Logan that Noah gate-crashed.

The door opens and Noah and Dad come in chatting still and smiling as they talk quietly about football. Noah's a die-hard Fremantle Docker fan and Dad's a one-eyed Port Power supporter so they're discussing how the teams are going. I know that if they've got to the football stage then Noah's definitely won Dad over for sure. I raise my face for a kiss as he bends to press his lips to mine softly.

"Hey Baby. You okay? You look like you've been crying. Is everything alright?" He asks a frown wrinkling his forehead.

"Yeah Hun. Just girl talk. We were just catching up. What have you got there?" I ask taking in a cardboard tray full of disposable cups and a paper bag.

"Oh right. I got you a chocolate donut, because I'm good like that, and a hot chocolate plus a round of coffees for the rest of us." He says as he hands me the bag and the cardboard cup carefully.

"Aww, thanks Hun. That's just what I need. It's nearly feeding time I think...and you know I just love chocolate donuts."

Julie looks from me to Noah and back again with a grimace. "Shit Mia. He really does need to give my husband some lessons!" She declares on a laugh. "It's not fair that you get Thor and I get the Hulk!"

"He does look like Thor doesn't he? I keep telling him that, but he doesn't believe me!" I tell her forcefully.

"No I freaken don't. I'm not some bloody airhead movie star. I don't care how many times you tell me." He says, sitting on the edge of the bed and lifting Alice from my lap to cradle her in his huge arms. The sight of those large biceps holding our tiny little girl has Julie and I drooling and nodding to each other in a silent agreement. He catches us and shakes his head with a smirk.

"Your Mummy's being silly baby girl." He tells Alice softly as she starts to stir, pushing her arms up in a stretch. He watches her as her eyes lock with his and a huge grin splits his face. "Hey Alice. You're gonna be trouble in about 16 years aren't you? I'm gonna have to buy a big shotgun to keep all them boys away." He coos at her using his baby voice, and we all laugh at him.

"Huh, try 10 years! I swear that Jacie is hormonal already and she's only 8!" Julie tells him as a shocked look covers his face.

"Nonononono. You aren't dating till you're at least 25 and even then I get to choose him for you." He tells our daughter as she stares up at him, totally in love already.

I look over at him in surprise. "You do realize that I'm 26, don't you?"

He turns to me with a wry grin and says, "Yeah, but you aren't my daughter. The rules change for her!"

"Just as well the boys are going to be around to look after her then eh?" Dad tells us, smiling widely. He's raised two girls so he knows how difficult they can be.

"Just don't ever expect to win an argument with her Noah. You may as well just give up now. She'll have you wrapped around her little finger in no time flat." He says, nodding to Alice.

"I think she already has, Dad." I say as Alice lets out a tiny mewl that means, "feed me, I'm hungry."

Noah passes her to me and I undo my gown to feed her discretely, conscious of Dad being in the room. She attaches immediately and starts suckling. Jake stirs and lets out a loud bellow at being left out of mealtime. Julie passes him to me and helps me to rest him on a pillow so that I can feed them both at the same time. I notice Dad looking out of the window, so that he doesn't intrude. He's old fashioned like that. Jules helps me attach him and I watch them both as they contentedly close their eyes and fill their bellies.

The nurse comes to check on my blood pressure again and notices the babies feeding so she decides to come back in about 15 minutes or so after checking that I don't have a headache or blurred vision and that I feel okay.

Chapter SIXTEEN

Noah

Mia spent the week in hospital and I barely left her side the whole time. Callan improved daily and by Friday he was able to leave the NICU, but they want him to remain in hospital for a few more days to gain some weight. He's feeding well and able to join his brother and sister in Mia's !!br0ken!! Unfortunately, her Dad and sister had to leave and I drove them to the airport yesterday, hugging them both as we said our goodbyes. They're great people and we got on like a house on fire, even if he does support the wrong footy team.

We're resting on the bed watching some daytime movie when Christine surprises us with the news that we can take the babies home in the morning and she'll arrange for a midwife to visit daily to check on Mia. She has had the suction drain, IV and catheter removed and is allowed to get up and shower or go to the bathroom, but she still needs to rest up and remain on medication for a short while.

I ring Mum who's still at our house and ask her to bring in the Sahara in the morning as well as Mia's SUV as they'll need to drive it home because mine will be full of babies. She's ecstatic about the news and promises to be in early so that we can get them organized.

Mia and I spend the night alone with the three of them, getting used to their routine. She feeds two of them at a time and I give the other one a bottle of expressed milk, then burp them in turn and change them and put them down.

We decided not to make a nursery at home because after some long discussions with Mum and Dad they decided to buy a small transportable cottage and put it near the big farm house for themselves, and we'll move into the big house as soon as I can arrange it with work and when Mia's strong enough. In the meantime, we've put one cot in our bedroom and plan to use that for the three of them till we move.

Mum and Dad's cottage is nearly completed and should be done in a month or so they think, and it'll probably take that long before we're organized. to move as well. The house in Perth will still be there for when we visit or when Scarlett comes home. The babies are going to need constant pediatrician check-ups for a while and I'll be commuting back and forth so it makes sense to keep it.

The morning arrives quickly and brings with it a dark rainy day, not very common, even in winter, in Perth. We're both excited and up early, showered and have the babies fed as we wait for Mum and Dad to arrive.

I already installed their car seats a while ago and we found a triple stroller for them that has seats, each one stacked higher behind the one in front, so that it doesn't take up much room and its light enough for Mia to use later on. Mum's going to bring it in for us to take the babies down to the car.

Callan's fussing this morning and I'm pacing the room trying to settle the crying baby. He's a lot more demanding than the other two, but it's because he was the smallest and needed the most care. We're hoping that he'll improve in time. Mia's worked out an ABC system for feeding with the help of the nurses. Alice is A, Jake is B and Callan is C and she rotates them all for each feed, so that Alice and Jake feed with her and I bottle feed Callan and then the next feed Callan and Alice feed and I feed Jake etc. It's a way that they all get to breastfeed and they get cuddles etc plus they get one on one time with me as well, which I love. I'm absolutely adoring feeding babies and getting to know their little personalities which are already showing through. Alice is the laid back one, Jake is the biggest so he's the loud boisterous one and Callan is the demanding fussy one.

Once they're all settled in the stroller we say goodbye to the staff and promise to keep in touch, and thank them for all of their help. Little do they know, but I've arranged for a banquet of Chinese food and pizzas to be delivered to each shift for the next week as a small gesture to thank them for all of their hard work, though we can never thank them enough for what they've done for us. Mia gets teary again as she hugs everyone and thanks them. We're so grateful to be able to take our babies home so soon and know that they're healthy and happy.

Dad drives Mia's car and I help Mia up into my large SUV after placing each baby into their car seat. I think it was the longest drive home ever. I didn't want to go fast and I think I came home doing 50kph instead of the normal 60+. I double checked every intersection and green light before proceeding with our precious cargo, who incidentally, remain sleeping for the whole trip.

Note to self – if Callan fusses, take him for a ride.

He was out like a light in under a minute I think. Mia and I chat quietly for the short trip home, happy to be out the hospital and enjoying the scenery as we near the beach. I pull into the garage and help Mia down from the car and walk her inside to the sofa before getting Mum and Dad's assistance with the babies. We take the sleeping infants upstairs and place them in their cot so that the three of them are lined up long-ways, wrapped up in their swaddling cloths and covered by a thick fluffy blanket.

I go and get Mia and carry her up the wide stairs despite her protests, and place her on the bed with strict instructions not to move. She smiles up at me and agrees, but I know as soon as my back is turned she's gonna be out of that bed and checking on the babies, so I get Dad to help me slowly move the cot over to the side of the bed and lower one side so that she can touch them or pick them up if necessary though I don't want her reaching out too far just yet. The look of contentment on her face fills me with happiness and I'm once again overwhelmed by the love I have for her and our gorgeous children.

Mum spends the day cooking and cleaning even though I've told her a dozen times that we have a housekeeper, she still insists on doing it so I give up arguing and leave her to it. I spend the day going up and down the stairs again, checking on Mia.

Just after lunch I go up to get her tray and find her sound asleep with two babies attached, supported on pillows. All three were asleep, so I gently lift Alice and put her back into the cot and then do the same with Callan. Surprisingly Jake hadn't woken for a feed yet and I scoop him up, trying not to disturb him and I carry him downstairs so that I can feed him and let Mia sleep for a while.

Mum and Dad take turns feeding one of the babies while Mia feeds the others and we all settle into a routine. It seems like poor Mia always has a baby or two attached or is expressing milk for the other one. She jokes that some days it's not worth putting on a shirt at all, which I wouldn't object to, but I'm sure Dad might! He's been going back and forth to the farm checking on things there and then coming back to help us with the packing.

We're just about to sit down to dinner when there's a loud knock on the front door. Mia has Callan in one arm and Mum has Jake in hers while Alice sleeps peacefully on a lambs-wool rug on the floor of the living area.

When I open it I'm greeted by a mass of pink and blue balloons and it takes me a minute to figure out that Logan's standing behind them, as he pushes his way through the door dragging the balloons along with him. He's been training the new Mine Manager at our Pilbara Gold Mine and this is the first time he's been able to get away since the babies were born, though we speak nearly every day. I give him a man slap/hug thing that we do and he walks out to the dining table as I'm hit in the face by the balloons trailing behind him.

"Hey pretty lady...and you too Ma...sorry!" I hear him laugh as Mum slaps at his free arm. Mia giggles at his comment and gets up to give him a one armed hug as he deposits the balloons on the nearby table. There must be at least a dozen of the bloody things and I glare at him as he extends the hug just a little too long. Mia laughs as she looks over to me and smiles at my obvious frown.

"So you'd better introduce me to my amazing new niece and nephews. Which one is which? Who's this little fella eh?" He asks as he scoops Callan out of Mia's arm and cradles him in his large one. Mia does the introductions and he walks slowly over to Alice who's fast asleep with a full belly. He gently kneels down and runs his hand down her tiny face in awe. "Oh we're gonna have to buy a bigger fucking gun Dude...and a chastity belt too I reckon!"

'LOGAN ALEXANDER BYRNE!" Maxine admonishes him. "Watch your mouth around these impressionable ears please."

"Mum she's gonna be a heart-breaker for sure! You can see it already. I bet she ends up with Mia's amazing green eyes as well. She'll have the boys dropping like flies before long." He glances back down to his new niece.

"Which is precisely why I made sure she has two big brothers to take care of her." I say, as though I deliberately impregnated Mia with three babies. She looks at me with a stunned expression and shakes her head.

"Right..." She drags out the word. "It was your plan all along wasn't it?! You were so sure they were all boys remember?!" She says on a laugh.

"When I realized my error, I made sure that she had some protection for when she gets older." I tell her seriously as they all fall about laughing loudly.

Logan sits down and Mum goes and gets him a plate and we all sit eating and passing around the babies, taking it in turns to cuddle each of them. After dinner Mum and Mia disappear to feed Callan and Jake and I'm getting Alice ready for her feed and changing. Logan keeps looking over and laughing at me as I hold my tiny daughter up on my shoulder as she mewls for her dinner. I warm up her milk and walk over to the sofa while Logan and Dad clear the dinner plates and stack the dishwasher. When Alice has drunk half of her bottle I sit her up to burp, resting my hand under her chin and extending her neck, gently rocking her from side to side and patting her back.

"I honestly never thought I'd see this day big brother. You holding an infant in your big paws and loving it. I'm just flabbergasted honestly. My flabber has never been so gasted. It's kinda surreal to think that you have 3 little mites, it really is." Dad brings us both a coffee and sits down with a bottle of beer and laughs at Logan's expression of disbelief.

"He's doing an amazing job as well." Dad tells him. "He's even been changing shitty nappies. Something I never had to do when you boys were little."

"Yeah that's the worst part about babies for sure. You put in good healthy tucker and it just don't look the same when it comes out the other end, that's for sure!" I tell them both as they laugh loudly, Logan's nearly falling off the sofa because he's laughing so hard. "Shush bro, you'll make her cry and then you get to settle her if she does." I gently place the teat in Alice's mouth and wiggle it around trying to entice her to have some more. I'm becoming an expert at this shit. After two weeks of this, I should be. They feed nearly every two hours or so. Callan's rapidly catching up and the midwife is pleased with how well he's doing lately.

"Can I try feeding her? It can't be that difficult if you two can manage it. C'mere Darl. Let Uncle Logan have some Alice time." He says, lifting her gently from my lap and placing her in his. Her little arms jerk around as she opens her eyes and looks up at him. I see him melt into a puddle as their eyes connect and I reckon he's a goner for sure. She just won his heart and now he'll be her slave forever.

I pass him her bottle and he grabs it, not removing his eyes from hers as she studies him and waves her tiny arms around.

"Hey Baby girl. You want some more dinner?" He coos at her, and both Dad and I laugh at his baby voice. This tiny little infant has us all wrapped around her finger and we don't care. Nope. Not one bit.

Mia soon appears and tells us that the other two are sleeping soundly. She sits on my knee and watches Logan feed Alice, smiling widely. "You're a natural Logan. You need a few of these yourself." She tells him as she nods to Alice who's now sucking slowly and staring up at him with a frown.

"Yep one day. Not yet though. Oh by the way. Heth and I met up for lunch today. I don't think she realized you were coming home today until I told her. She just got back into town for the next week. She said that she'll catch up with you soon."

Mia had introduced her friend Heth to Logan hoping that they would fall madly in love, but it doesn't look like it's happening the way she planned.

"Oh how is she? I did try to call her, but her phone was off. I missed her the last time she was home because I was stuck in bed all that time remember?"

He glances up at her, dragging his eyes away from Alice's as they close quietly. "Yeah she's good. She got in just after I did at the airport and we met up at the baggage carousel and decided that we needed food. Geez she has some funny stories to tell about Kalgoorlie. I really must get up there one day. In fact, they have a Diggers and Dealers conference that we should go to Bro. It's in October I think. People come from all over the world to attend. Might be worth looking into, I reckon."

Noah nods in agreement. "I've heard a lot about it, but I've never gone. We should see if we can make it this year. It's only a few days right?"

"Umm I think it's 3 or 4, but I'll look into it and let you know. Heth reckons it's a great time. Apparently they set up a huge marquee for all of the delegates and they take over the city for those days. Sounds like a good time to me, and it's only an hour by plane."

"Providing Mia's fine with it, count me in." I nod my head to him.

"Of course you can go. We'll be fine won't we Maxine? Rory?" She looks from one to the other.

"Sure we will Sweetie. You and Logan go and check out this conference. We'll keep an eye on Mia and the kids." Mum tells us as she sips on her coffee.

"Thanks Mum. Don't know what I'd do without you both." I tell them, meaning every word. Mum and Dad have gone over and above these last few months.

Logan stays till the babies wake up for their next feed and helps with Jake's feed, astounded at the rapid way he demolishes a bottle of milk. He can empty it in minutes.

After he leaves we all settle in for the night, Mia snuggling back against me in our large bed. A small squeal wakes me up in the night as Alice decides it's time for a feed. I get out of bed and change her then hand her to Mia to feed as she wakes slowly. Callan wakes up next and I repeat the procedure for him as Mia attaches him to the other breast. Jake starts fussing soon after and I take him downstairs for his bottle, while Mia feeds the other two. We have some quality guy time together as he gulps down his bottle quickly and emits a huge burp as soon as I place him on my shoulder.

I laugh at the surprised look on his face, as though he can't believe that noise came from him. I kiss him and go upstairs to get him settled for the remainder of the night. Mia's fallen asleep again so I carefully put Alice and Callan both back in the cot to sleep for the rest of the night hopefully.

Our daily routine revolves around feeding and changing. Bath time turns into a production line as one of us undresses the baby and the next bathes them, then they're handed on for drying and then dressing. We laugh as they all voice their distaste for the procedure. None of them are keen on this bath thing. Dad and I get adept at the undressing and drying part as Mia and mum take it in turns to bathe and dress them on our dining room table where the morning sun hits and warms the room against the cool weather outside.

We have the gas fire going continually to help warm the large area and it works well. The temperature inside the house is constantly warm. Mia's gradually doing more and more and getting stronger each day, luckily.

She's still being monitored daily by the visiting midwife who comes to check on her every morning. Her blood pressure has settled and doesn't seem to be a concern anymore thankfully, and the babies are all gaining weight and sleeping well with no problems. Callan is a bit slower than the others to gain weight and seems to tire more easily when he feeds, but she's hopeful that he'll catch up in a few months and she's pleased with his progress so far.

I can't put off going back to work any longer and even though I've been doing a lot from home between helping out with the babies. I need to get back to the office and sort some things. It won't be easy with Mia not there and I'm dreading actually walking out the front door and not being with them for a whole day, but I need to go.

Logan's transitioning between working at the mine and at the office in Perth so that I can move down to the farm and work from there, but we need to iron out the kinks of how it's going to work on a day to day basis. He'll be taking over in the office full time and I'll be commuting between Albany and Perth when necessary because it's an 8-hour journey. I'll do what I can by email, phone and Skype to help out, but he'll be the one on the ground, so to speak.

There's a lot of work to be done before I can actually step back a bit and the sooner we get it sorted the sooner we can move to the farm. Mum and Dad are ecstatic about us moving into the homestead and having their grand babies so close to them. Dad can still help out if he wants to, but he's employed a great manager and he'll do the bulk of the work and I'll help where necessary. It'll be good to get back into doing some hard labor again, seeing as I won't be able to get to the gym like I do now.

I'm actually looking forward to it. I never thought I'd be able to step away from the company, but your priorities change quickly when you start a family. I want to be there when they start talking and walking and do all that stuff that they're gonna do. I don't want to be stuck in the office working 12 hour days like I used to before Mia came into my life.

I don't want to miss a minute of their lives, and this way I can be home to help out and also be involved to a great extent. Logan will have no problems stepping in to fill the void and I'm always on the other end of the phone anyway.

So, Monday morning finally arrives and I get up early to shower and dress before Mia and the babies are awake. I'm not sure how I'm going to leave them today. I stand at their cot and look at my sleeping infants and my heart swells.

"Hey Hun. Morning. What time is it?" Mia asks, stretching and yawning widely. I lower myself onto the bottom of the bed and crawl up it, pulling her into my arms for a hug. "It's early. Just gone 6. Go back to sleep. You have another hour hopefully before they're awake and rush hour starts."

"Na, I'm awake now. I'll get up and make you some breakfast if you want." She tells me, as she wraps her arm around my waist.

"Stay here. I'll bring you up a coffee and some toast in a while." I say as I plant a kiss on her temple and unwrap my arms, getting off the bed quickly and going downstairs to start our breakfast. By the time it's done she's fallen asleep again. I just leave it on her bedside table for when she wakes up. Hopefully it'll still be warm enough.

I lean over the bed and give her another light kiss, gazing down her relaxed, gorgeous face for a long while, trying to get the courage up to walk out the door. Finally, I drag my feet over to grab my suit jacket from the chair and pull it on and without looking back at them all, I determinedly walk down the stairs and out to the garage and start the car quickly before I change my mind about leaving.

I actually have a physical ache in my chest as I pull into my car park space at the office. Logan pulls in beside me and we walk over to the elevator together. He makes small talk and I grunt in reply, my mind focused on what would be happening at home now. The babies will be waking up soon. I hope Mia's had a chance to have her coffee and toast before they wake up, because once their eyes open its chaos for a while. Maybe I should ring her to check that she's okay and that she's eaten. Yeah I'll do that as soon as I get upstairs.

"Did you hear a word I just said Bro?" Logan asks as he steps out of the elevator.

Shit. I didn't even know he was speaking to me! Fuck. I really need to concentrate a bit more.

"Sorry mate. I was miles away."

"Yeah I got that. You were back with Mia and the babies weren't you?" He says with a grin.

"Err...yeah, I was actually. You have no idea how hard it was to leave them this morning. Hardest thing I've had to do in a long time. I'm gonna worry about them all day."

"Okay I get it. I'm sure it was difficult. Hopefully tomorrow will be easier. Once we've done what we need to there's no reason for you to stay today. You can piss off early if you like. I don't want your moping bloody face staring at me all day."

"Thanks Bro. I'll just give Mia a quick call and make sure they're alright before we start, okay?" I tell him pulling out my phone as we walk into my office. Looking at Mia's empty desk fills me with even more unhappiness at being away from her. I feel like there's a lead weight pressing on my chest.

Logan just shakes his head and smirks at me as I dial Mia's mobile number. I know it's beside her on the bedside table so I expect her to pick up immediately, but it rings 5 times before Mum answers with a rushed, "Hello Noah."

"Mum why are you answering Mia's phone? Is she okay? Is something wrong?" I ask hurriedly, fear pressing that lead weight down even further on me.

"Calm down Son. She's just in the shower. I just happened to be walking past when I heard her phone ringing and I didn't want it to wake up the kids."

"Oh thank Christ. Okay. I was just checking in and making sure she found the coffee and toast I left for her."

"Yeah it looks like she did. There's an empty plate and cup here, so she must have."

"Good. Good. Okay Mum. Tell her I love her and give them babies a big kiss for me when they wake up alright?" I tell her, wishing I was home to do it myself. "Oh and Mum...can you please make sure to buy some more nappies today? I noticed yesterday that we're almost out, and don't forget to put Callan's bib on him in case he spills a bit. He's been doing it lot lately and..."

"Noah. Son. We have it all under control. Go back to work. We're fine. Mia's good and the babies are asleep. Stop worrying. I'll get Mia to give you a ring after we've fed and bathed them all okay?"

"Yeah thanks Ma. Love you. I'll see ya later okay?" I tell her, on a long sigh, rubbing my hand across my hair, messing it up even more.

"Love you too Noah. See ya." She says, hanging up.

I don't get to ring Noah till late in the morning once the babies are all asleep again. I know how hard it was for him to leave this morning. I feel bad about falling asleep and not seeing him off like I had planned. I should have got out of bed when I first woke up. Oh well. Not much I can do about it now. I'll make it up to him tomorrow morning by getting up and cooking him some brekkie before the rush hour starts with the triplets.

The days just seem to blur together at the moment. It seems like a never ending round of feeding and changing. I'm lucky if I get to sit and eat lunch. Normally I have a baby or two in my arms as I do, but I wouldn't change it for the world. I love these little munchkins more than anything in the world...except maybe Noah. He's been amazing. I don't know how I would have coped these past few weeks without him and his parents.

The babies are now a month old and are growing like bean sprouts. I can't believe how quickly they're gaining weight and changing. They've all filled out and have lost that wrinkly little newborn look now. Even Callan's doing great. He's still a lot smaller than Jake, but not much smaller than Alice now. I adore them all and I can't imagine my life without them, even though I hardly have a moment to myself any more. Seems like there's always at least one of them awake and needing some attention.

Maxine and Rory are going to go back to the farm on Friday for a few days to check on the progress of their cottage. I'm so grateful to them both for everything that their still doing for us. I've assured them that we'll be fine without them. Noah's going to be home all weekend so it's just Friday and Monday that I'll be alone. I'll manage somehow, even though I'm nervous as hell about it. They deserve a few days away to rest, recuperate and recharge their batteries. It's just a shame that Albany's so far away. It's a long drive down and back for them, but that can't be helped. Poor Rory's been commuting back and forth the last few months while Maxine's been here looking after me, so I don't begrudge them a weekend away. They've been incredible.

I ring Noah on his mobile and he answers on the second ring. "Hey Baby. How's things at home? You guys okay?" He asks quickly.

"Yeah Hun. We're good. How's your first day back at work going?"

"Good. Logan's been doing much better than I thought he would while I was on leave. He's not going to need much training to take over, but don't tell him that. We don't want his head getting too big." He laughs at his joke.

"Right. Noted." I reply on a laugh. "Seriously. How're you doing?"

I hear him take in a deep breath and blow it out again before saying, "I miss you. I hate being away from you and the kids. I can't concentrate on what I'm supposed to be doing here, I'm so distracted. This is harder than I thought it would be...Sorry I'm just being a big sook I know, but I'll be home in a few hours.

There's just a few more things I need to go through with Logan and then I'm out of here."

"Okay Hun. Have fun and we'll see you soon, alright?" I tell him. "Love you."

"Aw Baby you don't know how much I miss you right now. I love you too. See ya later." He tells me before hanging up. I go and check on the sleeping babies just to reassure myself that they're all fine, before going downstairs and making us all a coffee.

I relay our conversation to my in-laws and we quietly feel sorry for him. It really must be hard to be away from the infants. I can't imagine leaving them just yet. Not even for an hour or so. Luckily I haven't had to. Maxine and Rory have gone out to shop for us when necessary so that I didn't need to. I realize that I haven't actually left the house in the last three weeks and I'm good with that. It'll be easier to take them out when they're a bit older. I don't want to be exposing them to colds and flu's in a shopping center if I don't need to...especially Callan.

Noah arrives home about 3:30pm and immediately comes over and kisses me firmly and steals his daughter from my arms where I was cradling her. He peppers her face with gentle kisses and then proceeds to do the same to the boys as we laugh at him.

"God I missed them. It's pathetic I know...but I couldn't wait to get home to see them all. I need to cuddle them for a bit and then I'll be fine." He says as he gently kisses Jake's head before handing him back to his mother to finish feeding. Jake cries loudly at the interruption to his food and Maxine pushes the teat into his mouth and he immediately shuts up and sucks at it firmly.

"I missed you too Hun." I tell him as he sits beside me on the sofa, and wraps his arm around my shoulder. He picks up Alice's hand and runs his finger over the back of it as she grips his other finger.

"Hey Baby girl. Did you miss your Daddy as much as Daddy missed you?" He coos to her sweetly. She looks up at him and blows a raspberry unknowingly and we all laugh as he imitates her and blows a raspberry back. She's fascinated by his action as she stares at him, waiting for him to do it again. He does it over and over for her as she studies him and tries to purse her lips like his. It's incredible to watch her facial expressions as she looks at him as if she's trying to understand how he does it.

My phone rings from the kitchen bench and just as I'm about to pass her over and grab it, Noah gets up and answers it for me.

"Hello Mia's phone." He says. "No she can't come to the phone right now. I'm her husband, can I help you?" We watch as he listens for a while as someone talks. "Uh huh. Oh hi. Yeah. Okay...uh huh...right...yeah I'll let her know. Thanks for telling us so soon. Yeah, you too. See ya."

"Who was it Hun?" I ask as soon as puts the phone back down to finish charging.

"That was Chelsea. That cop from Albany that came and took your statement? She was just letting you know that there's a date for the trial. It's not till October, but she just wanted to tell you before someone else did."

At the mention of the trial I immediately feel my body go tense and I have trouble breathing. I shove Alice at Rory as I try to catch my breath, dragging in huge gulps of air, but still feeling like there's no oxygen in my lungs. My arms are tingling and my heart is about to jump out of my chest it's beating so hard and fast. Noah quickly strides over and sits beside me, grabbing my face so that I have to focus on his.

"Breathe Baby, you can do it. Just slow it down. In...one...two...three...Hold...one...two...three. Out...one...two...three...that's right...just like that. You're okay. I've got you...okay...slowly...yeah...good." He continues encouraging me for a while till I'm relatively calm, and my heart rate and breathing are almost back to normal.

Maxine and Rory watch me closely, a helpless look on both of their faces as they cuddle the babies in their arms, because they can't do anything else at the moment. I burst into tears and cover my face to hide it from them all. I sob till I can't breathe again and Noah has to help talk me down.

He holds me close, both arms wrapped around me securely as he whispers over and over that he's got me and how much he loves me between kissing the crown of my head. It takes me a long time to finally stop the sobs and I try to apologize between them for being such a baby. I finally sit up and Noah relaxes the grip that he has on me as I swipe at my eyes roughly.

"I'm sorry. It just caught me by surprise. Just when I finally stop thinking about it, something happens to bring it all back again. I'm okay now, I promise."

"Oh Mia. Sweetie. I'm so sorry. I know how hard this must be for you. The last thing you'd want to do is stand up in court and testify against them. That's understandable." Maxine tells me gently, her face full of sympathy.

"I never want to see them again, honestly. I don't want to be in the same room as them. Hopefully they won't make me. I can do it all from another room surely?" I turn to Noah beginning to panic again. He pulls me close and assures me that I can. I won't have to be in the court room if I don't want to be.

"It's 2 months away at least, so I don't want you thinking about it right now okay? We'll talk to Chelsea and that John bloke and make sure that you can do it all from another room. I'm sure it won't be a problem, and I'll be with you every second.

I promise you that you won't have to see them ever again, Babe."
He tells me firmly, and I believe him. I have to. I'm not sure how
seeing them both again would affect me. Especially
Jackson…that would just be too hard. I'm not sure I could handle
it, even with Noah beside me.

I try to put it out of my mind as we all sit there and talk about
something else as soon as I've composed myself. Maxine tells me
that she skyped Scarlett yesterday afternoon which was early
morning in London, and had Jake in her arms while she was
talking to her and now Scarlett's trying to see if she can arrange
some time off to come home for a few weeks to meet her new
niece and nephews.

We haven't seen her since January so it would be wonderful
if she could. I know that Noah misses her as well. They're all
remarkably close, and I adore Scarlett. We've been skyping as
well, but I normally leave it till the babies are sleeping so that I
can talk to her with no interruptions.

I can't wait to see her again. Noah tells me that he spoke to
Caleb today and he may be coming over for a conference and is
going to arrange a few days leave while he's in Perth so that he
can come down to the farm and visit. I haven't met Caleb yet. I've
only seen photos of him that Noah and Maxine have. He looks
like a cross between Noah and his Dad. He doesn't have Noah's
startling blue eyes, but he's just as handsome in his own way.
His hair is a bit darker than Noah and Logan's and he has that 3-
day stubble look happening, which suits him.

The rest of our day is uneventful as we continue with the
packing and sorting for the move to the farm. Well, I take care of
the babies while the others do all the hard work. Noah suggests

that we just get a company in to do it all for us and move it down to Albany as well and I'm good with that. I don't have much stuff. I sold most of it when I sold the apartment for a tidy little profit. I didn't have a lot of furniture anyway and all of my clothes are here and a few personal items that I couldn't part with.

The rest went on Gumtree for sale. I was glad to be rid of it actually. I just wanted to forget the part of my life with the arsehole and that apartment reminded me of him even though he was rarely there. It was my sanctuary and my independence from him and he never really liked it. Looking back now I realize that he wanted me to move in with him, so that he could just use me as a trophy wife. Something to show off to all of his friends like a shiny new toy. I was merely another possession, I think. Thank god I found out what he was like before I married him.

I'll never forget his face when I found him pounding his teenage clerk over his desk that day, not that he knew I was there till it was too late. I came back from lunch early otherwise I wouldn't have caught them. That was the last day I saw him and I hope I never see him again. God…why am I even thinking of him? What I have with Noah is so much more than I ever thought I had with Dylan…fucking arsehole. I laugh now when I think of how I thought he loved me. I have no idea how long his affair with the floozy had been going on and I don't care now. It doesn't matter anymore. Not now that I have Noah and my family.

Friday comes bright and early as Maxine and Rory get up at dawn to make the long trek home. They're as quiet as they can be, but I still hear them rustling around in their room across the hall and I throw on my robe, leaving Noah and the babies to sleep. I carefully walk downstairs and make them a coffee and shove a couple of bits of raisin toast in the toaster for them. It's the least I can do. They creep down the stairs not realizing that I'm already up awake and I can hear them murmuring as they make their way to the kitchen quietly.

"Morning Sweetie. What are you doing up so early? I hope we didn't wake you." Maxine says, gratefully picking up her mug of coffee and a slab of the sweet toast.

I smile over at her holding my cup in front of my mouth with both hands. "No I wanted to make you some brekkie before you left." I tell her as I watch them both eat quickly. Rory smiles and nods his head in appreciation as he bites into the thick toast. "Thanks for this luv. It saves us stopping on the road for some like we planned." He says around a mouthful.

Once they're gone, I wander around for a while and then head up to our bathroom for a quick shower before anyone wakes up. I hurriedly wash and condition my hair and run the soapy lotion over my body. Wrapping myself in a towel I open the bathroom door just as Noah opens it from the other side and I crash head first into his rock hard chest. "Oh shit...sorry! I didn't realize you were up yet. Did I wake you?" I ask as I push my wet hair back from my face, holding my towel together firmly.

"No Baby. The alarm woke me and then I couldn't find you. I didn't hear the shower going. I'm glad that I came in here to check first though. That towel doesn't look very secure...maybe you should give it to me." He says quietly as he leans forward and locks his lips firmly with mine. I try to keep the towel together at the front as his hand comes up and grabs hold of it. I pull back from him and raise my eyebrow at his action. "Uh

Uh…you know what the doc said…6 weeks…not just yet…still got another week till my check up." I remind him, tugging the towel out of his hand.

"Fuck me sideways…it's gonna be a bloody long week." He says scrubbing his hand over his face and up through his hair. I lean up to kiss him on the cheek, needing to stand on tippy toes to reach him, and move past him into the walk in wardrobe to get my clothes for the day. "I'm sure you can survive for one more week Hun." I tell him over my shoulder.

"The least you could do is come and help me take care of this problem Sweetheart." He calls back to me, turning on the shower.

Just as I pull on my yoga pants and hoodie, Callan wakes up squawking for his breakfast, which in turn wakes the other two. I change them all quickly and lay Callan and Jake on my lap to feed and leave Alice to Noah. He'll take her downstairs and give her a bottle. She lays relatively quietly in her cot while I concentrate on feeding the boys.

I'm getting the hang of feeding two babies at once, but I love it when they wake up one at a time and I get to feed just one of them. I make the most of our special time then and give them lots of attention. It doesn't happen very often. Normally if one starts crying the others are awake instantly as well.

Noah strides out of the bathroom with a towel wrapped around his hips, water still dripping down his body. He scoops up Alice and showers her with kisses as she reaches her little hands up to his face. She's definitely going to be a Daddy's girl. He continues to kiss her as he walks downstairs to warm up her bottle. He brings her back up to the room and lays beside me propped up on pillows as he gently puts the bottle to her lips.

"You good now Hun?" I ask with a smirk. He knows exactly what I'm talking about as he grins widely. "No thanks to you, but yeah. My balls are so blue that I could use them to sign my name

I reckon." I huff out a giggle at the image that jumps into my mind and his grin widens as he leans over to kiss me quickly, mindful of the squirming baby in his arms.

"You gonna be alright home alone today? I feel bad having to leave you like this, but I have that conference call with the Canadians, who want to pick my brain about the program we set them up with. They're having some issues and I need to see what the problem is, otherwise I'd stay home and help."

"It's fine. We'll be alright. They still sleep most of the day and I'll just bath each of them when they wake up next time. There's no rush. I have all day. I promise I'll take thing slow and be careful." I promise him.

"Make sure you do. And no lifting anything heavier than Jake. That means no laundry, no housework and no cooking either. I'll do it all when I get home. I'll try to nick off early if I can." He says as he lifts Alice to his shoulder and pats her back as she sleeps. Once she gets rid of her wind, he lays her on the bed between his legs and picks up Jake who's fallen asleep and burps him as well. I do the same with Callan and gaze around at my little family, all sleeping and surrounding me. Lifting them one at a time Noah places them gently back in their cot and continues dressing as I watch his every move. I love his body and every muscle ripples as he pulls on his clothes. I heave a big sigh as he covers himself with his shirt, and he smirks across the room at me. "You could have had this body this morning, but no...you want to wait and deny me my fun." He says cajolingly.

I laugh softly and don't bother to answer, knowing he's not serious. If I had jumped on him this morning, he would have been the first one to remind me that we still have another week till the postpartum check-up with the OBGYN and the pediatrician. My incision has healed already and itches like crazy, but other than that I'm fine. My belly's still a little podgy, but I know that doesn't disappear in a few weeks. I have more curves than I did before, but not enough to make any difference to my size or my clothes.

Noah makes us breakfast while I dry my hair and leave it down for a while till he goes to work. He loves it when I don't put it up. I'm seriously thinking of cutting it now as I don't have the time to care for it like it should be. I think I'll cry when the time comes, but I think it's necessary.

Maybe once Maxine and Rory get back I'll make an appointment and they can babysit for me so that I can go. I won't tell Noah. I'll surprise him when he gets home that day...or shock him....whatever. There's not much that he can do about it once it's done and he did once say that if I wanted to cut it, he would come with me for support, but I'd rather do it this way. I make a tentative plan in my mind and decide to cut it so that it's still long to my waist. That should keep him happy, and it'll be much easier to care for, I'm sure.

Maxine and Rory make it back Monday afternoon just as Noah arrives home from work. Luckily Maxine had been stocking up the freezer because I've hardly had time to scratch myself today let alone cook dinner for them all. The babies have been fussing and I've spent the day either feeding or rocking them all in turn.

I haven't even had a shower and I'm close to tears by the time they all walk in the door. Maxine takes one look at me and scoops the boys out of my arms, cradling them against her and Noah goes to carefully pick up Alice, rocking her gently in his arms, trying to calm her.

I'm too scared to speak because if I open my mouth, I'll cry, so I take the opportunity to go upstairs and have a shower and 5 minutes of peace and quiet. I hear Noah open the bathroom door and he leans against the huge vanity, watching me as I shower. He has his arms crossed and his legs are crossed at the ankles as he sits against the vanity cabinet.

"Rough day Baby?" He asks gently, with a frown.

"Uh huh." I reply, biting my bottom lip to stem the tears and stop my lip from quivering. I quickly wash myself and turn off the shower tap, stepping out as he grabs the towel and wraps it around my shoulders, pulling me in for a hug. The dam breaks and I sob loudly against his clean shirt, leaving damp patches. I hate crying, but I'm just a bit tired and overwhelmed today. Noah rubs my back and bends down to kiss my forehead, not saying a word, but just holding me close, his warm body wrapped around mine for support.

"I'm sorry. I shouldn't complain. They're normally so good. It's just a bad day." I tell him as I take some deep breaths and stop the tears forcefully.

"Hey it's okay. There are gonna be lots of bad days in the future, I reckon. Just think how much fun it's gonna be when they're all teething. I just need to know that you're really alright *today*. Why don't you take your time, and I'll start dinner while Mum and Dad get the kids organized? It looks like you need a bit of time out, so why don't you stay up here and rest up till I tell you that dinner's ready? How's that?" He says generously.

"No, I'm fine, honestly. I just needed a moment. I'm good now. I'll get dressed and come down soon." I tell him.

"Are you sure? You don't have to. We can handle it."

"No you've had a full day of work and poor Rory's been driving all day. I'm fine. I'll just finish getting dressed and I'll come and help you with them." I say walking away from him to the wardrobe to pull on some sweats and a fleecy hoodie. He waits for me at the doorway and takes my hand as we walk down the stairs together to the living area where the kid's grandparents are cuddling and rocking them softly. Callan's already asleep and the other two are battling to keep their eyes open. Of course, now they sleep...I've been trying to get them to sleep all afternoon and now they sleep. Typical.

Our week continues on, the days blurring together in a frenzy of feeding, changing, bathing. Wash, rinse and repeat. It isn't till Friday morning that I get a minute to ring my hairdresser and ask her to do the unthinkable and chop it all off. She tries to talk me out of it, but I'm determined now, so she makes an appointment for me for 2pm which coincides with the babies' nap time so it's perfect.

Noah won't be home till at least 5 or maybe 6 so it gives me time to get across town and back again. I explain what I'm doing to both Maxine and Rory and Maxine's horrified, but understands my reasoning. They promise to babysit for me as I go up and put some decent clothes on for the first time in a month. I want to look nice for Noah when he gets home, and I hope he understands like his mother. It's not like I'm getting a buzz cut. There will still be a lot of hair left, it'll just be half of what it was before.

Actually walking out the door for the first time and leaving them is the hardest thing I've had to do in a long time. I have tears in my eyes and nearly change my mind and walk back into the house. I force myself to get into the car and drive away before I have a change of heart.

"Are you absolutely sure about this?" Jilly, my hairdresser asks me for the tenth time since I sat down. "I really, really don't want to do this if you aren't 100% positive that this is what you want to do."

"Positive." I say definitively. "Go for it. Up to my waist is fine. That still leaves me with long hair, but it'll just be easier to manage. Braid it and chop it. You have my permission."

"Oh luv, I feel awful doing this. After all these years of growing it, this seems like sacrilege to cut it off now. Are you absolutely sure?" She asks as she starts braiding my long hair.

"Absolutely sure. I need to do this, so please just hurry up and do it now, before you talk me out of it." I plead with her, as she continues braiding. "Can we send the hair to be made into a wig for the cancer foundation? It'll make it easier knowing that it's gone to a good cause."

"Of course Honey. I have a contact who can arrange it. It's much too nice to just throw away that's for sure. I'll make absolutely certain that it gets there." She tells me as she finishes the braid and ties it off. "Okay here goes nothing." She says, picking up the sharp scissors and opening them as she decides how much to cut off. I hold my breath as she tightens the scissors around the large thick braid. "Last chance Mia. Yes, or no?"

Looking her in the eye in the reflection in the large mirror in front of me I nod slightly and take a deep breath as she closes the scissors on my hair and over half of it comes away in her hand. I slowly let out the breath that I was holding and raise the edges of my lips slightly at her, trying to smile, but not able to.

It's going to take me a little while to get used to this and she doesn't push, just leaves to go and make a cup of tea for me as I grab hold of the remainder of my braid and pull it over my shoulder, running my hand down it lightly. "Wow." I utter softly as I study my reflection. I don't remember my hair ever being this short and to anyone else this is still very long hair.

I drive home playing with my hair that falls around my body as I turn my head. I play with the ends of it, wrapping it around my finger over and over as I wait at the stoplights. She did a great job of styling it and even curled the ends so I have large loose curls all through it.

Maxine gives me a hug as soon as I walk into the kitchen, where she's warming bottles, and tells me how nice it looks and how much it suits me. I know she's being nice, but I need a lift so I'll take all the compliments that she throws my way. I'm slightly concerned about Noah's reaction, but I won't have long to wait. He'll be home soon.

Rory does a double take when he walks in holding Jake and gives me a quick kiss on the cheek, telling me how pretty I look before grabbing a bottle out of the warmer and striding back to the sofa and sitting to feed the crying baby. I help feed with the bottles and then go upstairs to express the milk I would have fed them so that I can save it for later.

Just as I'm taking the bottles downstairs to the kitchen I hear the front door open and Noah calls out a "Hi" as he notices me and then stops dead in front of me as I hit the bottom stair, his arm blocking my way. He grabs my shoulders and turns me around on the stair without saying a word, before picking up a handful of my hair and letting it fall from his hand in a silky curtain. "Baby I love it." He says gently kissing the back of my head. "Why didn't you tell me you were going to do this today? I would have come with you. Did you cry?"

"Almost, but I was actually much better than I thought I would be. It's still long, just not as long as it was." I say as I turn back to face him. "Seriously, what do you think of it?"

He studies me for a minute then runs his hand down the hair that's fallen over my shoulder and lifts it gently to his lips. "It's still amazing Sweetheart. I love it, and I know it's going to be easier for you, but promise me that you won't go any shorter?"

I smile at him as I hook my arms around his neck, still holding the babies' bottles of milk carefully in each hand, and pull him in for a kiss. "Deal." I say before our lips connect. He wraps his arms around my waist and lifts me up, so that I have to quickly slide my legs around him as he supports my butt and walks out to the kitchen, much to his parent's surprise. Rory quickly looks away, but Maxine raises one eyebrow as he leans over to kiss her cheek before depositing me in front of the fridge and opening it for me as I giggle softly.

"So... do you like it?" His mother asks, smiling and nodding in my direction.

He looks from her to me and back again as he grins. "Absolutely. It looks great."

"I agree. It's just different, but I'll get used to it. I wasn't sure about it even though it makes sense." She tells him as she smiles over at me.

"Right then I'm starving. Who's for some takeout huh? Mia? Dad? What would you like? We need to make the most of the next hour or two while the tribe are sleeping." He tells us looking around to his parents. "Mum what do you feel like?"

"Errr...how about some pizza or fish and chips? Either one sounds good." She replies as she walks over to the sofa with a glass of white wine and sits down next to her husband.

"Dad? Any preference? Noah asks him.

"Nah I'm easy. I'll eat anything, you know that." He smirks up at him, looking like an older version of his son. Now I know who Noah inherited that smirk from.

"Right, Mia it's up to you Baby. What would you like?" He turns to me, giving me his full attention.

"Okay um. Pizza I think. There's that place down at the shopping center. Those were nice when we got them before." I tell him indicating the pizza place not far away. He drags out his phone and scrolls through the numbers till he finds the one he needs and dials quickly ordering us all a pizza.

Luckily he knows our favorites. We chat for a while before he goes out to collect the food. When he comes back the house instantly smells of pizza and my stomach growls as I realize that I missed lunch and I can't remember if I had breakfast or not. I know I made some toast but I don't remember if I ate it or not. I'm going to have to be more careful and make sure that I eat regularly.

We spend the weekend getting ready for the movers to come on Monday. Even though most of the furniture is staying we're talking a few large items with us along with most of our clothes and personal items.

Rory and Maxine are moving a lot of their furniture into the cottage so we'll need some of ours to replace it. We're taking our bed because we both love it and a new one's been ordered for here, along with a new sofa and chairs. I bought them online because I didn't want to go out and spend an afternoon going from place to place when it wasn't necessary. Thank God for the internet.

Monday morning arrives quickly and I drag myself into the shower trying to wake up. I can hear voices downstairs and thank my lucky stars that I thought to bring my clean clothes into the bathroom with me as I get dressed quickly. The thought of being caught in just a towel scares the hell of me, so this morning I was prepared. Noah's been up and to the gym already I think as I slowly walk downstairs following the aroma of fresh coffee. I'm still not allowed to drink it, but that doesn't mean I don't love the smell. It's uplifting even if I can't have the caffeine hit. I make myself my decaffeinated cup and sip it slowly, enjoying the taste. Noah must be telling them what boxes to take. We packed a lot into Scarlett's room by the front door to keep them out of our way.

Noah strides back in with his coffee in hand, kissing me lightly as he puts it down on the bench to make some toast for us. I'm sure he's just checking to be certain that I'm eating but I appreciate the gesture. After breakfast we all organize the babies' bath time while the movers take boxes out to the truck, along with our newly stripped down bed and the sofa. The room looks empty with no sofa, but hopefully the new one will be here later today.

Once they're finished we feed the triplets and settle them for a nap while we all take a break for coffee. We aren't leaving for the farm till the morning and I'm not looking forward to such a long road trip. Noah offered to fly us down and he take the Sahara, but I wanted to share the experience with him and the thought of flying with the infants was almost as bad as the thought of driving with them.

It would have only been an hour by plane, but we'll manage. It may just take a little longer. I pack the car with the essentials for our trip and keep what I need handy behind the front seats on the floor, the only empty spot in the back seat. Their car-seats take up the whole wide bench seat so the floor is the only option. I pack them all a bag with extra clothes and nappies and stuff them into the small space on the floor, ready for the long road trip. Rory and Maxine are taking my car and following us and they'll fly up next time they want to come and drive their car back. In the meantime, they can use one of our cars as I don't intend to be going too far just yet, so mine will hardly get used.

Luckily the babies co-operate and wake up early so that we can feed them and get on the road quickly after breakfast. I was happy to wait and get something later, but Noah insisted we eat before we leave saying that he didn't want me passing out from lack of food.

The drive is relatively uneventful and the babies are very well behaved and sleep most of the way with a few stops for feeds. We're surprised at how well they coped with the long trip as we unload them from the car at the farm. Its dusk and we're all exhausted and in need of a shower and an early night.

Noah's parent's say goodnight and head over to their cottage which has minimal furniture at the moment, but they have their bed from the master bedroom. In the morning Noah and his friend Craig will move the furniture that they want to take over to the cottage, which is only a stroll away from the back patio of the main house. It has its own little fenced off yard and a back patio that faces away from our house so that they have some privacy.

It's the first time I've seen it and it looks gorgeous. They're really happy with it as well. It's ideal for just the two of them and if Scarlett or Caleb want to visit then they can stay in the big house with us. I'm still trying to get my head around the fact that it's our house and not Maxine and Rory's, but she's told me time and time again how happy she is to hand it over and for me to do whatever I want to it.

The only thing I really want to do is paint the babies' rooms for them. One in pink, one in pale blue and the other in mint green. I ordered their furniture online as well and it should arrive very soon, but till then Rory dragged out the cot that Noah used and he's put it in Noah's old room for them.

We transfer our sleeping babies to their new bed and stand watching them for a while as Noah pulls me back against him, wrapping his arms around my waist loosely. "Look at them Baby. They're just perfect. I think they're gonna love it here." He tells me leaning in to nuzzle the side of my neck.

"I think we all will Hun. I know I will, for sure." I say softly, leaning my head over more to allow him to get to my exposed neck. "How about tomorrow you take me for the grand tour? You said that there's a permanent creek close by? I need to see that so that I can keep the kids away from it when they start walking. I can just see it now, Jake will be the first one in and one of us will be dragging his sorry arse out of the water."

"Yeah you're probably right there! I promise that before they start walking we'll fence the house paddock so that they can't escape and no snakes can get in."

"Snakes? Are they a big worry? I hate snakes. I hate anything with no legs or more than four!" I tell him, shuddering at the thought of a snake near my babies.

"Not a big worry, but we are in the bush and that's where they live so you need to be aware when you're walking around in the paddocks, or even outside here, especially in spring and summer. We don't see many, but there are some killers around so watch where you walk and if you happen to see one, stand still and scream loudly. That's what we'll teach the kids as well when they're old enough. Normally the snake is more scared of you than you are of it."

I turn my head to look at him with a raised eyebrow in a, 'you've got to be kidding me' kind of way. "Wanna make a bet?!!" I ask him with a laugh. "There's absolutely no way that it would be as scared as I would be. Uh uh...nope."

"Okay Crocodile Dundee, come on and let's see what we can eat before we make our bed up." It's gonna seem strange being in this room with them. The last time I slept in this bed was when I left hospital after the attack and just looking at it brings back all of those memories. Noah must notice as he asks, "Do you want to change rooms? We can you know. We have a house full of empty rooms that we can use."

"No I wouldn't be able to sleep away from them and I don't want to drag the cot out now. I'll be fine." I promise him, sounding more confident than I actually feel.

"You sure? If you change your mind it'll only take a minute. Just let me know."

"Okay, let's go and find some food before you fade away to a shadow. I'm sure your Mum has a freezer full of food for us. Do you want to go see if they want to join us? They probably don't have a lot to eat over there yet if they aren't moved in."

"Yeah I'll be back in a sec. No doubt Dad will want some food. I'll go check on them." He says, as he pushes the back door open, and heads towards the new cottage.

Chapter EIGHTEEN

Noah

We're up early the next morning because the babies all wake up for a feed at 5:30am and now that we're awake there's no point in trying to go back to sleep, so we lay back in bed, playing and pulling faces at them, as they smile back at us with gummy grins. I don't realize how long we've been doing it until there's a loud knock on the door and I hear Craig yelling out as he knocks again. We've been mates since primary school and we catch up every time I'm down visiting and when he comes up to Perth. He has his own property about 15 minutes down the road, practically next door. Mia smiles at me as she realizes who's banging on the door and takes Alice, so that I can pull on some sweats and go let him in.

I greet him with a half hug/ back slap as I open the door to let him in. "Hey man. I thought you'd be up hours ago. Don't you have a heap of newborns now to keep you up all night?" He says as he walks into the kitchen and heads over to the coffee maker.

"Morning sunshine. Good to see you too." I tell him with a grin. "Help yourself to coffee. We haven't even had breakfast yet, so you'd best be making us one as well."

"Still white and two for you? What about Mia?" He asks grabbing cups down from the overhead cupboard. He's been in this house enough to know where everything lives in the kitchen. Hell he practically grew up here.

"Decaf pods are over there." I say pointing at the box that mum bought for Mia while she was pregnant. "She'll have one of those with some milk. She's still feeding so no caffeine for her."

"Seriously? She puts up with you and your crap and she doesn't even get caffeine? That's low man. I couldn't survive without my coffee...especially first thing in the morning." He says, shaking his head in disbelief.

"Me too. I love the stuff." I say as he hands me my mug and I take a big sniff of it, savoring the aroma. "So how's Bev? Mum said she's pregnant again. When's this one due?" Craig loves kids and he's trying to singlehandedly populate the south west while he still can. It's a family joke that he keeps Bev pregnant and chained to the kitchen sink. They have 4 kids already which keep her busy. This will make number 5 and he's the same age as I am.

"Yeah she's hoping for another girl this time. 3 boys are enough apparently, though I'd be happy with another. At least one of them will want to take over the farm right?" He asks, as he pulls the toaster out of the cupboard and hunts around for some bread. "Um. She's due in December and she reckons with her luck she'll go early and have a Christmas baby, which I don't see a problem with at all, but she does."

"Dude, 5 kids under 10. That's a handful. I don't know how you do it. Our 3 are still tiny, but I know how much hard work it is to care for them. I can't imagine another 2 as well."

"Yeah apparently this one will be the last because there's no more room in the car. It only seats 7, so Bev has put her foot down and told me I have to go for the snip." He says as we both cross our legs at the ankles unconsciously protecting the family jewels.

"Ah that's a brave move mate. Thank god we haven't made that decision just yet and hopefully it'll be a long time till we have to think about it. Mia had a hard time with this pregnancy, but her OBGYN assures us that it shouldn't happen again with the next one...if there is a next one. That's up to her."

"What's up to me?" Mia says as she hands over a squirming Callan to me and offers Alice to Craig. "Howdy Craig. How are you? Take this one for me please while I go and get Jake. Knowing him, he's probably rolled off the middle of the bed by now."

Craig takes Alice and immediately starts cooing to her and telling her what a pretty girl she is in that baby talk that they love.

Callan and I proceed to sit down at the huge wooden table that fills the middle of the room and I place my coffee away from me so that it doesn't get knocked over accidentally. I sit him up in my arms as he waves his arms around and looks around at the bright kitchen.

Sunlight streams in through the bare windows and warms the room. The scene outside is one that I never get tired of looking at. I can see cows off in the distance and green fields all around the house. Winter always brings a lot of rain and this year has been especially wet, adding to the lushness of the countryside.

I watch Callan as he studies the room and my best friend, wondering who he is. He seems to have a permanent frown on his face as though he's thinking very deep thoughts in his tiny brain. Always so very serious. Jake will be the goofball and

Callan will be the nerd I think. I love that their personalities are getting stronger as they grow. Alice is very quiet and uncomplaining, and always the contented one that's happy to wait a while if she has to.

I look down at my two babies and wonder if Mum and Dad ever had these thoughts about us when we were their age. I remember getting into a lot of trouble as a kid and dragging Caleb and Logan along with me, but nothing dangerous luckily. I always seemed to be the leader.

They would sometimes come up with ideas, but I would make them happen. Like the time that we decided to build a jetty out into the dam. We found a heap of old wood and made a rickety structure that collapsed as soon as Caleb stood on it and he fell down and broke his wrist. If I remember correctly, that was Craig's idea. It nearly worked!

I smile at the thought of these brothers doing what we did. Now I know how Mum felt. She must have been constantly worried about us, and normally with good reason. We all built a house in the huge gum tree out back one summer. It took us weeks to make and we were so proud of ourselves, till a heavy limb fell and crushed it. Luckily we weren't in it at the time.

"What are you smirking about over there?" Mia asks happily as she juggles Jake in her arms.

I laugh out loud as I look over at Craig. "Do you remember that summer we built the tree house? How old were we then? 10? Maybe 11? I was just wondering what I'm gonna do when these two start doing shit like that."

He laughs loudly at the memory. "That bloody branch fell down and wrecked it and you were so pissed you kicked the tree and nearly broke your foot. I remember that!"

"Oh Lord help me. I'm going to have to cut myself in three to watch them all 24 hours a day. Suddenly I'm rethinking our idea to move here. They're going to send me gray aren't they?!" Mia says, laughing along with us as she pushes some bread into the toaster.

Craig and I go and enlist Dad's assistance as supervisor for the furniture moving. It doesn't take long to transfer what they want and our furniture arrives shortly after lunch. Mia puts the babies in their stroller and goes to help Mum sort out where to put everything while they sleep.

While she's over at the cottage we help the two movers bring in all of our stuff and I place it where I think Mia would want it, but I'm quite aware that I may spend the next few days rearranging it for her till she's happy with it. I set up our bed and find the linen for it, enlisting Craig's help to make it, much to his disgust. He's more used to driving a harvester than making a bed and he lets me know as soon as I suggest it, though he does surprise me by picking up the sheets and arranging it neatly over the bed like a pro.

I want to have as much done as possible so that Mia doesn't have to do it when she's finished at Mum's. After the bed's finished, I start unpacking our clothes and hang them in the walk-in wardrobe that's nearly as big as the one in our house in Perth. Craig sits on the bed watching me as we chat as though we just saw each other yesterday instead of a few months ago.

Actually, it was before Christmas, so it was over 8 months ago. Our friendship has always been like that. No matter how long it's been we can just pick up where we left off. He'll always have my back and I'll always have his. He's as close to me as my own flesh and blood. The four of us were inseparable while growing up. There were other friends along the way, but we've always been close. I was his best man when he married Bev after meeting her in high school.

Mia hasn't met her yet so I suggest a BBQ tomorrow night and pray for a warm night so that we can sit outside and not freeze. Craig immediately agrees and rings Bev to confirm that it's okay with her, nodding to me when she says yes. Once the bedroom's done we go out and sit on the back patio and enjoy the afternoon sun. I pull out a couple of beers from the large fridge out on the patio and hand one to Craig.

Dad always made sure it was stocked when we came home to visit. He's not a big drinker, but like all of us, he enjoys a cold beer on a hot day...not that today is hot, but we reward ourselves for our hard work. I watch Mia walk across the small space between our houses and my eyes are drawn to her, dressed in tight jeans and a large pullover that does nothing to detract from her curves. If she's anywhere nearby I can't drag my eyes from her and Craig laughs at me as he notices me staring.

"Geez Mate. You've got it bad haven't ya? I admit she's a beauty. I don't know what she's doing with you...but I think she feels the same way as you do. I saw her staring at your arse before when we were inside the house. You haven't had your 6-week check-up yet have ya? You both have that look of desperation in your eyes!" He says on a loud laugh.

"Seriously Dude. It's all I can do to keep my hands off of her. We go into Albany tomorrow and see the pediatrician and she's arranged to see the lady who looked after her in hospital for her check-up. Actually her OB arranged it. They're friends, and rather than go all the way back to Perth to have it done she suggested seeing the Doc here, and the pediatrician's visiting tomorrow at the hospital so we'll go and see him there. Then if she gets the all clear I might see if Mum and Dad will babysit for a few hours for us." I chuckle as he spits his mouthful of beer out, trying to hold in his laughter.

"Why are Mum and Dad babysitting?" Mia asks hearing the last bit of our conversation and looking over at Craig who's wiping at his eyes and mouth.

"No reason Baby." I smirk at her as she frowns and obviously knows that she's missing out on the punchline somehow, but doesn't pursue the subject.

"Ah, I've invited shithead here and Bev and the kids over for a BBQ tea Saturday night. Bev's pregnant with number 5, but you two will get on, I think. She's a saint, putting up with this mongrel all these years." I nod in his direction and lift my beer bottle to my lips.

"Oh that'll be great. I've been looking forward to meeting her Craig. Tell her not to bring a thing. It's the least we can do to pay you back for all of your help today. You know we appreciate it. We'd still be trying to unload the truck if you weren't here to help Noah."

"Glad to help Mia. I was due for a day off anyway, and you've no idea how peaceful today's been for me. Normally when I'm home, I have the four kids yelling and screaming in my ear. I've enjoyed the quiet, believe me. You two need to make the most of it while these rugrats are still little. Once they start walking it's all downhill from there I reckon!" He says, standing up and draining the last of his beer, before placing the bottle firmly down on the table beside his chair.

"Well, that's me done. Better get home to 'She who must be obeyed'." He grins and nods goodbye to us both as I raise my bottle in a salute.

The air's starting to get a chill to it as dusk falls. We take the stroller inside leaving the sleeping infants in it so we don't disturb them. Mum and Dad make their way over to join us for dinner and help settle the babies after we moved their cot into our room.

Mia's looking forward to starting the painting in their rooms and Dad and I promise to help out. We'll go and pick up some paint while we're in town tomorrow if we have enough time, so that she can start, when she feels up to it. I know she's looking forward to their furniture arriving at the end of the week.

We'll finally be able to put them in their own cots in their own rooms, though I'll miss them when they move from ours. I've got used to their noises in their sleep. Mum warned us that it'd be years before we sleep well again and it's true. I hear every little cough and grunt that they make, even though I used to be one of those blokes that could sleep through a cyclone.

"Everything's going well with all of them. I'm pleased with Callan's weight gain already. He's nearly caught up to the others. Whatever you're doing with them, it's working. They're very healthy and contented." The Doc tells us, after examining them thoroughly. He's the same guy who checked them over before they left the hospital, and I'm glad that he's the one responsible for their ongoing care. I like him and I know Mia does too.

Alice smiles up at him, shoving her fist in her mouth and kicking her legs around, as he tickles her belly lightly, before handing her back to me to dress again in her pink onesie. "Do either of you have any concerns that you want to raise? How are you managing with the triplets Mia? Do you have help?"

Looking at him, cradling the boys in my lap I glance down at them and then over at Noah before replying. "Noah's only just gone back to work recently so he's been helping and his parents were staying with us in Perth and now they're on the farm with us as well. They've been amazing. I don't know what I would have done without them. We've worked out a routine for their feeds and we all do the rest of the care between us. So far...so good."

"That's great then. You know that there's help out there for multiples, though I'm not sure how much there is in Albany, but you should look into it. Even online support groups can help. A lot of those websites have some great ideas, so if you have some time check them out." He says as he stands to say good-bye. Noah shakes his hand before placing all of the babies in their new stroller and heading towards the door. "I'll see you all in a month at the same time. Take care."

We leave the hospital, after Mia and the babies being poked and prodded and stopping to feed them, we head to the paint store to choose some colors for their rooms so that we can get started with the decorating. That done, we head to the supermarket to pick up a few things and I wait in the car while Mia goes and shops, then I help load it in the back of the wagon.

Heading home I notice that Mia won't look at the accident site as we near it on the dirt road leading to our property. The fencing and post have been replaced from when Scarlett was run off the road and crashed into it, which lead to Mia's kidnapping and subsequent rape. She turns and looks over the seat at her sleeping infants rather than look at the new fencing.

She thinks I didn't notice, but she did the same thing when we passed the spot on the way into town. I hope this wasn't a mistake- bringing her back here, this time for good. That's if I can make it work for the company, otherwise we'll have to come up with a plan B.

Once we reach home, she seems fine again and chatters on about her plans for the kid's rooms and how she can't wait for their nursery furniture to arrive so that we can put it together. I figure the first cot's gonna be the hardest. They have to get easier after that surely. By the third cot I think I'll be an expert, and you're supposed to have bits left over after completion. It's a boy thing, my Dad told me.

We spend the rest of the day rearranging the furniture, then start on the painting while the rooms are still empty. We've put furniture a bit of everywhere. There is some in spare rooms, some at the cottage and some out in the garage, until we figure out what to do with it. Craig helped me move it all yesterday, and I'm glad that we did it then otherwise it would be Mia and I moving it and no way is she allowed to move heavy objects. Somehow I would have managed to do it myself.

Our BBQ ends up being delayed when one of their kids gets sick suddenly so we plan to try again next weekend. So instead of entertaining guests we decide to get stuck into the painting of the babies' rooms.

We work well together and get the first coat finished in Alice's room. It's a pale pink- very girly. She'll probably hate it by the time she's a teenager, but by then it'll need repainting anyway, so we'll worry about it then. Mia stands at the doorway after feeding the kids and admires our handiwork. "It looks great Babe. We did good." She tells me, looking around the large room. "I love it and I think with another coat it'll be perfect with her white furniture." I picture the room with a white crib and dresser and nod my agreement. "Yeah I think it will, too." I say hammering the paint tin lid back on firmly.

The rest of the week is more of the same. Mum and Dad come and help with the painting and we get it finished and dry before the truck pulls in to deliver their nursery stuff Friday morning. I've been trying to keep up with work at night, waiting till the kids are asleep before locking myself in the study for a few hours.

By the time I come to bed Mia's asleep already after falling into bed exhausted each night after a day of painting, feeding the babies and organizing the house. I have a plan for tomorrow night though. I want to take her into Albany to a nice restaurant and have some time for just us again.

Our days have been so completely overwhelmed by work and babies that I feel like we haven't connected as a couple for ages and I miss her. So I've arranged with Mum and Dad to babysit for the night so that we can have some 'us' time. Mum's happy about having them all to herself for the whole night, but Dad's not real keen on having to get up and help with the 2am feeds for the first time in 25 years. He'll manage though. I have faith in his ability.

Mia looks amazing in a deep blue dress that hugs her curves and stops mid-thigh. With black stiletto shoes she still only comes up to my shoulder but that dress is gonna look even more amazing on the bedroom floor later. The shoes can stay.

The babies are settled in over at the cottage and they're sleeping peacefully when we leave. It gives us a good feeling that they'll be fine while we're gone but I know Mia's nervous and I happened to tell Mum more than once to ring me immediately if there was any problem. In fact she actually pushed me out the door and closed it in my face after the third time, muttering something about me annoying her, which I thought was very rude!

The restaurant specializes in fresh seafood so we enjoy amazing fish from the harbor outside the door. By the time we leave I really need to undo the button on my jeans and Mia's holding her stomach. Not only did we have the appetizer and main course, but we finished it with a homemade cheesecake as well. I feel fat and bloated so I can only imagine how Mia feels. Luckily I parked a block away from the restaurant. The walk actually does some good, we reach the car and climb in. The drive home only takes a short while and I make us both a coffee as we sit and chat on the sofa and enjoy the peace of the night.

The only sounds from outside are the branches of the tree knocking against the house in the slight breeze. It's predicted to rain overnight and there's absolutely nothing better than the sound of rain on a tin roof, unless it's making love to the sound of rain on a tin roof, which is what I intend to be doing very soon. This woman completes me.

I love the way she looks, the way she moves, the way she speaks and thinks and most of all I love her heart. Plus, the fact that she loves me unconditionally, and even I know that sometimes I'm a pain in the arse and slightly overprotective and overbearing. She knows that she can't change me so she just accepts and moves on. She may not like it, but I'm happy that she's never made an issue out of it.

I slip my arm around her shoulders as we sit side by side on the sofa chatting. There's no noise coming from the cottage so that's a good sign that they're all sleeping. I'm sure we'd be able to hear the babies if they were awake. I know Mia's busting to go and get them and she's only restraining herself because she wants this night as much as I do. It's been perfect so far and it's only going to get better I hope.

"You look incredible tonight Baby. I don't think I told you before. I could hardly take my eyes off you all through dinner. In fact, there were a few guys who could hardly take their eyes off you. I was getting ready to beat the crap out of them. It's just as well we left when we did."

She chuckles lightly, pulling away to look me in the eyes. "You imagine things Hun. I'm sure they weren't looking at me. Maybe they were gay and looking at you!"

"Nope. I know what I saw. They wanted what's mine. Believe me. I'm a guy. I know how they think. It's not my body they were lusting after and as far as I'm concerned there's only one bloke allowed to lust after your body and that's your husband."

She surprises me with a smirk and nods. "Yes Dear." Then she bursts in loud laughter, holding her hand over her mouth to try to stifle it, even though the babies aren't here. Old habits die hard.

I lean over her, turning slightly as I grab a handful of her long hair and pull her head back so that I can kiss her soundly. Her laughter stops and she moans as my lips connect with her soft pink ones. I lick inside her mouth, tangling with her tongue as my arm moves down to lower the zipper on her dress slowly.

Her arms reach up and hold the sides of my head firmly, moving my face at a slight angle so that she can deepen the kiss. Our lips move against each other devouring our mutual sounds of pleasure. She moans softly over and over as I lower the shoulder of her dress on one side and then the other till she has to move her arms down so that I can slide it over them, exposing her to the waist. Her skimpy black lace bra shows her nipples as I glance down at her firm tits. I can't wait to get them in my mouth again. I've missed them both so much.

My dick's nearly bursting through the fabric of my jeans and I feel like a teenager who's on his first date as my breathing hitches when her hand brushes against the bulge. She reaches to undo the button and the fly quickly, grabbing hold of me with her small hand, pulling me out of my boxers. I'm so hard it's painful and I'm leaking pre-cum down the shaft as her hand moves up and down gently.

I drop my head back on the back of the sofa and take in a deep breath and let it out with a groan. I turn my head to look at her with glazed eyes. She leans down to kiss the tip of my dick lightly and her hair falls into my lap surrounding her. I place my hand on the back of her head encouraging her to go down on me.

She immediately opens her mouth and swallows the head of my throbbing length taking me as far as she can into her warm moist mouth. My hips jerk upwards on a reflex, and I let her head go so I don't choke her. She lifts her head slightly and then lowers it again onto me, and my control slips as I feel her tongue running up and down my pulsating shaft.

The familiar tingle starts in the base of my spine as I gasp in some quick breaths, trying to delay the inevitable. My hips rock up and down as she lowers her head and then runs her tongue back up me as she lifts it and then repeats over and over.

My chest starts heaving as my muscles tighten, almost to the point of cramping as I feel my release rush through me. She swallows every last drop and then licks me clean as I take a moment to recover. God I needed that! Having to sit across the table from her all night and try to keep my dick under control was hard as hell. It has a mind of its own where she's concerned and it knew that tonight was the night it was getting lucky.

I bring her head up to mine and kiss her softly all over her face, peppering light kisses on her eyes and the tip of her cute nose and then on the corners of her mouth before moving to take her lips in a bruising kiss. I reach around her back and undo the clasp of her bra pulling it off her quickly and cupping her gorgeous tit in my hand, my thumb rubbing over her large nipple.

I break away from her mouth and lift her slightly so that she's straddling my thighs, her dress bunched up around her waist. I bring her tits up to my mouth and lick the right one all over and then suck in the nipple, careful not to suck too hard or I'll end up with a mouthful of breast milk.

I run my tongue around her areola which has darkened with pregnancy and breastfeeding, and lightly grab her nipple with my teeth, pulling on it slightly. She utters a long moan as she lowers her head back on her shoulders, her hair cascading down behind her. I do the same to the other breast as she shoves it in my face, arching her back as I take the nipple firmly in my lips.

Fuck, I've missed them.

They're larger now and harder because it's feed time no doubt, but these tits have always been spectacular. My hands and tongue run over them simultaneously drawing deep groans from within her as I push them together with each hand and lave each nipple with my tongue, moving from side to side rapidly.

My eyes fly open as she pushes herself off my lap and it takes me a second to register her hand held out towards me. I shove my large one at hers and entwine our fingers as I rise up off the sofa, pushing my jeans and underwear down as I toe my boots off and raise my feet to discard my socks. Her dress drops to the floor and she's standing there in only her black thong and those goddamn stilettos.

I think I've died and gone to heaven.

Her body's even better now, if that's possible. She still has a soft belly from being pregnant, but it's almost flat again and she has curvy hips and larger tits than she had before. I study her, my eyes glued to every inch of her amazing body as I run them up and down, taking it all in and committing it to memory. She gives me a shy smile and turns, pulling me with her as I rip open my button up shirt, needing to be naked right now.

It hangs open as we walk quickly to our bedroom my eyes on her gorgeous arse, before she turns and reaches up to push the shirt off my shoulders and down my arms. I reach down and grab hold of each side of the scrap of lace and pull at it, ripping the delicate fabric easily so it comes away in my hand and I drop it to the floor.

She lets out a startled noise as she takes in my movement and then smiles up at me as she backs up to the king sized bed and lays back on it, legs spread wide and knees bent over the bottom of the bed. I stand where I am, allowing my eyes to roam all over her. Her legs look so long with those bloody shoes on, they go all the way up to her fucking ears almost! My dick hardens to stone as I just watch her, narrowing my eyes slightly. Her eyes are glued to my body as she takes it all in, roaming up and down my large frame. She reaches up her hand in invitation and I don't need to be told twice.

My mum didn't raise any fools.

I step forward, my breathing increasing rapidly as I drop to my knees between her legs and run both hands up her calves and then up over her silky thighs, still scarred with impressions of bites. I run a finger over them lightly as I make my way up to her core. I can see how wet she is already and I thank God that she wants this as much as I do.

I lower my head and kiss the caesarean scar reverently, running my tongue along it gently. It's barely a line now, but it'll always be a permanent reminder of the birth and the problems surrounding it. I thank God every day for her and the babies. My mouth lowers to kiss her bare mound then falls to her center as my tongue licks up and down her pussy lips. I move my hands to open her to me and pull back to study her, so pink and moist – and all mine.

I run my tongue up and down as I feel her clit harden, and I take it between my lips gently and tug on it. She arches her back and groans loudly, her hands reaching down to hold my head in place against her firmly. I use two fingers to push inside her entrance, finding her G-spot and rubbing it at the same time as I use my mouth on her clit, both actions sending her over the edge.

I feel her thigh muscles tighten rigidly and then she arches upwards on a cry as she cums suddenly, her body trembling, limbs shaking. She falls back to the bed again and removes her hands from my head, taking them up to scrub over her face, while her breathing settles back to normal. She's panting softly and trembling as raises her head and looks down, our eyes meeting and holding for a moment.

I drag myself up the bed, wrapping an arm around her waist and taking her with me, depositing us both in the middle of the large bed, my huge body covering hers completely. My dick's as hard as stone, anxious to get inside her at last. I think this is the longest I've been without sex for years. It's been 8 long weeks since the birth and it was a few weeks before then as well. My dick feels like it's about to burst, it's so hard. I need to be inside her...now!

"Noah wait." She says, still trying to catch her breath. "We need a condom. Do you have any? I started back on the pill, but for the next few weeks we need to be careful. We don't want another unexpected surprise."

"Shit, I think I have some in my old room. Hold that thought and don't move a muscle while I go and check." I say as I lift myself off the bed, my dick immediately protesting as I look down on her.

I stride quickly over to my old room and rip open the top drawer of my dresser and hunt around for the box that I know should be in there. I quickly check the date because they've been there a while and find that they're about to expire soon.

I'll need to stock up again, but these should be fine till I get back into town to do it. I quickly grab the whole box and almost run back to our room, throwing them down on the bed beside Mia as I climb back over her with a grin. "Found em!" I declare on a laugh. "Now let me at it. I need to be inside you Baby. I can't wait any longer. You sure you're okay?"

She nods, holding her bottom lip in her teeth and I reach up to free it gently. "Just go slow and I'll be fine. I'm ready Noah. I need you too. It's been too long."

Reaching out to the box I grab out a condom and rip it open with my teeth, quickly rolling it down my length. Just that action nearly has me cumming as I line up the head with her entrance and push slowly into her. She's so tight. We both groan loudly at the feeling of being connected like this, as I thrust my hips slowly forward, tunneling into her moist soft walls. She opens her legs wider and I grab her thighs pushing them up, opening her widely so that I can go deeper.

"Noah," she sighs, reaching up to pull me down for a long hard kiss, our lips crashing against the others, teeth meeting and tongues sliding together. I can't get enough of her. I slowly drag out my length and push forward again as I feel her tighten around me. "Noah....more...please!" She begs softly and I thrust back into her a bit harder. "Enough?" I ask breathlessly as a sheen of sweat covers me.

"Harder!" She tells me, pulling my head away slightly before locking her lips with mine again. I use my hips to push into her heat so hard that she moves up the bed slightly before grabbing hold of my back to steady herself.

I can feel her long nails scrape down my sides as I pull out of her and then immediately thrust back into her, our flesh slapping together as I increase the pace, rapidly drilling in and out of her as she gasps out my name, telling me that she's close. Thank fuck for that. It's taking all of my control to stop myself from spilling inside of her before she's climaxed.

I feel her orgasm overwhelm her, she throws her head back and screams my name as I thrust into her savagely and still, her pulsing walls taking me over the edge with her, as cum shoots out of me and fills the condom. I give another couple of jerky hip thrusts to ride out my climax before collapsing on top of her as she wraps her arms around me. I don't think I can move even though I'm probably squashing her with my weight. My limbs won't support me just yet.

We struggle to come down from our high as I pant rapidly, gasping in air, my heart beating at probably twice its normal rate and pounding so hard I think it's trying to jump out of my chest. I kiss her all over her face as she takes some deep breaths, her face and upper chest flushed with ecstasy, eyes glazed with passion as she opens them slowly trying to focus. I can't believe how good that was and how much I want to do it again.

I roll off of her and force myself up off the bed, moving to the bathroom to dispose of the condom. I know that they're necessary, but I hate wearing them, and who would have thought that a married man would need them? Seriously this sucks!

I wander back to bed and pull the covers up over us as she snuggles into my side, sliding her arm over my stomach as I wrap my arm around her. "I'm so relaxed I don't want to get up." She tells me sleepily.

I pull back a bit to look at her face. "Why do you need to get up? Sleep Baby. That was quite a workout."

"Yeah it was, but I have to get up and express this feed, otherwise I'm going to be in agony by morning." She says as she rolls onto her back. I can see what she means as her firm full tits sit high on her chest. I drag myself out of bed and head to the kitchen to get the pump that she uses and walk back quickly, because being naked in the middle of a winter's night isn't much fun if you aren't clinging to someone else.

She does that whole pump and dump which still fascinates me. I watch as the milk fills the bottles, amazed that she and every other female on the planet can do that for their babies. I'm still astonished that she can feed our kids like she does. I'm not sure I would do it if it was me.

Chapter NINETEEN

Mia

Noah gets up early to go and meet Logan at the airport, while I go and check on the babies, who happen to be sound asleep again. Maxine tells me that she only had to get up once, about 3am, to feed them all and they went straight back to sleep and she was just waiting for them to wake again for their next feed. I can't believe how much I missed them all, even though they were only 100 meters away, I felt like a part of me was missing.

I gently pick up Alice and kiss her soft little cheek as she opens her eyes sleepily, focusing on my face. A gummy grin spreads over hers as she waves her arms around excitedly. I think she missed me as much as I missed her. Just as I'm about to sit down with her Jake bellows loudly, upset that he isn't being cuddled as well. Maxine scoops him up quickly, hoping that Callan will stay asleep for a while longer so that I can feed these two before he wakes.

I make myself comfortable on the sofa as Maxine hands me a baby for each side, positioning sofa cushions under them to help. The relief at having them feed is wonderful. I brought over one of the bottles from last night. Maxine prepares it for Callan the minute he wakes up. Just as I'm finishing feeding we hear a knock at the door and Maxine gets up to answer it, carrying Callan in her arms, still drinking his milk.

The door is pushed open and Logan strides in followed by Noah, who walks over and sits beside me, I hand him Alice as I finish up with Jake. Noah carefully lifts her up on his shoulder to burp her as Logan pulls up a chair and takes Callan from his mother and proceeds to finish feeding him while she gets up to make us all a coffee. "So how have my nephews and niece been? They're growing like mushrooms Mia, what the hell are you feeding them? Fertilizer?" We all laugh at his joke as he smirks widely. His eyes lower to take in his smallest nephew who's staring up at this stranger who kidnapped him from his Nana.

"You know you're only here to help put all the furniture together right? You only get a small time to play with them and then we start work. It's gonna take us most of the day I reckon. Dad's gone out on the tractor to do the top paddock so it's up to us, and I've seen how you handle a screwdriver. It might even take us two days!"

"Oi! I'll have you know that I'm extremely handy around the house, thank you! Don't listen to him Mia, he tells lies." He says still holding Callan's bottle to his mouth as the baby drinks slowly.

"Well this should be fun. Do we need to pull up chairs to watch the show? What do ya say Maxine? Shall we go and supervise them and make sure they're doing it right?" I ask her as we giggle together at the thought of these grown men tackling a few bits of DIY furniture. "Surely they can get it right eh? Or do you think we should pitch in and help?"

"You can if you want to, but I intend to try out my new oven today and do some baking plus a roast for dinner tonight. We can eat at your place if you like, that way we aren't disturbing the kids. Do you want to help or you going to watch these fools trying to do a man's job?" She laughs at them as they both turn in her direction with a "HEY!"

I agree to help with the baking once I've put the babies to sleep and we all carry them over to the main house to their temporary cot in our room. Hopefully tonight they'll have their own beds, in their own rooms.

It takes them all day and most of the night plus a few black fingernails and a lot of cussing before the rooms are ready for their new occupants, but at least it's done now, and with only a few dozen screws and bolts left over. The guys assure me that they aren't needed and that the furniture is fine without them, but I have my doubts.

Logan stays with us for a few days helping his Dad with some work that he needs both of them for. All I know is that we looked like we had a lot of cows and then suddenly we didn't. Apparently they were helping Rory load them into trucks so they could be taken to the abattoir. I try not to think of their fate. When you're raising livestock like this you have to toughen up a bit, so I don't say anything, but I seriously contemplate becoming a vegetarian, so as I don't eat any of our animals.

Noah finally takes me on a tour of the property. We take the quad bike and make our way through the green paddocks, some full of beef cows and some empty. They rotate the paddocks where they keep them so that they don't overgraze one area. After some time, we come to the permanent creek, which has a deep waterhole with huge gum trees overhanging the banks.

The water trickles down over large rocks till it hits the deep pool, but it's so clear you can see the pebble covered bottom. I spy tadpoles in some of the smaller pools, and watch fascinated as they wiggle around and cling to the vegetation growing in the pools. A few small frogs sit on the rocks surrounding the pools and jump into the safety of the water when they notice us. I bend down to get a closer look, knowing that our kids are going to love this spot. There's a long stretch of grassy bank on each side and some of the gum trees stand in the water creating large deep pools between their roots. We sit on the grass and enjoy the solitude, the only sound coming from the water trickling over the rocks as it makes its way along the creek and the birds in the trees.

Noah tells me that they used to have a rope hanging from one of the large trees and they used it to swing over the deep waterhole and drop in. They would spend a lot of their summers down here as kids, and there was a permanent track worn from the house to the creek. It took them about half hour to walk to it and then the same home again, so they often brought down a picnic lunch and spent the day swimming when it was hot. I can imagine how serene it would have been for them back then. Poor Scarlett would have been outnumbered by 3 to 1. No wonder she grew up a tomboy.

I love the lush green countryside and there's so much land, that a few acres are planted with Jarrah trees. They take hundreds of years to grow fully, but since their grandfather planted them, they are a reasonable size. They make a shady retreat as we wander through them and I'm grateful that he had the foresight to make an effort at conservation even back then.

Noah tells me that these are scattered around the property and we've only seen a fraction of the whole place. It spans over a hundred acres apparently, quite a substantial size. I love that we have local produce on our doorstep and that our children will have fresh air and nature around them growing up. I'm going to ask Dad to come and stay for a few months if he wants to. There are more than enough spare rooms and I'm sure he'd love to see the farm and maybe help Rory do a few little things. We're all hoping that Rory will still be involved for as long as possible, but we know they also want to travel. Noah's happy to let him take a step back and leave the bulk of the work to him and Jesse the farm Manager.

I think Rory would be bored stiff if he couldn't help out so this is a great compromise. He can do as much or as little as he wants and Noah will be around to help him if needed. The work at the office is sorting itself out and Logan's handling most of it now with Noah advising or doing a lot from his office here.

I know that there will be times that he will need to go up for a few days and spend some time in the office in Perth, but at the moment we're both enjoying having some time together, and getting into a routine with the babies and the work needed outside.

Noah goes out to help Jesse with the cows early and I'm feeding the boys when the phone rings. I'd placed my mobile on the end table beside me and I quickly reach out for it and swipe across the screen without looking to see who it is, and say hello. A female voice introduces herself as Chelsea, the policewoman who took my statement after the rape and she makes small talk for a minute as I wonder why she's calling me at 8 in the morning.

Eventually she gets to the point of the call by telling me that the trial has been moved forward, apparently because they need to be tried separately they want to do it while the chief magistrate is visiting from Perth so that he can sit along with the jury for each trial. This means that I will be required to testify at each sitting as they've both pleaded Not Guilty, despite the huge amount of evidence against them. The date of the trial is two weeks from next Monday and I will be required on Tuesday she thinks as Monday will be set aside for swearing in the jury and the opening addresses from the Barristers. I listen to everything that she says, but it feels like I'm in a bubble of panic as I set the phone down after I end the call.

My chest is tight and my breathing rapid and shallow, and I can feel my body trembling as I look down on my boys, still feeding as though my world didn't just turn upside down. I concentrate on slowing my breaths by focusing on them, rubbing over their heads lightly with my hands as they open their eyes and stare at me. I adore these babies and I'll do whatever I have to do to get past this and put it behind me so that I can get on with being a good mother to them all. Nothing is too much for them.

I try to tell myself that the sooner this is over and done with the better, but I know that this won't be easy for me or for Noah. He'll have to relive it again just like I'll have to and I know that he didn't take it well the first time. I'm hoping that he'll be okay now because I'll need his strength to get me through this. I'm dreading being in the same building as those bastards and I pray to every God out there that I don't have to actually stand in the same room with them.

While I'm sitting there studying my babies with a million thoughts racing through my mind, Maxine knocks and comes in the back door. Immediately she knows that something's wrong by the look on my face and she rushes over to sit beside me, waiting for me to tell her. She just sits, as I compose myself and I relate the phone call and force my tears back down deep inside. I'm determined not to waste any more tears on those lowlife mongrels. When I'm done she wraps me up in her arms and promises to be with me every single minute that I need her to be. She'll babysit or come with me if I want to take the kids with us. I haven't thought that far ahead yet, but I'm grateful to her for the offer. I knew that she'd support me as well and I thank my lucky stars that I have such an amazing family who aren't scared to stand beside me in any way they can. I'm going to need them all as I find the strength to do what I need to do to make sure those filthy bastards spend a long time in jail.

Noah walks in cheerfully just before dinner and kisses my neck as I stand at the stove stirring the warm casserole that I made for us with Maxine's help. He takes one look at me after he turns me to face him and his body goes rigid, on high alert. "Baby what's happened? Are the kids okay?" He asks glancing around to see them all in their chairs on the lounge room mat fascinated by their hanging mobiles in front of them and quite content.

"No they're fine." I say quickly, reassuring him as I glance over to make certain that they are all okay. "Chelsea rang this morning. You know. From the police." He nods in understanding, encouraging me to go on. "So it seems that the trial's been brought forward so that the Chief Magistrate can be there. The first one is two weeks from next Monday and the other one follows straight afterward, probably the next week. She wants me to call in and go over everything sometime next week with the prosecutor."

"Oh Fuck. Okay. We knew this was coming, it's just a bit sooner than expected that's all." He says as he hugs me to him even though he's dusty and sweaty from whatever he's been doing all day. "You know that I'll be with you no matter what. Every minute of the day, I'll be there. You don't have to do this alone and we'll make sure that you don't. It's gonna be okay Babe. You can do this." He says as he rubs gentle circles over my back, calming me for the first time since the phone call this morning.

He continues to hold me close for a long time, knowing that I need him to do this without me actually asking. It's not until Callan starts whining softly that he lets me go and strides over to scoop him out of his chair and kisses him gently. Immediately he stops crying and stares up at Noah, his little mouth opening in a wide smile, arms reaching up to touch his face.

The day of the trial looms dark and bleak, thunder rolling in the distance and rain hammering down on the roof. It's a fitting day for what I need to do. We're all up early and Maxine comes over to stay with the babies along with Rory who delays his chores till the rain stops.

I think he actually loves being with the kids, but doesn't want us to know so he makes all these different excuses to be with them constantly. We all know what he's doing, but none of us say anything about it to him. Noah drives us into Albany and pulls up as close to the court house as he can.

We make a run for it, as we get out of the car and dodge puddles on the sidewalk. The courthouse is a large brick and stone building dating back to the time that the city was first settled. The entrances are surrounded by local stone brickwork and we race in through the doors as fast as we can to get out of the rain. I look around and see Chelsea and the other policeman John standing to one side chatting, heads close.

They notice us at the same time and lift a hand in greeting as we make our way over to them, dodging people standing around nearby. I'm nervous as hell and if Noah hadn't been with me I think I would have been running in the opposite direction by now – rain or no rain.

Forever Noah's

"Morning." Chelsea says, giving me a reassuring smile. We return her greeting and make small talk for a while till someone taps her on the shoulder and whispers something in her ear and she looks over to me with a concerned expression. She thanks them and turns back to face me, grabbing my other hand slowly and telling me that it's time.

A million butterflies swarm in my stomach as I hold Noah's hand tightly and follow her down a long hallway. She opens a door for me and ushers me inside taking a chair in the corner and showing me to a chair behind a table with a computer screen attached. Noah sits beside me as I lower myself into the chair slowly and focus on the screen. It's a video link to the court room and I can see the whole room from behind the public gallery as the Magistrate walks into the room and greets everyone solemnly.

A noise off to the side distracts me as I see Jackson being lead into the room by 2 security officers, a long chain joining his wrists till he gets to the long table where his lawyer sits, then he's released from the cuffs and the officers step back to one side, eyes glued to him as he sits. They go through the procedures about what the charges are and when he's asked about whether he pleads guilty or not guilty to them he says firmly and forcefully, "NOT GUILTY".

Noah and I exchange a look of amazement and he shakes his head, but doesn't say anything, just holds my hand tighter, his thumb rubbing over my knuckles again and again.

I listen carefully to the proceedings and after an hour or more Chelsea indicates that it'll be my turn next as the main witness and those butterflies turn into wedge tailed eagles and I wonder if I'm about to puke. I swallow over and over, forcing myself to take deep breaths and trying to settle my nerves. I know that he can't see me in person, but just the thought of him being able to see me on the large screen TV monitor that stands in the corner of the front of the court room is enough to terrify me. I can see him clearly from behind and I wonder if that view will change when I need to speak.

Will I be able to see his face as I tell them all what he did to me that day? I want to see his face, to see if he shows any regret for the harm he did when he changed my life by his actions. I want him to be sorry about the pain that he caused me and the suffering that I still go through and will constantly need therapy for.

I want him to see that he may have broken me that day, but Noah put me back together and keeps me that way by the enduring love that he and his family shows me, but the biggest anchor I have is my babies. I want him to see that he didn't break me completely. I want him to see that I came out of this a stronger person, one who doesn't allow anything to come between her and the people that she loves.

I want him to see that I survived and will continue to do so for the sake of my husband and my children.

That's what I want him to see, but somehow I think that if he could see me at all, he would see a terrified woman who's doing her best to make it through each day and so far doing a wonderful job of faking being brave and strong. I still wake up occasionally from the nightmares of the rape and I can clearly see him, feel him and smell him as he violates me repeatedly. I manage to keep my breakdowns to myself most times, only occasionally allowing Noah to see my fears getting the better of me. He's been an absolute rock and I wouldn't have come this far without him.

When my turn comes to speak I manage to answer each question with a coherent reply, telling the events as though it happened to someone else, trying to distance myself from the memories, as my new psychologist suggested. By the time I'm finished I'm mentally exhausted and strung out from the ordeal.

The defending lawyer tried to make it out that it was consensual sex and even tried to say that I wanted it and enjoyed it.

That argument fell apart when the court room was shown pictures of my injuries. I hardly recognize my face in the photos. I hear Noah take a sharp intake of breath as he sees the photo. I study Jackson as the photos are shown and there's nothing, no sign of regret, no looking away – nothing. No matter what the lawyer says I answer in the same even tone, not raising my voice or arguing with him as Chelsea and the Police prosecutor advised me. I turn around a few times to see Chelsea smile at me encouragingly. Once she even gave me a grin and a thumbs up sign.

Chelsea shows us out as Noah pulls me into his side and keeps me there till we get to the large wooden door that takes us outside. As soon as that door opens I fall apart and he scoops me up, carrying me through the rain to the car quickly, and shoving me inside to sit on the passenger seat.

Damn! I was determined to make it to the car before this happened!

I'm angry at myself for breaking down in public like that. I'll never let it happen again, no matter what. I sit and cry till I have no more tears, but I'm hidden from the outside by the teeming rain that continues to fall heavily. Noah just sits and waits for me to pull myself together, not saying a word till I swipe at my eyes with a tissue that he passes me and I apologize on a hiccup.

"Didn't I tell you once never to apologize to me for this? I know how difficult that must have been and I'm incredibly proud of you. That took courage and a lot more strength than I have. I doubt I could have done as well in your position.

You did an amazing job in there Baby, and I appreciate how incredibly hard it was for you. I get it. I do. I love you so much. C'mere, let me hug you." He says leaning over the console between our seats and wrapping me up in his large arms as more tears sneak out of my eyes and make their way down my cheeks. I just sit and enjoy the feeling of security that he gives me.

I'm no stupid helpless little girl who needs a man to do everything for her, but this grown woman appreciates having someone so wonderful by her side. He does more for me with his silence than anyone has ever done with words. His presence is necessary for my very survival. His kiss is the breath my body needs to exist. His arms are my security blanket. His words, my heartbeat. I depend on him to make me whole, something I don't think I knew even existed before I met him. With him I don't need to pretend, he just accepts me for who I am and I love him so much for it. I honestly don't know how I'd live without him.

I don't know how long we sit in the car, listening to rain beating down on the roof, our breathing the only other sound inside the large SUV. Outside the world carries on as normal but right here and right now, nothing intrudes on this moment. I pull back slowly after he kisses my hair for the hundredth time since I got in the car. My body is exhausted, mentally and physically. I can't believe that I have to come back next week and do it all over again for the next trial. Hopefully next time will be easier than this was.

Noah gives me a wry smile and keeps his hand over mine on my thigh as he starts the car and drives out of the parking lot. The wipers are barely keeping up with the amount of rain hitting the windshield and the other windows are fogged up slightly from our breathing. It's a slow drive home and the dirt road is muddy and slippery, taking extra time to negotiate. The rain continues for nearly a week as we all spend a lot of time inside around the fire in the living room. Luckily Rory had stocked up on wood before winter.

The day of the next trial arrives too quickly. Once again Noah and I make the drive into Albany in the rain and meet Chelsea and John and the Prosecutor in the large entrance area. We make our way down the long corridor again and watch the proceedings from the video link in the private room.

This lawyer is trying to blame everything on Jackson so that his client will get cleared of the charges. Both Noah and I look at each other and shake our heads at the stupidity of the notion. Noah is actually a witness against him as well and he stays with me until I've once again repeated everything that I could remember about the man that I now know arranged my kidnapping. He says that he was just an innocent party who was called to the motel room and found Jackson there with me. I scoff at Chelsea as we watch him lie under oath every time he opens his mouth.

Noah gets up on the stand and tells the court about how he was the cause of my kidnapping and what was said in the motel room which was a repeat of what the police officers had already said. He told them everything that happened from the moment he walked into the motel room to find me chained to the bed and his voice hitches a few times as he takes a moment to finish his testimony.

The Magistrate thanks him for his time, and he's allowed to go. We don't want to wait around for the rest of the trial to finish. Chelsea has promised to ring us as soon as there is a verdict like she did for Jackson's trial last week. He was found guilty of rape, deprivation of liberty and assault and will be spending at least 10 years in jail.

I'm a lot more composed as we walk out of the court house to the pouring rain. I think because I'd said and done it all before it was easier for me this time, plus this guy didn't touch me, he was the mastermind behind the plan, yes, but he never laid a finger on me. Jackson was the one who petrified me, because he was the one with no conscience about doing whatever he wanted to me. I was just a body for him to use as he wanted, and what he wanted was to inflict as much pain as possible. I'll never forgive him for what he did, and I'll carry the scars forever, both inside and out.

This time I make it all the way home before breaking down inside the house. I rush to our room and sit down on the bed as Noah goes to get the babies from his parent's cottage. I decide that I need a shower so that I can do this in peace and he won't know when he gets back. Stripping off all of my clothes quickly I close the bathroom door behind me as I turn on the large shower and walk in making the most of the hot water, finally feeling warm for the first time today.

I cry silently, stifling my sobs with the water and hope that Noah takes a while so that I can do this without him worrying about me. I just need a few minutes to get this out and then I'll be fine. I wash myself all over and take my time doing it so that I can cry without interruption. I hear Noah rustling about in the bedroom and I try to pull myself together in case he comes to check on me. I manage to control the sobs, an occasional hiccup the only sign that I had a meltdown, besides the fact that my eyes are red and puffy no doubt. I turn to face the wall so that if he comes in he won't see them.

I get out and dry myself and dress quickly in some sweats and a pullover and head out to find him and the kids. They're all in the living room by the warm fire. Noah's put them into their own little bouncy chairs and he's giving them all a good talking to about behaving for their grandparents. I get the idea that at least one of them wasn't good for them today. They all goo and gah at him while waving their arms around and kicking their legs as he tells them that when Nana's in charge, they need to listen to her when she tells them to sleep. I smile as I approach quietly, knowing that he has been using this as an excuse just to interact with them all, and they're all loving it. They watch him with smiles on their little faces as he bends to each of them in turn, seeking reassurance of their co-operation in the future. I can't contain myself any longer as I burst out laughing loudly at the demand. They see me and start kicking frantically with delight as I step closer to the sofa where Noah sits, with them at his feet. "Do I detect a note of dissension in the ranks?" I ask, not looking directly at him, rather I scoop up Jake out of his chair and cuddle him to me, kissing his head, eyes lowered so that Noah can't see the result of my tears.

"Not exactly. Mum said they didn't want to sleep this afternoon, so I was just giving them a reminder about who's in charge. Hopefully now it's all sorted." He says as he grabs hold of Callan's foot and rips his sock off to tickle it lightly, resulting in a screeching giggle from our boy. Alice joins in squealing loudly as he does the same to her as well. He goes to take hold of Jake's foot and our eyes meet over the baby on my shoulder. "Sweetheart?" He asks as he studies my face, taking in the watery, swollen red eyes that meet his. "You okay? Do you need anything?"

Gently pushing my hair back away from Jake's grasping hands, he leans in to kiss me on the temple and then does the same to Jake. One of his kisses nearly fixes everything wrong in my world...nearly. I just nod and look down at my giggling babies, too scared to open my mouth for fear of losing it again. I'm trying to be strong, but when Noah looks at me like that, eyes full of sympathy and concern, it's nearly the end of me. I swipe at my eyes as a stray tear falls and suck in a huge breath, determined not to shed another single tear over today's events.

"Mia? Talk to me Baby. I thought you were okay, but you've obviously been crying. What can I do?" He asks gently as he scoops Jake out of my arms and sits him in his lap and wraps his other arm around me tightly, pulling me into his side.

"Honestly there's nothing that you or anyone can do Hun, I'm fine. I promise." I tell him, trying to give him a smile, but only manage a small lift of one side of my lip. "I just had a moment...again...but I'm okay now. Now how about I start some dinner for us while you keep them occupied for a while? They'll be wanting their tucker soon, so I'll be quick."

He kisses the top of my head and I pull myself out of his hug and stand up, heading for the large kitchen. I love cooking in here. It has a homely feel to it, but with the latest appliances. I quickly get the chicken that I put out to defrost and start making sweet and sour chicken, one of the few dishes I know how to make by heart. I fill a pan with water and place it on the stove to heat for the rice as I gather all of the ingredients that I need. I can hear Noah chatting to the kids as I prepare our dinner, and I marvel at the domesticity of the moment.

The crackling fire in the living room fills the house with the scent of eucalyptus from the logs and I've realized that it's one of my favorite smells. I can hear the logs popping in the deep fireplace while Noah reads the babies a story about Aladdin. They must be totally engrossed in his words because I can't hear a sound from any of them and I'm grateful that they've given me time to do this before they start screaming for their dinner.

I've named this the 'Rush Hour', because at this time of day I'm trying to do a million things at once as well as feed them and get them ready for bed. They're all in their own cots now, which is great, especially at 2 am. It used to be that one woke up and then started crying which woke up the others who demanded a feed as well. Now I find that Jake and Alice may sleep through till 6 am if Callan doesn't wake them in the night. My boobs are still getting used to this change of feed times which varies from night to night, meaning I either have too much milk or not enough. Thank God I've been expressing each feed and we have a stock of milk in the freezer as well as the fridge. Jake reminds me of Noah with his appetite, he can drink twice as much as the other two already.

My little babies are growing quickly, and we've settled into a routine that works for all of us, with the help of Noah's parents. My Dad's decided to come over for a while and I'm so happy and excited. Noah's going to get him from the airport and bring him back next Friday when he comes back from Perth. He needs to spend the week in the office so he's leaving on Sunday and won't be back till Friday night.

I don't know how I'm going to manage a whole week without him but I will. I have Maxine and Rory to help and hopefully after tomorrow night I'll have a new friend, my first since we've moved here. Craig is bringing his wife and children for dinner and I'm looking forward to it. We've spoken on the phone and I know that we'll get on famously. She's friendly and outgoing and much like me, really...except with one more child and another on the way.

Chapter TWENTY

Noah

The big bastard arrives on time with poor Bev dragging behind him, organizing the kids. Typical boys, their rambunctious and noisy and need room to run around so we wear them out by taking them all out on the quads down to the creek, giving the girls time together to get shit organized. Mia gives me a grateful look as Connor and Lachie climb on the bike with me and Paddy and Blake climb on with their father and wave goodbye as we take off slowly, making the most of the ride. We go and check out the cows and make sure they're okay and then head on down to the creek for a quick look.

It's nearly dusk as we arrive back and offload our passengers who immediately start chasing each other around like lunatics. Craig just shakes his head as he strides over to Bev, who's ready with a beer for him, Jake resting on her hip as Mia carries out the other two babies for me to take. No beer in hand unfortunately. I go over to the fridge and carefully pull it open and bend down to grab a bottle off the shelf without disturbing Callan who's in that arm. I'm getting bloody good at this one armed stuff, I must say. I've had a lot of practice now and no doubt I'll get more.

Rory and Maxine wander over and greet Bev and Craig with a hug and watch the boys playing on the large back lawn as the sun fades and a chill hits the air. We're all rugged up in warm clothes, but it's decided that we'd be better inside, and I'm trying to figure out if the house is childproof enough for this lot of ratbags. I do a quick mental rundown and decide that there's nothing valuable that they can demolish in a few hours...I hope!

Craig sits and supposedly supervises the kids while Bev and I set the large table for us all. Mia cooked a roast leg of lamb and it smells delicious as she slices it and serves it up on our plates. We manage to get the kids to sit still and eat by promising them ice cream for dessert if they behave. Sudden silence hits the kitchen as they stuff their faces quickly, racing to see who can finish their dinner first. This is the first time they've shut up since they arrived.

Bev and Mia chat about kids, the farm, how we met, how Logan asked her on a date and what happened that night. I'm listening with one ear on their conversation trying to hear Mia's side of the story as Craig tells me about what's wrong with the Freo footy team and how he'd fix them if he were the coach. Somehow I don't think the coach's job's in any danger at the moment.

Bev's oohing and ahhhing as Mia tells her how we met at the office and then goes on about Brisbane and how she had to help nurse me after my broken leg and how I seduced her with my eyes...WTF? Is that even possible??! If I'd known that, I would have used my baby blues to better advantage and got me some back then.

Craig laughs when he realizes that I haven't heard a word he said since he started talking about the last derby between Freo and West Coast Eagles. By that time, I was concentrating on

Mia's story and I must have zoned out for a bit. It's great listening to her tell her version of what happened. If you listen to her it was all my doing how we got together, but I have to butt in and put in my two cents worth when I tell Bev how Mia 'accidentally' spilled coffee all over her see through blouse on her first day of work. Poor Mia turns bright red at the memory as she slaps my arm with the back of her hand. I lean over and kiss her pink cheek still chuckling, "It was gorgeous Baby. One of the best days at the office that I've ever had. I still love that bra…it's one of my favorites."

She sputters out a forceful, "NOAH!" as she looks around to make sure the kids are distracted and didn't hear. They're too busy eating their ice cream to worry about what we adults are discussing. I mean seriously, if Lachie shovels in that ice cream any faster he'll end up with a frost bite headache and it'll serve him right. He's the eldest and should know better.

I'm sure I didn't do that when I was his age. My mother would have tanned my backside if I had, but Craig's too laid back to care and poor Bev just looks totally exhausted. I suggest to him that we take the boys camping next weekend and have a boy's night with them to give Bev a break.

She looks at me gratefully, excitement in her eyes at the thought of a night to herself. That look makes me even more determined to do this with my oldest friend. I'd do anything for him, but I reckon he's completely clueless about how much Bev looks to be struggling at the moment. I might be able to have a chat to him that night as well. Anyone can see how tired and worn out she is…well anyone but him apparently.

We don't have to go far, there are plenty of good spots to camp here on the property and it's been years since I've pulled out my swag and slept in it. I'm sure we have a pup tent or two somewhere for the boys to use. Dad must have read my mind and tells me that he just saw them in the shed the other week so at least that's covered. The noise from the kids is louder than a jet plane when they realize what we're talking about. I shush them with my hands, telling them to take it down a notch before they wake up the babies.

I get up to clear the table and drag Craig with me, much to his surprise. I bet he doesn't lift a finger at home. Poor Bev would be doing it all while he sits back in his chair. She's just one of those women and he's the type of bloke who'll let her do it all without thinking about what her workload must be. I know how exhausted Mia gets from looking after the kids and the house.

I try to help her as much as I can, but I know Craig wouldn't be helping his wife. She looks like she's nearly ready to break...and maybe that's what she needs to do to get him to sit up and take notice. That might work. He's a bit slow on the uptake, my mate, always has been. He's a great bloke and he loves her dearly, but he's a bit old fashioned about men and women's roles.

He's fine with allowing Bev to do all the hard yards with the kids, the house, the shopping, the gardening and everything else he doesn't do while he's off doing farm stuff, and maybe it worked for them before, but from the look of her right now, I don't think it's working anymore. I make a mental note to help Mia out as much as I can, to avoid seeing that look of exhaustion on *her* face. I intend to be a hands on father to my kids, not leave it all to her. Even though she's still feeding them I do as much as I can in between farm and office work.

I drive up to Perth the next day after keeping Mia in bed for a late breakfast...well I ate and she starved...but it was soo worth it! She didn't object while I was exhausting her, but she needed food afterward so I made her some of my famous pancakes while she fed the kids. I helped her out in between feeding her bites of pancakes and berries and maple syrup. The breakfast of champions.

Our prolonged goodbye was my fault. It was hard to leave them, knowing I was gonna be gone for the week. A whole week without my babies...I don't know how I'm gonna cope...truly. I promise to Skype every night after work as I start the car and drive off, watching her retreating figure in my rear view mirror. I need her so much I feel like I'm leaving a piece of my own body behind. It's gonna be a very long week, that's for sure.

I barely make it through the 4 days in the office, and if it hadn't been for the fact that I was collecting Mia's dad from the airport I think I would have made the long trek home on Thursday night, no matter how late it was. I'm almost bursting out of my skin by the time Don arrives and I see him walk through the doors from the sky walk.

We walk downstairs to the baggage carousel to wait for his suitcase and make small talk about footy and his beloved Port Power team. I thought I was a staunch supporter for my team, but I'm nothing compared to him. Mia says his house is full of footy stuff collected over the years.

Making our way out to the car I drag his suitcase behind me to the parking ticket machine to pay for the time I spent waiting for him and then we hurry to the car. It's just after 12 so if we hurry we can be home by 7:30 or 8:00 tonight. I make a quick call to Mia to let her know that we're on our way as we drive out of the airport parking lot and onto the freeway through the city. We listen to the radio for a while till he finds an old 50s CD in the console and insists on playing it. I have no idea where the hell it came from, but I have a suspicion that Logan may have planted it. I know darn well that I never bought it.

Actually it isn't half bad. I don't mind some of the old songs and Don knows most of them and hums along with the music quietly. We stop for food and refueling about 4pm, knowing that Mia will have dinner ready for us when we get home. As anxious as I am to get to the farm I drive carefully and stick to the speed limit all the while conscious of the knowledge that every kilometer gets us closer to my family.

I intend to cuddle them all for the rest of the night....and you know that saying, "the second bang will be the closing of the door"? That'd be us if Don wasn't with me. I can't wait to get her to bed and spend the whole night making up for lost time. I don't care how exhausted she is tomorrow...I'll do everything that needs doing if I have to.

As soon as we pull up I jump down from the car and almost run to the door and pull it open, nearly tearing it from its hinges. Mia startles at the sound and a squeal escapes her as her shoulders touch her ears with fright.

She quickly covers her chest with her hand as she sees that it's me and not some ax murderer intent on doing her a damage. "Jesus Christ Hun, you scared ten years off my life! I didn't hear the car pull up." Noticing her father behind me she quickly pulls out of my hug and runs over to wrap her arms around him, those gorgeous eyes of hers tearing up.

I can see how hard she's trying to hold them in, but the dam bursts and she sobs into her father's chest, as he hugs her tight. "Hey now Gert. It's good to see you too. Stop with the waterworks will ya?" He says pulling out a tissue from his pocket and drying her eyes carefully.

"Sorry Dad, I didn't mean to blubber all over you. I'm just so glad that you're here at last. It's been a long day." She tells him on a hiccup, her bottom lip still trembling slightly.

"I know...for me too. Now where are my grand-children? I hope they aren't sleeping?" He asks looking around the kitchen hopefully.

"No. They're supposed to be, but I think they knew their Daddy was coming home so they all decided to wait up for him. They're in the living room on their mats having a kick around. Hopefully they'll tire themselves and sleep all night for a change." She says as she leads him into the spacious living room.

They're all laying on their backs on their activity mats, toys strung over them on a frame, their little arms reaching up to bang them around. I scoop up Alice and Callan and kiss them as they kick their arms and legs wildly, in delight. God, I missed them so much. Mia gently picks up Jake and I sit with all three of them in my lap as she places him on my thighs.

Don comes to sit beside me as he studies his grand babies carefully. Jake gives him a toothless grin and he returns the smile, looking to me for permission to pick him up. I nod and gesture to him as Jake starts squirming around till Don holds him up under his arms and stretches out his arms so that he's at the same height as his face, scrutinizing his grandchild. "Look at you. Such a big boofy boy aren't you huh?" He tells Jake, who grins up at him, his fist traveling to his mouth.

"Oh he's the piggy one Dad. If he had his way he'd spend all day on the boob." Mia tells him, as Don and I burst out laughing and share a look between us.

Hell, we're males...sue us! That's my idea of heaven actually, and I laugh at Mia's disgruntled look when she realizes what she said and why we're laughing. "Oh very funny the two of you. I can see that already you're getting along fine. Maybe this wasn't such a good idea after all! Now the boys definitely outnumber the girls. Alice...you and me...we stick together okay?"

"Na, we'll behave I promise." Don says with a smirk, bringing Jake down to hold him close against his shoulder.

"Of course we will Baby...well...most of the time anyway. It's gonna be good for Dad to have another man about the house to keep him occupied. I'm sure he'll be putting you to work first thing tomorrow. How much do you know about tractors? I think that was on his plan for the next few days. He wants to pull it apart and check something, I wasn't really taking much notice."

Dad smirks at him and declares, "I know as much about tractors as any other train driver...this should be interesting...I'll be his assistant...that I can do. I know my way around tools."

"You'll be fine. Just don't let him wear you out. You aren't here to work your arse off. Just do what you want to do....and if that means sitting down and watching TV or reading a book...then that's fine...you do it. Dad loves to potter and it keeps him out of our hair...especially Mum's...so we let him keep busy...but just because he does doesn't mean that you have to." Noah tells him as he swaps Jake for Callan and kisses him gently on his little face. Jake squeals up at him and blows bubbles with his mouth, his tongue poking out between his lips. His dark hair is growing and covers his head in a soft downy cap. Noah runs his hand over his hair lightly as Alice watches every move that he makes. She's certainly a Daddy's girl already. She has him wrapped around her little finger.

He worships her and the feeling's mutual. I'd say that she's Daddy's princess, but we don't use that word and I've noticed that Noah's careful not to use it in deference to me. It was what Jackson called me all afternoon in that seedy motel room, so it only has bad memories for me and I appreciate Noah not saying it.

At least I know that they're both behind bars for the next 5-7 years with parole, 10 years without. Chelsea rang a few days after the second trial and told me the verdicts. There really was no doubt. Two police officers, Noah, Logan and I all heard what they said that day so there really was no denying it. They each blamed the other in their confessions, trying to get a reduced sentence.

It should make me feel better, knowing that they're locked up, but really it doesn't. Nothing will help me feel better about what they did to me...nothing. I just need to deal with it the best way I can, but at least now I can try to put it all behind me.

Now I'm just happy that I won't bump into either of them at the supermarket or in town. I was always looking over my shoulder to make sure that they weren't around, so hopefully I can relax a bit knowing that they aren't out there anywhere. I never want to see either of them again. I've started seeing a visiting psychologist every 2 weeks and so far so good. We haven't got into much of the details of what happened that day and I know that we'll have to sooner or later but right now I'm all for later. I've had enough talking about it at the trials. I don't want to think about it anymore, or dream about it. I just want to try to forget about it. Sounds easy right?

It's not.

Dad and Rory are inseparable over the next few weeks. We've taken to calling them Tweedle Dee and Tweedle Dum, because where one is you will always find the other one. Normally in the machinery shed fiddling with some engine or part to the header or tractor or one of the cars. I'm loving having Dad here to spend some time with us, and I know that he's enjoying it as well.

He's loving having the babies close and watching them grow and change. I can't believe that they're four months old already. Jake is already starting to roll himself over. The others aren't too far off doing it as well. They keep me busy that's for sure, but at least they're all sleeping through the night now, which means that Noah and I get a lot more sleep than we did. Well, when we don't take advantage of them going to sleep early.

Dad thinks we go to bed at 9pm because we're exhausted and sometimes that's the case, but normally it's because we can't keep our hands off each other. Like tonight. Noah's been handsy all day, even though we woke up early this morning and I was worn out before I got out of bed. Nothing like waking up to find a blonde god between your thighs.

Actually I recommend it as a great way to wake up!

Now that I told him so, I'm a bit worried/delighted that he's intending to wake me like that every day from now on. The man has wicked skills with that tongue.

The kitchen's warm with spring sunshine coming through the windows and bathing the room in bright light and heat. Dad's already out helping Rory do something with the cows – fixing windmills or something like that. He's really enjoying his stay, and he and Rory are definitely life-long best buds I think.

Noah's heading back into Perth for a few days of office time so I intend to make us a large breakfast of eggs, bacon and toast and feed the kids while he's showering and dressing. The babies are playing with their activity mats on the large deep mat in the living room while I cook us some food.

Keeping an eye on them and the eggs and bacon takes a bit of work, but you learn to multitask when you become a mother...you have to...especially with three of them. You'd be amazed at what you can do while you're holding two babies and rocking another with your foot.

At the moment my focus is on Jake who's desperately trying to roll off his mat, but being stopped by the frame hanging over it that holds all of the toys. He's not happy about the apparatus preventing his freedom and he's telling it so loudly. I walk over and pick him up and cuddle him as he throws himself backwards and almost out of my arms as he flings his arms around in temper. I pat his back and soothe him, but he holds himself rigid and screws up his face as he continues to bellow his annoyance.

I race over to the stove and quickly lift the frying pan from the hot element before the eggs burn and shove two pieces of toast into the toaster, all the while jiggling Jake on my hip, trying to placate him. He allows himself to be calmed and stops screaming in my ear as he watches the scene outside. The lush green pastures fascinate him as his eyes are drawn through the windows to the fields beyond.

I watch the cows in the far field as they slowly meander around, eating the long grass slowly. I love watching the scenery out these windows. They wrap around the corner of the room so you can see a great amount of the area outside. I watch as Maxine waters her garden and even though I can't hear her I know that she's singing to herself softly as she walks slowly around the small yard.

The thought makes me smile. I scan the fields trying to locate Dad and Rory to see if they are coming down for breakfast any time soon, but I can't see them anywhere. They must have gone to one of the other pastures. I did hear them say last night that they intended to go over to Craig's farm to help him do something today, so maybe they've gone already.

Noah strides into the kitchen with a broad smile on his handsome face. "Was that you making all that noise little man? What's got you so upset huh?" He asks Jake as he takes him from me and holds him close. "What was all that screaming for?"

"I think that was his first temper tantrum. He couldn't roll over because of the bar on the activity mat, so he chucked a wobbly. He has his father's temper I think." I say as I lean over to kiss him gently and then reach up to touch lips with Noah.

"Me? What about his mother's? I think you're much worse than I am. I'm sure he's got it from you.

My side of the family are all placid and quiet." He says on a laugh, knowing full well that he's lying through his teeth. He has a bad temper when he wants to show it. I've seen it in action first hand. Luckily it doesn't get used very often, but when he does get mad...watch out. I raise my eyebrow in disbelief and just shake my head and walk over to the bench grabbing out the cooked toast and buttering it for him.

He manages to eat with Jake trying to pinch his fork every time he raised it to his mouth. He thought it was a great game and was getting mad that Noah wouldn't let him have any. I quickly ate my food and took my plate over to the sink as Noah stood up and handed Jake over to me.

"I have to go Baby. I've got a conference call with some guys from China at 4 today and I don't want to be late. Logan doesn't know enough to tell them what they need to know so I have to be there. The hard copies of the plans are in the filing cabinet otherwise I could just do it here. I hate having to leave you with this lot, but I really need to hit the road."

He leans down, kisses Jake, then walks quickly over to the other two and scoops them up in his large arms peppering them with kisses too as they grab at his face. He lowers them back to the floor and then comes to stand in front of me, holding his hands to the sides of my face as his eyes study every inch of it.

"God you're stunning. I could look at you all day. Have I told you that I love you yet today?" It's a rhetorical question because he knows that he spent a good half hour this morning telling me over and over as well as showing me.

"You may have mentioned it once or twice already, but I can never hear it enough. Now go, before I drag you back to that bed again for the rest of the day."

"You don't know how good that sounds…but I'm out of here. Be good for your Mum." He tells them all, giving them one last long look. "I'll be home by Thursday afternoon Sweetheart. I love you and I'll Skype you tonight." He leans in for a long kiss, his mouth pressing firmly over mine again and again. "Miss you already." He tells me as he turns and opens the screen door and before long I hear the large SUV start up and pull out of the driveway. I let out the breath I was holding and look at Jake, his eyes fixed on the closed door.

I think he's waiting to see Noah walk back in again. "No my baby boy. Dad's got to go to work. It's just you guys, me and Poppa for the next few days. We'll be fine though eh?" I say as a grin breaks out over his chubby face and his hand reaches up to pull at my bottom lip, giggling as he does.

I bathe them all and put them all down for their morning nap then tidy up the kitchen quickly before deciding to do some baking while they're asleep. I mix up a batch of chocolate chip muffins and bake them in the large oven, setting the timer to remind me to take them out if I get distracted. We can have them for afternoon tea and what we don't eat I can freeze for later on. Noah loves muffins and chocolate chip are his favorite, so I make some extra large ones for when he gets home.

The first batch is perfect, so I pull them from the oven and place them on the stove top to cool. I happen to glance out of the window and notice Maxine walking quickly over to our door, yanking it open quickly as she looks around for me. I take one look at the pinched worried look on her face and immediately know that something bad's happened.

"Noah?" The question escapes me quietly as I slide into a chair at the large wooden table. My face shatters as I feel my heart breaking into a thousand pieces and I think I'm about to pass out. "NO! Not Noah Sweetie…I'm afraid it's your Dad. Rory just rang me from the hospital. They took him in there from

Craig's place down the road. Apparently he had some kind of turn and they think it might be his heart. Rory said to tell you that he's with him and he's okay, but I knew that you'd want to go and be with him. I'll stay with the kids. You go."

The blood drains from my face and my legs barely hold me up at her words. I struggle to think straight, fear piercing my heart immediately. "Right. There's muffins in the oven. Milk in the fridge and more in the freezer if you need it. I'm sorry to do this to you, but I have to go and see what's happening. I'll be back as soon as I can." I stand on shaking legs and walk to the door, grabbing my handbag on the way out, promising her that I'll ring as soon as I know anything.

I barely remember the drive in to the hospital, but I remember the nurse in Emergency opening the door for me so that I can go and be with my Dad. All the way in I was telling myself over and over that he'll be fine. He's tough, but I know that he has a bad family history with heart disease, and I wonder if this is the first time this has happened or if he's keeping something from me.

The friendly nurse pulls back the curtain allowing me to enter the cubicle where Dad lays hooked up to a heart monitor on a small trolley. I hear the constant beeping of the machine and I pull my eyes away from it to study Dad's pale drawn face. He looks to be in pain and I almost run to his side, grabbing at his free hand and enveloping it with both of mine. The shock of seeing him like this almost has me speechless. His face has a gray tinge to it and he doesn't look right. His skin is clammy when I touch it lightly.

"Dad?" I ask scanning his face for a clue as to what's going on. I glance up to the guy standing on the other side of the bed and notice him for the first time. He's tall and dark with hazel eyes and a ready smile which is aimed in my direction. "Nate Barnes." He says kindly as he looks down to the chart that he's holding in his hand. "I'm your father's doctor. You must be the Mia he's been telling me about. You're right about her Don." He tells Dad as he glances my way again.

I immediately wonder what he's right about, but push it to the back of my mind for another time, as I ask him what's happening, a note of panic in my voice. "Your Dad's had a heart attack and luckily they got him in here as quickly as they did so that we could start him on some drugs to help him. That's what's in the IV over there." He nods to the bag of clear fluid running into Dad's other arm.

My shaking legs almost collapse under me as I pull in a chair and sit, not letting go of the hand I'm holding. "A heart attack?" I repeat incredulously. "Dad?" I whisper and he pulls his head around to look at me, trying to smile, but only managing a small grimace. "How are you feeling? Are you in pain? Have you had heart problems before?" I fire questions at him as he closes his eyes for a moment, before reopening them and focusing on mine.

"Yeah Gert I have. Just a few angina episodes, nothing drastic. I normally keep my spray with me in case I need it, but I forgot it this morning when we went to Craig's. I just thought I'd pulled a muscle. Been doing a bit of heavy work the past few days and I thought it was from that. Thank God they wouldn't listen to me and dragged me in here to be checked. Did you know that Nate here is Craig's brother?" He says directing my attention to the good looking man in blue scrubs again.

"Oh I didn't realize. Sorry. I can see the resemblance now." I tell him, our eyes meeting across the small space.

"Yeah I'm the good looking one though." He says with another smile, showing even white teeth. "I knew my dumb ox of a brother had a brain in there somewhere. If they'd waited any longer to bring him in he may not be here doing as well as he is." He tells me solemnly, turning to study the beeping display on the monitor.

Even to the untrained eye I can see that his heartbeat's erratic with normal beats interspersed with an odd beat here and there. I watch it for a minute wondering if I should panic now or if this is normal. "So what's happening now? Is that okay?" I ask Nate as I nod to the display. He knows immediately what I'm talking about and gives me a reassuring smile.

"Yeah that's fixable. He had the best day to have a heart attack. It's the day when the Cardiologist visits so he's been to see him already and the bad news is that Don's probably going to have to go to Perth for a while so that they can do an angiogram and put a small stent into the damaged artery in his heart. I'm just about to go and let Craig and Rory know what's going on if that's okay with you. They're out in the waiting room. No doubt the whole district knows about it by now so at least they can tell Max and Bev that he's alright." I quickly nod my assent as he walks out leaving the machines beeping noise the only sound filling the silence. Surprisingly there's not a lot of noise from the area outside the curtain, which I'm grateful for.

"Dad, how are you really?" I run my hand down the side of his face. "Is there anything I can get you?"

"No Love, I'm okay. Just tired now. The pain's eased off thank goodness. I felt like a lead weight was pressing on my chest, but that's eased now as well. Once I have this shunt thing put in I'll be good as new apparently....so the specialist says."

"Is it a major operation? Did he explain what they do?" I ask, my face contorted with a deep frown at the thought of him undergoing heart surgery.

"Not exactly, but he did say it was a routine procedure. Not cutting my chest open or anything. Apparently they go in through a vein in my leg and it'll only take an hour or so. At least that's good news. A few days in hospital post-op and I can go home."

"I'll be with you for the whole time Dad. I'll get the kids and drive up today if they're moving you straight there. I'll ask Nate when he comes back."

"There's no need for you to do that Gert. Noah's there and young Logan. I'm sure they'll come to visit. It's too much for you to do the long drive alone. It's not necessary, I'll be fine." He says as his eyes close slowly, he tries to drag his eyelids up, fighting sleep.

"You rest up and don't worry about a thing okay?" I say, leaning in to place a kiss on his cheek, as I mentally make a list of things I need to do and what I need to pack for the babies to go to Perth. Oh shit Noah! I pull out my phone from my bag and dial his number. He answers after a few rings. "Hey Sweetheart. I'm still on the road. Do you miss me already?"

"Noah, something's happened. Where exactly are you?" I ask, my voice rising with panic. I take a deep breath to calm myself as I hear his worried reply.

A note of panic audible in his voice as he mutters into the blue-tooth. "Hold on. I'm just gonna pull over and talk. What's happened? Is it the kids? Is someone sick?!!

"No it's Dad. He had a heart attack this morning at Craig's farm. They brought him into the hospital and he's okay, but he needs to go to Perth for surgery." I tell him, trying my hardest not to cry, as I move silently out of the room so I don't disturb Dad. The hallway's deserted so I prop myself up against a wall as I wait for Noah to reply.

"What the Fuck?!! A heart attack? What caused it? What were they doing? Is he alright?" He fires the questions at me, and I can hear the worry as he barks out the words. "Baby, he'll be fine. He's a tough ol' bastard. I can go straight to the hospital when you find out when he's being moved up here. Let me know as soon as you know anything. Okay? I'll ring Logan and see if he can rearrange things in the office so that we can meet him as soon as he gets here."

"Okay. I'll ring you when I find out from Nate. He should be back in a minute."

"Nate's there? He's in good hands if Nate's caring for him. He's one of the good ones Babe. He'll make sure that he's okay." He says with certainty, his tone reassuring me.

"Yeah he's been taking good care of him. He looks awful Noah." I tell him as a tear slips down my cheek and I brush it away. "His skin's a gray color. I've never seen him like this. I'm just glad that the Cardiologist was here today. He's checked him out already and he's the one that's organizing for him to have the procedures as well. Nate said it was a good day to have a heart attack, if it had to happen." I tell him on a half laugh half sob.

"Baby calm down. He's in good hands and I'll meet him at the hospital as soon as he gets here I promise. Just keep me posted."

"I'm going to drive up this afternoon once he's on the plane. They're arranging with the RFDS to take him up as soon as possible. Once Nate has a time I'll ring you and let you know straight away and then go home and pack up the kids and drive up with them."

"No. That's crazy." He says firmly. "I'll arrange a jet for you, it'll be easier than taking them on a commercial flight and there's no way you're driving up with them alone...especially today when you're upset." He pauses to make sure I'm not going to argue, but I'm not stupid. That's the best plan. I'm in no condition to drive. "Okay as soon as you know what's happening let me know, but I'll arrange the jet so that it's down there on standby for you and I'll meet you at the hospital later today. Oh and Babe....try not to worry, he's tougher than you think. He'll be fine."

"Okay. I love you, you know that?" I ask him as I see Nate returning.

"Not half as much as I love you Sweetheart. Forever and eternally. Now go and let your Dad know that we'll be here for him and I'll see ya later okay?"

"Righto. I'll see you then Hun. Bye." I tell him and disconnect the call, stuffing the phone back into my pocket as Nate stands next to Dad and checks the heart monitor again.

"It's all arranged with the RFDS Mia. The Ambulance will be here shortly to take him to the airport, but unfortunately they have to take a sick kid and his mum as well so there won't be room for you to go with your father. I'm sorry, but sometimes this happens." He tells me apologetically. "Oh and he'll be going to Royal Perth Hospital."

"No it's okay. I taking the babies up with me as well, so I can't go with him anyway, and thanks, I'll let Noah know." I tell him as he grabs his chart again and starts writing in it.

"Oh that's right. I heard you guys had twins...or was it triplets? I remember Mum telling me something about it. "How are they doing?" He asks, raising his head to look over the bed at me.

"Triplets. Two boys and a gorgeous girl. They're wonderful. Growing like sprouts at the moment. They're five months old now. It's gone so quick I can hardly believe it myself."

"Babies tend to do that. So no sleepless nights for you anymore? I'm having trouble picturing Noah with an armful of babies, I must admit. I never thought it'd happen honestly."

"Yeah he's great with them all. Absolutely adores them and they worship him as well. He's a hands-on Dad you know? He gets up in the middle of the night and changes nappies, helps with bath and feed time as well. He can't get enough of them."

"Wow. Hard to believe. You must have softened him. I'd never have thought he'd have anything to do with babies. He's always been such a blokey bloke, if ya know what I mean." He says with a laugh. "Oh do you mind if the guys come in for a minute? They've been out in the waiting room all this time and asked if they could see him before he left. I said I'd check with you before I said yes."

"Of course they can come in." I say, realizing that I should have thought about it before. "Shit I feel bad. I completely forgot about them out there. I'll go get them now if you like?" It's not really a question because I'm already out of the room. I feel awful about them waiting all this time. They could have been in here with him and I.

I return with them following close behind and I stand back out of the way so that they can stand next to the stretcher. Dad opens his eyes and gives them a small smile as he notices them. "You buffoons come to give me a farewell party or a wake? If it's a wake, you're too damn early. I'm not going yet."

I smile as he jokes about his situation. At least he hasn't lost his sense of humor. We all laugh at his comment. Rory answers with a smirk. "Only the good die young, you stubborn old bastard. You'll be around for a long time yet." He says with a tilt of his chin, his concern for his mate showing on his face plainly.

Craig speaks up after clearing his throat quietly. "I've got to get back to the farm, but I just wanted to make sure that you're alright before I left. Nate's pretty good at his job apparently, even if he is a degenerate Bum." He looks over to Nate daring him to say something. Nate just smiles back at him and lets it go. Must be an inside joke I figure.

Before Craig can say anymore the curtains pulled back sharply by a uniformed paramedic dragging a small stretcher behind him. We all step out so that they can transfer Dad onto it and organize him to leave for the plane.

Craig waits till he's safely on the bed before saying goodbye to him and gives me a pat on the shoulder as he walks out to leave. Rory stays with me and we follow them all out to the waiting ambulance. Dad's carefully loaded into the back of the van and I climb in beside him to give him a kiss on the cheek and tell him that I'll see him soon. He gives me a wan smile and promises to behave.

As the door closes and the paramedics climb into the vehicle, the dam breaks and Rory holds me tight as I sob loudly into his flannel shirt. He runs his hand over my head gently, muttering platitudes as his other arm tightens around my back. After a few minutes I finally get myself under control again, apologizing profusely for falling apart on him. He just smiles and nods understandingly. He holds my arm as we walk over to the large SUV and I give him the keys so he can drive home. Noah's right. I'm in no fit state to drive home let alone for 8 hours to Perth.

When we make it back to the farm I open the door as soon as the car stops and jump down, striding quickly into the house. I yank open the door forcefully, looking around frantically to find the babies. They're all in the living room on their activity mats, as Maxine watches over them from the sofa. She immediately gets up and comes towards me, concern deepening her blue eyes.

"What's happening? How is he now?" She asks quickly.

I give her a rundown of what happened and what the plan is for today and she helps me to pack as Rory stays with the kids, chatting to them. I don't pack much for me as I left a lot of clothes in the house, but the babies will need quite a bit. We don't know how long I'll be there for so I end up throwing things into suitcases and resign myself to buying whatever we forget.

They all behave wonderfully on their very first plane ride. Maxine and I watch them as they sleep in their car seats strapped into the deep leather chairs. Noah told me that he's arranged a minivan to take us home from the plane and I'm grateful for his planning, I'm having trouble thinking past getting to the hospital right now.

The car drops me off at the front door to the hospital and I practically run inside to the inquiries window to find out where he is. I don't want to use my mobile to ring Noah in the hospital in case it disturbs Dad. Once I get directions I find the elevator and stand inside pressing the close door button, anxious to get up to him.

I find his room quickly and knock quietly on the door before opening it and poking my head around. Noah walks over to me with a grin and pulls me into his arms as I open the door wider and walk to him. "Hey Baby." He says kissing me lightly on the lips.

"Hey you." I say gripping his shirt in my fist, needing to feel him against me to give me strength. I turn to face Dad who's looking better already. His color's coming back and he's not clammy anymore, though he's still got nasal cannula giving him oxygen piped from the wall. I smile broadly at him, holding back the tears that threaten to fall. "Hi Dad. How are you feeling?" I ask as I finally let go of Noah and walk the few steps to the bed. I bend down to kiss his cheek again as he assures me that he's feeling much better now.

I take the chair beside the bed and Noah takes the one on the other side near the window. I grab hold of Dad's large gnarled hand as we chat for a while, making small talk. The nurse interrupts us to do his Obs and tell us that he'll be going down for his angiogram soon and someone will come and get him shortly.

We nod our thanks as she leaves and the door closes softly behind her. Noah gets up and starts pacing quickly, nervous, but trying to cover it. We watch him as he wears a path from one side of the room to the other.

Luckily it isn't long till the orderly comes with a wheelchair to take him down for his procedure. Dad got changed into his hospital gown before I got here, much to his disgust and I cover his legs with a thin blanket for the walk downstairs. We're going to head home for a while and check on things there. They told us that it'd be at least an hour and a half to two hours, but they'll call us and let us know as soon as he gets back to the ward.

The car ride to the house is silent except for the radio music. I'm trying hard to keep calm and I know that Noah is as worried as I am.

Logan must have come home early, we realize, as we open the door to the house from the garage. The delicious smell of Chinese food hits us as we walk in. At the same time Jake lets out a screech of protest and I hurry into the living area and scoop him up from the floor, sitting down on the sofa and lifting my shirt to undo my bra to feed him. Just as I manage to do it Logan walks in and smiles in greeting at us both, his expression changing to stunned embarrassment as I attach Jake to my breast to feed.

"Holy shit...sorry...errr...um...I...shit!" He says trying to tear his eyes away from my exposed breast. "I was just gonna let you know that we're having stir fry for dinner and Mum's upstairs putting the other two down for the night. They could hardly keep their eyes open for their bottles before. She shouldn't be long. I'll just go and keep an eye on the food. Your housekeeper did a great job of stocking the fridge Mate, there's even beer in there if ya want one."

Noah walks over to him and slaps him upside the head on the way to the kitchen. "Eyes off Dickhead, and stop fuckin staring.

Anybody think you'd never seen a boob before!" He grumbles in warning, as Logan finally drags his eyes away and follows Noah to the kitchen.

"NOAH BYRNE. I HEARD THAT!" Maxine yells from the stairs as Noah mutters about her stupid Vulcan hearing. I laugh quietly at him being told off like a five-year-old, but he knows his Mum hates him swearing. He'll be the next one to get a slap upside of his head if he does it again in her presence. At least he has the decency to look embarrassed as she glares at him as he gets two beers from the fridge and hands one to Logan.

"Sorry Ma." He tells her contritely, as he walks past her to come and sit down with me and Jake.

Dinner's delicious and the boys do the dishes while I have a quick shower and change to go back to the hospital to see Dad. It's been almost two hours since we left and I keep checking my phone constantly for any missed calls, but there's just a blank screen still. I'm anxious to get back, especially now the kids are all asleep, hopefully for the whole night. They're all sleeping through most nights which I'm
grateful for. The extra sleep is welcome now, because my days are still incredibly busy.

Noah drives Logan and I back to the hospital for a quick visit. I just need to see Dad and check that he's fine. Logan wanted to come as well so all three of us walk down the hallway to his room, knocking softly before entering. His bed's empty and I have a bad feeling in my gut. "Noah, I'm going to go ask a nurse to find out what's happening. They said two hours' maximum but it's been longer than that and now I'm worried."

"I'll go Babe. You stay here with Logan. Maybe they were late starting the procedure or something. There's bound to be a simple explanation. Don't panic just yet." He says as he walks out the door leaving Logan and I studying the empty bed. I look up at him and he gives me a small smile.

"He'll be fine Mia. Just wait and see. I'm sure there's a reasonable explanation like Noah said."

"I hope so Logan, but I have a bad feeling about this. Something's wrong, I just know it." I tell him as I walk over to the window and look out at the lights of the city in the distance.

Chapter
TWENTY
ONE

Noah

I walk down to the Nurse's station in the middle of the ward. It's surrounded by beds and encased in glass above the benches so that they can see everyone while they're there. At the moment there's only one nurse in there writing in a chart. She looks up and her eyes devour me as I lean against the door jamb. She looks like a cougar about to eat a small animal. She's attractive in a hard kind of way. Too much makeup and too bleached blonde for my taste though.

"Can I help you?" She says with a sultry look, telling me that she'll help me with anything I want.

"I'm Don Drummond's son-in-law. We were just wondering why he's been gone so long? Is there any way to find out what's happening?" I ask her, her shoulders slumping slightly as she takes in my words. She realizes that I'm off the market and I make a point of showing my left hand, so that she can see my wedding band clearly as I hold up my hand to my chin and rub it lightly.

"I'll ring down and see I can find out for you." She says as she lifts the phone receiver, dials a number and waits. Nobody picks up at the other end and her face is contorted into a deep frown. She eventually hangs up and looks over at me worriedly. There's no mistaking that look, and mine mirrors hers no doubt. Maybe Mia's right. Women's intuition and all that.

"I'll keep trying and I'll let you know as soon as I hear anything okay?" She says going back to writing in her chart.

"Right. Thanks. I'll be in his room waiting for him. Appreciate it if you could come tell us as soon as you have any news. My wife's stressing out about him." I say as I turn to walk away.

"Will do." She replies, head still down, concentrating on what she's writing. "I'm sure he's fine though."

"Yeah I hope so." I tell her over my shoulder.

Mia's eyes fly to mine as I walk in the door. She was looking out the window and turned quickly at the door opening. "The nurse is gonna keep ringing them. Nobody's answering at the moment, but she'll come and tell us as soon as they do." I say walking to her and wrapping my arms around her as she buries her head into my chest. "It's okay Baby. He's alright. I'm sure they just got delayed. You know what hospitals are like. Shit happens and holds everyone up."

She raises her head and looks up at me with those huge green eyes and I pray to everything holy that what I say's true. I don't know that she could handle another knock down. She might never get up again. I lower my head to kiss her softly, rubbing my lips over her full pink ones, getting lost in the feel of her against me like this.

If it weren't for Logan clearing his throat, I'm not sure I'd be able to pull away from her. I pull back and look over at him as he gestures to the door. I hadn't even heard it open, but the Nurse stands there in her pale blue scrubs and gives Mia an appraising look as I hold her tightly.

"Err sorry to interrupt, but I thought that you'd like to know that Mr Drummond will be on his way back shortly. One of the tech's got delayed in the OR so they didn't start on time. Apparently it went well and he's fine." She looks around the room and her eyes fall on Logan and he returns her look of interest and smiles at her. "Okay well I'll leave you to it, but I'll be around till 11 if you need anything at all." She says, her eyes glued to Logan's, as she smiles and leaves the room.

"You know that there's no justice in this world when I ended up with Nurse Ratchet and your Dad gets cared for by someone like that." I smile down at Mia as she finally relaxes in my arms, letting out a long sigh of relief.

"You'd never have needed me if you'd had her, and that would've been a shame now wouldn't it?" She says, teasingly, her fingers reaching up to trace the outline of my lips lightly. I open my mouth and suck on her finger as a smile breaks over her face for the first time in hours. "You were the best nurse ever Sweetheart." I say, letting her finger fall from my mouth.

"Right, and if I remember correctly you owe *me* a nurse now after stealing Mia practically out of my arms. I think I'll go and collect. She looked interested didn't she? I didn't imagine it did I?" Logan asks, looking from Mia to me quickly.

"No Logan she was definitely interested. Go and ask her out. I'm sure she'll say yes." Mia tells him as she cuddles into me further and closes her eyes for a second, breathing in my scent.

I nod to my brother and he quickly opens the door and looks both ways in the hallway before walking out. While he's gone I just stand there and hold Mia tightly, peppering her head with kisses. Thank God her dad's alright. I couldn't handle her heart being broken again by grief. She's just getting back to the old Mia and her nightmares have almost stopped. She rarely had one till the trial, then they started again, but that's understandable.

We both pull apart as we hear the sound of people approaching and the door opens again to allow the orderly to push in the stretcher. Mia walks quickly over to her Dad, who's pretty groggy still, but awake. She grabs his hand and lifts it to her chest, holding it between both of her own.

"Thank God you're okay. I was beginning to panic because you were gone for so long." She tells him quickly, swiping at a stray tear. "How are you feeling?"

"I'm alright Gert. No need to worry. I'm fine. Just sleepy." He assures her, struggling to keep his eyes open.

The orderly and I help him over to the bed and Mia straightens out his blankets for him. He looks very pale, but I'm sure that's just due to the procedure. I stand back and allow her to fuss over him for a while after the orderly leaves. Don grumbles about it, but I can see that he really enjoys her attention, even if he doesn't say so.

"I'm good now Luv. Go home to your babies. I'm probably just gonna sleep for the rest of the night anyway. Noah, take her home boy." He mutters as she smooths down the blanket one more time.

"He's right Sweetheart. There's no reason for us to stay. We can come back in the morning and talk to the Cardiologist then." I take her hand and pull her up from the bed and into my arms. "We need to go rescue Logan from that Siren's clutches I think. I bet she already has his bank account numbers by now. We'll be back first thing in the morning Don." I tell him as we walk to the door and I pull it open. We both look back when he doesn't reply, he's sound asleep already.

We walk out to the Nurse's station and find Logan surrounded by four females clad in scrubs. He looks quite at home amongst the giggling nurses. I raise an eyebrow at him as he turns and introduces us, but I don't remember their names seeing as I'll probably never see them again, but I nod politely at them all in turn.

Mia tells him that we're leaving for the night and he tells the blonde bimbo, who's name's Hannah apparently, that he'll pick her up tomorrow night at 7 and says goodnight to them all.

We walk briskly out to the car enjoying the cool of the night after the heat of the day earlier. A cool breeze wafts over us all as we climb into the Sahara. By the time we get home Mia's asleep and Logan decides to stay the night rather than drive back to his house. He has a few clothes that he leaves here for such an occasion as he often stayed over after a long day or a few too many beers. Mia sits up slowly as I turn off the car and looks around groggily.

"C'mon sleeping beauty. You need your bed. Do you want me to carry you up?" I ask softly, getting out and walking around to her side of the car and opening her door.

"No Hun, I'm fine really. Shit sorry. I didn't mean to fall asleep. Must be more tired than I thought." She says, her voice rough from sleep. "What time is it anyway?"

"Just gone 11, and you know that those kids are gonna be awake at 6am no matter what, so you need to go up and get ready for bed. I'll be up in a sec. I'll just grab a drink and then be up to tuck you in okay?" I say as we walk into the house together, Logan following behind. She nods at me, but doesn't say anything, instead walking over to the stairs to slowly walk up them to our room. Logan follows me into the kitchen and leans against the bench as I get two beers from the fridge and pass one over to him.

"I hate to do this to you Mate, but I'll need tomorrow morning as well to spend at the hospital with Mia and Don. She wants to see what the Cardiologist says about the angiogram and just in case its bad news I want to be with her. You gonna be alright without me at work?" I ask as I lift the beer to my lips, taking a long gulp of the cold liquid.

He nods and takes a drink before answering. "Yeah I'll be fine. I can rearrange those calls again and move the meetings. Shouldn't be a problem. Shit happens Bro. Right now you're needed here more than at the office. Don't stress about it. It's all good."

"Thanks. Appreciate it." I tell him scrubbing a hand up over my face. I'm exhausted too. It's been a long day and my body's telling me so. "Well I'm off to bed. See ya in the morning." I say setting down my empty bottle on the counter.

"Yeah. Night." He says with a tip of his beer in my direction.

When I get upstairs I find Mia already fast asleep, curled up in a ball in our huge bed. She almost looks like a kitten. I go and quietly check on the kids and they're all sleeping soundly. I stand beside each of their cots and just watch them sleep. They look like cherubs when they're sleeping.

Tiptoeing back to our room I quietly close the door and creep over to the bathroom by the light of the small bedside lamp that Mia left on. I hurriedly clean my teeth and strip out of my clothes, walking naked over to the bed and climbing in behind her, wrapping one arm over her waist and taking in a deep sniff of her hair, before kissing the back of her head lightly. She snuggles back against me in her sleep and lets out a long sigh. I fall asleep almost immediately.

She has that effect on me. Just being around her relaxes me. Holding her, comforts me. Kissing her makes me content, and making love to her fulfills my wildest dreams of happiness. I don't know how I ever thought my life was great before she and the babies came along. Looking back now it was empty and selfish. Now my whole universe revolves around the four of them and I can't imagine my life any other way.

I'm woken with a hand on my morning wood. As I slowly come to consciousness, I realize that Mia's already awake and sliding her hand up and down my shaft slowly. My eyes open to lock on hers as she kisses me on the chest lightly then her mouth moves over to my nipple and bites it gently, flicking her tongue over it as I groan from deep in my chest.

The sound draws her eyes up again and she deftly moves to straddle my hips as I reach down and grab her hips, surrounding them with my large hands. As she leans forward, her hair falls around her, enclosing us in its curtain. I raise my face to meet hers and a long sigh escapes her as our lips touch, our mouths pressing together. I slide my tongue over hers as she pushes herself down on to my rock hard dick.

The feeling of her surrounding me like this is just amazing, and the only sound in the room is our skin slapping together, as she raises and lowers herself on me, and our moans of ecstasy as her rhythm quickens and she sits up giving me the best view in the world. Her hair falls over her and I can see myself disappearing into her each time she lowers herself down. I move my hands from her hips up to her gorgeous tits and knead them forcefully, rubbing my fingers over her large nipples.

God I love these tits.

They're just as incredible now as they were before the pregnancy. I lick my lips as I raise my body up, putting one hand outstretched behind me to support myself as I use the other to bring her tit closer so that I can engulf the nipple in my mouth. I flick my tongue over and around it as it hardens in my mouth. I do the same for the other one as Mia's hands come up to hold the back of my head, her fingers digging into my scalp.

I look up to see her throw her head back as her hair falls over her shoulders and down her back in a glossy waterfall. I watch her raise herself up and lower herself, her movements becoming more frantic. I groan loudly as she squeezes my dick with her muscles before releasing them. Her thighs tighten around me and I know that she's getting close. Her rapid breathing matches my own as my chest heaves, while I try to hold back my release.

As I feel her muscles contract around me again she lets out a loud, "Oh FUCK!" and shatters against me, her body jerking wildly as she climaxes. My own follows quickly as I hold myself deep inside her and grunt a few times, my eyes closing from the sheer pleasure. She falls forward onto me as I lower us back down, still connected. I pepper her face with light kisses as she comes back to earth slowly, still panting hard from her workout.

"Good morning to you too." I tell her softly once I can speak again, kissing the crown of her head. "I love the way you say good morning Baby. In fact, I'd go so far as to say I wouldn't object to being woken like this every day."

She turns her face up to mine with a glazed sated look and smiles at me. "Geez Hun, that was amazing! So morning sex is becoming my favorite thing as well as night time sex, and that's right up there with shower sex too."

"You'll exhaust me completely if you want sex twice a day forever, but I'd die a happy man Sweetheart. So give it your best shot!" I chuckle at her, leaning in for another kiss. Just when I think we might be good for round two a bellow sounds out and we both fall back on the bed and she rolls to one side, getting up quickly and throwing on her robe.

"Bloody Jake." I say exasperatedly. "Remind me to do this to him when he's a newlywed will ya Babe? I was hoping to have my turn on top this time."

I hear her giggle at me as she walks out the door and closes it behind her. I lay back and prop myself up with pillows, straightening the covers over my lower half. Soon she's back with Jake and Callan, laying them in my arms as she turns to go back and get Alice.

Pretty soon all three are squirming all over the bed, laughing and giggling as I blow raspberries on their bellies and bare legs and arms. Jake kicks me hard on the chin when I move in to give him another raspberry on his chubby thigh and I pull back and rub the sore spot on my stubbled chin.

One by one Mia feeds them as I play with the other two. This is becoming the best day ever. Morning sex and giggling babies...who knew?!! I have everything I need right here in this bed with me. I smile over at Mia with a lazy grin and she asks me what I'm grinning about.

"I'm just thinking that this has been a perfect morning so far. It doesn't get any better than this Baby." I say, smiling broadly at her.

"Yeah I agree." She says returning my smile and looking over at her babies, who are grabbing their feet and trying to roll over while babbling non-stop. "Where's your Daddy Alice?" She asks her as Alice continues stuffing her toes in her mouth and drooling over them. Alice immediately looks over to me and a definite "Daaaa" comes out of her mouth around her toes.

"Did you hear that? She said Dad! Oh my fucking God! She said Dad...I can't believe it!! She's such a clever girl. I always knew it. I knew you were Daddy's favorite baby girl for a reason Alice. Yes, I did." I tell her as I scoop her up and lay her against my raised thighs as she kicks me in the stomach, pushing herself up with her legs.

"Say it again Baby girl. Say Dad for Daddy." I coo to her as she giggles loudly at me and stuffs her fist into her mouth now before pulling it out with a long line of drool attached. Mia's laughing at us, but I'm seriously claiming that one. She said Dad. Not Mum...Dad. I'm fifty foot tall and bulletproof right now. I think my chest is gonna burst with the amount of emotion that I'm holding in as I look at each of our children and I couldn't be more proud of them or love them anymore than I do.

"Thank you Mia." I say seriously as I lean in to kiss her forehead.

"What for?" She asks, a frown creasing her face.

"For giving me these three. I don't know what we ever did before we had them, do you?" I say running my hand over Callan's little legs. "They're perfect, just like their Mum."

"Well I remember we had a lot more sex before the babies came along, not that I'm complaining at all. They're angels and I don't know what I'd do without them now, and their Daddy's pretty perfect as well."

"On that note, this one's done a crap in her nappy and I'm naked under here, so I'm so not changing her." I say quickly as I hold Alice up at arms-length towards Mia. She puts Jake down on the bed and takes Alice from me and kisses her softly on the cheek, while Alice grabs a handful of hair and tugs it hard. "OW! Let go Baby girl. Come on, we'll change your bum and bring you back for more cuddles with your Daddy in a while."

As she walks away I watch the boys playing and laughing on the bed. Jake pulls at Callan's lip and he laughs as he does it. Callan retaliates by grabbing Jake's arm and raking his nails down it, causing Jake to pull it back and drop his bottom lip with a bellow of pain. I laugh as I scoop him up and kiss his arm softly. "See little brother's not such a pushover is he huh? Be nice to him, he's smaller than you." I tell him as he stops crying and looks at me, his bottom lip still trembling, before he reaches up to slap at my mouth, his cries turning into giggles as he slaps at my face over and over.

"Hey little man! I get it. You want some attention. Okay well show me that belly so that I can tickle it." I say as I pull his onesie apart over his stomach, bearing his pink naked belly. I get my fingers and tickle him lightly as he squeals in my ear and then pulls at it with his little hand, trying to shove it in his mouth. I lower my head to his stomach and blow raspberries all over it, which results in him grabbing my hair and pulling it while he giggles loudly. Callan joins in as I reach over to him and tickle his belly too.

Mia comes back in and stands in the doorway taking in the sight of us boys all laughing together on the bed and a smile breaks over her face.

"Look at Daddy being silly with your brothers Alice. Isn't he a funny man?" She asks as she rocks her slowly. Alice replies with a sharp squeal, shoving her fist back into her mouth again.

"C'mon Hun. Can you bring down the boys for their breakfast while I go and get it ready for them? I want to get back to the hospital as soon as I can." She says smiling at us all, then turning to walk downstairs. I can hear her chatting to Alice as she walks away.

Once the babies have had their breakfast we take it in turns to shower and put them down for their morning nap. Mum assures us that she'll be fine and we promise to be home at lunchtime to feed them again. Now that they're eating real food it's all hands on deck at meal times.

Don looks much better than he did last night when we left him. He has more color. in his cheeks today and smiles widely as we enter his room. Mia bends in to give him a kiss and then sits down in the chair beside his bed as I make my way over to the window to look out quickly before turning back to him. "How are ya feeling today Mate?" I ask him.

"Yeah better. Yesterday knocked me around a bit, but I'm good today." He says as he looks down on his daughter. "You didn't need to come in so early Gert. I'm fine really."

"No we wanted to be here when the specialist does his rounds. I want to find out what happens now Dad. Did they say anything last night?" She asks worriedly.

"Nothing that I remember clearly. I was a bit groggy afterward so I don't remember much."

"It's okay." I say. "We'll find out when he gets here."

We make small talk for a while till there's a knock at the door and Dads cardiologist strides in, followed by another couple of residents and the blonde nurse from last night.

"Well how are ya today Don?" He asks briskly, glancing down at his chart.

"Good thanks Doc. Anxious to get this over and done with and get home again." He tells him on a chuckle.

"The good news is that we won't have to send you to St Johns after all. The angiogram showed a blocked artery as we expected, but luckily it's not too bad, and a spot opened up here later today so we can slip you in there and hopefully you'll be able to get home in a day or two, barring complications."

"That's great news isn't it Dad?" Mia beams at him and then across to the Doc.

"Yeah Gert it is. I'll be glad to get home, that's for sure." He agrees.

"Right, well the girls will be in later to prep you and hopefully I'll see you around 5 tonight Don." He says as he turns to leave again as the residents follow like sheep trailing behind him.

"Oh I forgot to tell you Dad. Julie's flying in today. She'll be here after lunch. Noah's going to get her from the airport and she can stay with us for as long as she wants to. She just wanted to be here for your procedure and make sure that you're okay."

"Aw she worries too much. You both do. She didn't need to come. I could be home tomorrow. She should be home with her girls." He protests.

Mia looks at him and says, "No we should be here with you. There's no way we wouldn't be here. You don't get rid of us that easily."

I hear a "Harrumph" from the bed, but he doesn't bother saying any more about it. He knows that he's fighting a losing battle.

"Give up Mate. You know you won't win against these females. *You* did raise them after all." I tell him with a smirk, and he laughs as he looks over to me.

"You're dead right there Son. They'll win every time. Her sister's just as bad as she is. You just wait till she gets here. We'll be fighting a losing battle then, that's for sure!" He says shaking his head. I think he's pleased that both of the girls will be here with him despite his protests.

"Well Mia why don't we leave him to it and go home and then we can come back later today after we've collected Julie from the airport. I'm sure she'll want to come straight up here and see for herself that he's okay." I tell her as I walk over to the door.

"Okay. We'll be back later on Dad. You rest up. We'll go home and see the kids and make sure Mum's alright with them still then we'll go meet the plane and be back."

"Okay Love. I'll be here. Don't plan on going anywhere just yet." He says with a laugh as she leans in to kiss him again.

Chapter TWENTY TWO

Mia

We wait for the crowd of people exiting their specific planes to clear. As I wait for Julie, I anxiously hold Noah's hand and I try to stretch, to see over the crowd. Finally, I see her push her way through the crowd of people, she sees me and starts running, she throws herself against me and we hug tightly. When she pulls away I have tears in my eyes and so does she. It's been a while since we've seen each other, but we keep in contact with an email or text or call every day or two.

She's my big sis and I love her dearly, I'd do anything for her as she would for me. My sister looks like me except she's the total opposite of me, if that makes sense. She's got short blonde hair and mine is long and dark, but other than that we have the same features and body type and when we're standing together we look very similar. At the moment her hair is cut into a short bob which suits her. It's been dyed a light blonde and the glossy strands are pushed around when we hug each other.

She pulls back and swipes at her cheeks, she pulls Noah in for a hug as well. He wraps his huge arms around her and pats her back lovingly, before standing up and smiling down at her.

"Hey you. Good flight?" I ask as she lets go of Noah and turns to me.

"Yeah it was fine. I'm not very fond of flying though. Give me a car any day." She laughs. "I have visions of the plane falling out of the sky and taking me with it...not a good thing when you're thousands of feet in the air."

"I'm glad you made it in one piece then." Noah says with a chuckle.

"So am I Noah....so am I!" She tells him with a giggle. "You cut your hair girl! I can't believe it...after all these years. I know you sent a pic, but I still didn't really believe that you'd done it." She says, picking up a handful of my hair and studying it for a minute before letting it fall again.

We all walk over to wait for her suitcase and I give her an update on Dad and what the Cardiologist said this morning. She nods and asks questions while we make our way to the car in the short term parking lot after paying at the machine for the parking costs.

We go back and have a quick lunch at the house while I feed the kids and Julie clucks over them all. They've grown and changed a lot since she saw them last. They were just newborns then and even though I'm sending lots of pictures of them all it's nice for her to be with them, even if it's just for a short time. They all lap up the attention, but before too long we put them down for their afternoon nap and drive back to the hospital.

Julie practically runs to Dads door and pushes it open forcefully when she finds it. We follow her in to the room as she throws her arms around Dads shoulders and bursts into tears again. He pats her back in comfort as she clings to him and sobs for a while. Noah and I stand back and let her have her moment. I've had plenty of moments since this first happened so we allow her time to recover before moving in to take her place, giving Dad a quick kiss on the cheek in greeting.

"Hey Jules. You didn't need to come Love. I'm fine, but I'm sure that Mia's been telling you a lot of nonsense to the contrary." He says over my shoulder as I squeeze him in a tight hug.

"Hey I don't do that!" I say with a laugh as I pull away and Noah grabs me, pulling me in to lean against him, my back to his chest.

"I had to come Dad. Needed to see for myself that you're okay. Plus, I wanted to be here for the stint, which I thought would be in a few days, but now it's been moved up to today. So I'm glad that I got here in time." She says as she grabs his hand and holds it tightly. "So how are you doing old fella?"

He snorts with derision at her question. "Not so much of the old thanks Missy. I'm fine. I just want to get this over and done with and get home again. The sooner the better."

"We can stay in Perth as long as you need Don." Noah says looking to me for confirmation and I nod in agreement. "Whatever you need you just tell us and it'll happen."

"I think the nurse said before that I'll need to stay in Perth for a few days at least, but until I actually have it done there's no way to know, but she did say that I'd spend the night up in Special Care."

"If that's what you need to do then that's what you do. Listen to the Doc and do what he says." Julie tells him as she sits in the chair beside his bed, still holding his hand.

"What time are they taking you down Don? Do you know?" Noah asks as he leans down to kiss the top of my head. We always need to be touching somehow. It's like a physical craving. If we had our way we'd never leave the bed and never get dressed again. His fingers run down arms and then wrap around me again. I look up at him and he leans down for a kiss.

"Alright you two cut it out or get a room!" Julie says sarcastically. "Geez, people would think you were newlyweds or something!"

"Not quite, our wedding anniversary is coming up just after Christmas, so I suppose technically we are still newlyweds for a bit longer." Noah tells her with a wry grin.

"It's quite obvious. I wonder if you'll still be doing that after twenty years together." She says.

"Somehow I think we will, wont we Baby?" He replies as he focuses on me and our eyes lock. I nod and smile up at him before turning in his arms and getting up on my toes to reach him for a kiss. My hand runs down the side of his face as I wonder to myself how I could ever stop wanting him or needing him close. It's just not possible. My love for him shows in my eyes as I pull away and look up at him. Like they have a mind of their own my fingers run over his lips, tracing the outline of them lightly.

"Never. It's never gonna happen. When we're old an gray and wrinkly, I'll still want you as much as I do now." I tell him softly.

"Oh please…get me a bucket! I think I'm gonna be sick." Julie teases, making retching sounds behind me as Dad laughs loudly.

"Shut ya face, you two! You're both just jealous." I tell them with a laugh.

"I can assure you Gert, I'm not jealous in the least bit. He's definitely not my type. Sorry Son." Dad says still laughing loudly.

"All good Don. You're not my type either, but your daughter here…well she's more than enough for me for the rest of my life.

Definitely my type, aren't you Sweetheart." I tell her as I look down into her eyes, lovingly.

"Better be." She says quietly with a small smile.

"Dad make them stop!" Julie wails looking for support.

Dad laughs again at us and shakes his head. "Don't think they would anyway. Leave them be Jules. You'll get used to them. I have, they're like this all the time. Ah, young love."

"Oh please. Noah you look like you want to devour her right here." She tells him indignantly.

"I DO!" He laughingly replies, as I swat his arm and blush deeply. Everyone laughs at his words and I hug him to me even tighter.

"Right well I don't know what the joke is, but it looks like we've missed it anyway Joe." A medical orderly says from the doorway as he turns to his mate behind the stretcher.

"You wouldn't get it if I told you." Dad tells them from his bed.

"You ready for this Don?" He asks as he moves the stretcher into place beside the bed so that Dad can just slide across on to it. "That's the way. Don't worry, we'll have you back here in no time." He says as he covers him with blankets and grabs his chart from the end of the bed. "He'll be fine, guys, I promise we'll look after him. The ward nurse will let you know when he gets up to Special Care. You know that he'll have to spend the night up there don't you?" We all nod in reply as they push the stretcher out to the hallway for more room. I follow quickly as they stop outside the door.

Leaning in to place a kiss on his cheek, I tell him I love him and I'll see him soon. Julie does the same, but with tears filling her eyes. Once they move down the corridor to the elevators we follow them till they're out of sight. Still standing in the hallway Julie and I link hands for support, Noah pulls me back into his chest again and wraps his arms around my shoulders. "He'll be fine Baby. Just wait and see."

"I hope you're right Noah. I really do." Julie tells him over her shoulder, her head still facing towards the elevators at the end of the hallway.

He unwraps one arm from around me and lays it along her shoulder pulling us both in for a hug. "He's a tough ol' bastard. He did fine yesterday, so there's no reason to think he won't today. Why don't we go downstairs for a coffee while we wait for him?"

"Yeah good idea. I need a drink, but I'm too nervous to eat anything. C'mon Sis, my shout." I say, pulling her behind me, Noah lets us both go and follows us to the elevators.

Two hours later and I've began pacing the floor. Noah's at the window, looking out at the city lights and Julie's half asleep in the chair beside the bed. The nurses know that we're waiting for news and keep coming in to offer us a drink or a sandwich. Noah accepts, both gratefully but there's no way I could stomach any food right now. My is churning madly and I'm worried that my coffee's going to make a surprise return.

I walk over to the window and stand beside Noah who turns to study me. "He'll be fine Babe." He says reassuringly rubbing a hand up and down my back.

"It's taking too long Hun, I'm beginning to panic." I tell him quietly, conscious of Julie slumped in the armchair next to us.

"Don't. He'll be alright. Look what happened yesterday. Maybe the same thing happened today? Maybe they were late starting and that's why he's been gone so long. Or maybe they want to get him settled upstairs before they let us know that he's okay."

"I'm trying to be positive, truly I am…but it stopped working about an hour or so ago." I tell him softly, wrapping my arms around my waist, mainly to stop my hands from shaking. Noah moves forward and wraps his arms around me and kisses my forehead in support.

"I know Sweetheart. It's been a long day for all of us. Once we know that he's okay we can go home and rest easy." He whispers back to me.

"I'm glad that you're here Baby. I don't know what I'd do without you." I say as I lift my face for a quick kiss.

Our lips meet tenderly and I savor the taste of him. He tastes like coffee, even though it's been a while since he had one. I rub my lips over his softly as our tongues meet in the middle.

"Oh god not again! Do you two ever stop?" We hear from the arm chair and we pull apart with a smile. His eyes are dancing with laughter as he looks down at Julie. "Nope I don't think I could if I wanted to. Sorry Jules, like your Dad said…you're just gonna have to get used to it."

"Get used to what?" We hear from the doorway and turn to see Logan standing there looking confused.

"Get used to us kissing constantly. Ask Logan Jules. He'll tell you that it doesn't stop." Noah says with a smirk at his brother's expression of disgust.

"He's right Julie. They're always doing it…like…ALWAYS doing it. It's really sickening sometimes." He says shaking his head with a laugh. "I keep telling Mia that she chose the wrong brother, but she doesn't believe me for some unknown reason."

"That reason would be because she chose the *right* brother, Dickhead." Noah tells him.

"I definitely did. Sorry Logan, I did choose you to be my brother-in-law, but I absolutely chose the right man for my husband." I tell them all as I look up to meet Noah's grin.

"So where's Don?" Logan asks, changing the subject.

"Still not back yet. He's going up to Special Care for the night so he won't be coming back here at all, but we're still waiting to hear that he's up there and settled so that we can all go and visit." Noah tells him.

"Oh right. What time's he due back?" He asks, looking around to all of us in turn. "I just thought I'd pop in because Hannah moved our date from tonight to tomorrow, she said she had a headache or something like that. I thought I'd come and check on him instead. I got caught up at the office otherwise I'd have been here earlier."

"Problem at the office Bro?" Noah asks with concern and a bit of guilt. I know that he's been torn between staying here with me and going in to the office with Logan. I'm glad that he's here, but I know that he needs to go in to do some work as well.

"Nothing I couldn't handle. Don't stress Dude. It's all good." He says giving Noah a reassuring look. I'm grateful for the attempt. but I doubt that Noah's reassured at all. His face confirms it.

"How about you go in tomorrow and Jules and I'll come to the hospital to stay with Dad. I know that you need him Logan and I'm sorry I've been monopolizing his time like this." I tell him on an apology.

"Na it's fine Mia. I've managed okay without him this week. Shit happens as I told him before, but I'll be glad to have him back for a while if you don't need him hanging around." He says on a nod.

"Oi you two...I'm right here! I can decide for myself if I come in or not Logan. You aren't the boss of me." He says like a petulant child and we all laugh at him. That breaks the tension in the room and I laugh as loud as the rest of them. Just then the door flies open and a scowling nurse tells us all to keep it down. Apparently we're being very loud and noisy. She then tells us that Dad is about to be taken up to the ward and she'll let us know when we can go and visit.

Immediately we're contrite and apologetic for laughing so loud. I'm also relieved and clinging to Noah as he slides his arm around my waist, otherwise I may well have fallen to the floor and he knows it. Julie's crying in relief as we all say a silent prayer of thanks that he's okay. I'm itching to see him and make sure for myself, I know that everyone else in the room feels the same. At his age anything could go wrong at any time so it's amazing that he's come through this unscathed. Lucky for him, it wasn't much a worse heart attack. We are lucky that he's always been healthy and fit.

After what seems like hours and two trips down to the cafeteria for coffee later, a nurse finally comes in and tells us that we can go up for a quick visit. The guys wait outside while we go into the Special Care ward to find him. He's sleeping peacefully and I glance up to his heart monitor to see his heart rate is steady and fine. Thank god for that, and I'm sure Julie's thinking the same as she follows my gaze.

He's lying flat on the bed with one pillow supporting his head. He hates having one pillow to sleep on. He needs more than that. There must be a reason that he only has a very flat one. The nurse comes over and smiles at us both as she quietly tells us that he's fine and he's had a sedative and he needs to keep his legs straight over night, but other than that if he's okay tomorrow afternoon then he can be discharged. So far he's doing all the right things. His heart beat is steady and slow and he's not bleeding from his entry site.

Just as she finishes speaking Dad's eyes open slowly and he focuses on us both standing on one side of his bed. I lean in to kiss his cheek lightly and he has trouble keeping his eyes open as he says, "Hey Gert."

"Hey yourself old man. You've had a big day. How are you feeling now besides tired?" I ask him quietly, so as not to disturb everyone else around him.

"Hey Jules." He says, looking over to her. "I'm okay Love. No pain or anything. Just tired. I feel like I've been hit by a bus. I'm totally exhausted." He says, slurring his words. The nurse assures us that it's just the sedative that's making him so groggy. Apparently they drug them well after the procedure so that they rest and recover and don't move around too much. It's important that he keep his legs flat on the bed all night so that his wound heals and he doesn't bleed out from the groin incision that he has.

Julie and I leave after five minutes or so as he falls back to sleep almost immediately. I've seen him and made sure for myself that he's fine so I'm happy to go. I walk over to the nurse to ensure that she has our contact details if she needs us for any reason and she grabs his chart to check and assures us that she does.

I follow Julie out the door to the two large males waiting on the other side, leaning against a wall near the elevators. As soon as Noah sees us he straightens and walks over to me enveloping me in his arms. "How is he Babe?" He asks anxiously.

"He's good. Very drowsy, but other than that the nurse said he's doing well. He can't keep his eyes open so we thought we'd leave him to sleep." I tell him, snuggling into his warm chest.

"Yeah I'm surprised that he's doing this well. At his age every procedure is risky." Julie tells us as she presses the button for the elevator and the doors slide open immediately. We all follow her into the large space and lean against the wide rail that surrounds the stainless steel interior.

"Did he have any history of heart problems at home Jules?" Logan asks her curiously.

"No not that I know about, though since he carries a spray for angina, he must have and not told me. I had no idea. The first I knew about it was when Mia rang me to tell me that he'd had a heart attack. I couldn't believe it. I was totally stunned." She says, shaking her head at the memory. Logan follows us home for a beer with Noah and to catch him up on the work problems I think.

We chat as we drive home, we're still talking when we walk in to the chaos of our home. Alice and Callan are screaming loudly as Maxine hurriedly feeds Jake his bottle, all the while trying to shush the other hungry children. I run over and scoop up Alice as Noah strides over to Callan and does the same.

They settle for a minute, but soon start demanding their milk. I sit down on the sofa and get a cushion for my lap as Maxine gives a sigh of relief that we're home while I pull up my t-shirt and start feeding the hungry babies. Once again I hear Noah slap Logan upside of the head as he mutters, "Eyes off Dickhead. How many times do I have to say it?"

Poor Logan looks like he wishes the ground would open up and swallow him as he sputters, "Shit...sorry Mia...oh shit...sorry Ma! Ah Fuck!"

His mother gives him the one eyebrow raised look which tells him to shut up immediately and he obeys her silent command. I laugh at him and Julie joins me as he blushes a deep pink and quickly makes his apologies and leaves. We hear his car start up and drive away in the silence of the night.

"Noah stop being cruel to him." I admonish him with a scowl.

"Fu...sorry, bugger him Sweetheart. He's obsessed with your boobs, the little perv, and only I have that privilege." He says as his mother gives him the evil stare at his near slip of the tongue. I put my head down as a smile breaks over my face and I focus on the hungry babies in my lap.

"Thank God you all got here when you did. I was trying to figure out how I could feed the other two with my feet! Won't be long and they'll be able to hold their own bottles, but they aren't quite there yet." She says, looking a bit frazzled. I apologize for staying so long at the hospital and, she immediately stops me with a ,"Shush Sweetie. It's fine. I'd have coped somehow."

The next morning Noah leaves early for the office and Julie and I feed and bathe the babies and put them down for their morning nap and then drive to the hospital in Scarlett's new BMW, which replaced her old one that was written off in the accident. It drives well and we find a car park easily, thank goodness. I'm not sure if Dad will be allowed to go home this morning or not.

I rang Special Care when I got up this morning, they said that he had a comfortable night and may be moved back down to his room this morning, once the Cardiologist had a chance to review him. We make our way there first and check to see if he's back in his private room yet. Unfortunately, he isn't so we go up to Special Care and wait for the Doc to arrive. The nurses are pleased with his progress and make a fuss of their "Star patient", who's lapping up all of the attention.

Once he's settled back into the private room he falls asleep again as Julie and I chat quietly amongst ourselves. The Specialist wants him to stay for another day so we make our way home at lunchtime to eat and feed the kids while he's still sleeping.

Once they're fed Julie makes some lunch for us all and then we leave Maxine to play with them while we go back to sit with Dad for a while longer, promising to be back for their next feed.

Dad's awake and feeling better when we get back to his room. Noah texted to check how he was doing, which I appreciate because I know how busy he is at work today. It's the small things like this that make him a wonderful husband.

The next day is much the same. More waiting around for Dad to get discharged from the hospital. Its lunchtime before all of the paperwork is done and we actually walk outside, keeping a close eye on Dad as we walk slowly to the car.

Once he's home, we rearrange things so that Julie shares a room with Maxine for the remainder of her stay. The babies take up one bedroom, we have another and Dad has the last downstairs bedroom. That way he doesn't have to exert himself climbing up the stairs.

At the end of the week we go back for his check-up before driving Julie to the airport for her flight home. There are a few tears as we say goodbye, but Dad's grateful that she came over to keep an eye on him. Saying goodbye again was hard for all of us, I'm not sure when she'll be back over again for a visit. I know that Dad planned to stay for another month or so before going back to Adelaide. I ask him about his plans on the way home from the hospital, luckily his plans don't seem to have changed. He can relax and recover from his surgery here on the farm.

Noah left early for the office and I haven't heard from him by dinner time, so I'm assuming that he's been caught up at work. I've tried ringing, but it just goes straight to voice mail. He must be *really* busy, he always answers. By 10pm, I'm beginning to get worried. It's not like him to be so late without calling me. I've sent numerous texts, but they've gone unanswered as well. I read my book until my eyes can't focus anymore.

I realize I just can't keep this up and settle in to the bed to sleep. Maybe he just had a late phone conference or meeting. I can't complain after all of the time that he's spent with me the last few days. I don't want to be one of *those* women. I know that he's needed in the office, and I have to get used to him working long hours like he used to before we met.

The morning light shining through the blinds wakes me and I automatically reach across the bed for Noah. I find his side of the bed empty. I sit up quickly, listening to hear if the shower's on, but there's no sound from the bathroom. I get up and softly walk down the stairs to see if he collapsed on the sofa so he wouldn't disturb me, but there's no one downstairs either. I glance up at the clock and see that its 6:15am.

I try his phone once more and it goes straight to voice mail, yet again. Now I'm *really* starting to panic. He's been gone all night with no phone call, which has never happened before. Where the fuck is he?

I leave a terse message on his phone for him to call me immediately and start pacing the living room, my anger taking over any concern I have about his wellbeing. How thoughtless of him. Why couldn't he just text me and tell me that he was going to be late and why the fuck isn't he home now? All night and no word. After more pacing I'm fuming. I try his direct number at the office, but it just rings out. Now I'm pissed AND worried, not a fun combination, if you ask me.

I decide to try Logan's mobile and he answers right as I'm about to hang up. Groggily he says, "Hello?" I ask him if he's with Noah. "Not now. I left him at the bar with the others last night. I'd had enough and needed my bed. Why what's up? He asks as he yawns loudly.

"He didn't come home and he isn't answering his phone. I'm getting worried and pissed off. Who was he out with?" I demand, getting angrier by the minute.

"Ummm we all went out together for a few drinks, a couple of clients and a mate. They were all standing upright when I left them, but they'd definitely had more than their fair share of drink. Noah was pretty merry, last I saw of him, but I thought he was heading home soon after me. Let me try to track him down and I'll give you a call back. He's probably sleeping it off somewhere."

I give him a terse "Thanks," and end the call. I look down at the phone in my hand and will it to ring and let me know that he's alright. My stomach is in knots and I feel like I'm half a breath away from a full blown panic attack. I sit down on the sofa and concentrate on my breathing, trying to slow it down before I hyperventilate. My heart's racing a million miles an hour and I rub my chest as I take a deep breath and hold it before letting it out slowly. My phone rings loudly in the silence. I grab it and quickly answer with a panicked "Hello?!" Logan says "Sorry no luck. Dave said that they left him at the bar alone, but apparently he was gonna catch a cab home. You sure he's not there anywhere?"

"NO! He's not home, you moron! Sorry...I'm freaking out here! He hasn't slept in his bed and he isn't on the sofa. Where the fuck is he?" I ask angrily pacing the floor biting my bottom lip in frustration.

"He won't be far Mia. I'll go in to the office extra early and see if he's passed out on a sofa. I'll let you know as soon as I get there. Give me half hour or so okay?" I can hear the worry in his voice as he ends the call.

With nothing better to do till the babies wake for their breakfast, I use the remote to turn on the television, catching the end of the morning news headlines. I'm so deep in thought that

I almost miss it when the newsreader starts telling about a prisoner escaping from a jail in Perth overnight. It's only when I hear Jackson's name mentioned that I sit forward and take notice.

Oh my Fucking God. That's him! My worst nightmare. His face fills the screen as the newsreader warns everyone not to approach him as he may be armed and dangerous. Fuck, Fuck, Fuck! My almost panic attack develops instantly into the worst one yet. I'm trembling all over and I feel like I can't get any air into my lungs. I open my mouth to gulp in some oxygen, feeling like a goldfish. Pins and needles travel down my arms and my heart's pounding so hard I'm worried I'll have a heart attack at any moment.

'Where's Noah...where's Noah? Where the Fuck is he?" I'm really freaking out now. I need Noah...now! Right this minute. Tears stream down my face as adrenaline floods my body and I feel like I need to run far away...but I can't run and I can't stay like this.

From upstairs, I hear Callan crying to let the world know that he's awake. Trying my best to ignore the story on the television screen I rapidly pull myself together and walk up the stairs to get him before he wakes the whole house. I'm sure he's already woken the other two.

I run into the nursery and almost trip as my foot connects with a large pile of blankets. "Who the fuck left these here?" I think as I steady myself from the almost fall. I hear a pained groan and my husband's drowsy, stubble covered face emerges from the lumpy pile of blankets. He has a large red mark, in the same pattern as his shirt, which tells me he used his arm as a pillow all night.

"Fuck! Noah, you damn near killed me! What the hell are you doing in here?" I screech at him, as my anger reaches Def-con 5. It's not often I explode, but watch out when I do, and now he's *really* pissed me the fuck off. My rage is the only thing I can think about. How dare he worry me like this?! What a fucking arsehole!

"You goddamn son of a bitch! Where the fuck have you been all night?!" I hiss at him, conscious of where we are. All the kids are awake and gibbering quietly. They're watching us intently, wondering what's going on. They know by the tone of my voice that I'm not happy, but they don't know why.

"Fuck Baby, calm down. Inside voice remember." He says groggily as he runs his hand up over his face and through his hair, while he sits up slowly, groaning loudly as he does. "Ohhh shit, my head feels like it's about to explode," He complains softly.

"I can't believe this....do you have any idea how worried I was? I thought you were dead in an alley somewhere! How dare you not let me know that you're okay? That is not acceptable Noah. No way, no how. Right now I hope your head does explode because you deserve it!" I yell at him, blinded by rage. I can hardly think straight, I'm so angry with him.

I hear Maxine come in and watch as she takes Callan and Alice downstairs for their breakfast, but doesn't look at us as she does it. I wait until she leaves before lashing out at him again viciously. "You fucking bastard. Did you even think about how worried I'd be huh? Did I enter your head at all as you were partying with your mates while I was here with our children? I can't believe you never answered my calls or texts. Why would you deliberately worry me like that? Well?! Say something!"

"Fuck me. I would if you'd just take a breath for a minute." He says getting to his feet unsteadily. His eyes are red and bloodshot and he looks like shit, but I don't care. I continue to rant at him, getting angrier by the minute.

"Give me one good reason why I should? As far as I'm concerned you deserve everything I give you right now. You inconsiderate, lowdown mongrel. I can't believe that you thought so little of me that you didn't even text me or come to bed when you got home at least. How could you let me worry like that? Where the fuck were you?" I say as I pick up Jake who's now crying in his cot at the raised voices. I kiss him gently on the cheek and rock him on my hip as I turn back to Noah.

"If this is how it's gonna be for the rest of our lives, you can count me out. No way am I putting up with you disappearing all night. This is *not* how it's going to be...I can guarantee it." I tell him loudly, trying to get my anger under control for Jake's sake. He's picking up on the tension in the room as I berate his father, whom he worships.

"Geez Sweetheart, give me a fucking break. I could explain if you'd let me." He says, getting angry himself now as he runs both of his hands up through his hair messing it up.

"Go on then. Tell me why you couldn't be bothered calling me or texting last night to let me know where you were or what time you'd be home?" I say defiantly, lifting my chin slightly, waiting for him to come up with a good excuse. Nothing he says is going to calm me at the moment. There's no excuse in the world that will make this right.

"I left my phone at the office to charge it." He says pinning me with his bleary eyes.

"And you couldn't have borrowed Logan's to tell me where you were? Give me a break." I say harshly, jiggling Jake on my hip even though he's stopped crying now.

"Logan's was at the office too. He forgot it and didn't go back for it till he was going home. I didn't intend to be so late, but things just kinda got out of hand. On drink lead to another and another and we were chatting, before I knew it I was pissed out of my brain. Everyone deserted me so, I eventually flagged down a cab and came home, but I didn't want to disturb you so I thought I'd stay in here with my babies and keep them company." He looks down at the pile of blankets at his feet and shakes his head. "It seemed perfectly logical at 2am."

I take a few deep breaths and walk out of the room heading downstairs with Jake, who's getting impatient for his breakfast, totally ignoring Noah. I'm too angry to speak to him right now. I'll wait till I've calmed down, which may be never or eternity. That's how enraged I am. I feel worthless and betrayed.

"Morning Maxine, Dad." I say as I flop down on the sofa to feed two of them. Seeing as Jake is the most impatient, I attach him first then Maxine passes over Alice while Dad feeds Callan a bottle. After they've all finished we place them in their high chairs for their cereal and fruit. They love sucking on bits of fruit at the moment, but they make such a mess I don't know if it's worth it some days. We each feed one baby and I watch Callan as he rubs a strawberry through his dark hair, leaving a trail of red goo as he does.

Dad and Maxine have been talking amongst themselves and leaving me be, which I'm grateful for as I run over the conversation in my head. Or rather my ranting at him as he stood there and took it all. I'm still too angry at him to be concerned about how he's feeling as he wanders downstairs slowly still looking like crap.

"Hey Mum. Don." He says with a small lift of his chin in greeting. "Babe do we have any painkillers? My head feels like someone's stomping on it from the inside."

I walk over to the kitchen and yank open the cabinet where the medicines are kept out of the way. I grab the bottle of painkillers and almost throw them at him as I walk back to my seat at the dining table.

"Thanks." He mutters filling a glass with water and gulping them down quickly, draining the glass as he drinks. I'm sure he's dehydrated. He certainly smells like a damn brewery. Alcohol seeps out of every pore and he definitely needs a shower.

"Big night last night Son?" Maxine asks him with a smirk. I'm sure she's seen him like this before, but I haven't and I don't appreciate it.

I raise my eyes to glare over at him as he lowers his head, not meeting my eyes.

"No it didn't start out like that despite what my lovely wife thinks. We just went out for a few drinks and got a bit carried away."

My snort of derision is audible all the way across to the kitchen as he raises his head sharply and fixes me with his blue eyes.

"I tried to tell you upstairs, but you were too busy yelling to listen to anything that I said. I never ignored your calls or texts, my phone's still at the office, if you want to check. I'm sure Logan's there by now. Ring him and find out." He says waving his hand to my phone on the bench.

"Shit Logan!" I say as I fly out of my chair and over to grab up my phone. "He's still looking for you. I should let him know that you're home. He was as worried as I was. Another person you need to apologize to."

"Is that what this is about?" He says angrily, glaring at me from the other side of the kitchen island. "You want me to apologize?! Well Fuck! Sorry if I had the audacity to be considerate and not wake you in the middle of the night by coming to bed. It won't happen again I can assure you. Next time I'll bring home a fucking brass band to announce my arrival!"

I hear Dad say quietly behind me. "Shit, he's done it now!" as Maxine answers with a quiet giggle, almost immediately stifled by her hand over her mouth.

I glare back at my brooding husband, as I unlock my phone and quickly dial Logan's number. He answers almost immediately and waits while I tell him that his brother made it home last night after all and he can call off the search party. He picks up from my tone of voice that I'm furious and just tells me that he's glad that he's home safe and sound, and doesn't ask any questions. I'm in no mood for small talk, so I rapidly end the conversation, but not before he says, "Tell him his phone is still on the desk charging, will you? He must have forgot it like I did. I left mine in my bloody suit jacket because I didn't put it on when we left. It was a nice warm night, never thought about it to tell you the truth."

I look over to Noah with a slightly less icy glare realizing that he would have heard the conversation, because he raises one eyebrow expectantly. I turn my back on him, knowing that I'm being a bitch, but I need to get my anger under control before I say something else that I'll regret later. I see a quick look pass between Maxine and Dad, but neither of them says a word, allowing us the time to work through this without interference.

I sit down and wipe off the worst part of the goo on Callan before taking him upstairs for a bath. I half fill the bathtub with warm water and bubble bath and place some toys in it before stripping Callan down and carefully lifting him into the water. He splashes excitedly as Maxine brings up the other two and we do the same with them. The kids love bath time and I love watching them play happily in the water. Jake picks up a small cup and fills it with water and tips it out over and over again, laughing loudly as he does it.

Alice loves to slap at the water getting everything wet that sits in a meter radius of the tub. She shrieks as she hits the water and it splashes onto Callan's face, but he doesn't look impressed and bangs a small plastic boat on her head in retaliation. Her shrieks instantly turn into cries and I soothe her by wiping her over with a soft sponge which she loves. She constantly tries to take it from me to suck on.

Everything goes into their mouths at this age. They're all teething after all. Drool is constantly running out of their mouths and each of them has a huge bib on or one of us wiping at their chin to clear it.

I feel Noah enter rather than hear him. We always know when the other is in the room, even if we can't see them. It's like a sixth sense. Maxine gets up from the floor beside the bath tub and leaves the room as Noah takes her place, picking up a sponge and running it over Callan's head lightly.

We sit in silence for a while just enjoying play time with the babies till the water starts to get cold and I pick up Alice and dry her quickly before wrapping her in her hooded towel. I then quickly do the same for the others. Noah manages to balance both of the boys on his hips as he walks them into our bedroom and places them gently down on the bed before climbing on with them. It's quite warm in the room, it gets that way with the morning sun. I can tell it's going to be a hot day because the sun already has some heat in it as it streams through the sheer curtains.

I place Alice down with her brothers and turn away to get their clothes for the day. I return from the nursery with clean nappies for them all and their clothes. Once they're dressed I climb onto the bed as well deciding that now is a good time to clear the air, despite still being angry, even though I know he told me the truth about last night.

"So have you calmed down enough to talk about this like rational adults?" He inquires as though we're discussing the weather. I realize that he's keeping his tone light because of the kids. He doesn't want to upset them, which I'm thankful for even though I was the one who scared them this morning with all of my yelling and screaming.

"Not really, but I know we have to do it." I tell him with a sigh of resignation.

"I'm sorry if I worried you. That was never my intention, you have to believe that. I feel bad that you were so upset by me not calling or waking you when I got home. I thought I was doing the right thing, in my beer addled brain, by not disturbing you."

"So why didn't you sleep downstairs on the sofa? It would have been more comfortable than the floor surely?" I ask as my anger finally diminishes and common sense prevails at last. "It must have been really uncomfortable even with the mat on the floor."

"I was too drunk to notice. I don't really remember much after I got home. I honestly had no idea that you'd be waiting up or worrying like that. As I said, I was pissed. I'm not a big drinker and these guys kept plying me with it. I think they wanted to finally see what I looked like after a few too many. Yeah that worked out well for me didn't it? Remind me to kick their arses next time I see them." He says with a smirk. Obviously the painkillers are working, because he has a bit more color. in his face now and his eyes have cleared. Jake climbs all over him and pulls at his bottom lip firmly, running his fingers over his teeth and scratching over his bottom gums.

"Ugh, come here you big bruiser. Play nicely with your siblings." I say as I pull him away from Noah and place him back on the bed with his toys. He immediately grabs two wooden blocks and bangs them together loudly, laughing at himself as he bangs them harder and harder. Noah blinks each time the blocks connect and I know that it must be hurting his head. I was wrong about the painkillers. His grimace as Jake knocks the blocks together confirming my thoughts.

"Steady on Buddy. Daddy can't take much more of that. Can't you find a teddy bear to play with?" He asks him as he swaps the blocks for a toy car. Jake raises it to his mouth and proceeds to drool over it, but at least he's momentarily quiet.

"So it never occurred to you that I'd be worried? You couldn't ask one of the other guys to borrow their phone? One text to tell me that you'd be late. That's all it would have taken. You have no idea the thoughts that were running through my head. I thought that Jackson had somehow tracked you down and everything that went through my mind wasn't pretty, I can tell you." I say, my voice quavering with emotion as I talk about my deepest fear about Jackson punishing me for testifying against him by getting back at Noah or the babies.

"What the hell are you talking about? How could hurt me from maximum security prison?" He asks with a deep frown, not understanding.

I look at him, my eyes haunted and filled with tears. "He escaped yesterday and they think he's armed and dangerous."

I'm not prepared for the explosion as Noah flies off the bed and stands beside it with his fists clenched. I can see the vein in his neck pulsing as he clenches his jaw tightly. "Why the hell didn't someone let us know as soon as it happened? How did you find out?"

I look up at him as I relay the news broadcast and how I panicked at the thought of him getting to Noah somehow.

"Oh shit...Baby I'm so sorry. You know that if I'd known, I would have been home immediately. Fuck, of all the nights to not have my phone on me. It'll never happen again." He says fiercely as he paces the floor of the large room. "God, I had no idea! I can't believe it. How the fuck does a monstrously big guy like that escape from maximum security?" He mutters.

"They didn't actually say, but I got the impression that he hurt a guard and maybe stole his gun as well. They did say that at least one guard had to be taken to hospital." I tell him matter of factly. "Noah I'm a bit worried about this. What if he's coming here? Dad doesn't know anything about the attack and I don't want him to. He can't be worrying about that at the moment with his heart issues."

"I know, but we'll need to tell him something. We can't leave him in the dark." He says thoughtfully. "How about we just tell him that he's in jail because he was Carl Brown's accomplice in a lawsuit against me. Hopefully he won't ask too many questions, but at least then he'll be aware of the danger and look out for you and the kids if I'm not here."

"Okay that works. I really don't want him to know the whole story though Hun. It's not like he can change the past. He'd just get upset and angry and that isn't good for him right now. He's supposed to be resting and recovering."

"I agree." Noah says on a nod. "We're still telling him the truth, but not the whole truth. It's your story to tell if you want him to know the rest. I'll abide by whatever you want to do." "Thank you." I say sincerely. "Now let's go downstairs with these munchkins and wear them out for their nap. I think a tickle session's needed right now." I say on a laugh, but inside my gut is churning violently and I feel like I'm going to be sick. I'm determined to put on a brave face and pretend that nothing is wrong, that way Dad won't worry. A smile covers my face as I descend the stairs with Jake, while Noah carries Callan and Alice down in his arms.

Dad and Maxine share a look, then both of them look over to us with a questioning gaze. "Sorry guys. I was being a bitch earlier, but I'm fine now. I was just totally freaking out when Noah wasn't home, but we talked and it's all good now." I say as Noah nods in confirmation.

"It wasn't just me staying out late that she was worried about. Don, we haven't been entirely open with you." He says as Dad raises an eyebrow and looks over to him, waiting for him to continue. "Fuck...sorry Ma." He apologizes as soon as the word leaves his mouth. Maxine nods for him to continue. "The truth is that there's a guy who's pissed off at me because of some shit that happened with the company and he ended up in jail because of it. Mia found out this morning that he somehow escaped and they reckon he's armed and dangerous. That's why she was having a meltdown."

I hear Mum's exclamation of surprise as her shocked eyes fly to meet mine, with a knowing look. Instantly she understands what Noah's doing and gives me a slight nod of her head to confirm that she'll stay quiet.

"Exactly how dangerous is he?" Dad asks, realizing that Noah didn't give details about the charges against Jackson. "Is he likely to come after you Son?" A frown creases his forehead as he waits for Noah to reply.

"He might, but we have a security system as you know and I honestly doubt that he'll come here. It'll be the most obvious place so he wouldn't be that dumb." He tries to reassure them both, but I can see it isn't working as the frown on Dad's face deepens even more.

"Have you talked to the police yet?" Maxine asks worriedly, looking from Noah to me with concern etched on her face.

Noah shakes his head, replying "Not yet no. I'm gonna ring them now and see what's happening. It's entirely possible that they apprehended him since the broadcast this morning. I can't believe that they didn't even ring us to let us know. That's just crap and I'll tell them so as well." He vibrates anger as he strides quickly to his office, slamming the door behind him after he enters.

Startled, Callan begins crying from his activity chair in the living room where we put them. This starts the other two as well and we all walk over to scoop them up and settle them. They quiet down after a few minutes and we all sit on the sofa and wait for Noah to return. I lean in and tickle Callan's stomach lightly as he giggles and throws around his arms and kicks wildly. Dad and Maxine follow suit and soon they're all laughing loudly as we play.

The office door opens eventually and a calmer Noah walks over to the sofa. He sits down next to me and picks up Callan placing a kiss on his forehead as he does.

"So what happened? What did they say?" I ask quickly.

He looks over to me and says, "Not much. It took me forever to actually talk to someone who knew what was going on, and even then they don't know much. Nobody rang us because they were going to send out an officer this morning to tell us in person apparently. They did say that they have a couple of leads that they're following up, but they assured me that they're also doing frequent patrols up our street as a precaution. He advised us all to stay in today and have the alarm set, but they doubt that he'd attempt to come here. They think he's long gone, but they're not sure where exactly."

He finishes by scrubbing his hand up over his face, and I pick up on the anxiousness of the movement.

He's not telling me the whole story and he knows that I know it, I don't push it because of Dad, but you can bet your ass I'll ask him when we're alone. I hate not knowing when something involves me and this certainly falls into that category. I give him a nod of understanding as he turns back to play with Callan.

Dad looks over to him with concern. "Do you have any weapons in the house Noah? Just in case the bastard does do the stupid thing and come here?"

Shaking his head, Noah gives him a wry smile. "Never needed any before Mate. Not even a baseball bat unfortunately. Believe me though, if that bastard shows up, I'll be doing everything in my power to make sure he doesn't leave alive."

Maxine huffs out a breath. "Noah that's not the way to be thinking. I agree that he'd be pretty stupid to come here, thinking of killing him is understandable, but not necessary. We'll just ring the police and hope that they're close by."

Noah shakes his head rapidly as he says firmly, "No Mum. If he shows up here he's a threat to my family and then he's a dead man. I'll do whatever I need to do to stop him and I won't bat an eye about it. Mia, the kids and you guys are my world and **nobody** messes with what's mine."

"Well let's hope it doesn't come to that Son. Surely he has more brains than to come here. Do you think we need to tell Logan if this involves your Company?" Dad says as he rubs over Alice's soft dark hair.

Noah and I look at each other quickly, realizing that we've forgotten about Logan. Noah hands Callan back to me and heads to the office to ring his brother and let him know what's going on.

I hear the murmur of voices as I put the baby into his chair again and follow Noah into the room, closing the door behind me. He raises an eyebrow in query, but doesn't stop his conversation as he turns back to the window again and tells Logan about what the police told him this morning while I stand waiting patiently in front of his large wooden desk. I hear him tell Logan that they warned him Jackson that could come here for retribution. They found a notebook in his cell that contained both Logan's and our addresses. Noah wants Logan to come here – safety in numbers and all that. Logan gets the unsaid message that says Noah wants backup just in case the big biker manages to break in despite the precautions. Now I'm really worried, but trying to hold it together and not show it. I wait until Noah's finished his call before interrogating him about what else they said that he didn't tell me.

Chapter
TWENTY
THREE

Noah

I know what she's asking me and I'm torn between telling her the truth and protecting her. Deciding that if it were me I'd want to know the truth. I start by telling her that the police have grave concerns for us and wanted us to move to a hotel for security until Jackson's found and dealt with.

They didn't want to alarm us, but apparently he'd been boasting in jail that he was gonna cut out my heart and finish what he started with Mia. As she listens the color. drains from her face and I can see her trembling and tears fill her eyes, but she doesn't let them fall, instead taking some deep breaths and steadying herself, taking the time to get her thoughts under control. I see fear flash across her face for a moment, but I blink and it's gone. Despite being immensely proud of how brave she's acting I know different. I know how terrified she is and I don't blame her.

Trying to make her feel safer, I also tell her that at this very moment there are two undercover cop cars parked in the street keeping an eye on the house for the rest of today. Logan agreed to come and stay over and I thank God that he understood my unspoken words.

If that bastard gets in, I'll do what I need to do to protect Mia and the babies, but I'd rather do it with his assistance. He's a member of a pistol club and has a license to own a firearm.

Working in the Pilbara there were times when a stray animal had to be humanly dealt with after being hit by a car or hurt somehow. I know that he has a pistol in his safe in the apartment and I hope he discreetly brings it with him when he comes.

I'm not an advocate of firearms, but this is an extenuating circumstance. Believe me right now if Jackson showed his face I could easily shoot him between the eyes. I've been to the pistol range with Logan and I know how to handle a gun.

I'll kill the mongrel with my bare hands if necessary, but it'd be quicker with a bullet. No, on second thought, my bare hands might be better because he'll suffer longer. I know that he's big, but he's fat and slow. I have fitness and speed on my side – all he has is bulk and brute force.

I gather Mia in my arms and hold her close while kissing the top of her head gently. "It'll be fine Sweetheart. I won't let him hurt you or the kids. I'll die first."

Instantly looking up and locking her gorgeous bright green eyes with mine she says, "That's what I'm afraid of Noah. That's my worst nightmare. I couldn't survive if something happened to you."

"Nothing's gonna happen to me Baby. This is suburban Perth. It's never gonna happen. They'll catch him soon, don't you worry." I say as I lean in for a kiss and lift my hand to run the back of my fingers down the side of her face. She closes her eyes at the touch and sighs deeply, before opening them again.

"I hope you're right Noah, truly I do. I want this pig out of our lives for good. I thought he already was," She tells me taking a deep breath in and letting it out on a long sigh.

"I know Mia, I know. Me too, but I still think that he wouldn't be dumb enough to come here. He'd have to know that it's the first place that the cops would look for him."

We stand there for a long while just holding each other and gathering our thoughts. A knock at the door tears us apart. I pull open the office door and tell Mia to stay there. I know it's probably only Logan, but I'm not about to take any chances. I approach the door gingerly before putting in the code to disarm the security system, turning the lock and pulling the handle, allowing my brother to enter quickly.

"Hey." He says as he passes me and I close the door and lock it again.

"Hey. Thanks for coming over Mate. I didn't want to alarm Mia, but I appreciate you being here just in case there's trouble. I hope you came prepared." I ask him knowing the answer before he speaks. He nods to tell me that he knows exactly what I'm asking about.

"Of course. It's loaded and ready in the back of my shorts. Hopefully nobody will look that closely at me. Never thought I'd need it for this Bro, gotta tell ya." He says with a shake of his head as we walk down across the entrance to the office.

I open the door and Mia immediately rushes over to me and smiles at Logan in greeting. "Thank god you're alright Logan. I was worried. I hope you realize that this's is probably a big fuss for no reason, but I'm glad that you're here. I'll sleep better tonight knowing that you're safe too."

He envelopes her in a bear hug, and tells her that he's glad to be here too. I can't help but notice that his eyes fly to the window and mine follow his and take in the fact that the shades aren't drawn. I quickly walk over and pull down the blind, then walk out to the other rooms and do the same, I don't want to leave anything to chance. If he's out there somewhere then I don't want him to be able to see us or know where we are in the house.

Thankfully Don and Mum doesn't ask questions about what I'm doing, though I've never closed the blinds facing the back yard before, it has a lot of privacy. I can feel Mum's eyes on my back as I walk from window to window quickly securing the blinds.

Mia walks out and puts on a brave face, hiding her fear well. Don gets up and walks to the kitchen with Alice on his hip and reaches up into a cupboard to get coffee cups for us all and proceeds to use the coffee maker passing one to each of us as they're ready. I give mine to Mia and then wait for the next cup patiently as I watch Mia carefully. I can see how much tension she's holding in and it scares me a bit that she's terrified right now and I can't do anything to help her. I won't let her out of my sight today, I don't care if I have to follow her to the bathroom and wait for her. There's no way I'll allow him to get close to her, though I still have my doubts about him coming here. He would have to know that we'd be waiting for him along with the police outside. He couldn't be that stupid could he?

We all chat while we drink our coffee and watch Logan on the floor playing with the kids. They're crawling all over him and slapping at him with glee as he tries to fend them off, by tickling them and blowing raspberries on their stomachs. Laughter fills the room and I realize that I love the sound of them all being so happy. Besides the sound of Mia as she cums around me, my kid's giggles are the next best sound in the universe I think.

As they all begin tiring and rubbing their eyes I scoop them up into my arms and walk with them upstairs for their nap. I put Alice in her bed while I change Jake's nappy and then do the same for her. Callan comes up with Mum and she does the same before putting him down and covering him over with a satin bound rug.

All day we sit around, Logan on the phone as he handles some work stuff and me in my office with the door open so that I can still see Mia as she watches television with her Dad and my mum. Intermittently we all take it in turns to go and check on the kids while they sleep and each time it's Mia's turn I follow her on the pretext of having to pee anyway.

Nightfall brings an anxious feeling and I know that I won't sleep tonight. I double check the alarm and every window to make sure that they're all locked. I feel a bit of cabin fever as I pace the large living room while everyone watches a movie, or pretends to watch it. I know that Mia's eyes are following me as I take long strides back and forth. I must be making her dizzy because she finally gets up and comes to me, halting me with a hand on my chest. I stop and look down at her as she raises her eyes to meet mine.

"Noah you're making me nervous. Please stop it. Come and sit and watch this DVD with us. Pacing the floor isn't going to help anyone." She says quietly pulling me over to sit down next to her on the large sofa. I have no idea what the movie is about, as I can't concentrate on it. Mia holds my hand with hers and periodically squeezes it to comfort me. I have a tingle in my spine and I don't know why...just a bad feeling.

I tell myself that it's just my paranoia getting the best of me, but I can't shake it. Mum and Don are the first to say goodnight and head off to bed and Logan goes to his room to take a call from overseas where it's early in the morning there. Mia snuggles into my chest and I wrap my arms around her. She doesn't seem to have the same bad feeling that I can't get rid of. I will myself to relax as she gives a deep sigh and her eyes finally close, despite her telling me earlier tonight that there was no way she'd be able to sleep.

I gently kiss her head and try to focus on the television, but my spider sense just won't allow me to relax completely. I stare at the glowing screen for a long time, but I have no idea what I'm looking at, my thoughts occupied elsewhere as Mia's warmth seeps into me. She's softly breathing, slow and deeply, so I know that she's fast asleep. I move slightly trying not to wake her as I slide my arm from around her and lay her back on some cushions. She stirs, but remains asleep. I stand up and decide to do another check of all the windows and doors.

Starting with the front door I twist the knob to check that it's locked, but then realize that I didn't check the security door when Logan arrived. I don't remember locking it. I slowly pull open the heavy wooden door and reach over to check the lock on the outer door when I'm thrown backwards by a force and searing pain tears into my right arm as I register a loud bang.

What the fuck?!!

I'm lying against the bottom of the stairs as I hear chaos erupt around me. Mia screams and starts running towards me as the babies wake up terrified by the noise and scream loudly joining hers.

I yell at her to stay where she is as Don comes flying out of his bedroom not 4 feet from where I'm lying. They both get to me about the same time as I see the front outer door almost fly off its hinges. Jackson looms in the doorway and it takes a minute to register what's happening.

I hear footsteps pounding down the stairs as car doors slam out in the street. He doesn't say a word just smiles and lifts the pistol in his right hand aiming it at me slowly. Mia sees him at the same time as he pulls the trigger and somehow yanks me over to her out of harm's way.

The bullet tears apart the bottom stair and Don is knocked backwards to the wall, by the splintering wood. Bits of timber ricochet around the entrance hitting us all and I feel a piece embed itself into my thigh. I stand up, pulling Mia with me as Logan bursts into sight with his gun raised and aimed at the figure in the doorway. I hear two shots ring out and Jackson drops instantly, but he's not dead.

One of the shots was his, as his gun fired when he fell.

I hear Mia scream with terror as blood covers the floor in an ever increasing pool. Jackson gives me an insane grin and lifts his gun again as he tries to sit up. I push Mia behind me and rage fills me now that disbelief has passed. I'm so angry that I can't think straight as I run over to him and kick his arm, hearing it snap as a bullet lodges in the ceiling as the gun fires again.

He laughs at me and slowly says "You're gonna fucking die tonight cocksucker, but not till after I have her again, she was so sweet that last time!"

Blood oozes out of his mouth, and he pulls the gun down trying to aim it at me, but I'm too quick for him and kick at his arm again as he finally lets go of the gun with a grunt, and it flies across the room, landing at Don's feet.

I hear the sound of people running and the door flies open as two shots ring out nearly deafening me as Jackson falls again, this time staying down. I look up to see two plain clothed cops with guns drawn and we all look over to see Don with a gun in his hand, supported by his other hand and Logan with his arm outstretched with his weapon also.

The smell of caudate is strong in the room and nobody says a word for a minute or two allowing the events of the last few minutes to sink in. Finally, I drag my eyes away from the dead body on the floor in front of me and turn back to see Mia falling to the floor. I run to her, catching her just before she hits the floor. Her leg is covered in blood and it's dripping everywhere.

"Somebody call an ambulance!" I yell in panic as I realize that she was hit by the stray bullet, but I'm not sure where. My own shirt is covered in blood, but I don't feel anything at the moment.

My body is so full of adrenaline that there's no pain as I carry her away from the drama in the entrance, and place her on the sofa gently.

I grab the leg of her cotton pajama pants and rip it open revealing a wound in her thigh that's bleeding profusely. By this time Mum has arrived downstairs and is barreling towards me, screaming at the top of her lungs, asking if I'm okay...trying to figure out who has what wounds. We all have blood covering us for different reasons.

Don was hit by shards of timber and he's covered in bleeding cuts, Logan was sprayed as one of us got shot and his polo shirt is speckled with blood. Mum's face drains of color. as she takes in the sight of Mia unconscious and bleeding as I press my hand to her wound trying to stop the flow of blood.

"Mum get me a towel or dishtowel...anything!" I yell at her as she finally tears her eyes away and hurries over to the kitchen pulling open a drawer and coming back with an armload of clean dishtowels.

I can hear the cops in the entrance as they bark into their mobile phones. Where the fuck were they???? They were supposed to be protecting us...what the fuck happened?? I don't have time to think about it right now. I watch the blood ooze through the clean linen towel and replace it with another, pushing it firmly into Mia's thigh with my hand.

"Where the fuck is the ambulance?!" I scream out to the cops, panic overtaking me. Mia's so pale. God she has to be alright. We haven't come this far to have her snatched away from me now. The universe wouldn't be that cruel surely. I need her like my next breath. I'll shrivel up and die without her.

Logan lifts his head at the sound of sirens approaching as the cops come in to check on us at last. I'm still feeling no pain, but I know that I've lost a lot of blood as I start feeling faint. I fight the darkness and focus on keeping my hand firmly pressed against Mia's small thigh.

We hear the sound of doors opening and people running outside as the doorway is filled by a large paramedic who gingerly steps over the obviously dead body blocking the doorway and runs into the living room carrying a bag of essentials. His eyes quickly scope out the room and focus instantly on Mia as he drops beside me and tells me to keep applying pressure to the wound.

He snatches out an IV bag of fluid and quickly pokes a cannula into Mia's wrist and hooks up the IV line. Her color. is getting worse now. She's so pale that she's almost the color. of the white sofa, and my body starts to shake as the adrenaline drops and terror fills me at the thought of losing her.

Logan stands beside me and pushes me back out of the way as he takes over holding the towel on still bleeding wound as the paramedic yells to the cops to get the stretcher in here ASAP. As he swings his gaze back to me he notices the front of my sleeve and the oozing blood dripping down onto the clean floor. He quickly assesses the wound and places a thick wad of gauze and a heavy dressing over the wounds, one in the front of my bicep and an exit wound in the back of it. I allow him to do what he needs to do, but only so that I can get back to Mia.

I make my way over to her as Logan changes the dishtowel for another because blood is dripping out of the old one. He chucks it to the floor with the pile of others and presses with all of his might against Mia's leg trying to stop the bleeding. She still hasn't made a sound or woken up and I'm panicking more and more by the second. She can't leave me...she just can't.!

I fall backwards as I see the paramedic drag her onto the floor and scream at the cops to get the other paramedic in here, for a Code Blue.

He starts CPR on my wife who's now turning an awful tinge of blue. I can hear Mum crying and Don trying to comfort her before he realizes what's happening. Logan mutters a curse and I hear his voice hitch as he tells me to stay calm.

Stay fucking calm!!!

How can I stay calm as the love of my life is having hers ripped from her?! I wish Jackson wasn't dead so that I could go out there and kill him over and over again. How could this happen...not Mia....it can't be real. I nearly lost her once before....it can't be happening again...not my gorgeous Mia. I need her...her kid's need her...they have to save her.! I'm screaming loudly at them to save her as the other paramedic drops to the floor and helps with CPR, quickly getting a tube into her throat and using an oxygen bag thing to pump air into her lungs while the other guy presses down in a rapid rhythm on her chest. Logan tries to block my view by moving, but I can still see her lying there lifeless on the cold white tiles

I start negotiating with God...begging him to give her back to me...I promise anything and everything I have if he'll just make her better. I can feel the tears stream down my face as my mind goes blank. I feel like I'm in a fog...everyone sounds like they're in a padded room far away as my brain shuts down, unable to comprehend what's happening.

I hear someone say about the femoral artery being severed as one guy attempts to put in another IV line in the other arm, but can't seem to find a vein between squeezing life giving oxygen into my wife's lungs.

I don't know how long they work on her for. Time is irrelevant at the moment. I sit and wait for them to tell me that she's gonna be fine...I wait and wait.

I hear Don's sobs as he keeps repeating that she can't be dead...she can't be dead...over and over again. His words finally filter through the fog surrounding my brain as I fall apart completely and hear a feral primeval scream before realizing that it's coming from me.

NO....NO...NO...NO...no way!

They can't stop...they have to continue...they can't give up...I scream at them all to do something...save my girl.

We're meant to grow old together.

They look at me with sympathetic faces, but they step back away from her. I manage to crawl over to her on all fours, as Logan shuffles backwards and I hear him crying softly. I shove an arm under her shoulders and bring her up to my chest as her head falls back.

NO!!!

My mind just can't fathom that an hour or so ago she was cuddling into me on the very sofa in front of us. I can hear Mum, hysterical with grief and Logan getting up to comfort her.

A scream escapes me as I roar with rage and emotion.

This can't be happening...it can't be.

That's all my brain can focus on at the moment...this can't be real.

No words can describe my pain as my heart shatters into irretrievable pieces, never to be whole again.

I'm rocking her with me.

I sit back with my legs folded under me.

I can't let her go...they need to keep trying...they're wrong...she's not dead...she hasn't left me...she wouldn't do that...she couldn't leave her children.

We're her life…she's got to stay with me.
We need her…

I need her.

This can't be happening!

I hug her close to me as I cry like no man has ever cried before. The roar of grief can't describe the pain that I'm feeling.

My heart is ripped open and shredded as I cling to my gorgeous, lifeless wife.

My soul has cracked and broken as my angel flies to heaven.

Mia's and Noah's story continues in Always Noah's, available now on all platforms.
For more books by this author, please turn the page.

The land of shadows wilt thou trace
And look now know each other's face
The present marred with reasons gone
And past and present all as one?
Say, maiden, can thy life be led
To join the living with the dead?
Then trace thy footsteps on with me:
We are wed to one eternity.
~John Clare

Acknowledgments

Firstly, thank you for reading and I hope you continue to enjoy the series.

Next, I have to thank my husband for putting up with me while I was busy writing and not cooking or doing housework. He's been my rock.

My sister, for her daily texts needing updates on the story, and for supporting me through every book.

My wonderful Editor Melissa Van Natta for once again doing a fantastic job.

Tracey from Soxsational Cover Art for her amazing covers which everyone raves about. I'm so grateful for finding you.

My friends, for their support and understanding every time they asked me out and I declined, because I had writing to do. Luv you guys.

The next book of the series is due out September 2015, so I hope you continue to enjoy the story.

Thank you for reading Country Hearts.

Books Available
Eternally Mia's (The Western Australian Series Book 1)
Forever Noah's (The Western Australian Series Book 2)
Always Noah's (The Western Australian Series Book 3)
Country Hearts
Dalton's Haven

Website
http://www.lillybarrett.com/

Twitter
https://twitter.com/Lilybarrett10

Forever Noah's

Email
lilly.barrett@outlook.com

Facebook
https://www.facebook.com/authorlillybarrett01

Goodreads
https://www.goodreads.com/author/show/13819165.Lilly_B
arrett

Instagram
https://instagram.com/Lilly.Barrett

About THE AUTHOR

Lilly Barrett is a fifty something mother of two grown children, two fur babies and a large male. I live in Outback Western Australia among gum trees, red dirt, emus and kangaroos...and flies!

When I'm not writing, I'm reading or looking after foster dogs till they find their forever home. My 'to Be Read' list gets longer each day, and I already have more books than I'll be able to read in one lifetime.

Work as an Office Manager for a global accounting firm keeps me busy, and I'm lucky to love my job and work with some fantastic people.

I love Western Australia's vastness, and there are so many different facets to this state, that I'll never run out of material for my books.

Please leave a review on the site you bought this book. I promise, I read every one of them, and appreciate your comments and suggestions.

Thank you and I hope you enjoyed my story.
Lilly

www.ingramcontent.com/pod-product-compliance
Lightning Source LLC
Chambersburg PA
CBHW070104120726
47909CB00002B/492